CAPTURED

THE FINLAYS & THE FAE

THE FINLAYS & THE FAE

LISA M. BIRK

TALE WEAVER PRESS

First Printing: 2016

Cover image by Lisa Victoria
Book design by Joni Stringfield
Author Photograph by Kristen Davis

ISBN: 978-0-692-66880-1

Tale Weaver Press
10942 Canyon Mesa Lane
San Diego, CA 92126

www.lisambirk.com

Ordering Information:
Special discounts are available on quantity purchases by
corporations, associations, educators, and others. For details, contact
the publisher at the above listed address.

U.S. trade bookstores and wholesalers:
Please contact Tale Weaver Press Tel: (619) 200-3836
Int'l.: 001 619 200 3836 or email sales_taleweaverpress@twc.com.

for Jerry, my supportive & loving husband
Kristen & Matthew, my inspiration & fellow adventurers

· table of contents ·

· preface ·

Captured: The Finlays and the Fae is told through the eyes of its five main characters. Point of View symbols have been added to indicate when the story changes from one character's perspective to the other. They also provide the date and time when events take place.

KING OSERON

CAITIE

LEANNAN

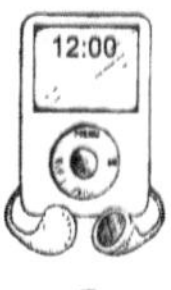

ROBBIE

MUNGAN

THE DARA CELTIC KNOT

Symbolic of the root system of an oak tree.
The Dara Celtic knot can be used to represent strength, endurance, wisdom, leadership and destiny.

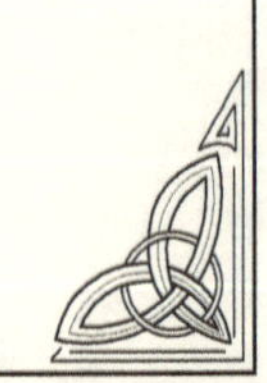

the thirteenth peregrination before it all began...

· the necessary tribute ·

DEAD OF NIGHT
MARCH 31ST

KING OSERON DREADED EACH RENDEZVOUS WITH THE Unseelie Court, but on this bone-chilling, starless night, a sense of foreboding settled over him deeper and darker than a kirkyard grave. Sharp gusts of wind whistled in his ears, whipped his cloak, and thrust his wooden wheelbarrow at a precarious angle as he pushed it across the lonely Scottish moor. Oseron vowed this would be the last chest of gold he delivered to the vile Unseelies. He had more than paid his debt to them. This night, he would take a stand.

The Daoine Shi deserved a stronger king. While the prison of Oseron's guilt kept him from breaking free from the Unseelies' hold, his people paid the greater price. Not only had he caged them in the mountain for a century and a half out of distrust of the Unseelies, he had twisted his words to deceive his queen as he feared her love for him was not strong enough to bear the truth. But with Tianna's revelation that a wee babe fluttered within her, the world changed. Oseron would not burden his heir with the blackmail Salucevil and his court demanded.

High above the monstrous dead oak that marked their meeting place, the Unseelies began their spiraling descent, slow and agonizing, like misshapen vultures circling over helpless prey. The silvery screecher alighted first on the uppermost branch and screamed, "Yereeeeeeck!"

Oseron clamped his hands over his ears, but the deafening cry pierced the very core of his fey being.

Salucevil glided on scaly wings to the most prominent limb in the tree, the putrid smell of death descending with him. The howling ghouls of lesser stature then trickled into the gallery, fanning out among the smaller branches.

"Silence!" Salucevil bellowed in a rasp of tortured voices that curled Oseron's toes. The leader's pale green eyes, more chilling than the wind, came to rest on the king. "I trust ye brought the required tribute."

Oseron stood tall and clenched his quaking hands. "I have," he said, feigning confidence.

"Open the chest."

Oseron twisted the brass latch free and squinted as he lifted the hinged lid. The magic of the Daoine Shi gold bathed them all in a brilliant orb of light. Hideous enough in the dark as ashen specters, the illuminated Court now chilled Oseron's blood to where his heart barely beat.

"Ciaran, bag our treasure," Salucevil ordered.

The stooped creature not worthy of a place in the tree, scowled at Oseron as he padded over from his post at the trunk's base. He sprang atop the treasure on birdlike legs. With bony fingers the length of a man's forearm, the red-eyed minion scooped up the glowing coins and a golden stream flowed into as many sacks as there were Unseelies, the treasure clinking like a bell rung with fury.

"Why should I forever do their bidding?" the creature muttered through drooping jowls. "'Tis high time I joined the Court and got a share of what is mine." The nostrils on his square muzzle flared and contracted as he tossed each bloated bag to the ground.

Oseron refrained from shaking his head in disgust.

A chorus of insults and curses trumpeted from the flock as the pile of golden coins under the minion's taloned feet disappeared from the chest. The light orb shrank with the filling of each sack till at last, Ciaran bagged the final coin, snuffing out the golden glow. The underling delivered the first share to Salucevil with a bow and then jumped down for the others' treasure.

"Faster!" Salucevil thundered.

The flustered creature flew in and out of the oak, distributing the sacks to the ungrateful ghouls. As Ciaran hoisted the last bag of gold, Salucevil announced, "This treasure has bought your people thirteen more years of peace."

Oseron took a deep breath, steeling himself. "Thirteen times over the last one hundred and fifty-six years I have paid the Court for my offense. My restitution should be complete. The Daoine Shi should be free!"

"Ye are in no position to bargain. And for your impudence, ye shall now deliver two chests every three years." Salucevil circled his hands and thrust his dagger-sharp nails high above his head. A ring of fire erupted from the ground surrounding Oseron.

"My people know not of our arrangement. I cannot gather so much gold in so little time without it being noticed."

"'Tis not my concern." Salucevil curled a finger and the flames inched an arm's length from Oseron's cloak. "Ye will find a way."

Sweat beaded Oseron's brow. His heart hammered. "I shan't abide by such terms."

"Then a fine bonfire ye shall make before we invade your mountain and destroy every last one of the Daoine Shi." Salucevil rippled his fingers. The flames rose to a dancing curtain. "Agree or burn!"

The king darted to and fro in the ring, vainly searching for escape from the scorching tongues.

Oseron envisioned his people ablaze, Tianna begging to be spared as the flames leapt toward her. "I agree!" he cried. The fire vanished. The smell of his singed hair and cloak hung heavy in the air.

Salucevil's lips curled in a gruesome smile. "I knew ye would see how reasonable I am."

At his master's signal, the screecher shrieked and spiraled skyward. In the order they arrived, the Unseelie Court flew from the tree, leaving Ciaran to trail after them. They swooped downward under the weight of their blood money before ascending. Oseron ducked and raised his hands to his face to deflect the blow from a ghoul's sack, but the treasure struck his palms and drove the royal ring's facets into his lip. The ruthless creature's cackle echoed in the night.

Alone once more, Oseron straightened and touched his fingertips to the welt rising in his mouth. He licked the bruised lip and tasted his blood. Eyes narrowed, he spat at the gnarled tree. He closed the lid on the darkened chest, turned his back on the disappearing flock, and lifted the wooden handles of the wheelbarrow for the long journey back to the mountain.

He had bargained with evil to spare his people, and Oseron hated himself almost as much as the Unseelie Court that trapped him into the deal. The helplessness of his predicament flooded his mind as he picked his way through the rough terrain. The occasional beating of a bat's wings intruded upon his thoughts. Each time he flinched and peered into the darkness, searching for the wretched source of the noise. Every time his gaze was met by a pair of glowing red eyes.

At last, Oseron reached the familiar mountain path and drew comfort at being nearly home. He knew every turn, dip, and rise like a ewe knows the cry of her own lamb, as this was his mountain.

At the inconspicuous cairn that marked the hidden trail, he left the path and guided the wheelbarrow through the brush and boulders to the mystic portal. The axle caught in an alder bush a few feet from the entrance. He cursed his carelessness and ripped the wheel from the shrub. The dim lantern hooked on the pole nailed to the front of the wheelbarrow jangled wildly and then settled, casting its pale light on the huge stone masking the entrance to Oseron's realm. In a hoarse, half-whisper, he uttered the spell to open the secret door, *"Fosgail an dorus drùidheil."* The black outline of the portal appeared as the rock swung noiselessly into the granite hillside.

Oseron scanned the sky for the vile bat, but thankfully 'twas gone. Exhausted, he pushed the wheelbarrow across the threshold and past the curve in the narrow tunnel, resting it against the rough-hewn wall.

Lantern in hand, Oseron returned to the portal and spied a rusty red and black spider crawling through the opening. He raised his fist to smash it, but the notion of the crushed spider's plentiful remains fouling his hand stopped him. Too tired to remove his boot for the deadly task, he sighed. "This night your fortune is finer than mine, for I shall spare your life and require nothing of ye." The spider crept across the tunnel wall. *"Dùin an dorus drùidheil."* The portal began to close as Oseron turned and plodded up the passageway.

The vague heaviness of lurking eyes pressed against the back of Oseron's head and neck. He spun round and thrust the lantern toward the portal. The only movement was the shadows on the stone cast by the flickering lamplight.

"Who is there?" He strained to listen for a sound, but only silence answered.

1 *the tale to be told is a collision of two worlds*

· the departure ·

8:30 PM
JUNE 19TH

CAITIE FINLAY'S FINGERS RAKED ACROSS HER SOGGY passport as she shoved her dead cell phone, her severed lifeline to home, into her backpack. If her little brother hadn't ratted on her, Plan F for flush might not have failed. Her passport would be floating through some San Diego sewer, and she'd still be in California unable to leave the country. But thanks to Robbie, Mom caught her bent over the toilet with a coat hanger trying to poke the passport down the skinny hole and made her fish it out.

Plans A-E hadn't worked any better. No amount of arguing, Plan A, swayed Mom. Attempts to convince the couple buying their house that the place swarmed with paranormal activity, Plan B, only got her grounded. She'd been sure that camping out by Dad's grave to prove she was too emotionally unstable to make the move, Plan C, was a winner, but at fifteen, none of her friends had their licenses yet, and their parents wouldn't drive her the 45 minutes it took to get to Ft. Rosecrans National Cemetery on Point Loma. Her best friend Sara's family refused to adopt her, Plan D. And Plan E, to run away, never got off the ground since she didn't have the money to pay her cell phone bill, and that was the one thing she wouldn't live without.

Now, some twenty hours after the flushing incident, the three of them stood at a kiosk in London's Euston railway station waiting on some kid with hair and skin as greasy as the sausage rolls he finally tossed into a paper sack for their dinner. Caitie's eyes burned after spilling a bottle's worth of tears on the long flight, and her chest ached from a million silent sobs. All her friends had said she was the lucky one. She was leaving, not being left. Wrong! They had each other. She was stuck with Mom and Robbie, moving to a country famous for haunted castles, kilts, and a loch monster. She wanted nothing to do with any of it.

"Relax, Robbie," Mom said. "Every twelve-year-old—no, everyone has something they're insecure about." She passed Cokes to Caitie and her little brother before grabbing the paper bag from the counter. "You'll fit in just fine."

"Easy for you to say. You're not me." Robbie lowered his eyes.

Caitie rolled hers.

He grabbed Mom's arm, his face all worried, and his eyes checking out the floor. "Why didn't you tell me?"

"Tell you what?" Mom asked.

"My shoes. They're neon white. Why'd you let me get them?"

"Because that's the pair you liked," Mom said as they weaved and cut through the crowd.

Caitie lagged behind not in any hurry to get to Platform 1.

Still clutching Mom's arm, Robbie stopped. She spun halfway around. He gritted his teeth. "Everyone's gonna say, 'Look at the American kid in the loser, white shoes.'"

"You forgot short," Caitie said.

Mom shot her a laser-hot glare before focusing on Robbie. The three of them faced off in the busy station like boulders in a swift-flowing stream. Mom lifted her eyes, looking for help from heaven. There wasn't any. She closed them, combed her fingers through her short coffee-colored hair, and counted to ten. Her lips barely moved.

Robbie snorted long, loud breaths in and out while a woman with a British accent announced over the loudspeaker, "The 20:55 train to Chester with connections to Holyhead now departing from Platform 12."

How could her brother be such an idiot? "You're worried about your shoes when our lives are coming to an end?"

Mom's eyelids popped open and her face froze so her words came out slow and icy. "They're not, and now is not the time."

"It is the time, and my life might as well be over! You're taking me away from everything and everybody that matters to me." Caitie's chin quivered.

Mom's anger melted and tears puddled in her eyes. "You think this is easy for me?"

"You're such a brat, Caitie. All you think about is yourself," Robbie said.

"At least I'm not acting stupid like you."

Mom raised her hands like a ref breaking up a fight. "Stop it now! Both of you."

"Just 'cause I don't want to stick out like you do," Robbie pointed to her board-shorts and flip flops, "doesn't make me stupid!"

"I want everyone to know where I belong. And it isn't here." The lump as big as a baseball rose in her throat again.

Mom bit her lips so hard they disappeared, leaving a straight, dark line across her face. She turned and marched toward the train. Caitie stormed after her.

"Hey wait!" Robbie yelled.

Mom stopped to check the train tickets and then squinted at the letters on the blue railcars with Caledonian Sleeper printed in big white letters. She pointed to the third on their right. "Robbie, ours is carriage J. Queue up behind the woman in black. Caitie, follow your brother."

Robbie dragged his feet. The fresh tread on his shoes squeaked as he led the way over to the white-haired woman. The old lady in front of them wore a pancake-shaped hat cocked to one side, a short black cape, and skirt. A flowered carpetbag with leather handles hung on her arm. She twisted her wrinkled neck and stared at Robbie's feet. Her lips puckered like she'd eaten a sour pickle.

"Your shoes are quite nice, young man," the lady said.

Caitie studied the old woman. That was a little weird. How did she know Robbie was stressed over his shoes? She hadn't been anywhere near them when he'd had his little fit. No way the lady could've read his mind.

"No one else's are white," Robbie muttered.

"A wise man appreciates what makes him unique."

"But I don't want to stand out."

"Brave men always do," the old woman said. "And that is indeed your destiny. Just as your sister's is to learn to see what she will not believe, even about herself." She reached for the silver handle next to the doorway and boarded the railcar.

Caitie eyed her brother. What was the woman talking about? Robbie brave? And the stuff about her—the only thing she couldn't believe was that they were moving to Scotland when all she wanted was to go home.

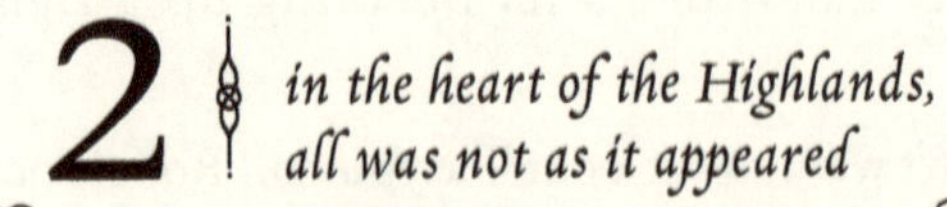

2 *in the heart of the Highlands, all was not as it appeared*

· to be or not? ·

STANDING ATOP A BANQUET TABLE, LEANNAN BIT A knuckle on her clenched fist, willing Mungan, the queen's brother, to win the Daoine Shi tournament.

With his liquid copper eyes focused on the chessboard, Mungan straightened in his chair at the ancient table centered in front of King Oseron's throne. He wrapped his palm round the crystal rook and pushed it across the giant board to capture the wizard Earnan's black onyx queen. The clink of crystal on stone reverberated in the Great Hall. Earnan's cheeks flushed. The cobalt blue glow of his robe shifted to scarlet. Leannan let out her breath.

Mungan glanced at his pocket watch, a mortal marvel that none of the other Daoine Shi, except Earnan, could understand. "A quarter hour." An enchanted quill rose from the table and recorded the time on the tournament scroll.

After shilly-shallying for what seemed a fortnight, the wizard smiled, his thin lips barely visible between his generous mustache and long snowy beard. His eyes glistened behind crescent spectacles, and his robe darkened to a deep shade of violet. The tension built in Leannan like an unscratchable itch. Earnan cradled a pawn in his hands and drove the heavy piece diagonally across the pearl and black marble squares to take Mungan's bishop. Leannan gasped.

Nuala, who sat amongst the kingdom's nobility on the bench below, jerked her neck round, whipping her long black locks behind her. Under the dancer's withering stare, Leannan wished she could hide like a tortoise in its shell. She turned her eyes away and stepped down from the table. With feather-light footsteps, Leannan left the Great Hall. She longed to see the end of the match, but feared Nuala would discover her secret merely by reading her face at its conclusion. No, 'twas best for her to leave. Perhaps she would tidy Mungan's chamber.

Leannan slipped into the corridor lit by the royal blue torchlights and twinkling stars conjured from Earnan's magic crystals. Silver clouds rolled into the Highland paintings lining the passage walls. It looked like a beautiful night. If 'twere not for the evil Unseelies roaming the skies, she would seek solace out in the fresh air. Nearing Mungan's teardrop-shaped door, Leannan glimpsed back to ensure she was alone. Gossip would fly like a bumble bee flitting from flower to flower if anyone spied her entering Mungan's chamber at such a late hour. She ducked inside, and her tension eased in the presence of his belongings. The garnet and emerald pieces of his beloved chess set sparkled in the rainbow firelight, and the clock Mungan found long ago in the mortal realm ticked steadily on the mantel.

She picked up the cloak laid at the foot of his sleigh bed, raised it to her face, and caressed her cheek with the soft cloth. His scent lingering on the fabric curved her lips in delight. Leannan swung the cloak round her shoulders and freed her wavy auburn tresses trapped at the nape of her neck. A sweet and powerful melody flooded her heart. She imagined Mungan's commanding presence, curtseyed, and lifted the folds of her long skirt to dance in an impossible reverie.

"Leannan, why did ye not tell me?" came a soft voice.

She spun round to see the queen resting against the door, her arms crossed and her blue eyes wide as cornflowers.

Leannan cringed as she slipped Mungan's cloak from her shoulders and hung it in his wardrobe. "Tell ye of what, Ma'am?"

"That ye are in love with my brother," Queen Tianna whispered with a sly smile.

Leannan was mortified. If anyone else found out she would be the laughing stock of the kingdom. "No. The cloak. I...I was tidying up and slipped it round my shoulders to…" She licked her lips, "free my hands while I straightened the bedcover. I merely forgot to hang it up." With a composing breath, she eased the wardrobe closed before facing the queen's probing eyes.

"Come now, Leannan. I saw ye gaze with closed lids into an invisible face and tenderly clasp the imagined hand of the one who holds your heart. Do not be ashamed. I have known and cared for ye since we lost your mother when ye were a wee child. Ye are more than my maidservant. Ye are a kindred spirit." Queen Tianna glided to the bed. She patted the jade covering, beckoning Leannan to join her.

Leannan sat on the edge of the cloud-soft mattress, her heart pounding with the force of a mountain waterfall. "I beg of ye, please do not speak of this to him," she pleaded. "He must never know."

"We Daoine Shi have an order amongst us to be sure, but exceptions have been made. Remember the sculptor Failbhe and Mairi, the laundress? 'Twill be difficult as Mungan is the Searsanach. But with the proper persuasion, Oseron might condone the match."

Leannan's pointy ears burned at the possibility. "But many others are far more worthy."

"Being noble born does not promise good character. And a fine piece of crystal with a flaw will soon shatter. Mungan needs a wife, who like a worthy chess opponent, will be quick of wit and strong to keep him on his toes, and lovely to distract and keep the game interesting."

The fire in Leannan's ears spread to her cheeks. "But what of Mungan's desires?"

"My little brother has had more than a hundred years to express them. He has merely shown protective concern for all the Daoine Shi maidens as is decreed by his role, nothing more. 'Tis time I aided him in matters of the heart." Queen Tianna's eyes sparkled.

A glimmer of hope sent a giddy ripple through Leannan. "I fear 'tis a wish too grand to come true."

Queen Tianna stood and squeezed Leannan's shoulder. "Put your trust in me and be patient." She tucked a folded note under the candlestick on the table next to the bed.

Leannan wondered what the note said, but knew 'twas not her place to ask.

"Now let us see if our Mungan shall be the victor." Queen Tianna ushered her from his chamber as the time torches turned to the silvery blue of moonlight, marking the night's waning hours.

Together they strolled into the Great Hall ablaze with the light of a hundred candles on each wheel-spoke chandelier. They skirted the glowing crowd and climbed the steps to the dancer's stage where the polished birch gleamed like honey in sunlight. Queen Tianna ascended the stairs to the royal platform and took her place at the smaller throne next to King Oseron's.

The dancer Nuala glowered at Leannan from her seat on the end of the oak bench, closest to Mungan. After the queen's encouraging chat, Leannan could not help but grin in return.

Earnan moved his rook forward one space diagonal to Mungan's king. Whispers broke out amongst the Daoine Shi like a den of hissing snakes.

Mungan bolted forward in his chair and slid his queen to the black square adjacent to Earnan's bishop. "Checkmate."

Leannan crossed her hands on her chest and let out a deep sigh, the smile on her face so broad her cheeks tingled. The Daoine Shi burst into cheers.

"Well done." Earnan extended his hand in congratulations.

Mungan reached out and shook it. "'Twas a fine game."

Queen Tianna raised her arms. "This calls for a celebration." She and King Oseron rose, and with her hand atop his, they descended the platform stairs, she as graceful as a wildflower yielding to the breeze. Leannan hastily withdrew to the cask room to gather a round of drinks for Earnan, Mungan, and the others. Moments later, she offered a chalice to the victor, the vanquished, the king, and queen.

Her chin held high, Queen Tianna raised her goblet. "To my brother, Mungan, whose strategic skill has this day won him a great Daoine Shi honour."

"Here! Here!" the crowd shouted.

"Aye. Ye have proved yourself a worthy adversary, Mungan," King Oseron said.

The towering triplets waddled up arm in arm. Without a word, Alvy and Ulvy stooped their bulky frames, each grabbing one of Mungan's thighs, and hoisted him in the air. Mungan ducked to avoid the chandelier. "Here's to Mungan!" Elvy shouted.

"Aye, here's to Mungan!" Alvy and Ulvy jiggled him up and down. The heather ale in Mungan's chalice splashed about, showering his hand, sleeve, the three brothers, and the floor.

"My victory is not worthy of such a grand gesture," Mungan sputtered.

The simple trio beamed up at him with toothy grins and round eyes like huge hazel marbles. Ale trickled through their wild, red hair onto their rosy faces. They shook him harder.

"Put him down!" King Oseron ordered with none of his typical tolerance for the trio.

They dropped Mungan like a boulder and Elvy gave him a hearty slap on the back. "Ye done good," Elvy boomed in a gravelly voice, his eyes never leaving the floor as he swayed from side to side on legs stiff as trees.

"Aye, ye done good," Alvy and Ulvy echoed. They swayed in unison with Elvy, their eyes focused on the same spot. All three bobbed their large heads, linked arms, and waddled back to the edge of the gathering, grunting in satisfaction as the musicians began a merry tune.

Mungan's patience with the brothers raised him higher on the pedestal of Leannan's admiration than the trio had lifted him in the Great Hall. "Congratulations," Leannan said, wishing she had thought of something witty instead. She refilled his cup, not allowing his warm eyes to distract her, for fear she would spill the ale.

He gave her a gracious nod in return.

Nuala stepped between them, her back to Leannan. The graceful dancer swung her swanlike neck, flicking her long black locks against the backdrop of the *Faerie Forest of Roles* painting that spanned the entire width of the Great Hall. To the dancer's right, the king and queen's mighty oaks and Mungan's proud rowan glistened. Behind Nuala were the graceful willows of the dancers. Leannan glanced at the maidservants' tiny scrub hazels far to the left and backed away from the confident and stunning dancer.

"To your victory," Nuala purred and held up her goblet. Mungan clinked his chalice against the dancer's and grinned.

"Perhaps we can play a wee game, and ye can teach me your most wicked moves." Nuala swished a hip to the side, and her cat-eye green dress hugged the curve.

Queen Tianna glared at Nuala, her eyes the icy blue of snow at twilight. She reached for Mungan's arm and kissed him on the cheek. "I am weary, dear brother, thus I bid ye goodnight." She turned a cold shoulder to Nuala and pushed her long skirt back, avoiding the dancer.

Nuala wrapped her lithe arm around Mungan's, nuzzling close to him.

"I cannot give away all my secrets," he answered with a crook of his brow.

Leannan's heart ached as she watched him look deep into Nuala's hypnotic eyes.

The king turned to his guards, the surly Cormag and wily Ballard. "I am off to the treasure room to ensure all is well before I take my leave for the night."

"Shall we stand watch?" Cormag dripped with deference.

"'Tis late, and there is no need for both of ye."

"Then I shall be the sentinel, Your Majesty." Cormag looked down his nose at Ballard, who swaggered over to a bench, his eyes fixed on Nuala.

As King Oseron left with Cormag at his heels, Leannan retreated to the alcove to prepare her nightly tray for Tianna. She filled one of the queen's silver chalices with elderberry wine and placed an assortment of cheese on a plate. With a linen napkin threaded through a Celtic ring, the salver was complete. She left the alcove with the tray on her outstretched hand just as Mungan exited the Great Hall. Their eyes met, and she stepped on something other than the floor. She looked down and spied a white mouse clawing at the slippery marble in a mad attempt to escape, his tail trapped beneath her foot. "Ahh!" Leannan jumped. The tray tipped. The cheese took flight and the queen's cup toppled, splattering the purple wine on Mungan's saffron shirt.

"Oh, your pardon I do truly beg. A wee mouse frightened me."

He studied her, his head tilted down, and his eyebrows raised in disbelief.

"'Tis true!" She scoured the floor for the creature. "He was wee and white as a star and right beneath my foot."

"Leannan, ye need not craft such a tale. No harm done." His eyes twinkled with amusement.

"The only tail here, kind sir, belonged to the wee mouse I stepped upon. But I am truly sorry about your shirt." Leannan offered up the napkin from her tray.

"Ye best keep that for later. Ye may need it more than I." He winked. "I bid ye a fine night, Leannan, and I hope ye have seen the last of your mysterious mouse."

"Good night." She stooped to wipe up the wine puddles.

Nuala strolled through the archway. "Where are ye going, Mungan?"

"To my chamber."

"What has happened to your shirt?" The dancer outlined the purple stain with a finger.

"A wee mishap," Mungan said with a chuckle.

"She is a ham-handed fool, Mungan. As Searsanach, ye should relegate Leannan to scouring pots and floors while the rest of us sleep. 'Twould be safer for ye and better for us all."

Leannan felt the invisible daggers Nuala hurled with her eyes. She skittered to the enclave to prepare a new tray for Queen Tianna and fought back a flood of stinging tears. How could Mungan ever think of her as anything but a clumsy dolt?

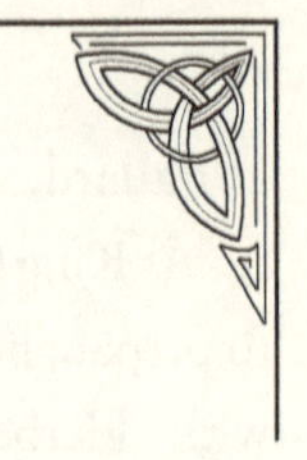
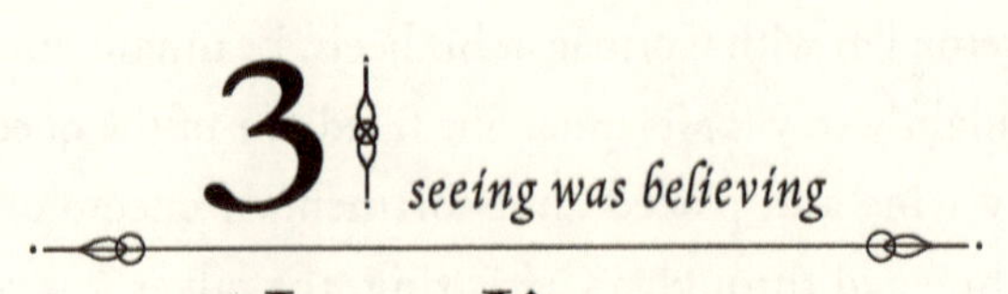

3 *seeing was believing*

· the glimpse ·

1:50 AM
JUNE 20TH

A HAND CLAMPED TIGHT ACROSS HIS JAW JOLTED Robbie awake. "Mmmmmmmph!" He clawed at the fingers to yell for help.

The shadowy hulk muzzling him lunged toward his head. "Shhh! Robbie, it's me," Caitie whispered, her breath tickling his ear.

His rigid body went limp. She released her grip. "What are you doing?" he whispered.

"I can't sleep. I want to get some milk. Come with me."

"We can't sneak out. Mom'll kill us."

"Don't be such a wuss!"

He shook his head no.

"I'll buy you M&M's."

The offer was tempting, and he was up anyway. "Make it king-size and it's a deal."

"All right. Just don't make any noise." Caitie handed him his jeans, T-shirt, and shoes all wadded up together.

A minute later he was dressed and down the ladder from the top bunk, his shoes under his arm. Caitie cracked open the door, and a sliver of light from the corridor sliced into the compartment. He tip-toed out after her and watched her ease the latch closed. "Aren't you going to lock it?"

"I don't have a key."

"We can't just leave it open. Someone could get Mom." He wiggled into his shoes without untying the laces.

"Take a look around. Do you see anybody else? We'll be lucky if someone's still working the lounge car."

"But…"

"Stop worrying! We'll be back quick." She took off before he could say anything more.

Robbie wobbled after her, jostling his way through several sleepers. They came to a long room with tables and chairs at one end and four blue couches at the other.

"This has got to be it," Caitie said.

The spooky old lady who'd boarded the train before him sat on one of the sofas holding up a small cloth bound book. In her other hand was a silver disc tethered to a chain around her neck. Her head nodded up and down as she looked out the window and checked the thing in her hand. She reminded him of Coach Khale timing kids as they ran the mile for P.E. Robbie tugged on Caitie's arm and jerked his head in a signal to leave. They needed to get out of there before the old lady saw them.

"No," Caitie said in a harsh whisper.

Still wearing the creeper cape and flat black hat, the woman looked over at them as they walked in.

A pretty woman in a Scotrail uniform sat at a table next to the doorway leading to a tiny kitchen. She put down her paperback and stood. "What can I get you?"

Caitie tousled her sun-streaked, wavy hair. "Do you have any milk?"

The woman nodded. "I think I can find you a carton."

"What about M&M's?" Robbie asked.

"No, but will chocolate-covered biscuits do?"

"That'll work."

The woman pulled a shiny red and blue package from a cabinet and a carton of milk from the small fridge. "Two pounds, please."

Caitie slid out a bill from the front pocket of her jeans. "Will five dollars cover it?"

"I'm sorry, but we don't take U.S. currency."

"But I haven't had any time to exchange my money yet."

Great, she'd woken him up and risked them getting into trouble for nothing.

"I will treat them their midnight feast." The old lady set her book down on the table. She dug through her funny bag, pulled out a bulging coin purse, and pinched the clasp open. The money jingled as she rummaged through it.

"Come here, young man, and give this to our attendant."

Robbie's chest tightened and he shot Caitie his *You do it* look.

"Go or else," she said, like a smiling ventriloquist.

Dressed in a black skirt, gray stockings, and clunky shoes, the old lady could have been a librarian from one of the black and white movies Mom liked to watch.

Her hair was pulled back in a twist, and her strong perfume smelled like spicy flowers. She dropped three coins onto Robbie's sweaty palm.

"Thanks." Robbie closed his fist around the money and hurried back, glaring at Caitie as he exchanged it for the biscuits. "These are called Digestives," he said in a low voice. "How can I eat something with a name like that?"

"You'll manage, I'm sure."

"But it sounds like something you take to get rid of a stomachache."

Caitie ignored him and headed toward the other end of the lounge car before he could stop her. "That was really nice of you to pay for our stuff." She offered up the bill. "Can I give you my American money?"

"No, thank you, dear, but do sit with me a wee while." She reached for the tattered map lying beside her on the sofa and set it on her lap. It was marked up with numbers and a thick squiggly line. She peered through her reading glasses at a locket watch on the end of the chain around her neck. "'Tis two o'clock in the morning. You two should be sleeping." The old lady tilted her chin down and studied them over the glasses resting low on the bridge of her hooked nose.

"I know." Caitie sat down, opened the carton of milk and swallowed a big gulp.

Slouched on the opposite sofa, Robbie tore open the plastic wrapper and wriggled a chocolate covered whatever-it-was out of the package and into the palm of his hand.

"One would guess you are too excited about being on holiday to sleep, but—" the woman raised her penciled eyebrows and looked into each of their faces—"his misty-blue and your stormy, sea-green eyes betray you. They each have seen much sorrow, and that I suspect is the reason sleep eludes you."

"How can you see that?" Caitie took another swig of milk.

"I may be ancient, but my senses are still sharp, very sharp indeed."

Robbie flashed back to the stuff she'd said about him and Caitie before they got on the train. It was too weird to even go there, but he did want to know how she'd read his mind. "How did you know I was thinking about my shoes earlier tonight?"

"The same way the salmon knows which river will lead him home."

"I don't get it." He nibbled at the wanna-be cookie. It was like a Ritz cracker with chocolate coating. He wrapped his mouth around the rest of it.

"Then let us just say I knew you were troubled about them."

"That's kind of creepy," he said, still chewing.

"Robbie!" Caitie shot him a dirty look. "I'm sorry. He didn't really mean it."

"Do you want one of these?" He held the package out to make up for being rude.

"No, thank you." The old lady smiled.

"I do." Caitie crossed the aisle and stuck out her hand.

He handed her one, and she curled up on the couch again.

"So why are you still up?" Caitie asked.

"I enjoy the rocking of the train, my book of Burns poetry, and the scenery too much to miss a minute of it."

"But it's dark outside. There's nothin' to see," Robbie objected.

"You'd be surprised." She gave him a mischievous grin.

What was that supposed to mean? The digestives sucked his mouth dry. "Can I have some milk?" He got up and reached for Caitie's carton.

"Don't drink it all."

He downed half the milk and wiped a wet mustache off with the back of his forearm before plopping back on the sofa.

"We used to live in California. It's a really great place." Caitie slumped down and flopped her head back. Her chin started to tremble—a sure sign she was about to cry.

"Tell me, Caitie, why are you so sad?" the old lady asked.

Robbie settled deeper into the leather cushions. This was gonna take a while.

"Our dad died six months ago." She hesitated and bit her lip, her eyes all watery. "His jet was shot down in Afghanistan."

The words still stung like a fresh rug burn, and he wondered if they always would.

"I am so sorry for your loss." The woman squeezed his sister's hand.

Caitie exhaled, the air puffing out her lower lip as it whistled by. "Mom sold the house and furniture, packed up our stuff, and shipped it to our grandparents' place in Scotland." She wiped a tear from her eye.

"We had to give away our dog, Gunner, too," Robbie added. Something else he didn't understand.

His sister swung the paua shell on her hemp necklace back and forth, pulling the string taut. "We have to go live with people we don't even know… in the middle of nowhere."

"And where exactly is the middle of nowhere?" the old lady asked.

"Drumnadrochit," he said.

"That's not so far from Inverness. 'Tis lovely there."

"But we're from San Diego. It's got the beach and a ton of other fun things to do." Caitie looked at the woman like she was crazy for not getting it.

"The village lies on Loch Ness, the largest body of water in Scotland."

"Yeah, the famous one with a monster," Robbie said with zero enthusiasm.

Caitie rolled her eyes at him before returning to her pity party. "It's not the same. My friends and I had planned to spend the summer at the beach. We were gonna boogie board. Have bonfires. My friend Santi even promised to teach me how to surf."

"Aye, you're right. It will be different for you." The old lady pursed her lips the way she had before they got on the train. "Now why do you suppose you don't know your grandparents at all?"

"Our mom never really talked about them," Caitie said.

"There's an old Scottish proverb that says, 'A misty morning may become a clear day.' Perhaps Caitie, there is a mist for your mum that you can help to clear. And as for friends, surely you will make new ones in no time."

"But it's my old ones I want to be with." She combed her bangs back with her hand.

"Me too." Robbie lay down, wondering if they were gonna stay here all night. The couch was comfortable. The lights were soft. All he needed was a pillow.

"My friends back in San Diego are the only people who understand me. And I still really need them." Caitie tilted her head back and drank the last of her milk. "Why can't my mom see that?"

"I'm sure she had her reasons for the move. Give it a chance and you may grow to like our country. The Highlands are a wonderful place. It's beautiful and magical."

Robbie thought of how she'd read his mind and wondered if the old lady really meant it. He propped himself up on his elbows. "Magical?"

"No, Robbie. That's just something people say to make you want to go there."

"I'm afraid you're quite wrong, Caitie. Scotland truly is magical."

The woman's words made him shudder.

Caitie crossed her arms. "I'm sure it's pretty, Ms. …."

"Miss Moncrieff. So you do not believe me?"

Caitie shook her head. "Not really. I don't believe in magic."

"Do you, Robbie?" Miss Moncrieff asked.

"I don't…I don't know."

Miss Moncrieff studied him with the tip of her tongue sticking out between her cherry red lips. She glanced down at the map resting in her lap and checked her watch. "Robbie, look out your window and tell me what you see far to the left in the distance."

He turned to the big glass pane behind him. They were way farther north so it wasn't black like night in San Diego, but all he could make out were dark outlines of the hillsides. "Nothing really."

"Come quick or you'll miss quite a treat."

Uneasy, he didn't move. He was torn—scared but curious. Miss Moncrieff's eyes pierced his, and he felt like his thoughts were written on the pages of a book she could read.

"Indecision becomes a decision, and time lost never returns. Be brave, Robbie, like your father."

He crossed the aisle way slower than his racing pulse. Miss Moncrieff peered around him and grinned. He turned his head again. It didn't look any different.

"Bend down. I want you to wear my tam for a bit." She took off the funny black hat.

He bent over enough for her to place the flat cap on his head.

"Now spin round and tell me what you see."

Robbie straightened up and turned back to the window. His eyes widened and his brows shot up. "What the…" He blinked hard. "There are hundreds of gold lights out there." He raced to the couch and pressed his nose against the glass. "It looks like a gigantic snake uncoiling and slithering up the hill. It wasn't there before. Can you see it, Caitie?"

"Nope. There's no light snake out there." He could hear that *Don't be stupid* edge in her voice.

"Quickly, Robbie, come. I want your sister to see as well."

"That's all right," Caitie said.

Robbie froze; his nose glued to the cool pane. Why hadn't he seen them a second earlier? Was Miss Moncrieff a magician? She sure didn't look like the flashy ones he'd seen on TV, but it was the only way to explain what she just did. The lights disappeared from sight as the train rolled north. He walked over to her and handed back the soft tam. "What was that?"

"That hill you caught a glimpse of is home to a southern clan of the wee folk."

"Wee folk?" Robbie asked.

"Aye, the fae. Although you would know them better as fairies."

"No way." He wished she'd admitted to being a magician instead. Fairies belonged in stories, Disney movies, and little kid video games, but not in real life.

"You needn't be frightened if you keep your distance. Most mean no harm to humans that don't disturb them. Only the Unseelie Court should be avoided at all costs."

Goosebumps rose on Robbie's arms. "Who are they?"

"The worst, most evil of the fae, known for roaming the midnight skies in search of victims to snatch for their heinous pleasure."

"Well, I'm not getting near any of them!" he said.

Caitie bit her lip. He knew she didn't believe Miss Moncrieff but was trying to hide it.

"Why did I have to wear your tam to see the lights?" he asked.

"That is a wee bit of Highland magic. Now, you two best be off to bed before your mum wakes up, and you give her a terrible fright for being gone."

"I s'pose you're right." Caitie stood to leave. "Thanks again for the cookies and milk."

"Goodnight, Miss Moncrieff," Robbie added.

"Oh, and Caitie, be patient with your mum. She's suffering too and may not have shared everything with you yet."

Robbie led the way. Once inside the next railcar, he stopped and grabbed his sister's arm. "Caitie, I really saw those lights. How did Miss Moncrieff make that happen?"

"She couldn't have."

"I'm not lying. They were there, hundreds of 'em!"

"Robbie, there was nothing to see. It was all in your imagination." She tapped his temple.

"It was not. I saw it, I swear!"

Caitie shrugged. "Look, she's probably got ESP or something which is how she knew you were paranoid about your shoes."

"Okay, but how did she make me see the lights?"

"It's simple, she put her hat on your head and sent you subliminal messages telling your brain to think you were seeing lights that didn't exist. I saw a show about ESP on the Discovery Channel. That's got to be it." Caitie started down the narrow corridor.

"You really think so?"

"Sure. She was kind of weird. Really nice, but weird."

"But..."

"But nothing! Let it go!" She crossed the threshold into the next railcar.

The vision of the light snake haunted Robbie. Caitie was wrong about Miss Moncrieff playing games with his head to create the lights. He was sure of it. Now his long list of things to be paranoid about just got longer as he added fairies to it. What would Dad think? How could he ever be anything but a coward compared to him?

4 *hearts were broken*

· the unwelcome surprise ·

EARLY MORN
JUNE 20TH

WITH CAREFUL BRUSHSTROKES, LEANNAN ADDED THE wistful branches of a willow to her painting of the valley before her. If only Mungan could see her as strong and graceful like the tree, not clumsy as she was last night when she doused him with Tianna's wine. She stood tall to dispel the weight of her troubles and chose to dwell on such thoughts no longer.

The woods around her awakened, and the birds filled the valley with a steady chorus. Though she longed to stay outside and paint the crisp morning away, she raised her hand toward the sky to measure the time. The sun peeking through the clouds had risen four finger-widths above the horizon. There were only moments more to be free and revel in the smell of the pines before she had to return to the mountain.

Her painting needed a patch of wildflowers before she would be satisfied though. She searched for the perfect shade to complement the scene.

"Ahh, 'tis there." With her arm stretched in the direction of deep fuchsia foxgloves a stone's throw away, she swished and dabbed toward the flowers, drawing their color and scent into the unicorn hairs of her brush. Then with delicate strokes she painted the flowers on her canvas.

"Much better." She tilted her head and studied her work. Somehow her babbling burn looked and sounded a little too serene. She touched her brush to a dew drop and added it to the dusky blue she had pulled from the dawn sky. The stream now glistened and its verse rang true. "Aye, 'tis nigh perfect."

A strange horn wailed in the distance as it did nearly every morn, only this day, it sent a shiver down Leannan's back. Was it a sign of trouble to come? A sudden movement caught her eye. Her heart thumped wildly as she strained to see what it was. Two long ears twitched. Only a hare loped out of the tall grass.

She drew a calming breath.

A twinge of guilt pricked her conscience as she wrapped her paintbrushes. Her ventures into the outside world each summer morning at dawn violated the Daoine Shi code. The king's decree for no one to leave the mountain without his approval was for their own protection. 'Twould have been more prudent to be wee on her outings, but doing so would slow her journey to the valley. The perils in the outside world were very real—humans and solitary fae with nasty dispositions, and most dangerous of all, the marauding Unseelie Court. But she could not help herself. The freedom and true beauty in the outside world could not be conjured inside the mountain. Every moment was worth the risk. She dropped the paintbrushes in her muslin bag and slipped its wide strap over her head and shoulder.

Leannan lifted the painting from the boulder that served as her easel. She called to the red squirrel watching her from the lowest branch of a nearby rowan, "I shall see ye on the morrow." He twitched his bushy tail and scampered up the tree.

The song of summer in her heart brought a bounce to her footsteps that seemed to shorten the distance up the path home. Why was it her most treasured time always passed too quickly? She entered the dark cave and skittered up the boulders to the portal. *"Fosgail an dorus drùidheil."*

The mystical door concealed in the granite cavern wall swung slowly into the mountain. The soft peach light of sunrise spilled upon the stone near the entrance. The torch flames had not yet shifted to the gold that marked the morning hours. With her eyes on the painting so as not to smudge the colors, she passed through the portal.

"Leannan?"

Faster than a spinning wheel with a stick thrust in its spokes, she halted at the unmistakable voice that whispered her name. "Uhh..." Her heart fluttered. Her mouth went dry. She concealed the painting behind her back with one hand.

"Where have ye been?" the Daoine Shi Searsanach demanded, his arms crossed, his black boots spread far apart.

Why was Mungan at the portal? The tiny chance she had of winning his heart vanished before her eyes. "Mungan, I can explain."

"No, ye cannot. There is no worthy reason for what I now behold."

"I was careful. No one saw me." She could not draw her gaze from the floor to look upon his face.

"No one leaves the mountain without approval from the king." His voice was dagger sharp. *"Dùin an dorus drùidheil."* The portal closed at his command.

"Aye, I know 'twas a breach of our code." She wished to melt into the floor.

"Do ye not realize the Unseelies could have snatched ye?"

The urge to confess her many ventures and to assure him she rarely sensed danger was powerful, but Leannan resisted. She looked into his face. "But they did not."

"What are ye trying to hide, and may I add, quite poorly behind your back?"

"A wee painting." She brought the canvas as wide as her arm was long and taller than her torso out from behind her.

Mungan studied the mountain valley, his eyebrows crooked in puzzlement. "Did ye go and steal it?"

She raised her chin. "No, of course not. I painted it myself."

He took the picture from her hands. The grim expression on his face softened. He shook his head. "Leannan, 'tis not the first time ye have left the mountain to paint, now is it?"

She hesitated, fumbling for a way to twist her words, but there was none. She had to speak the truth. "No."

Silence. She looked round at the rough-hewn walls of the wide passage as she could not look him in the eyes.

"Your painting ventures are acts of rebellion. The king will lock ye in the dungeon or worse. Remember Mordrigg? Because of his wanderlust, he was condemned to a hideous fate." Mungan turned her chin to face him. "How have ye forgotten his agonizing screams as he died in the stocks from the iron's poison?"

She did not answer. Mordrigg had been foolhardy.

"Does Queen Tianna know?" Mungan asked.

"I believe not."

Mungan shook his head as if he knew not what to do with her.

"What reason brings ye to the portal when all others are asleep?" Leannan asked.

He sighed. "Tianna left me a note. She requested I meet her here as she is troubled over something. I suspect after this encounter, 'tis ye. After all, what better way for me to uncover your rebellion than to arrange a meeting here at the time ye come waltzing through the portal?"

Leannan could not imagine how her mistress could have found out. Every morning when she brought a breakfast tray to Tianna's chambers, she found the queen asleep. "'Tis something else Mungan, for she knows not what I have done. Perhaps she suggested ye meet here as she believed the passageway to be the one place ye would never be seen by anyone."

"I have my doubts."

"Mungan, what will ye do now ye know I have broken the code?"

"I am befuddled, for 'twill bring me no pleasure to report your rebellion."

"Then perhaps ye can overlook this wee indiscretion."

"I regret my sister's summons. Here I stand, at her request, a witness to her maidservant's rebellion, yet where is she at this early hour? 'Twould be better to be blissfully asleep."

"I wish ye were as well." Leannan hung her head.

"Come, we will go to Tianna's chambers. Your fate can weigh heavy on her conscience."

Leannan hoped somehow the queen would forgive her. Mungan, however, did not appear as willing. She could not blame him.

With the painting in one hand and her arm in the other, Mungan ushered her down the passageway.

He paused at the entrance to the corridor surrounding the Great Hall. Sensing no one, they quickly crossed the corridor and entered the hallway that led to the queen's chambers.

"Mungan, may I stow my painting?" she whispered, as they approached her teardrop door.

"Fine, but do not tarry." He handed her the canvas.

Leannan entered her chamber, and Mungan followed. She whisked her way to the wardrobe and opened the door just enough to slip the painting inside. He came behind her and swung the door wide. His eyes scrutinized the cupboard floor.

Her chest tightened, strangling the breath out of her. She had not anticipated he would be so bold. She backed away. He pushed aside her dresses and stooped down. If he searched the back of the wardrobe, he would find her one and only portrait—the one of him. She could not bear the humiliation. With shaky hands she slipped the bag of brushes from her shoulder and stashed the satchel under her bed.

Mungan pulled out several canvases and examined them. "Ye have quite the gallery in here. I am afraid, however, they are the result of far more than a wee indiscretion." He returned the landscapes and closed the wardrobe. "Och, Leannan."

She breathed easier with the portrait undiscovered. "The outside world calls to me, and through painting, I can bring home the joy I find there."

Mungan shook his head, pleading with his eyes. "Ye must rein in your passion or it will be the death of ye. And others of us, no doubt." He grabbed her hand and pulled her to the door.

His strong grip stirred the butterflies in her stomach to a flurry. He grasped the handle and paused before freeing the latch. He looked at her, and his copper irises left her moonstruck. Why did the thrill of this moment's pleasure, alone and so close to him that she could see the flecks in his eyes, have to come wrapped in such shame? Her dream was dead, and no measure of help from Queen Tianna could redeem her in Mungan's mind. Her only hope was to be saved as the maidservant she had always been—else she would descend to the dungeon as a criminal—perhaps banished and forgotten.

"When we reach Tianna's chambers, I will wait outside, and ye shall go in to wake her. I shan't enter without knowing she is alone. For if the king is there, I would know not how to explain myself."

"But—"

"Leannan, ye will do as I say. Now go first into the corridor to be sure no one is about. We have more than enough to explain as 'tis." His gaze lingered, and he gave her hand a gentle squeeze.

She knew Queen Tianna would be alone but thought it better not to argue with him. Leannan opened the door and peered into the corridor. She signaled with a nod, and Mungan slipped quickly from her chamber. He took the lead as the two stole through the passageway. Leannan silently released the latch on the queen's door and tiptoed inside. The time torch hung near the door cast its soft peach glow. The only other light was the flame of a single candle on the table next to the canopy bed and the chamber's everlight, the orange molten crystal shifting in shape like a tongue of flame suspended from the ceiling in its blue lapis sconce. She gently leaned against the polished wood to push the door closed.

The queen lay alone. Her eyes were open, but Tianna did not move her head. "Ma'am?" Leannan called softly.

No response.

A flash of heat radiated through Leannan from her pointy ears down to her toes. "Queen Tianna?" Her voice broke as she reached her mistress's bedside. The queen's once sparkling blue eyes were now opaque and dull. Leannan's hand flew to her mouth. The elderberry wine she'd drunk the night before came up and burned the back of her throat. She spun round and dashed back to Mungan.

Her quaking hands flung the heavy door open. She clutched his forearm and drew him inside.

"What is it?" he demanded. He looked to Tianna's bed. Without waiting for her reply, Mungan rushed to his sister's side.

"She is dead," Leannan sobbed.

"Tianna, oh Tianna! This cannot be." He shook her shoulders. "Awake!" His fingertips frantically probed her temple for a pulse.

Leannan knew there was none to find. Queen Tianna's glow was fading.

Mungan's hands went to his head. He pulled back his hair and grimaced with pain. "I am too late," he whispered.

Leannan's heart ached for them both. She stepped to his side, searching for the right words, but they eluded her.

"Tianna was fine last night. Weary, but fine," Mungan said.

"Aye, she was."

"Wait." His copper eyes met hers, and she felt him strive to see inside her heart. "Ye brought her a glass of wine, after I bid ye goodnight."

"Aye, and she was very much alive." Her whole body quivered with grief and fear at what she suspected he was thinking. "I loved her as I would my own mother."

"Tianna was too young to die. She was troubled, and ye have ventured out of the mountain. Repeatedly."

"I would take my own life rather than harm the queen."

"Could anyone from the outside have followed ye back into the mountain?"

She shook her head. "No. I have been careful not to endanger anyone else."

Mungan began to pace.

"We must go tell the king," she said softly, wiping the tears from her eyes.

"Not just yet. 'Tis too early in the morning. Ye have no proper reason to have come to these chambers. Nor do I."

"But he must know."

"Aye. But alerting him now will raise too many questions I am not yet prepared to answer. Ye have broken the code, but I do not believe ye have done this to Tianna."

The relief swept the breath from her chest. "Perhaps she was fading, and we did not know." Leannan looked once again at her dead queen through bleary eyes.

He returned to the side of the bed. "No. 'Tis obvious from her note my sister knew something. And I am certain she paid the price for that with her life. I will find who murdered her, and the one responsible will pay dearly for their deed."

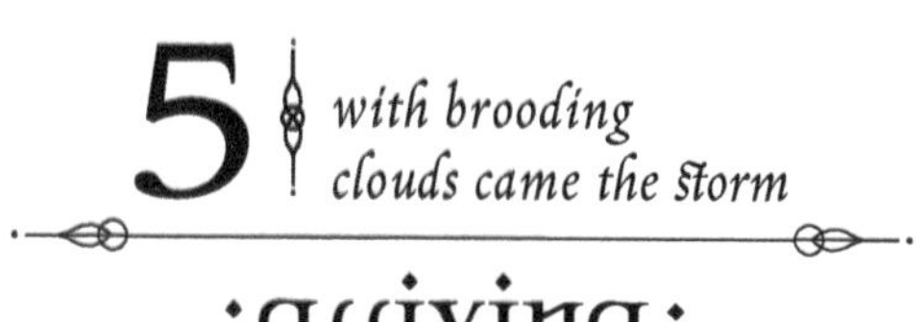

5 *with brooding clouds came the storm*

·arriving·

8:15 AM
JUNE 20TH

THE VIEW OUT THE TRAIN WINDOW CHANGED FROM rolling, sheep-dotted pastures to a blur of stucco houses before Caitie shimmied all the way into her jeans. She grabbed her hot pink tank top with buttons on the front and scooted away from the open door adjoining their two compartments so Robbie couldn't see her when she changed. She'd tossed and turned until dawn, worrying about why their grandparents were total strangers. Now she wished she hadn't ignored Mom's early wake-up calls, choosing instead to sleep until the last possible minute.

She yanked the brush through the tangles in her long hair. "How soon will we be there?"

"In just a few minutes." Mom carefully folded her nightgown.

Caitie tousled her hair for that beachy look, even if she felt far from carefree on the inside. She grabbed her toiletry bag and stepped to the sink beneath the window. Industrial buildings flew by way too fast as she squeezed a strip of blue gel onto her toothbrush. "How come you never told us much about our grandparents?" The tingly mint shocked her mouth awake.

Mom folded yesterday's shirt. "Caitie, we really don't have time for this right now."

"I don't get how there's plenty of time to pack your suitcase just perfect. But not enough to talk about something important."

"Why do you always pick the worst possible moment for a serious conversation?"

Caitie shook her toothbrush at Mom. "'Cause when we get off this train"—she whirled around to spit and spun back to look Mom in the eyes—"we gotta move in with strangers. We deserve to know."

"Yeah." Robbie climbed down from the top bunk and stepped into the doorway wearing jeans, a long-sleeved T-shirt, and his old skate shoes.

"Where are your new shoes?" Mom asked.

"They're in my bag. These feel better."

They all knew why Robbie wasn't wearing the white pair, but this wasn't the time to call him out on it. The stuff with their grandparents was way more important than her brother's stupid shoe issues. Anyone was gonna know he was American the minute he opened his mouth. "Nice try at changing the subject, Mom, but it didn't work."

"It's complicated." Mom zipped her overnight bag shut.

"We're listening," Caitie said.

"When you were younger, it was too hard to explain. When you got older, you stopped asking."

"We're old enough now to understand complicated. So what's the story?" Caitie wiped her mouth with a washcloth and put away her toothbrush and paste.

The train groaned and rolled to a stop. The muffled sound of compartment doors opening and closing seeped through the walls.

"We've got to go. I'll explain it all later," Mom said.

"I want to know now." Caitie stuffed her pajamas and toiletry bag in her suitcase and plopped down on the lower bunk. "And I'm not leaving until you tell me."

"Caitie, the attendants must clean in here for the next passengers."

"Did they do something horrible?"

"No, your grandparents are good and decent people. There was just a big… misunderstanding. I promise everything will be okay."

"Not good enough. At least give us some clue what happened." The silence in the compartment roared. No way she was gonna give in on this one.

The light in Mom's eyes faded and her shoulders sagged. "Caitie…"

The door swung open, and a Scotrail attendant barged in with a trash bag in one hand. "Oh, excuse me. I thought the compartment was empty."

"We were just leaving." Mom pulled her suitcase off the bed. "Let's go."

Caitie shot Mom a dirty look and jammed her arms through the sleeves of her tie-dyed hoodie. Her mother skated again. It wasn't fair. She stood up, slipped on her flip flops, and grabbed her overnight bag.

The sky was gray like her gloomy mood. She was in Scotland, and there was no going back. The cool breeze and new life she couldn't escape made Caitie shiver as she stepped from the train. They passed a white sign on the bleak concrete platform with the words "Inbhir Nis" printed in blue letters.

"That's not how you spell Inverness," Robbie said.

"It's in Gaelic," Mom said.

"Don't they speak English here?" The panic of a preschooler was in his voice and eyes.

"Most do, but some of the older folk still speak Gaelic."

Caitie envisioned a pruney old man and woman babbling at her in a language she couldn't understand. "Our grandparents speak English though, right?"

"Yes. They speak both," Mom said.

"Whew!" Robbie couldn't have sounded more relieved if he'd just dodged detention. They entered the terminal. An older woman rose from her seat on a row of metal mesh chairs. She looked like a grandmother, with short gray hair, oval glasses, plump cheeks, and a kind smile. A man way too young to be Mom's father stood up with her. The older woman straightened the bottom of her pale blue cardigan and waved.

"There's your Gran," Mom's face beamed as she waved back at the woman.

"Where's our grandfather?" Robbie asked.

Mom took a shaky breath. "I don't know."

"He probably didn't want to come here either," Caitie said.

Mom glared at her. "Catriona Anne Finlay. That's enough."

She'd pushed a button with that remark. Too bad it wouldn't win her a trip to her old room back home.

"Who's the guy with her?" Robbie asked.

"I have no idea," Mom said, in a near whisper.

The man was close to Mom's age with dark hair and a nice outdoorsy face that went well with his broad shoulders and flat abs. If Caitie were old, she'd probably think he was hot.

"Oh, Maisie! I am so sorry." Their grandmother threw her arms open wide. Mom rushed into them.

Grandma MacGregor's eyes got watery, and her chin trembled as she held

Mom tight. So that's where I get it from. Caitie's own chin quivered as she watched the two of them.

Mom wiped her eyes, smudging her mascara. "Mum, this is Caitie, and that's Robbie." Her grandmother drew close and cupped Caitie's face in her warm, wrinkled hands. "I'm so sorry you lost your father. I want you to know, though, I'm very glad you're here."

Caitie choked back the lump in her throat and blinked away tears, but as she looked into her grandmother's pale blue eyes, she felt welcome. "Thanks, Grandma." That felt weird to say.

Grandma MacGregor took Robbie's hand in both of hers. "I have waited a good long time to meet you, even if it's under such hard circumstances." Her Scottish brogue was way thicker than Mom's.

"Thanks." Robbie looked down at the tile floor and scuffed his shoe.

Their grandma took a deep breath and turned to the guy with her. "Maisie, Caitie, and Robbie, this is Mr. Alistair Ross MacLeod." She patted his arm affectionately.

"It's just Ross." He smiled and gave Grandma a patient glance with eyes the color of gingerbread.

"Ross is your father's right-hand man."

Mom's eyebrow's furrowed for a second with surprise.

Ross nodded to her and Robbie and extended a hand to Mom. "It's a pleasure to meet you, Maisie."

Mom clasped his hand and shook it. The corners of her mouth twitched. Caitie hadn't seen her this nervous in a long time.

Ross turned to Robbie. "I'm going to bring the car round. Would you like to come? You can tell me of your trip."

If Robbie said anything about the fairy lights Miss Moncrieff helped him imagine, she'd kill him. The second person they met in Inverness didn't need to think their family was crazy. Ross went for Mom's suitcase. "Don't you dare say a word about last night," Caitie whispered to Robbie.

Her little brother's eyes narrowed. "I won't." He took off for the exit with Ross.

"You never mentioned Dad needing help or Ross, for that matter," Mom said.

Grandma MacGregor shrugged her shoulders and tilted her head. "You never asked."

Mom crossed her arms. "But a person should let one's daughter know about such things."

"Perhaps the person's daughter should not have waited four long years to write if she wanted to know those kinds of details."

"But I did write after that."

"Five letters in twelve years, Maisie. Ross had become like a son to your father. Me too. I wasn't about to say anything that could drive you further away." Grandma MacGregor wrapped her arm around Mom. "But there's much time to talk, now that you've come home, and well we should."

The two headed for the glass double doors. Caitie followed close behind. Four years? Mom didn't talk or write to her parents for four whole years? She could get plenty mad at Mom, but it never lasted more than a couple of days, tops. What could've happened?

"How's Dad?" Mom stopped. "Why didn't he come?"

"You'll have to ask him yourself," Grandma said with sadness in her voice.

What were they getting into?

They stepped out of the station into a plaza surrounded by dingy, old buildings with tan bricks blackened around the edges like over-roasted marshmallows. High on a pedestal in the square stood a statue of a man in a kilt holding a rifle. Even without the seagull perched on top of its head, the guy looked silly with his super tall lumpy hat.

An old Volvo station wagon pulled up to the curb. Robbie waved from where the driver would sit in an American car. Ross got out and extended a hand. "Can I put your suitcase in the boot?"

"Sure." Caitie didn't know what boot he was talking about, but she gave him her bag anyway and he stowed it in the back of the car.

Moments later, they were driving through the narrow streets with Grandma MacGregor pointing out landmarks along the way. "There's the High Street, Caitie. It has lots of lovely shops."

They passed a road blocked off from cars and filled with people in drab colored clothes. She doubted they'd have Pac-Sun, her favorite store, here. Everything looked so different. Compared to San Diego's glass and concrete skyscrapers, the low stone buildings with pointy roofs looked ancient.

"That's the River Ness," Grandma MacGregor said as they crossed a bridge. "And up on the hill is Inverness Castle." She pointed to a red stone fortress with round towers.

Before long, they were driving through wooded countryside with a skinny lake on the left side of the car. "Is that Loch Ness?" Caitie asked.

"'Tis," Grandma MacGregor answered.

"Have you ever seen Nessie?" Robbie blurted out.

"No." Their grandmother chuckled. "Many people say they've spied the creature though. Your room has a window overlooking the Great Loch, so you can keep an eye out for her."

Caitie studied the choppy water. "The monster's just a legend, Robbie."

"A fair number of folk here believe in her, dear, and all sorts of other mystical creatures. It's very much a part of Scotland's culture. You should ask Ross about that." Grandma MacGregor patted Caitie's arm.

What was with everybody in Scotland?

"So, Mum, how are the McLean's?"

With the conversation steered to people she didn't know, Caitie let her mind wander. She had to admit their grandma seemed pretty nice. There might be some good things to come from this move after all. Up 'til now, she hadn't given that any thought. Maybe their grandparents' place would be a lot bigger and nicer than their old house in San Diego. Mom did say it was on Loch Ness, and in California homes by the water always cost a lot and were usually fancy. She didn't want her grandparents' place to be a castle with lots of creepy paintings of strangers and furniture that looked old and uncomfortable. But a big house with plenty of space would be pretty sweet—especially one with her own bathroom. Maybe they could even talk their grandparents into converting a spare bedroom into a media/game room where she and her new friends could hang out. That is, if she could find new ones as good as her friends back home.

Ross turned from the road onto a gravel driveway, lurching Caitie back to reality. To the right, stood a small white stucco house with little windows that seemed to pop out of the gray roof. It reminded her of the dwarves' cottage in Snow White, only way plainer. To the left, lots of red curly-haired cattle with broad heads, huge brown eyes, and wide pink noses grazed in a fenced pasture, swishing their tails. Several calves stood near their mothers, all watching the car as it passed by. Their new home was no estate, just a tiny, old farm.

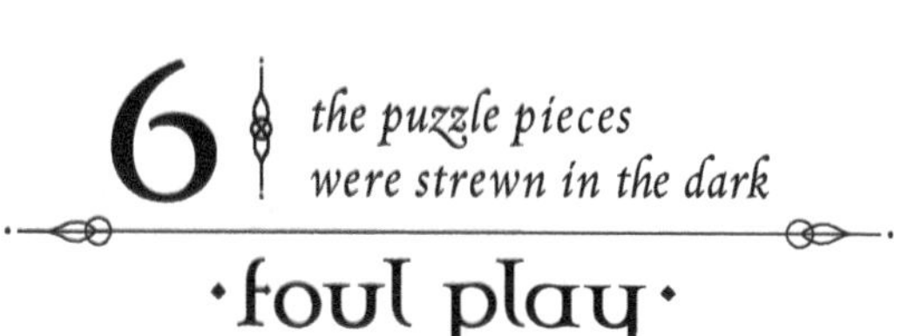

6 *the puzzle pieces were strewn in the dark*

· foul play ·

MUNGAN LOOKED DOWN AT TIANNA'S LIFELESS SHELL, torn between grief and a desire for vengeance. He had failed his sister. But what could he have done to prevent this? He racked his tortured mind, but there were no answers. If only Tianna had spoken with him last night, then perhaps things would be different.

As Searsanach, Mungan ensured all in the kingdom carried on as reliably as the sun rising, only this dawn brought a nightmare from which he could not awake. First Leannan, risking her life in the mortal realm, and even worse, threatening every other Daoine Shi by her irresponsible action; and now, Tianna dead, and most likely at the hands of one of their own. He felt as though the weight of the mountain above had collapsed on him, and he knew not how to prop it up.

Leannan wrung her hands at the queen's bedside. "What shall we do?"

"First, say nothing of Tianna's note. If the murderer knows not of her attempt to speak with me, they may tip their hand in a wee manner not noticeable to most, but I will be watching."

"Then I shan't, not even to Lileas."

"Good." He hoped Leannan would be true to her word for the two were as inseparable as dancing from music, and Lileas was a known gossip. "I need to know how they took Tianna's life. Only I must have Earnan's help."

"Then I shall fetch him." Leannan turned toward the door.

"No, not yet. 'Twill be best for ye to pretend to discover Tianna when ye bring her breakfast. After that we can alert him." Mungan opened his pocket watch. "The torch lights will change to gold in an hour and a half, and the cooks will arrive in the kitchen." He unclasped the watch chain from the loop on his breeches. "How long will it take ye to prepare a tray?"

"Only a few moments," Leannan said.

"Ye shall bring it at quarter past nine." He closed the cover and handed her the watch.

Leannan bit her lip, confusion clouding her pretty face. "Mungan, I do not know what is a quarter past nine. I only know the time by the changing color of the torches."

He sighed and opened his hand. "Of course not."

She placed the watch back in his palm. "Ye press the crown to open it like so." The engraved cover popped open, exposing the face. "The hands move as time passes. The short one marks the hours and the long, the minutes. At this moment, 'tis half past seven. When this hand," he tapped the glass above the long black pointer, "is here on the three, and the small hand is just past the number nine, that is when ye shall bring the tray."

She looked up at him with huge, dark blue-green eyes and nodded obediently.

"When the long hand reaches the four, ye shall leave to notify the king. At the same time I shall ask Earnan to breakfast. We shall meet in the corridor, and ye will share with us the wretched news. We will come here, and then ye shall fetch the king. Do ye understand?"

"I believe so."

He snapped the cover shut and offered her his prized possession once more. "King Oseron must be convinced ye have just discovered Tianna. If he finds out ye left the mountain, ye shall be imprisoned for breaking the code. Of that, I have no doubt. And I shall lose my position as Searsanach for not preventing it, and perhaps my life for instigating this deception."

Fear furrowed her brow. "I shall do my best, but I am afraid. Ye know we cannot lie."

"Aye." Mungan nodded. "But if ye do as I say, ye can speak true words to the king, and no one will be the wiser as to how and why we found Tianna earlier." He kneaded the back of his neck. "Now be off and do not fail me."

Leannan glided to the door, peeked out, and slipped from the chambers.

Turning to Tianna, he cupped her cold face in his hand. "Ye have left me all alone now."

MUNGAN PACED IN HIS CHAMBER AND WITH EVERY TURN OF HIS heel he read the mantel clock. Thirteen past nine. Leannan should be in the alcove preparing the tray. Fourteen past nine. Would his plan even work? Quarter past nine. She should be leaving for Tianna's chambers. Sixteen past nine. Did Leannan's flowing skirt even have a pocket for the watch? Seventeen past nine. If someone spotted it in her hand, they would know something was amiss. Eighteen past nine. She should be at Tianna's door. Nineteen past nine. 'Twas nearly time. Twenty past nine. He left his chamber, thoughts of the events to come tumbling through his mind.

Mungan rapped thrice on the wizard's door.

Earnan answered. "How are ye this fine morning, my friend? Still basking in the glow of your victory?" The wizard's robe undulated between cobalt blue and deep purple.

Mungan chuckled and tried to look as if he had not a trouble in all the fae realm. "I am hopeful my worthy opponent will breakfast with me."

"A fine idea." Earnan slipped his wand into the pocket of his robe and entered the passageway.

Leannan rushed toward them, her hands clutched to her chest and her face pale. "Mungan, Earnan, I beg of ye come quickly."

"What is troubling ye?" The knot in Mungan's stomach grew.

"'Tis the queen." Leannan's voice sounded as strained as a high fiddle string. Her eyes met his first and then flitted to Earnan's.

"Then we must go in haste." Earnan turned to close his door.

Mungan saw glints of gold in Leannan's clasped hands. With his heart thumping madly in his chest, Mungan reached his hand out to hers. She slipped him the watch. He hooked the clasp to the loop on his breeches, slid it into his pocket, and took a quieting breath. Earnan's door latch click closed, and the wizard turned to leave, his robe now violet-red.

"Tell us, Leannan, what is the matter?" Mungan asked.

"I fear Queen Tianna is dead." Her voice broke.

Mungan's mind conjured up his sister's lifeless eyes. "Say 'tis not so!" The three raced down the corridor to Tianna's chambers.

"Ye must be mistaken," Earnan said, breathless. "She was fine last night."

Leannan stopped in front of the queen's door. "I wish that I were."

Mungan flung the birch teardrop open. He rushed to his sister's bedside. Fresh waves of grief washed over him as he retraced his steps. "Tianna!" Her body was white as a pearl, her glow completely extinguished.

Earnan drew to the opposite side of the canopy bed and gently touched the queen's temple. "Her fire within is gone."

"When did she leave us?" Unspilt tears blurred Mungan's vision.

"By the glaze of her eyes and the absence of her glow, at least six hours or so." Earnan pulled the brocade duvet and silk sheet back from her chest.

Tianna's folded hands rested oddly on her stomach, the tips of each thumb touching as well as her pointer fingers. She looked eerily beautiful like a white marble statue about to speak. The gathered neck of her silk chemise exposed her smooth shoulders, and her golden mane framed her delicate face. The blossom of her life had just fully opened. She should have lived another four hundred years, at least, and her wee babe known the gift of life.

Mungan looked up and found Leannan standing close to the table by the door where she had set the queen's breakfast tray. "Leannan, go to King Oseron's chambers. Tell him I request he come at once."

"I know not if he is able," Earnan said. "The king slipped last night in the treasure room and injured his back. Cormag and Lileas assisted him to his chambers. I gave him a potion for the pain and asked Lileas to tend to him and call for me in case he took a turn for the worse."

"I was not aware," Mungan said. "Nevertheless, he must be told."

"Aye." Leannan curtseyed and left, quietly closing the door behind her.

"May I call upon ye to lift Queen Tianna's body?" Earnan asked.

Mungan coaxed his palms under her shoulder blades and knees and gently scooped Tianna up, cradling her in his arms. She was icy and limp. Her head lolled back. A dagger thrust through his heart could be no more painful.

Earnan cleared the drooping fabric of her nightclothes off the sheet and bent down to inspect her head and back. "There is no wound. Ye may lay her down."

Mungan leaned over the bed and placed Tianna's body back where she had lain. He tenderly pulled down the hem of her gown.

Earnan studied her vacant eyes then gently closed them.

"What are ye doing?" King Oseron hobbled into Tianna's chambers following Leannan. He leaned on a carved hawthorn cane, supported on one side by Cormag and hefty Lileas on the other. His salt and pepper hair was disheveled, and his velvet robe hung open. "What has happened here?" His reddened face contorted as he moved.

Mungan had not expected King Oseron to be so impaired.

"Queen Tianna is… dead, Your Majesty," Earnan said softly.

King Oseron halted with the cane frozen in mid-air. He covered his mouth with his other hand.

Leannan winced at the words, Lileas's mouth gaped, and Cormag wore his typical sullen expression.

"No, 'tis not possible. I cannot believe it. I will not believe it! All was well with her last night." The king braced himself with the cane and limped toward Tianna's body. He grasped the queen's hand and raised it to his cheek. "Awake, my beloved, awake!" He kissed her hand and laid it down at her side. His devotion to Tianna for over two hundred and fifty years never wavered. "How could this have happened?"

"It appears there was no struggle," Earnan said.

"So she died in her sleep." King Oseron stroked Tianna's hair.

Mungan shook his head. "That makes no sense. Tianna was vibrant and still so young."

The king's eyes flashed disapproval at the strong contradiction of his words.

Earnan scissored his snowy beard between his fingers and glanced at the table by Tianna's bed. He raised his bushy brows. "She could have been poisoned."

"With what?" King Oseron demanded.

"Perhaps iron or St. John's wort," Earnan said. "And I noticed last night when I made a potion for your pain, Your Majesty, that my vial of wort was not where it should be."

Mungan stepped to the table by the bed and studied the silver tray next to the candlestick. The napkin free from the braided silver ring hung off the tray. "Could either have taken her life with such haste?"

Earnan's robe undulated between burgundy and black. "Iron is more potent than the St. John's wort. Even so, I would suspect her to have suffered a few hours."

"But ye believe her fire died more than six hours ago." Mungan picked up the silver chalice to smell the remaining drops pooled at the bottom. There was nothing but the fruity bouquet of elderberries.

"Aye, I still do."

Lileas engulfed Leannan in her arms. The hefty maidservant gently patted the back of the grief-stricken maiden who buried her face in Lileas's generous shoulder.

"When did ye bring Tianna her tray last night?" Mungan asked.

Leannan pulled away from Lileas. "Mere moments after ye saw me in the corridor."

"I left for my chamber shortly before two o'clock." He reached in his pocket for the watch and opened the cover. "'Tis now roughly half-past nine. If my sister has been dead for six hours, then she left us somewhere close to half-past three."

The king pounded his cane on the stone floor. "Tell me in terms I comprehend."

"Over half the span for the silver-blue torches, Your Majesty." Mungan turned to Earnan. "Then she could not have lingered for several hours. It must have been something else."

The wizard raised his pointer finger as if he seized a solution to the puzzle from the ceiling. "St. John's wort and iron together could have acted quickly."

Perhaps someone had tainted a cask with iron filings and the wort. "Where did ye pour the wine from, Leannan?" Mungan asked.

"The same cask of elderberry wine I have used the past fortnight. I had a wee dram of it myself before I brought the tray."

"And the cheese?" He picked up a slab from the salver, smelled, and pressed it to the tip of his tongue. Its delicate flavor with the hint of woodland moss was unspoiled.

"From the blocks prepared for the chess match. That cheese was served to all," she said.

"What was Tianna doing when ye brought in her tray?"

"She sat there, brushing her hair." Leannan nodded toward the dressing table.

Mungan spied his sister's gown draped over the painted screen that segregated her dressing area from the rest of the chamber. "Had she changed into her bedclothes?"

"No. Queen Tianna was still in her gown." Leannan's distraught gaze went to the screen where the lavender sleeves hung limp over the forest scene.

"Did she say anything unusual?" Mungan asked.

"Merely that she was tired. I set the tray on the table, turned down the bedcover..." Leannan bit her lips and wiped a tear from her eye. "And bid her pleasant dreams."

"Can ye tell if the wine or cheese is tainted, Mungan?" King Oseron asked.

"It appears not. Leannan, come, look carefully. Is everything on the tray as ye remember?" He stepped back from the table. She picked up the goblet. Her eyes grew as wide as the eyes on a peacock's feathers. "'Tis a different chalice than the one I brought." Leannan pointed to the engraving on the cup.

He went to her side. "How so?"

"'Tis one of Queen Tianna's, no doubt, but the engraving on each is slightly different. This one has a posy of foxgloves. Yesterday was the first day of the week so I served her wine in the chalice with bluebells. The foxgloves are for the second day."

"Perhaps ye are mistaken, Leannan. 'Twas very late last night. In fact 'twas truly the second day, was it not?" Mungan asked.

"Aye, 'twas late, but last night after tipping the tray, I wiped elderberry wine off bluebells, not foxgloves."

"Then go to the alcove, Leannan, and search the cupboard to see if the chalice with bluebells is missing."

Leannan nodded and curtseyed to leave.

"Cormag, accompany her. And Leannan, keep your tongue as guarded as the Daoine Shi treasure," King Oseron said. "I shall be the one to tell the others of our loss."

"Aye, Your Majesty." She hurried off.

"Leannan was the last to see Tianna alive," the king said. "Could she have done this?"

Earnan shook his head. "Leannan is loyal and kind. She would gain nothing by it."

Mungan swallowed hard. Were her ventures out of the mountain reason enough? No, he had looked in her eyes. There was guilt in them at the portal, but none at discovering Tianna—only grief for a lost loved one.

"Then how was the cup poisoned without Queen Tianna's knowledge?" the king asked.

"Perhaps they slipped in while Tianna changed into her bedclothes, added iron and St John's wort to her chalice, and left unnoticed. Once they were sure she was dead, they returned and exchanged the poisoned cup with this." Mungan picked up the goblet.

"It seems more likely that Tianna's maidservant did the deed than someone else as ye propose, Mungan. Perhaps Leannan was disgruntled and—"

"Your Majesty," Lileas interrupted. "'Twas not Leannan who had cause to commit this crime. Several days ago as I prepared the alcove for dinner, I heard something most disquieting. My serving spoon slipped between the back wall and the table, heaped with food. In a rush, I ducked beneath the table to retrieve the spoon. I heard the queen tell Ballard to step into the alcove as she needed to speak to him in private."

The king tilted his head and wrinkled his brow. "And they did not see ye?"

Lileas flushed. "No. 'Tis a very large table and the linen covering it touched the floor."

"Oh." The king's eyes narrowed with doubt.

"Go on," Mungan urged.

"Queen Tianna said, 'I know what ye are doing, Ballard. Ye had better put an end to it, before I tell the king.'"

The king straightened and grimaced. "Surely ye are mistaken. Ballard is a trusted guard."

She hung her head low. "I am certain of what I heard, Your Majesty."

"And how did Ballard reply?" King Oseron asked.

"He told her, 'I am guilty of nothing.' And she said, 'I saw ye come out with bloody hands, and I know how it happened.' Then he said, 'Ye do not understand.' And she said back to him 'There is nothing to understand! And your actions shan't be tolerated.' Then Ballard demanded, 'Do not speak of this to the king or anyone else, Queen Tianna, for ye are sorely wrong.' And she spat back at him, 'We shall see about that!'"

"Did the queen ever speak to ye of this, Your Majesty?" Mungan asked.

The king gazed down at Tianna and shook his head. "No, nary a word."

"Lileas, where had Ballard been that upset the queen so?" Mungan asked.

"I know not, but I tell ye the fire in Queen Tianna burned with rage, and at dinner I noticed scratches and puncture wounds on Ballard's hands."

"Only murder or thievery would prompt such ire in my sister."

King Oseron shook his head. "But no one is unaccounted for." He took a step and winced. Lileas rushed to his side and helped him limp to a chair. Once seated, the king rested his hands on the crook of his cane.

"Then Tianna must have caught Ballard stealing." Mungan crossed his arms. "Perhaps he was in the treasure room."

"I cannot believe it." King Oseron thumped the cane on the floor. "Mungan, we must confront Ballard at once on this matter. Bring him to my chambers."

"Aye, Your Majesty. I shall go in haste."

"And have Cormag join us, in case Ballard is indeed guilty and attempts to escape."

"What shall we do with Queen Tianna's body?" Earnan asked.

King Oseron looked mournfully at the queen but said nothing.

Mungan was torn between fear for their safety outside the mountain and his desire to honour his sister. A proper funeral was the last gift he could give Tianna. She would want to rest next to their parents. "Our tradition calls for her to lie in state in the Crystal Garden till midnight, when we shall leave the mountain and bury her in the kirk cemetery with every Daoine Shi honour."

Earnan's robe shifted to red-violet. "But we have not left for a funeral in nearly two hundred years." He looked in Mungan's eyes, and the story of that dreadful night went unspoken.

"What then would ye propose?" King Oseron's voice was sharp, his countenance grim.

"We have laid the other five in the dungeon at your command, the risk too great of an encounter with the Unseelies." Earnan paused. "Or mortals."

King Oseron raised his folded hands to his face and tapped them against his chin. "Perhaps 'tis best not to leave."

"'Tis not fitting for our queen to rest in the dungeon. There will be an uprising amongst our people," Mungan said.

King Oseron glanced at Earnan. "'Tis not a time for discord. We shall speak to Ballard before I announce our grievous loss to all in the kingdom. Then, Mungan, ye shall make the arrangements for Tianna."

"And now I shall take my leave and confirm my St. John's wort is indeed missing." Earnan bowed and left in haste.

'Twas the right decision for Tianna, but for the rest of the Daoine Shi, Mungan was not so sure.

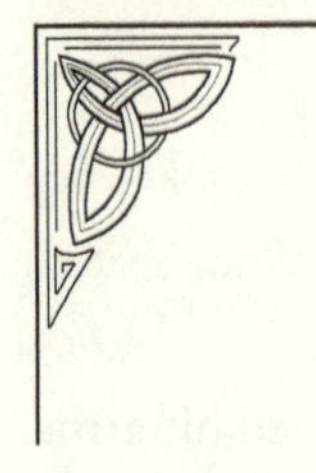

7 *if wishes were horses, two beggars would ride*

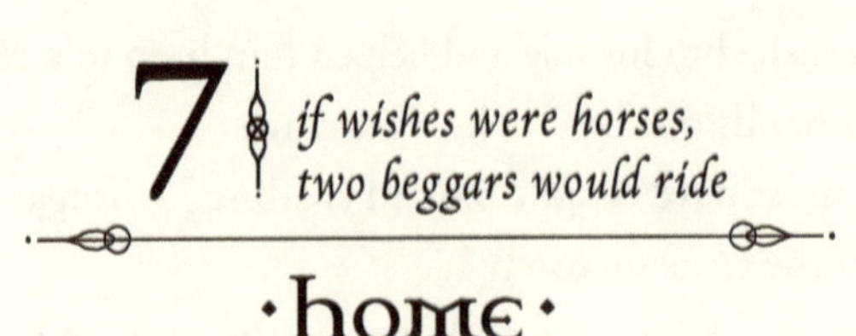

·home·

9:30 AM
JUNE 20TH

CAITIE'S HEART SANK AS ROSS PULLED THE STATION WAGON up to the end of the driveway between the back of the house and an ancient stone barn.

Mom smiled. "It's just as I remember."

Caitie reluctantly unbuckled her seatbelt. Why shouldn't it be? Anything this old can't change much, except to fall down. The car doors clunked open, and the smell of cow manure bombarded her nose. No wonder Mom didn't tell them their grandparents lived on a farm. She would've run away instead of getting on the plane.

The gravel crunched under her feet as Caitie got out of the car. Pines and some other kind of trees with white bark bordered the big backyard all the way down to a strip of rocky beach along the lake. An orange-stained wood boat with a small cabin was tied to one side of an old gray dock and a small white dinghy was on the other. The dock was as far away from the cows as she'd be able to get, and it looked like a good place for her to sit and hope that someday, someone in a big, shiny boat would come rescue her.

A stocky old man in overalls, a plaid flannel shirt, and khaki cap walked out from the other end of the barn carrying boards and a saw. That had to be their grandfather. He stopped near a stone shed and laid the wood on the ground, picked up the top one from the stack, and set it on a pair of metal stands. Mom shut the car door. He glanced over his shoulder and then turned back to saw the board. *How rude.*

Ross took her and Mom's suitcases into the house while Robbie struggled to roll his bag over the loose gravel. "Is that our grandfather?" her brother asked.

Mom sighed. "Aye." Caitie could hear the stress in Mom's voice, and it made her own stomach tighten.

Clap. Clap. "Get out of there!" Grandma MacGregor shouted as she opened the backdoor. A bunny, not in any hurry, hopped out of a huge garden on the opposite side of the yard.

Ross walked back out the door. "Was that directed at me?" he asked with a big grin.

"No, I was scolding a wee rabbit feasting on my carrots."

"Lucky for me, you weren't watching when I nicked a radish the other day," he teased as he sauntered toward the shed.

Grandma MacGregor shook her head, pretending to be mad, but her eyes sparkled.

The comforting smell of something fresh out of the oven filled the air as Caitie stepped inside the house. She closed her eyes and breathed deep. The scones Mom baked smelled like that. Her suitcase was next to a wood chest opposite the backdoor. On the chest was an old fashioned phone with a cord and a disk you twirled to dial. The only time she'd ever used one like that was when she called Mickey in the Disneyland Guest Services Center, and he wished her Happy Birthday.

She checked out the kitchen with its old cabinets and appliances. Something was missing. Where were the dishwasher and microwave? How could anyone live without those?

"We're giving you my old sewing room, Maisie, and Caitie and Robbie can have the bedrooms upstairs," Grandma MacGregor said.

"That's fine." Mom left her bag in the hallway outside the laundry room. "And where does Ross stay, Mum?"

"When we heard you wanted to come home, he decided to move into the shed."

Mom cringed like she'd just found moldy leftovers in the fridge. "The shed?"

"I know it sounds rather dismal. But he and your father have worked on it night and day for the last two months making it livable in time for your arrival. It turned out quite well, too."

Grandma MacGregor led them across worn hardwood floors to the living room with old people recliners and a boring beige couch. There was a TV, but it wasn't a flat screen. They followed her up the creaky staircase in the center of the house. She reached the landing and pointed to the left. "There's the bathroom. You'll be sharing it with your granddad and me. I cleaned out the bottom two drawers so you each could have one."

One drawer couldn't hold much more than her hair dryer. She turned to Mom behind her. "How many bathrooms are in this house?" she mouthed.

"One and a half," Mom mouthed back.

Caitie's jaw dropped. "No!" she said silently.

Mom nodded yes.

This is just great. At the top of the stairs, they turned right heading toward two bedrooms.

"Robbie, this is your room," Grandma said, pointing to the first one. It looked out on the lake. No, the loch. "Yours is at the end of the hall, Caitie. I hope you like them."

"Thanks, Grandma." Caitie said, trying to sound grateful.

"You're quite welcome. I'm going to let you two get settled now. There are scones in the kitchen when you get hungry." Grandma MacGregor disappeared down the stairs.

Caitie walked into her new bedroom. It looked old-fashioned and smelled that way. Mom pushed back the lace curtains and cranked the window open to let in some fresh air. The twin bed with its flower-speckled spread was way smaller than the double she had in their old house. There was a dainty lamp on the nightstand, a wardrobe instead of a closet, and crocheted thingies on every flat surface. Her heart sank to a new low.

She rolled her suitcase close to the wardrobe and sat on the bed. The springs squeaked under her weight. The room was okay for a little Scottish girl a hundred years ago, but she couldn't make this place her own. Her string of mini-surfboard lights and band posters wouldn't work in here.

Mom rubbed her back. "This used to be my room, Caitie. I remember waking up under my toasty duvet and looking at the snow covered hills on winter mornings. In the summer, the trilling of the skylarks would wake me. It's really a great room."

"Not for me, Mom. None of my stuff goes with a frilly lamp, all this crocheted stuff, and a girly-girl bedspread."

"In time, I'm sure you'll be able to make this room your own, Caitie. I'm going downstairs to unpack. Call me, if you need anything."

Caitie opened up her overnight bag. She pulled out her iPod, the charger, and electrical adapters Mom bought in the U.S. before leaving. Her iPod died somewhere over the Atlantic, but with it plugged in and the *Do not disconnect* message displayed, she knew it wouldn't be long before she'd at least have her music.

She dug back in her bag again and retrieved her cell phone. Now that she'd finally be able to get a signal, she'd text her best friend Sara. Caitie plugged the dead phone into her charger and hit the power button, fingers poised to press the keys.

No Service appeared on the bright blue phone display.

"Mom!" Caitie yelled.

Her mother dashed up the stairs. "What is it, Caitie?"

"I can't get service here." She held the phone display so Mom could see it.

Mom covered her mouth like she was thinking but didn't say anything.

"Don't you get it?" Caitie cried. "I can't call anybody. This can't be happening to me."

"I was afraid of that."

"It's because you got me the cheapest phone in the world."

Mom crossed her arms. "Are you paying for it, Caitie?"

"No."

"Then don't complain. When we got your phone, I had no idea that we'd be moving here. We'll drive back into Inverness tomorrow and see what we can do."

"Tomorrow! I promised Sara I'd text as soon as I got here. I haven't texted anybody since we changed planes at JFK."

"We haven't been here fifteen minutes. It would be incredibly rude to turn right around and go back to Inverness. You'll just have to wait."

"Mom, I can't live without my phone. I didn't want to come here in the first place. I don't know anyone. I need my friends back home."

"Tomorrow, Caitie," Mom said.

"Hey, can I get a phone too?" Robbie called from his room.

"No, Robbie, we've already been over this a hundred times. Not 'til you're 13." Mom retreated down the stairway.

"You got me disconnected from the world!" Caitie shouted. "I gotta be able to text my friends. And I promised I'd call Alicia the day of the party." Caitie scrolled through the few pictures she had on her old flip phone. Maybe it was going to work out better for her this way. At least, now Mom might let her get a smartphone.

I wonder if I can get these pics transferred to my new one.

If she couldn't call, she'd get on Facebook. She looked for the computer amongst the moving boxes stacked in the corner. It wasn't there. She found it in Robbie's room.

With the monitor in her arms, she started for the door. "I use this way more than you do."

"But the desk is in here," Robbie said.

"I'll set it on the floor."

"That's stupid."

She bit her lip and squinched her eyes tight. She hated it when her little brother was right. This house sucked! "Okay, it can stay in here," she agreed, "but only as long as I can use it whenever I want." They started plugging everything in. "Where's the internet connection?"

"I don't know," Robbie answered.

She raced from wall to wall frantically searching, but couldn't find it. She took a deep breath. "I'm so stupid. It's somewhere else in the house." She booted up and searched for a wireless network. Only one popped up.

Robbie hovered over her shoulder. "What do you think the password is?"

"I'll go find out." She bounced down the stairs and into the kitchen. "Grandma?"

"Yes, dear?"

"What's your network password?"

"Password?" Grandma's crinkled eyebrows and tilted chin straightened as she stood taller and smiled. "Here in Scotland you don't need a password to watch the telly."

"No, Grandma, your computer's password for the internet."

Grandma seemed to deflate. "We don't have a computer, Caitie."

This couldn't be happening! "You don't?"

Mom walked in the kitchen and gave her that *I don't believe you're doing this* look.

"Is an internet important?" Grandma MacGregor asked.

"It's not 'an' internet, Grandma. It's 'the' internet and my computer's worthless without it."

"Well then, where does one get the internet?"

"The cables for it must be installed. It's a service, Mum."

"We could pay for it, so it wouldn't cost you anything," Caitie offered. "And it helps a ton with your homework."

"I see," Grandma MacGregor said. "Since we don't have a computer, I never learned about them. Your granddad is a bit thrawn and doesn't care much for such newfangled things."

"What's thrawn mean?" Caitie asked.

"Stubborn," Mom said. "And in your granddad's case, not always right but never in doubt."

Grandma MacGregor raised her eyebrows and eyed Mom with pursed lips. She turned to Caitie. "Perhaps we can look into it, if it will help with your schooling."

The backdoor opened, and her grandfather came in without saying a word or even looking in their direction. He disappeared down the hall, and a door creaked shut.

What's with him?

"There might be an internet cafe in the village, Caitie. Maybe you'd like to go after you finished unpacking your things." Mom flashed her a nervous smile then turned and moved toward the backdoor. Heavy footsteps plodded across the wood floor.

"Hello, Dad," Mom said, her voice quiet and little girlish.

He stopped by the back door and looked at Mom. "Maisie."

"Thank you for letting us come."

"You're my daughter. This is your home. I wouldn't turn you away." He stared deep into her eyes.

"I'm sorry for hurting you when I left. I loved Tom and had to make a choice."

"That you did."

"He was a good man, Dad."

Grandma MacGregor whispered in Caitie's ear. "Why don't you go upstairs and ask your brother if he'd like to come down in a bit for some scones?" She gently ushered her out through the doorway to the dining room. Caitie stopped at the bottom of the stairs to listen.

"That's debatable. Tom Finlay was an American who came to Scotland, found what he wanted, and took it."

You freakin' jerk! Caitie wanted to slug him for talking about Dad that way.

"It wasn't like that, Dad, and you know it. You never gave Tom a chance," Mom said.

"He never let me. You barely knew him, Maisie."

"I knew him well enough to know I didn't want to spend the rest of my life without him."

You go, Mom!

"It looks like you will now anyway, Maisie. We all eventually pay for wrong choices."

What wrong choices? Caitie peeked around the stairwell. Mom's cheeks glistened with tears.

"You callous—" Mom cried.

"Don't you speak to me that way," her grandfather roared.

"Tom tried to ask you for my hand in marriage and your prejudice kept you from hearing it. We had no time to wait for you. He had orders to return stateside."

"I am not stupid, Maisie. He got you pregnant, and there was no proper kirk wedding."

What? No wonder Mom never told them.

"I never said you were. We were married at the Registrar's Office in Inverness. You can check the records." Mom stormed down the hallway to her room. Her grandfather hung his head and went back outside. The door slapped shut behind him.

Caitie stood there stunned. She'd been sure she was a honeymoon baby that came early.

Robbie rushed down the stairs past her and raced to Mom's room. He'd heard it all. They probably did in Inverness too.

She hated it here! How could Mom have been so stupid to move them a million miles from home and dump them into this mess?

8 *the truth was sought*

· the suspect ·

EVERY FIBER IN MUNGAN'S BEING WAS TAUT WITH tension as he marched Ballard through the golden lit corridor leading to King Oseron's chambers.

"What is this about?" the guard asked as he swaggered toward the gilded door.

Mungan did not answer. 'Twas best to let him stew. He ushered Ballard inside the spacious chambers and up the steps to the circular alcove where King Oseron sat at his great walnut burl table, eyes closed, his forehead resting on his hands. Cormag leaned against one of the five marble columns and stared at the mural of Loch Duntelchaig surrounding them. Gulls skimmed the dark water's surface and shifting winds rustled the leaves in the trees.

"Ye called for me, Your Majesty?" Ballard asked.

King Oseron opened his eyes and lifted his head. "Proceed, Mungan."

He inched the guard backwards toward one of the columns. "The queen has been poisoned, Ballard. And we have a witness that heard ye threaten Queen Tianna several days ago."

Gone was Ballard's perpetual smirk. The guard's black eyes widened at the accusation, and he looked as frightened as if cornered by a mongrel in the mortal realm.

"Your witness is wrong," Ballard said, his neck muscles tight, his eyes shifting between Mungan, the king, and Cormag.

"The witness is reliable," King Oseron said, his face stern, the whites of his eyes lined red with grief.

Mungan thrust his face inches from Ballard's crooked nose. "The witness heard Queen Tianna accuse ye of an act of impropriety. She saw your bloody hands, confirming in her mind ye had done the deed she suspected."

Ballard backed against the column. He raised his hands for an instant and glanced at them.

Mungan spotted the remnants of scratches and puncture wounds. So Lileas was right. He would take great pleasure in firing the flaming arrow to take this blaggard's life. "Is it not true that Queen Tianna caught ye coming from the treasure room after trying to steal gold?"

Ballard shifted his weight uncomfortably, his facial muscles twitching. "'Tis true Queen Tianna found me with blood on my hands, but I had been in the Glassblowers' Shoppe long after the craftsmen left for the day. I made a fine crystal goblet for Nuala to win her heart but dropped it, shattering the gift into a thousand shards. I cut my hands whilst gathering the pieces in haste."

Ballard was wily, but the ease with which these words rolled off his tongue took Mungan by surprise. Could there be some truth in them? Even though the Daoine Shi could not lie, they could be masterful at twisting words to their advantage. The Daoine Shi code declared roles to be respected and a cobbler not a painter be, but for Tianna to be so livid over Ballard trying to fashion a gift to woo the dancer did not ring true. Mungan studied Ballard as the guard looked to the king, begging for mercy with his eyes.

Ballard raised his hands close to Mungan's face and turned them over. "These hands did not steal treasure or life from Queen Tianna. After the chess match last night, Nuala and I went to the Crystal Garden. 'Twas nearly dawn before we left. She will bear witness to the truth of my words."

"Ye can be sure I will seek out Nuala to do just that," Mungan said. He thought of the night before and Nuala's attentiveness to himself. She was quite like a beautiful cat, loyal to none, but attentive to the one who at the moment held the sweetest cup o' cream.

King Oseron stared hard at Ballard. In all the years he had reigned, Mungan had never seen him rush to judge one of the Daoine Shi.

"Ballard, ye may take your leave for now. However, Cormag shall accompany ye at all times until we have verified ye were indeed with Nuala last night. And one more thing, neither of ye will speak a word of what has been said within these walls to anyone," King Oseron said.

"Aye, Your Majesty," Ballard said.

The guard was hiding something to be sure. Perhaps Ballard had stolen away, done the deed, and then spent the rest of the night with Nuala. He must not be allowed to get word to the dancer to bolster his story. Mungan had to speak with Nuala first. He fixed a smoldering eye on the guard. "Perhaps, King Oseron, 'twould be better for Ballard to remain in the dungeon until we resolve this matter with Nuala."

"Ballard has been a trusted guard for years. 'Twould be unjust to lock him away when he has a reasonable explanation for the wounds on his hands and the encounter with Queen Tianna. Cormag will ensure he does not speak with Nuala before we do."

King Oseron's unwillingness to detain Ballard was too generous.

"Aye, I will, Your Majesty," Cormag said.

"Now take your post outside the queen's chambers and make certain no one else enters them," King Oseron said.

Mungan reluctantly stepped aside.

Ballard swallowed hard and bolted from the king's chambers without his typical swagger. Cormag filed out after him. Mungan pulled him back.

"Ye best ensure Ballard's silence or ye will find yourself in as much trouble, Cormag," Mungan said in a low voice.

The sour guard sneered before leaving.

Mungan turned to the king. "I shall go in haste to find Nuala and speak with her."

"Ye must wait a wee while, Mungan. All in the kingdom must be gathered in the Great Hall that I may share our most grievous news. I need ye at my side as I make the announcement. The Daoine Shi must see that despite our unspeakable loss, the kingdom is not in disarray." The king tilted his head back and grimaced. "Do not fear, Mungan. Ballard would not be so foolish as to speak with Nuala when he has been forbidden to. Cormag will see to it."

He wanted to argue—to ask why the king did not see Ballard was hiding something—but thought it best to hold his tongue. "Aye, Your Majesty."

"Then ye must see to the bier. I want everything to be beautiful for my Tianna." The king looked into his eyes. "I am grateful that I can rely on ye Mungan, in my hour of grief." King Oseron took a deep breath before he hobbled out the door.

Mungan felt as though his own grief, the pursuit of Tianna's murderer, and his duty to oversee her funeral were like three strands of a rope unraveling despite his effort to hold it together. Each demanded his full attention, yet he was unable to give any concern its due.

9 *the value of the gift was underestimated*

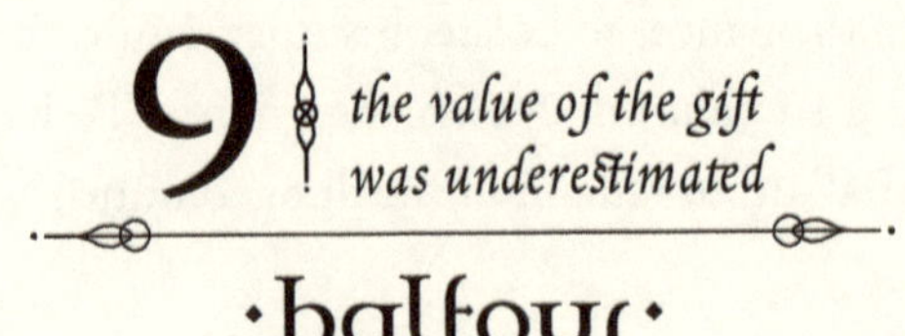

·balfour·

1:09 PM
JUNE 20TH

ROBBIE FOUND MOM SITTING ON THE SIDE OF HER BED IN front of the picture window that looked out on Loch Ness. Her head was in her hands. Her back shuddered with each faint sob. He knocked softly on the doorframe. She turned and tried to smile, then wiped away the tears streaming down her face.

"Are you okay?" He couldn't stand to see Mom cry. He snatched a tissue from a box on the nightstand, scrambled onto the bed, and handed it to her.

"Yes, Robbie. Thanks." She opened her arms for a hug.

He held her tight.

"Your granddad and I just have to work through our differences."

"We could always go back to California, Mom."

"Running away won't fix a problem. I did that sixteen years ago, and it only made things worse."

"He didn't even say 'Hi' to me and Caitie. He doesn't like us 'cause we're Americans, like Dad."

"You and your sister are his only grandchildren. He just needs to get to know you."

"I don't want to get to know him. Not if he's going to hurt you."

He heard barking. And where there's a bark, there's a dog. His heart beat faster, and he craned his neck, looking out the window to find it. He couldn't hide his excitement. "Do they have a dog, Mom?"

"Sounds like it. Why don't you go and see."

"Sure you're okay?"

"I'm fine, Robbie, really."

He ran out the bedroom and through the backdoor. His grandfather stood talking to an old lady inside a silver car, idling in the driveway. A black dog sat obediently at the old man's side. The backdoor banged shut behind him, and the dog cranked its neck around. It had deep brown eyes and a fluffy white chest.

Ross came around the far corner of the barn carrying an egg carton. He opened the passenger door and put it on the seat. The lady handed Ross some money and thanked him.

"See you Saturday night, Fiona." His grandfather gave a quick pat to the roof of the car.

"Give my best to Ina." The lady rolled up the window and drove off.

Ross disappeared into the barn, and his grandfather strolled back to the sawhorses with the Border Collie alongside. The old man lifted the handsaw and started cutting a board, sawing back and forth, smooth and steady. Robbie got down on his haunches and patted his knee, trying to call the dog over without his grandfather noticing. The dog's ears perked up, and he cocked his head. His grandfather stopped and turned around.

Dang!

"Come here, Robbie," his grandfather called.

He didn't want to, but he didn't want the old man yelling again either. Robbie got up, put his hands in the pockets of his jeans, and fingered his pocketknife as he ambled toward his grandfather.

The old man frowned with his whole face and waved Robbie over. "Pull those hands out of your pockets and move. It's downright disrespectful to dally like that when you're called by one of your elders."

"I'm sorry," Robbie took his hands out and walked faster.

"You want to meet my dog?"

Duh wasn't going to be the right answer. "Yes, sir," Robbie said in his most respectful tone. "Where was he when we got here earlier?"

"Checking on the sheep in the pasture." His grandfather crossed his arms.

"What's his name?" Robbie asked.

"Balfour."

"Never heard that one before," he said. "I used to have a Golden Lab." He wondered if the old man was the reason they had to leave Gunner behind.

"Balfour's a fine name for a herder. It means from the pastureland."

"Can I pet him?" Robbie asked.

"You'll have to ask him yourself."

Robbie slowly squatted down with one knee in the grass. He reached his hand out patiently. Balfour didn't move a muscle, so Robbie raised his palm and brought it gently to the dog's nose, allowing him to sniff it. Balfour checked out each finger, his wet nose twitching. Robbie stretched his hand further and scratched under the dog's chin.

"It looks like my dog thinks you're all right. What do you like to do, Robbie?"

"Play video games and…"

"Video games! They're a waste of time. You should be out in the fresh air."

Video games are a lot more fun, but there wasn't much chance he'd convince the old man of it. "I also play the guitar."

"Playing an instrument is a fine skill." His grandfather put his hands on his hips and crossed one foot in front of the other, resting the toe of his work boot in the grass. "Do you play any sports?"

"I played baseball for a couple of seasons. I was okay at it, but not great." Robbie inched closer to Balfour and scratched the dog behind his ear. Balfour closed his eyes a little and stretched his neck. His tail swished back and forth.

"The boys play shinty here in the Highlands. Ever heard of it?"

"No," Robbie said.

"It's a very old game going back before the history of Scotland was ever recorded. In America, the closest thing to our shinty would be field hockey. We have a fine team here in the village. It's an honour to be a part of it."

He could see where this was headed and didn't like it. "I never played hockey, ever."

"No reason that should stop you from trying shinty. We'll have to build up your muscles, but that should easy enough. There's always plenty of work to do on a farm."

"Great," Robbie said, not knowing what else to say.

"You want to show me what you can do?"

Robbie felt cornered. If he said yes, he had no idea what he was signing up for. Saying no didn't seem like a good idea either. "Uhh."

"Come here, lad, let's see you finish the cut on this board."

Robbie stood up and walked over to the sawhorses. He gripped the handle on the saw and jerked it back and forth. The saw caught in the slot each time he pulled and pushed. He couldn't get any kind of rhythm going. Five minutes later he was wiped out and had only managed a half inch more on the cut. He started to put down the saw.

"You're not going to stop now, are you? Why, when your mother was your age, she'd have had the board sawed through by now."

"My mom?" He couldn't remember ever seeing her with even a screwdriver.

"Aye, she was a strong girl."

"Don't you have a power saw to do this?"

"I have one, but I use it for big chores. This one's fine for building a wee hen box. It helps to keep me strong."

"Whatever." He sawed the board until his hand hurt. He left the saw in the groove and gently pressed on the red, puffy skin. "I got a blister."

The old man looked down his wide nose at Robbie's hands. "We'll toughen you up and turn that into a callus in no time. That's enough sawing for now though. There's a bucket of tennis balls just inside the barn door. Balfour likes to play fetch, and the exercise will do you both good."

Robbie really wanted to lie down in the grass instead, but Balfour jumped around when he heard fetch, so he sauntered over to the barn. It was cool and dark inside, and the strong smell of manure, hay, wood, and old leather caused his nose to tingle. He grabbed the thick wire handle and brought the metal bucket full of bright yellow tennis balls outside. "Come here, Balfour."

The Border Collie loped over and danced, his tail wagging.

The metal handle clinked onto the bucket as Robbie plunked it down in the middle of the backyard. He picked up a ball and aimed for the woods. Balfour raced after the yellow streak and caught the ball mid-air. He trotted back and dropped his drool-covered prize at Robbie's feet.

"That was pretty good, Balfour." Robbie picked it up and tossed the ball again. Their easy game only lasted about a minute.

"Come on, Robbie. You're throwing like a young lass," his grandfather said.

"I am not."

"Turn a wee bit and use your body to pull your arm like a whip." His grandfather pretended to throw.

Bet the old man wouldn't complain I was throwing like a girl if I hit him with one. Robbie cranked his arm back and threw as hard as he could. The speed and distance surprised him as the bright ball flew into the woods. Balfour tore off after it.

"That's better," his grandfather said, nodding his head. A second later the dog was barking like crazy. "Balfour's found something. You'd better go see what it is."

You go see. This whole game was your idea.

But before he could muster up the courage to tell him that, his grandfather said, "You're not afraid of the woods, are you?"

He sure wasn't gonna admit it, or he'd never stop hearing about it. "No wonder Mom left," he said under his breath as he trudged into the woods. He picked his way through dense brush, following Balfour's bark. A ways in, he found the dog pawing at a thicket. He could see bits of yellow buried deep in a mass of tangled branches. "What's the matter, Balfour? Can't get the ball?"

The dog looked up and barked again.

"I'll get it out for you."

He stooped down and thrust his hand into the bushes several inches. Thorns pricked his skin. He slowly backed out his hand. It was lined with white scratch marks. He stepped on stalks to clear a bigger opening and slipped his hand in again. Leaves rustled, small twigs snapped, and a flurry of fur whirled in the small space surrounding the tennis ball. His heart jumped to his throat. He jerked his hand back and the scurrying stopped. Peering into the small open space, he spied a cottontail rabbit, its whiskers twitching and sides heaving.

"So the bunny's what's got you fired up, huh, Balfour? Poor guy's caught in a snare." The trap was probably set by the old man. Here was a way he could get even with him for the blister. "I'm gonna cut the rabbit loose, Balfour, and you gotta leave him alone. He's a lot smaller than you. And scared too."

Robbie reached in and pulled out the ball. The terrified rabbit scurried around unable to escape. He pulled Dad's knife from his pocket, flipped out the biggest blade, and struggled to cut the shiny gold wire loop around the bunny's mid-section. The rabbit's claws scratched his hands worse than the thorns. Pop! The wire loop sprang open. The bunny bounced around the tiny space 'til Robbie's hands cleared the thicket. "Come on, Balfour."

The dog stayed low to the ground, his ears perked up, and his eyes fixed on the opening, waiting for the rabbit to jump out.

"You don't want that bunny. Let's play ball instead." He looked over his shoulder and patted his thigh. The dog looked back once more at the hole and then trotted over. "That's a good boy." He bent down to pat Balfour on his side. Out of the corner of his eye, Robbie spotted two ears twitching near the opening in the thicket. He cupped Balfour's head in his hands so the dog couldn't see the rabbit and scratched him behind the ears. "I think you and I could be buddies."

The frightened bunny jumped through the hole and scampered off in the opposite direction. With the rabbit gone, he let go of Balfour and headed back to the yard. Robbie fingered the rich mahogany casing of his pocketknife the way Dad used to, the way he did the night before he left on deployment.

Dad had sat down on Robbie's bed. "I have something special I want you to take care of, bud."

"What is it?"

Dad opened his palm and held out the pocketknife. "This was my Dad's. He gave it to me the day I left for Officer Training in Quantico. His dad gave it to him when your grandpa left to fight in Vietnam."

"So it was my great-grandpa's?"

"Uh-huh. During World War II, his infantry division invaded Southern France. Your great-grandpa met a woman there on his way to Dijon. She was so grateful that he and the other American troops had come to free her country from Hitler, she gave him this knife and told him she hoped someday it would help him or his family, the way he had helped them."

"So why give it to me now?"

"I'm leaving, Robbie. I want you to carry it with you, and when you do, I'm hoping it will remind you of me and how much I love you."

"I love you too, Dad. But I don't need anything to make me think of you. I always do when you're away."

Dad smiled and tousled Robbie's hair. "I'm glad, but I want you to have it anyway."

Robbie studied the knife. On its side was a glass inlay the size of a small button. "What's the brown speck under the glass in the handle?"

"It's a mustard seed."

"It's awfully small."

"That's the point. The mustard seed is so tiny, yet it grows into something so much bigger and stronger."

"I'll never be tall, Dad. The doctor said so."

"But with just a little faith you can be strong and courageous, Robbie. You can do great things." Dad had wrapped his strong arm around him and squeezed tight.

Robbie stepped back onto Grandpa MacGregor's freshly mowed lawn, wondering if Dad would have been proud that he used the pocketknife to free the rabbit. It wasn't really courageous, but the bunny was probably happy.

"What was troubling Balfour?" his grandfather asked.

"He found a rabbit. It was trapped in the thicket where the ball landed."

"I see you got the ball, but what of the rabbit?"

"He was caught in a snare, so I cut him loose."

"You what?" the old man shouted.

Robbie tried to stand a little straighter. "I cut him loose."

"You were a right numpty to do that! I would have expected as much from your sister, but not from you. Rabbits destroy your gran's garden. They must be snared to keep the population down, or they'll eat every green plant they can reach. If you had fetched me, we'd be enjoying rabbit stew for dinner tomorrow and done the woods a favour."

The old man had no heart. Robbie picked up the bucket of tennis balls and headed toward the barn.

"Your mother may have raised you in the city, but you're in the Highlands on a farm now, and there'll be no coddling you here. Death's a part of life on a farm, and the sooner you come to understand that, the better off you'll be, Robbie."

There was no pleasing this guy. He looked over his shoulder at his grandfather, standing there, full of himself, like he was king. Balfour sat beside him looking up at the old man, like he really was king.

10 seeking the old, & finding the new

·getting connected·

CAITIE THREW HER OVERNIGHT BAG ON THE BED IN HER room. The springs squeaked a complaint. She was an accident. How could she have been so stupid not to figure it out? Her mom's secrecy about their grandparents—suddenly it all made sense. Getting pregnant and running away to get married wasn't something her perfect mother would want to share. She tore open the zipper and rifled through her bag. Her grandfather hated Dad. He hated probably her too. And her own parents had lied to her for her whole life. They didn't say the words, but they never set her straight either, which was just the same as lying.

Had Mom and Dad even wanted her when they found out? Maybe Dad married Mom just 'cause he thought he had to. "You'll make plenty of mistakes in life, Caitie," he always said, "but it's what you learn from them and do from there on out that counts." She may have been his mistake, but he loved her. She knew it. He didn't lie about that. She picked up the shirts wrapped around the most important thing that belonged to her and carefully unrolled them to get to the camera case. It was the last gift Dad ever gave her.

He knew how much she loved to take pictures. It was the one thing she was really good at. She was always borrowing Mom's camera without telling her and getting in trouble over it. Mom would need it for something and come storming into her room 'cause the camera wasn't in the desk drawer where it was supposed to be. Dad had fixed that though the day before he left for Afghanistan.

"Caitie, sweetie, I have something for you." He pulled the most beautiful package she'd ever seen from behind his back. It was wrapped in shiny paper with pale yellow and peach roses. A sparkly, gold fabric bow on top made the box almost too pretty to open. She knew instantly the gift was special. Dad was great, but he couldn't do anything like this. He must have paid someone to wrap it.

"What is it?" She tingled all over with excitement.

He beamed. "Open it and see."

She tore off the heavy paper. "Oh, Daddy!" Her eyes blurred when she saw it was the Panasonic Lumix she'd wanted. "I love it!" She held the box to her chest and threw an arm around him.

"I want you to record your world for me while I'm gone," he'd said tenderly. "All those little moments often turn out to be the really important ones in life."

"I will. I promise."

Caitie unzipped the black vinyl case and pulled her Lumix out. She curled up on the bed next to the suitcase and cradled the cool silver camera against her cheek. Her cupped hands sunk into the pillow. *I miss you, Daddy.* Tears streamed down her face 'til there were no more left.

She took a deep breath. Feeling sorry for herself wasn't making anything any better, but taking pictures and getting connected with friends would. She got up and plodded over to the vanity mirror. The smudged mascara streaked across her face made her look like some bad actress in a scary movie. With a little spit on a tissue, she wiped the black away. If only her life could be fixed that easily. She grabbed her camera and phone and traipsed down the stairs. "Mom?"

"Yes, Caitie."

She followed the voice until she found Mom in her room at the back of the house, unpacking the suitcase lying on the bed.

"Are you okay?" Caitie asked.

"I will be." Mom fingered the frame of a family picture with the four of them at the beach.

"You should've told me what happened instead of keeping it this big secret," Caitie said.

Mom turned to look at her. "You're right. I'm sorry. I wanted to protect you."

"Then why bring us here? Your dad hates all of us." Caitie stepped into the room.

"No, he doesn't, Caitie. He's just very hurt. With your dad gone, and his parents too, this is all the family we've got. It may not seem like it, but we need them." Mom pushed the suitcase toward the pillows and sat down on the bed. "Come here."

Caitie joined her on the red and cream patchwork quilt, curling one leg under her, and dangling the other off the side of the mattress. She laid her camera and phone down and looked Mom square in the eyes. "We don't need him. He's a jerk."

"Don't say that, honey. He's still your granddad." Mom sighed. "And I can't be Dad for you and Robbie."

"Nobody can!" Caitie's voice cracked.

"What I meant was you two—" Mom bit her lip, "especially your brother, need a father figure. I can't be that, no matter how hard I try." She shook her head and her voice faded to a whisper. "Your granddad and I didn't work out our differences long ago. It's time we did, before we lose him too. I'm just sorry you've been hurt in the process."

"I've been through worse." Caitie's chin trembled. She leaned over and hugged Mom. She wanted to tell her Homer Simpson seemed to be a better father figure than her grandfather, but it wouldn't help.

"I love you, sweetie."

"I love you too." Caitie pulled away. "Can I go for a walk?"

"Sure." Mom brushed Caitie's cheek with the back of her fingers. "But be careful."

"I will." She picked up her camera and phone. "I'll be back." Not that she wanted to.

Hearing the faucet tap running, Caitie poked her head into the kitchen. Grandma MacGregor was washing some kind of purple and white stuff with leafy green stalks. She hoped it wasn't part of tonight's dinner. "Grandma, how do I get to the village?"

"There's a path close to the road on the left side of the garden. Drum's about a mile away."

"Thanks." Caitie stopped by the chest near the back door. In the center of the clunky old phone was a clear plastic button with the telephone number printed by hand on a yellowing paper disc beneath.

She added it to her Contact list, slipped her cell into her back pocket, and escaped out the front door.

She found the trail through the trees at the end of the yard and headed down the dirt path, trying to decide who she'd message on Facebook first. The gray skies brightened the wildflowers. Caitie stopped and snapped a close-up of yellow star-shaped flowers. Yellow was Alicia's favorite color. She'd start with her. A little further down the path, she photographed purple flowers on spiky stems. They looked like sea anemone with tentacles floating on the breeze. It made her think of the school field trip to the Birch Aquarium she'd gone on with Sara when they were little. She wondered if Sara was missing her as much as she missed Sara. She'd give anything to vent to her best friend about this whole mess.

The path ended at the outskirts of the village. The first building she came to was a gothic mini-castle, home of the Loch Ness Centre, complete with a statue of Nessie in a side pond. Drumnadrochit was nothing like her old neighborhood with its strip malls, box stores, and fast food restaurants. The buildings here were like the ones in those miniature villages people put on blankets of fake snow at Christmas. The park next to the main street had a sculpture of a fortress made out of rocks and mossy stuff. In the flowerbed at the base of it, Urquhart Castle was spelled in clipped-bush letters. She snapped more photos and focused her camera one last time for a postcard picture of a street lamp with hanging baskets of pansies. She'd love this sleepy little place if she was just on vacation.

Caitie strolled into the Bank of Scotland and up to a teller behind a glass wall. "Can you exchange $10 for me, please?" She took two bills from her pocket and slipped it into a tray under the teller's shield.

"Certainly," the woman said in a Scottish accent as thick as her French braid. The teller dropped three gold coins and two silver ones into the tray. "Six pounds, twenty pence."

"I'm new here. Is there an internet cafe in town?" Caitie stuffed the coins in the back pocket of her jeans.

"Are you by any chance Ina Macgregor's granddaughter?"

"I am," Caitie said. "How did you know?"

"Your gran told me you were moving here. I'm Elspeth McLean. We don't have that kind of cafe but the library has the internet." The woman checked her watch. "It's closed now though. You might try the hotel. I know they have it for their guests."

"Thank you." Finally, something was going right.

Maybe they'd let her use the computer if she bought a drink there. Caitie marched to the hotel with new hope, followed the signs upstairs to the cafe, and sat down at a window table. A girl about her age with curly red hair and brown eyes came up to take her order.

"What can I get for you?" the perky waitress asked, a pen poised to write down what she wanted on a small pad. On the girl's wrist was a woven floss bracelet, the kind she and Sara liked to make.

"Can I have a Coke?" Caitie asked.

"Nae bother."

The waitress returned carrying the soda with a lemon slice. "Are you here on holiday?"

"No. It's permanent," Caitie said, unable to muster any enthusiasm. "My family just moved here from California." She wrapped her hand around the cold glass.

"Are you the MacGregor's granddaughter?"

"Yeah." She nodded. "Does everyone here know we were coming?"

"Pretty much. It's hard to keep things quiet in a village. Everybody knows your business, even if you don't care to share it. My name is Rose. Rose Matheson."

"I'm Caitie..."

"Finlay." Rose finished with a big smile on her freckled face.

"Yeah. So how old are you?"

"Fifteen."

"So am I. Do you live in the village?" Caitie hoped she did.

Rose nodded. "Just down the road. When did you arrive?"

It felt like forever ago. "This morning."

"It doesn't sound like you're very happy to be in Drum."

"It's a lot different from where we came from. Stuff I used to take for granted doesn't work here."

Rose tilted her head. "Like what?"

"My phone and computer. I need to tell a friend in San Diego something important, but I can't. I'd go to the library to use the internet there, but it's closed." Caitie picked up the glass and took a long drink.

"My uncle owns this place. There's a computer in the hotel lobby for the guests. I can ask if he'll let you use it."

"I wouldn't want you to get in any trouble."

Rose shook her head. "I won't."

"I'd really appreciate it. How much do I owe you for the Coke?"

"£1.35"

Caitie jammed her hand into her back pocket and pulled out a gold coin. "Keep the change." Three bucks was a lot for a Coke, but meeting Rose was the best thing that happened to her today, and she deserved a good tip.

"Thanks." Rose looked around the cafe, eyeing the few customers. "Come on. I'll take you to the lobby."

Caitie stood.

"I like your jumper," Rose said.

Caitie scrunched her eyebrows, clueless as to what Rose was talking about. The waitress reached out and tugged on Caitie's sleeve. "Oh, you mean my hoodie. Thanks. I like your bracelet. The colors go good together. Did you make it?"

"Aye."

"I make those too. Maybe we can hang out and braid sometime."

Rose's eyes grew as wide as her smile. "Sure."

They left the cafe and headed down the stairs to the lower level. A cute boy carrying a case of mineral water passed them on the staircase. He looked at her and nodded in greeting. Caitie grinned.

"Where are you going, Rose?" he asked.

"Don't worry. I'll be back."

"Who's he?" Caitie asked in a whisper.

"Why?" Rose asked.

"He's cute."

Rose wrinkled her pug nose. "You think?"

"Yeah, but don't tell him I said so."

"He's my cousin, Willie." Rose beamed. "I won't say a word."

Caitie followed her into the reception area. In a corner, out of the way, was a desk with a computer.

A man probably a little older than Mom stood behind the registration counter.

"Uncle Donald, this is Caitie Finlay."

"Maisie's daughter?"

"Yes sir," Caitie answered.

Rose's uncle looked her over. "You can be glad you favor your mother and not that granddad of yours." He winked.

"Caitie just arrived. Neither her phone nor computer work. She has to get in touch with someone back in California. Can she use the guest computer?"

"Did I hear right, there's a computer in the MacGregor house?" Rose's uncle boomed.

"We brought it with us." She crossed her fingers behind her back, figuring what she was about to say would be the truth eventually. "We're going to get the internet, but probably not in time for me to get a message sent to San Diego before Friday."

"Angus and Ina MacGregor are going to have the internet too? I'd sooner believe Nessie came waltzing up on the village green for a cup of tea and biscuits." Rose's uncle crossed his arms.

What if what she'd said got back to her grandparents? "Grandma knows it's important for school, so I'm pretty sure we'll get it sooner or later."

"Ahh, I see. Rosie, I believe we can accommodate the village's newest citizen and make an exception to the hotel rules." He wrote down the password. "Here you go, Caitie," he said, handing her the slip of paper. "You're welcome to use our computer."

"Thank you, sir! And thanks, Rose." She logged on and her fingers flew across the keyboard.

hey alicia,

so I got to my grandparent's house this morning. everything is horrible here. my grandpa hates us and my phone doesn't work. there's no internet and I had to go to the hotel by their house to send this. I wouldn't have even gotten on here if my friend rose (a girl our age who works at the hotel) hadn't helped me out. i'm super bummed I can't be at sara's party but I know she's gonna be so surprised! since my cell doesn't work here please please pleasssee call my grandparent's phone during the party! their number is 44 0306 9990165. i'll be waiting for your call. I miss you guys!

caitie

11 *last respects were paid*

·silver bells·

MUNGAN STEPPED INTO TIANNA'S CHAMBERS AND held the heavy door open for the guards Cormag and Ballard, the silversmith Durell, and the cobbler Corc. He stared hard into Ballard's eyes as the four filed in, two by two, carrying the queen's alder bier, their cadence slow and somber. Ballard avoided Mungan's penetrating gaze.

Bathed in the rose glow of the time torch, Leannan leaned over Tianna's body. Though the maidservant's face was frozen with grief, her hands moved busily as she carefully wove forget-me-nots into her mistress's golden hair. Across the canopy bed, Lileas arranged a posy of bluebells and placed them in Tianna's porcelain hands, cascading the blue bouquet down upon his sister's green gown. How different the scene this day from several fortnights ago when he came to Tianna's chambers to consult with her about the May Day festivities. He closed his eyes for a brief moment and pictured Leannan chattering happily with Tianna as she helped ready her queen. Now, joy had turned to sorrow, and peace among the Daoine Shi dissolved to distrust as the rumors spread of a murderer lurking in their midst. All day, Mungan had seen the unrest and suspicion in their eyes as they whispered to one another.

Mungan approached Tianna's body. "She looks lovely."

The two nodded in response. Without a word Leannan glided to the dressing table, lifted the two large silver bowls of rose petals, and handed one to Lileas. Coming alongside the bier, they spread handfuls of velvety petals onto the polished wood and formed a fragrant pink bed for the queen.

"'Tis ready, Mungan." Leannan's voice was as soft as a summer breeze. She gracefully reached for Lileas's empty bowl and placed them both back on the dressing table.

"Corc, help me move Tianna," Mungan said.

The silversmith Durell took hold of both handles at the foot of the bier, and Corc stepped to the bed.

Mungan slipped his hands under Tianna's shoulder blades to lift her. He could feel the cold of her body, and her waxen complexion reminded him again she was truly gone and not just asleep. Corc gently picked up her ankles, and they laid her carefully on the rose petals. Leannan straightened the queen's gown, her fingertips lingering as though she could not bear to let go.

Wood tapping on stone announced King Oseron's arrival as he hobbled in leaning on his cane, followed by the piper. "My beloved Tianna, ye are still so very beautiful." The king bent over and kissed her cheek.

The piper began a mournful dirge, and Cormag and Ballard led the procession out of Tianna's chambers. King Oseron limped after the bier. Mungan took his place behind the king, and the piper followed. As they advanced along the passageway toward the Crystal Garden, Mungan studied the paintings on the walls. Cloudy, but no rain. Hopefully, the weather would hold for the night's journey to the kirk cemetery.

The funeral guard reached the junction of corridors bordering the Great Hall, and Mungan saw the Daoine Shi lined up in the archways. Each stood with head bowed in respect as the bier passed and waited their turn to join the procession. The piper's song was the only sound except for the occasional tinkling of the silver bells each Daoine Shi carried for a final gift to their queen.

Mungan looked to the great *Faerie Forest of Roles* painting. The artists had changed the leaves on Tianna's oak tree from vibrant green to gold. Her tree now matched the glimmering hue of their father's rowan and mother's willow, signifying their departure from the living. Loneliness as deep and cold as winter's snow on the Highlands settled upon him as he realized his was the only green tree of his kin remaining on the painting.

Down the corridor to the craftsmen's galleries, they processed until they reached the archway into the dim Crystal Garden, brightened by the time torches and the candlemakers' tribute to Tianna. The backside of the wide column near the entrance held candles on every outcropping of limestone. Their flames shone through the selenite crystals making the column glow like a rose-colored honeycomb. Hundreds of candles lined the path in the massive cave. Their lights shimmered on the green crystal leaves of the vines adorning the stalagmites. The wizard's tribute illuminated the quartz sculptures hewn from the cave's own rock—the doe near the turquoise waterfall glowed sunshine yellow, the fox between the two bridges that spanned the spring was a flaming red, the hares here and there were a bright snow white, and dotting the garden walls, the perched swallows were a brilliant blue.

The cascading waterfall competed with the piper's dirge as the procession crossed the arched stone bridge over the rushing spring. The funeral guard proceeded to the secluded alcove where they laid Tianna's bier on a broad, black-draped pedestal in the center of the small cloister surrounded by flow stone drapery. Ballard and Cormag took their places at either end of the bier and stood as sentinels with their hands behind their backs. Ballard's refusal to look Mungan in the eye convinced him more than ever the guard was guilty of something. Corc and Durell withdrew from the bier and lined up behind Mungan.

King Oseron looked into Tianna's face once more. With a trembling hand, he hung his silver bell on one of the bier's golden hooks near Tianna's head. He hobbled away; his shoulders slumped as if all joy and purpose in life had been drained from his body.

The candlelight danced on the cavern walls as Mungan approached Tianna. The piper's doleful music and the smell of rose petals overpowered him. "Oh, dear sister, may ye dance on the wind when the forest bluebells ring," he whispered. He hung his silver bell on a hook near her feet and went to take his position on the looping path leading out of the garden.

The king, now seated on a stone bench near the second bridge, waited to receive the condolences of his people. Mungan bowed to King Oseron before crossing over the turquoise water. He too, would stand as expected to receive their sympathy, but he planned for more. This would be his best opportunity to study each mourner hoping to see a trace of guilt for Tianna's murder in one among them.

Durell walked by shaking his head. "'Tis a true shame, Mungan."

"I am bereft of words," Corc added with nothing but sorrow in his eyes.

"I know," Mungan said.

Lileas draped her arm around Leannan as they crossed over the arched bridge.

"Mungan, I am truly sorry for your loss," Leannan said.

He looked into her innocent eyes. "And I for ye as well."

Leannan bit her lip and dropped her head.

Lileas rubbed Leannan's shoulder. "My heart goes out to ye, Mungan." She ushered Leannan from the garden.

With his hands clasped and his head bowed, the wizard approached. "Your sister made a fine queen, Mungan."

"Aye, she did. 'Twas kind of ye, Earnan, to give her such a lovely tribute. The illuminated statues are truly beautiful."

"As was she." Earnan nodded wistfully. "Are ye prepared for the journey down the mountain?"

"'Tis only right to bury her by our parents, but my intuition warns of impending danger."

"Perhaps 'tis not your intuition, but bad memories from the last funeral. Fate would not be so cruel again."

"I hope ye are right, Earnan." He tried to squelch the worries that fought to overtake his thoughts.

One by one, the Daoine Shi came to honour his sister and express their sorrow, but Mungan did not see in any eye a hint of guilt. The line of mourners dwindled. Alvy, Elvy, and Ulvy approached, swaying in time and unison to the piper's dirge, their massive shoulders hunched and their hands wringing their giant tunics.

"Queen Tianna's dying has—" Elvy sniffled loud and long, "has ripped out our hearts."

"Ayyyeee, ripped them out hard," Alvy and Ulvy echoed. All three dissolved into blubbering waterfalls.

"Tianna is honoured by your grief, for it speaks of your devotion to her," Mungan said, raising his hands high to pat Alvy and Ulvy's shoulders.

"No. No. No," Elvy said, "'Tis we who should be consoling ye."

"Aye. No. No. No," Alvy and Ulvy said in unison. The trio encircled him, squeezing so tight Mungan could barely breathe as they sobbed.

"Alvy," he gasped as they eased their grip for a collective shudder. "Elvy and Ulvy, I am most consoled."

"Good." Elvy stepped back, nodded, and wiped his nose with the back of his hand.

"Aye, good," his brothers echoed. They nodded and wiped their noses too.

"We'll do a fine job tonight. Our best for Queen Tianna." Elvy straightened his shoulders.

"Aye, our best," Alvy and Ulvy said. Elvy linked their arms and the trio, resolute in purpose, left the Crystal Garden.

Mungan turned to see Nuala marking the last of the mourners. She spoke her regrets and curtseyed deeply before the king. Nuala then slinked across the bridge.

"I know 'tis a dreadful sorrow ye must bear, Mungan. And if I can be of any comfort in your grief, I would find it an honour." She grasped his hand in hers.

"'Tis a gracious offer, Nuala, and there is a way ye can be of assistance."

"Tell me how," she said with a coy expression.

"Ballard said ye were here in the Crystal Garden with him last night. Is that true?"

Her smile soured into a pout, and she looked at him with those spellbinding eyes. "I have no interest in Ballard." She batted her long black lashes. "Why would he speak such words?"

Mungan battled to concentrate. "I know not."

Her full lips curved with mischief. "I think I know why." She paused and came close to his side. "Ye must know that rumors are raging." Her voice was as silky as her gown.

"I imagine they are."

"Well, with Queen Tianna so…so young and appearing so vibrant last night, for her to die in her sleep like that, 'tis quite suspicious." She pressed closer.

"Aye." He took a deep breath.

"So if she was murdered, whoever did the deed would be trying to hide it." Her words trailed off to a whisper; her steamy breath tickled his ear and sent a shiver down his spine.

"Ballard said that ye were with him…."

"So ye would not think him to be the guilty one, of course." She grasped his other hand and looked at him with hungry eyes. "Ye must not believe him, Mungan." She kissed him lightly on the cheek. "Do not forget, I am here if ye need me."

As he watched her sashay away, he tried to clear the fog she stirred in his mind. *What exactly were her words?*

King Oseron's cane tapped the stone bridge as he limped across. "Nuala appears quite fond of ye."

"She is distracting."

"Did ye speak to her about last night?"

He nodded. "Nuala says she was not with Ballard."

"Then Ballard could have been the one..." Concern spread across the king's face.

Soft scuffling across stone drew Mungan's attention back to the cave entrance. Leannan, rushed up the path, her hands clasped at her chest. "Forgive me, your Majesty, but Mungan is very much needed in the Great Hall."

"Why, do tell?"

Leannan's chest heaved as she caught her breath. Her eyes were wide and concern creased her brow.

"There is a riot unfolding."

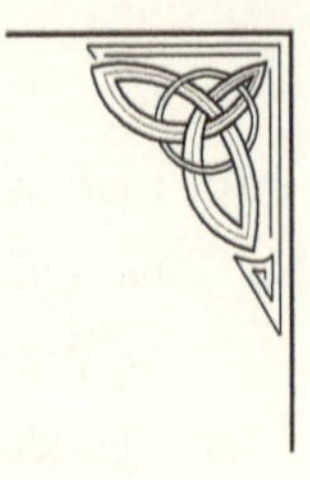

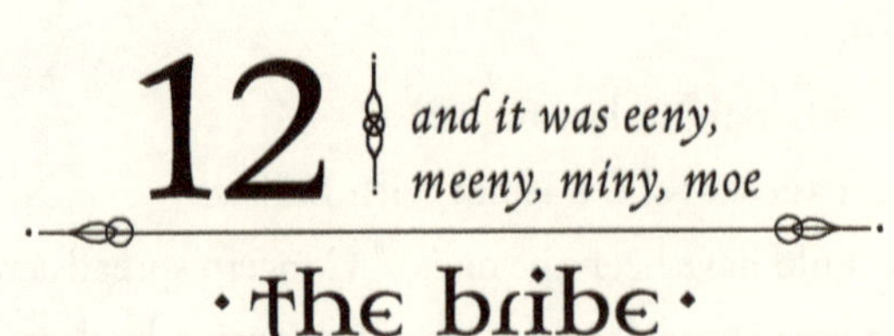

12 *and it was eeny, meeny, miny, moe*

· the bribe ·

ROBBIE FINISHED WASHING HIS HANDS AND WIPED them on a towel at the sink. He was starved and nothing the old man could say was going to wreck dinner.

His grandfather sat down at the head of the dining room table. "You're in for a treat tonight, Robbie."

Why was the old man suddenly being nice? "Oh yeah?"

A grin spread across the old man's face. "A finer Scottish meal, you'll never have."

Robbie's stomach rumbled. "I can hardly wait! Where do I sit, Grandma?"

"You and Caitie can take the seats next to the front window."

He picked the spindle-backed chair furthest from the old man. Te-dum, te-dum. Caitie bounced down the stairs, and he gave her his *lucky you* smile. "We're on this side of the table." The chair legs complained to the hardwood floors as he scooted in so she could get past.

The old man crossed his arms, and his smile evaporated. "I went to the bathroom to get cleaned up before tea, but was sure I must be in the wrong home. There were clothes and a towel on the floor, a hair dryer and make-up on the counter, and the mirror was frosted with toothpaste."

"Sorry about that. I took a shower," Caitie said.

"Go clean it up. It won't take but a moment or two." There was no arguing with the look on his face.

Caitie sighed and went back upstairs.

At least, he wasn't the old man's only target. His grandfather seemed to be more than happy to give grief to every one of them.

Ross sat down at the other end of the table as Mom brought in two large bowls. One was full of mashed potatoes. The other stuff had the same texture, but the bright yellow was all wrong like a bottle of food coloring got dumped into it. "I'm sorry about the bathroom, Dad. I didn't know she'd left it a mess."

"She'll learn," the old man said.

Caitie returned as Grandma MacGregor walked in holding a platter with something that looked like a steaming alien from a movie. The bloated, gray ball had huge veins and dark junk inside. Robbie's jaw dropped. Suddenly the gnawing in his stomach stopped. He glanced at Caitie. She looked grossed out too. The old man's eyes were so fixed on the platter that Grandma MacGregor set in front of him though, he didn't even notice them.

His grandfather sucked in a deep breath. "The haggis looks wonderful, Ina."

"Thank you, Angus." Grandma MacGregor's worry lines turned to deep creases. She gazed at him and Caitie and wiped her hands on her blue and white checkered apron. "Your granddad was determined your first tea at our house be Scottish."

"And rightly so," the old man said.

"Oh," Caitie's voice wavered.

Robbie bit his tongue. Mom's words played over and over in his mind from warped slow to chipmunk fast, "If you haven't got anything kind to say, don't say anything at all." He pointed to the blob. "What exactly is this?"

"Chopped up heart, liver, and lungs, oatmeal, onion, suet, and spices all mixed together and stuffed into a sheep's stomach. In fact, a blackie raised right on this farm." The old man made it sound like each ingredient was some kind of delicacy.

And this is supposed to be a treat?

Grandma MacGregor and Mom joined them at the table.

"Thank you, Lord for the bounty you have provided. Bless the hands that prepared it and the food to our bodies. Amen." The old man held up a knife and meat fork like he expected a drum roll before he poked the sheep's stomach with the fork and sliced open the steaming blob. The contents erupted like the guts of a space monster slashed by a light saber.

The stinking smell of liver made Robbie's stomach spasm, his eyes water, and his gag reflex go hyper. He brought his hand to his mouth and looked to Mom for relief. Her tired eyes managed to say "Stop that right now!" He put his hand down and realized she was expecting him to really eat this. The old man reached into the slashed blob with a large serving spoon and scraped out the inside like he was gutting it. Another dry heave squeaked deep in his throat and jolted Robbie forward.

"Are you all right, Robbie?" Ross asked with more sympathy than Mom was willing to dole out.

From the look on her face, "no" was the wrong answer. "Uh-huh." He couldn't understand why she was so concerned about the old man's feelings when her own son was on the verge of heaving all over the dining room table.

One by one—Ross, Mom, and Grandma MacGregor passed their plates to the old man who plopped a helping of the steaming horror on to it. Caitie took a deep breath and handed her plate to him too. Robbie pleaded with his eyes for Mom to grant him pardon from this torture. She silently delivered the clear message that her verdict wasn't up for negotiation and to pass his plate. Caitie kicked his calf and gave him a sickening sweet smile. He flicked his plate like a Frisbee to her waiting hand and the old man slugged a heaping serving of sheep gut oatmeal onto it. Robbie thought of all the times he'd fought with Mom and Dad over salmon. Right now, he'd give anything for a plate full of fish instead. He picked up the bowl of yellow gunk. "What's this?"

"Turnips," Mom said, "only here they're called neeps."

Robbie scooped a tiny spoonful, leaving lots of room for the potatoes which was only thing that looked edible.

"I spoke with the head teacher at the high school today about registering you two," Mom said. "She invited you to join them this Friday for their last day. She thinks it will be good for you both to meet some of the kids in the area. I think it's a great idea. It will be a long, lonely summer, if you don't know anyone."

"We've already finished school once this year. Isn't that enough?" Robbie asked.

"Just listen for a minute. They're going on a weaselling field trip."

He looked at the old man and envisioned kids two feet taller than him chasing rodents with hockey sticks. "What's weaselling?" he asked pretty sure he didn't want to hear the answer.

"It's boulder climbing and caving from what I understand." Mom tried to look and sound enthusiastic. "They never had such a thing when I was your age."

Caves were cold and dark. His skin went clammy.

"Sounds kind of fun, but I can't go." Caitie said it the same way she told Mom she was not moving to Scotland.

"Why not?" Mom asked.

"'Cause Friday's Sara's birthday party! I already told you, Mom. They're kidnapping her in her pajamas and taking her to Alicia's for breakfast, remember? Everybody's going to be there. They're going to call me so I can still be part of it."

Thank you, Caitie!

"But, sweetheart, we haven't resolved your phone issue yet," Mom said.

"They're going to call me on Grandma and Grandpa's phone."

"How'd they get the number?"

"I sent it to Alicia on Facebook while I was in the village," Caitie admitted.

"So there's an internet cafe here?"

"No, but I met this really nice girl named Rose, and her uncle let me use the computer in the lobby of the hotel."

Somehow Caitie could always figure out a way to get what she wanted.

Mom sat back in her chair and put her hands in her lap. Her eyes flickered between the old man and Grandma, before focusing on Caitie. "I know you don't want to miss that phone call, honey, but if you're willing to go on the field trip and your gran and grandad don't object, I'll call about getting the internet."

The old man stared at Mom. "Maisie."

"I'll pay for it and all the installation costs. We have Tom's insurance."

"You're bribing the lass."

"Angus, the children have sacrificed a great deal coming here," Grandma MacGregor said quietly. "And the internet is crucial nowadays for schooling."

"So you both think the answer is to keep spoiling them, just like they were in the States."

"The internet could help us here on the farm, Angus," Ross said between bites. "Up-to-the-minute market reports, the weather, and then, of course, you could keep up with shinty scores better and fishing news."

"Hmmmmph." The old man stuffed a huge forkful of yuck in his mouth.

"But, Mom, that's an impossible choice," Caitie said.

"You've just been given more than a generous offer, sweetie. I would very seriously consider it, if I were you."

His sister's lips gave way to let out a loud breath.

"You haven't touched your haggis. What's the matter with you, lad?" the old man asked.

"I don't really care for it," Robbie answered in a low voice.

"How can you know when you haven't had a bite?" the old man boomed back.

Grandma MacGregor put her hands on the table and started to stand. "I'll get you something else, Robbie."

"You will not," the old man ordered. "You're not running a pub here, Ina. When I was a lad, I often helped hunt our dinner." Grandpa MacGregor glanced at him with disapproval over cutting the rabbit loose; Robbie was sure of it. "And I ate it gratefully, no matter what it was."

Well, good for you! Robbie wanted to shout back. "And I'm not going weaselling either," came out instead.

Mom sighed. "And why don't you want to go?"

"I don't like caves."

"For heaven's sake, Robbie. It's going to be a lot of fun," Mom said.

Everybody else ate in silence, while he and Caitie stared at their Scottish breakfast barf wishing for American food. The only sound was the clinking of forks on the white plates.

The old man wiped his mouth with the cloth napkin and set it on the table. "Ross, have you noticed #42? Looks like she's losing weight."

Ross nodded. "She appears to be."

"It's been two weeks since she calved. I say Friday we cleanse her, and if Robbie's here, he'll provide an extra pair of hands for the job."

Ross sized Robbie up. "Suppose his arms are long enough?"

What would he need long arms for?

"I believe so. And being thin like that, it will be a lot more comfortable for the heifer."

This wasn't sounding good. "What do I need long arms for?" Robbie asked.

"To clean out the afterbirth rotting inside the cow."

Robbie's spoonful of mashed potatoes never made it to his mouth, but clanked instead on the plate. "Gross! I'm not cleansing any cow."

"If you're here, you will. The job takes every pair of hands available."

Robbie knew the old man meant what he said. Deep down he was sure his grandfather wanted him to stay on the farm that day, just so he could take a shot at making a man out of him. He steeled his eyes against the old man's. "I gotta think about it." His was the impossible choice, not Caitie's—scared to death and humiliated in front of his new classmates, or grossed out beyond his ability to even imagine.

"What do you want to do, Caitie?" Mom asked.

"What kind of a friend will I be if I'm not here when they call?"

"I'm sure they'll understand."

"I'm not, but it doesn't look like I've got much of a choice. I'll go and Robbie, you're coming with me."

Could this day get any worse?

13 *and there was mourning at night*

· the fae funeral ·

WITH HIS PULSE POUNDING AS FAST AS HIS FOOTSTEPS, Mungan sprinted from the Crystal Garden and into the corridor bordering the Great Hall. Beyond the marble arches of the half-walls, the Daoine Shi flailed at one another, benches flew and tables turned, sending plates clattering. The artist Taog, faced an easel in the corridor, feverishly painting the riot before him with wild brushstrokes.

"What is going on here?" Mungan shouted.

"A monster of a fight!" the artist exclaimed with a gleam in his eye. "Such movement! Such life! How could I resist capturing the scene?"

A porcelain plate sailed through the archway toward Mungan. He ducked and the plate crashed into the wall, shattering into a hundred jagged pieces.

"Mungan!" King Oseron limped toward him with Leannan at his side.

"Do not enter, Your Majesty." Mungan raised a hand and gestured for the king to retreat. "'Tis not safe."

King Oseron nodded, his eyes filled with a fear Mungan had not seen before. The king raised his palms as if he knew not what to do.

Mungan cupped his hands and shouted, "Take refuge in the laundry, Your Majesty."

Leannan opened the double door a few feet away and ushered the king inside. Moments later, she emerged.

"Fetch Earnan, quickly!" Mungan ordered.

Leannan scurried through the bordering corridors and disappeared down the passageway toward the wizard's chambers.

Mungan leapt over the half wall into the fray. "Stop! Stop!" he cried, but the musicians playing louder than the rabble, drowned out his voice. The

Daoine Shi in front of him ducked, and a tankard of ale splashed Mungan in the face, stinging his eyes.

Alvy's fist met Garbhan's stomach with an uppercut that sent the mason skyward. Garbhan landed on the wheel-spoke chandelier, knocking down candles and setting his cloak ablaze. The mason dove back into the churning crowd and rolled on the floor to put himself out, just as Lileas doused him with a pitcher of ale.

"Enough!" Mungan shouted. But the Daoine Shi paid no heed, hollering, yanking great clumps of each other's hair, hurling tankards, and stabbing one another with forks. Mungan fought his way, ducking punches and stepping over rolling bodies to the archway across from the treasure room. He escaped as the wizard emerged from the passageway with Leannan.

"Earnan, I need a brief, but large hailstorm," Mungan shouted above the din, just as Niall the chief torchman slid in their direction atop a banquet table.

The wizard pointed his wand toward the ceiling in the Great Hall. *"Dòirt a nuas clachan meallain!"* Black clouds formed and roiled, raining a torrent of hailstones as big as hazelnuts on the fighting mass. The shock of the pelting ice balls silenced the fracas. The throng stopped swinging at one another other and raised their arms instead to fend off the painful assault.

Mungan jumped onto the half-wall. "Enough!" he shouted. "I know not what started this riot, but it shan't begin again. The next to throw a fist or push a neighbor will spend a good long while in the dungeon, contemplating their misdeed. Am I understood?"

"Aye," the crowd shouted collectively, flinching and ducking as the hailstones struck.

Mungan turned to Earnan and nodded.

The wizard pointed to the black clouds. *"Sguir a clachain meallain!"* Earnan flourished his wand in a grand upward sweep. As quickly as the hailstorm started, it stopped.

"Until I sort this out, no one says a word unless ye are spoken to!" Mungan bellowed in his most commanding voice. He pointed to a little boy standing on the half-wall near the artist. "Friseal, who threw their fist first?"

"Elvy, sir."

"Does the boy speak the simple truth, Elvy?"

"Aye, 'twas me." Elvy hung his head so low it seemed to touch his belt.

"Aye, 'twas him." Alvy and Ulvy echoed with their heads hung just as low.

Without looking up, Elvy pointed to the singed mason Garbahn, standing in front of him. "He disnae want to go to the kirkyard for Queen Tianna."

"'Tis dangerous, Mungan." Garbahn held his stomach. "The Unseelies. It has been over a hundred and fifty years since all in the kingdom left the mountain for fear of them."

"Dangerous or not, we will honour our beloved queen," Mungan said with finality.

MUNGAN GLANCED AT HIS POCKET WATCH AS HE STRODE DOWN THE PATH in the Crystal Garden, a quarter past ten. They would soon leave to bury Tianna. He had only a few moments to confront Ballard about Nuala's denial of his alibi. After hearing of the conversation with the dancer, the king granted Mungan permission to throw the guard in the dungeon—a quick task sure to bring a great measure of satisfaction.

Mungan lurched at the sight of Cormag standing guard alone over Tianna. "Where is Ballard?" he asked in a sharp whisper.

"In his chamber. The night will be long. He claimed to be weary already. I told him to snatch a few winks," the sour guard said with cool disdain.

"Who gave ye such authority?"

"I did." Cormag narrowed his coal grey eyes. "Need I remind ye, Mungan, that I am the captain of the king's guard, and I answer to King Oseron, not to ye."

Mungan clenched his fists and gritted his teeth. "Need I remind ye, Cormag, that the king ordered ye to stay at Ballard's side."

"I indeed ensured Ballard spoke nary a word to Nuala, not even when she passed by to pay her respects. Then I watched the two of ye converse. Ye took no action, thus I assumed the matter with Ballard cleared."

Mungan fought the urge to slam Cormag against the cavern wall. "Ye are not to assume anything when it comes to obeying the king's orders." He spun on his heels and stalked away.

"Where are ye going?" Fear and contempt mixed in Cormag's voice.

"To find Ballard," Mungan said without looking back.

"He will be returning any moment," Cormag said. "Of that I am sure."

Mungan spun round and marched over to Cormag, bringing his face within inches of the guard's bulbous nose. "Ye be the guard and I shall be the Searsanach. Be silent and do your job."

Moments later, Mungan stood in the royal blue glow of the time torches pounding on the guard's door. No answer. "Ballard?" Still no response. He burst into the dim chamber. "Get up, ye blaggard!"

Ballard lay sleeping on the bed.

"Wake up!" He raised the guard by the shoulders and shook him hard. Ballard's head dropped lifelessly back on the pillow.

"Mungan, stop! What have ye done?" Lileas asked, filling the doorway.

A sickening pit grew in Mungan's stomach. "I came to wake him up, but something is wrong. I believe...I believe he is dead."

"First Queen Tianna and now Ballard?"

Mungan combed the hair back from his brow with his fingers. "Find Earnan and hurry." He listened for a breath, but there was none. Ballard still had the glow, so he could not have been dead long. 'Twas too dark in the room, so he tipped the candlestick on the small table next to Ballard's bed in the direction of the chamber's orange everlight. The molten crystal sent sparks back, lighting the three candles. Suspicious of another poisoning, Mungan searched for a tankard or goblet, but there was none to be found. He drew his fist to his lips and concentrated. There had to be evidence of some kind to explain Ballard's demise.

He pushed back the guard's long curly hair and pulled the collar away from his neck. No bruising from strangulation. Mungan twisted Ballard's shoulder to check his back. The guard's head flopped to the side. There at the base of Ballard's neck was a red and white bull's-eye the size of his smallest fingernail.

"Mungan?"

Earnan's voice startled him. "Ballard is dead. I believe I know why. Come and see."

The wizard's robe shifted from violet to scarlet as he came alongside Ballard's bed. "What have ye found?"

Mungan pointed out the red mark with the white ring. "There appear to be two bright red specks in the center of the mark."

The wizard bent over and studied Ballard's neck through his crescent spectacles. "Aye, there are." Earnan's brows quirked in surprise.

"I suspect a spider bit him."

Earnan nodded. "I believe ye are right."

Ballard deserved to die, but Mungan wished he had gone at the hands of the Daoine Shi and not by the venom of a spider. Was it merely a strange coincidence? He looked at his pocket watch. The eleven o'clock hour was fast approaching. "We must go. The time for Tianna's procession draws near, and King Oseron must be told of this."

"What shall we do with Ballard?" Lileas asked.

"Nothing much can be done for him now," Earnan said.

"On the morrow, we'll lay him in the dungeon with the others." Mungan ushered them from Ballard's chamber.

BACK IN THE CRYSTAL GARDEN, ALL THE DAOINE SHI EXCEPT FOR the torchmen, gathered in a line, silently awaiting the start of the procession, a good many of them sporting cuts and bruises from the Grand Elvy Brawl.

"Taog, I need your assistance," Mungan said. "Come with me."

"Certainly," the artist said.

Entering the secluded alcove, Mungan found King Oseron at Tianna's side. Cormag stood at his post while Durell and Corc waited nearby to take their positions as pallbearers.

"Your Majesty, Ballard is dead," Mungan said in a low tone. Cormag, Taog, Durell, and Corc snapped their heads in his direction.

The king's jaw dropped, and he took a step backwards. "Cormag told me Ballard slipped away to catch a few winks."

"I found him lying on his bed, but—"

The king's eyes narrowed. "Did he take his own life?"

"I think not. It appears Ballard died of a spider bite."

The king looked mournfully at Tianna. "Then the spider has rendered judgment in my place. I believe Ballard has received what he deserved. Now come, Mungan, our devotion this night belongs to Tianna."

"Taog, I need ye to replace Ballard as pallbearer," Mungan said.

The artist nodded. "Of course."

With Cormag and Taog at the front and Corc and Durell at the rear, they lifted Tianna's bier. The silver bells tinkled as the king led the procession out of the Crystal Garden and through their mountain's corridors. At the portal, the torchmen stood ready to pass torches to all the Daoine Shi.

"Fosgail an dorus drùidheil," Niall, the chief torchman commanded. The portal opened, and he led the way to the floor of the cave below.

Taog and Cormag raised their end of the bier and sidestepped down the boulders while Corc and Durell lowered theirs so nary a rose petal fell. The pallbearers marched toward the opposite cavern wall and waited for Earnan.

The wizard flourished his wand. *"Beagaich!"*

Tianna, the bier, and the pallbearers all shrank in an instant to one sixth their size. Then Mungan, Earnan, King Oseron, and Niall made themselves wee as well.

Niall guided them to the cavern's main entrance where Earnan tapped a large boulder with his wand. *"Thig am fianais eich sithich!"* A miniature white horse came forth from the rock with silver bells woven into its silky mane. Niall grabbed the reins of the horse's golden bridle and led it to King Oseron. The king winced as Mungan assisted him into the bejeweled saddle.

One after another, Earnan brought forth silver-belled steeds for each of the wee Daoine Shi nobility. With the task finished, the wizard mounted his own horse.

The pallbearers marched in unison to their place behind the king. The piper stepped in line following the bier. Their nobility—Earnan, the artists, dancers, poets, and musicians along with the elder fae—reined their prancing steeds into position behind the piper. Each held a torch on a long pole secured in a scabbard on the saddle. The silver bells on the horses' manes jingled as the steeds waited impatiently. The silversmiths, wood craftsmen, and masons came next. The spinners, seamstresses, cobblers, candlemakers, torchmen, and cooks fell in behind them. Leannan and Lileas took their places ahead of the towering trio who marked the end of the procession and bore shovels on their shoulders.

When all were in order, Mungan mounted his steed and joined the line behind the piper.

Niall stepped back into the cavern. "The path is clear."

The piper began a doleful dirge, and the chief torchman led them out of the cavern and into the cool night. The Daoine Shi snaked down the mountain path, raising their torches high in honour of their beloved queen.

The rhythmic clap of the horses' hooves on the mountain path reminded Mungan of the triplet's cadence as they dug the grave that night one hundred and fifty years earlier when they left the mountain for the last funeral. His father, the Daoine Shi Searsanach, more social than serious about his duty, positioned himself graveside, closest to the grieving family. He should have been stationed on the periphery, watching for danger. Mungan, rather than his father, first sensed the movement beyond the stone wall. A two-wheeled metal contraption, propelled by its seated rider who seemed to run in place, skidded on the gravel, collided with the wall, and flew into the kirkyard.

Mungan pushed Tianna and others within reach out of the way, but his father and mother were crushed by the plummeting mortal. The human, reeking of whiskey, lay oblivious as the Daoine Shi worked to free those trapped under him. The funeral was cut short. Mungan took charge as Alvy, Elvy, and Ulvy worked feverishly to bury his parents and the other body while the injured were helped back to the mountain.

From that night on, Mungan despised mortals. The drunk would survive, but Mungan would do what he could to get even. He crawled on top of the giant, searched his pockets, and stole the only thing of value on the careless fool, a golden object that at Mungan's wee stature was as big as a platter. It had a cover that popped open to reveal a clock. In time, the pocket watch had become Mungan's most prize possession, for it served as a constant reminder of the importance of each passing moment and the responsibility entrusted to him as Searsanach. The role demanded diligence, for in an instant of neglect the Daoine Shi could pay the price with their lives, as his parents had that night under his father's watch. Mungan vowed that would never happen again as long as he was Searsanach.

The sound of the horses' hooves disappeared as they left the path at the base of the mountain and marched on the grass across the valley, through a pass in the hills to the east, and onward to the cemetery on the outskirts of the village. Round the stone wall and through the kirkyard gate, the procession made its way.

The triplets began to dig near his parents' grave. Forming a faerie ring, the Daoine Shi sang their mourning songs, arms entwined and torches raised for their queen. Mungan's eyes and ears strained to sense danger in the dark, but the night was quiet.

With the hole finished, the trio passed two ropes under Tianna's bier. Leannan unfolded a black silk shroud. Lileas joined her, and the two covered Tianna's feet. With unspeakable sorrow spreading over Leannan's face, they drew the rest of the sheet over the bluebell bouquet, past her emerald pendant, and over Tianna's lovely face. The silver bells tinkled as Taog, Cormag, Corc, and Durell lowered the bier inches from the ground. Elvy on one side, and Alvy and Ulvy on the other, took up the slack on the ropes before lowering the queen into the grave.

"Tianna, my beloved, may this night bring ye peace," King Oseron said. "Your life has been taken from us too soon, and our hearts are filled with grief. Let us take comfort in knowing that the one who stole your life has been justly repaid."

A collective gasp rose from the crowd.

"Aye, Ballard, who committed this evil upon our queen, is himself dead. And we can be grateful to the spider which has avenged the deed. So we bid ye a final good-night, dearest Tianna. Sleep well forevermore."

"'Twas a very wise spider," Elvy said.

Alvy and Elvy nodded. "Aye, very wise."

Mungan could not help but wonder if somehow the words of these simpletons heralded the truth.

He closed his eyes as the trio shoveled the first clumps of earth back into the grave and winced as the dirt thudded on his silk entombed sister. An unsettling breeze raised the hair on the back of his neck. It whipped at the torches, and they fought to stay aflame. Mungan jerked his head at a faint howling from the west. "Earnan," he whispered. "Do ye hear anything?"

The wizard tilted his head, straining to listen. Earnan's amethyst eyes grew wide.

"Mungan," the king said, with urgency. "The howling. 'Tis the Unseelies."

The crowd stopped singing.

"Earnan, the horses. Dispense with them now," Mungan ordered. The wizard rushed to the torchmen who held their reins. He waved his wand. The steeds stampeded toward the rock wall and vanished.

"Snuff the torches! And take cover in the bushes," Mungan commanded.

The fae each blew a rainbow puff that doused the light as the howling grew louder.

King Oseron limped toward a nearby alder bush while the rest of the Daoine Shi dispersed round the kirkyard. The trio continued to shovel dirt into Tianna's grave.

"Ye must stop, Elvy! The Unseelies, they are approaching," Mungan urged.

The three continued shoveling. "We must hide Queen Tianna," Elvy said.

"Aye, hide her, we must," Alvy and Ulvy grunted.

"But if ye do not stop and take refuge, they will see ye!"

"No! No! No! We cannot let them get her," Elvy said, breathless.

"Aye. No! No! No!" the brothers echoed, just as winded.

A pewter mass in the clear sky like an evil cloud drifted toward them. Mungan scanned the kirkyard. Through the bushes he spied the faint glow of each Daoine Shi. "Earnan, we cannot hide ourselves, the glow will betray us."

The wizard raised his wand. *"Fàs dorcha!"* Black sparks shot from the tip of his wand, and the glow of the Daoine Shi turned black as coal as Earnan waved his arm in an arc. The wizard pointed the wand at himself, Mungan, and the trio who continued to shovel, and their skin blackened in an instant.

"That helps, but a sharp eye, will still spot the trio's movement," Mungan whispered. The howling Unseelies were less than a half a mile away. "Turn them into statues on a headstone."

Earnan raised his wand. *"Bi 'nad ìomhaigh!"* The triplets froze—Elvy stooped, the tip of his shovel in a clump of dirt, Alvy and Ulvy tall with their arms thrust forward in a suspended toss. The trio and ground beneath were now smooth white marble.

"Well done," Mungan said in relief. They slipped into the alder bush where King Oseron had hidden. Mungan peered through the openings in the leaves.

A shriek pierced the heavens as the Unseelies began to descend in a slow spiral. A foul smell drifted downward and settled on the kirkyard. Mungan feared his heart beat as loud as a musician pounding on his bodhran.

"Mama!" a terrified young bairn nearby cried. Mungan willed the mother to silence her child.

A creature with sickly, pale green eyes and a goat-shaped head glided on scaly wings to the kirk spire while the rest of the flock landed on the rooftop, pushing and cursing at each other to make room for themselves.

"Silence!" the creature on the spire ordered in a voice that sounded like many tortured souls.

"The Daoine Shi are out this night."

"How do ye know, Salucevil?" a warted spriggan asked.

"I can smell them," the leader said. His gleaming eyes searched the kirkyard.

A stick-necked kilmoulis with his rat-shaped head, two beady eyes, and no mouth clung to the edge of the roof, twitching his nose as he sniffed the damp, cool air.

The one-eyed fachan balanced precariously on the rooftop with his single leg and arm. "If they were here, we would see their glow."

"I suggest we take our leave, Salucevil, for the Daoine Shi are gone and all that virtue seeping up through the kirk roof makes my scales crawl," the spriggan hissed, spewing sparks.

"Fine," Salucevil answered. "I can be patient."

The creature cackled long and deep, shattering Mungan's frayed nerves.

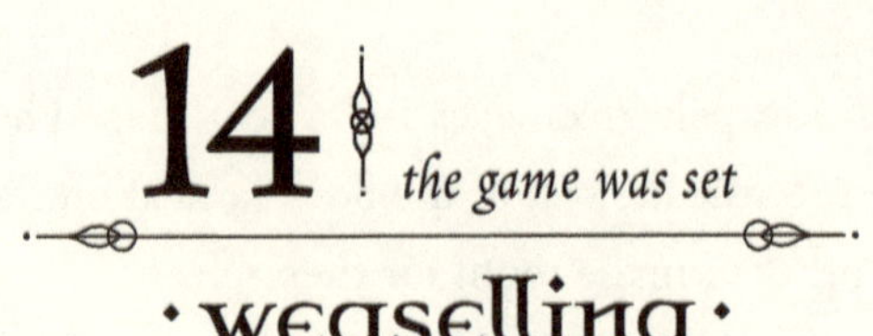

14 *the game was set*

· weaselling ·

MOM PULLED THE CAR UP IN FRONT OF GLEN URQUHART High School and shoved her open palm in Caitie's direction. "Hand it over."

"But, Mom…"

"I'm not going to let your brand new phone get broken or lost while you're weaselling."

"I'll keep it safe. I promise." Caitie clutched the phone in the pocket of her hoodie. She didn't want to miss the call from Sara's party and hoped somehow there would be service wherever it was that they were going.

"No." Mom sounded just as firm as if Caitie had asked to fly back to San Diego.

With a huge sigh, she pulled out the cell phone and slapped it on Mom's hand.

Mom half-turned to Robbie in the backseat. "Don't look so glum. You're going to have a great time."

"Mm-hmm." Robbie sounded totally unconvinced.

Caitie opened the car door. "You're sure Grandpa MacGregor isn't going to back out on the internet deal, right?"

"He won't. Loch.net will be at the house tomorrow morning at ten. Now let's go."

Caitie scooped her lunch sack off the floorboard and got out. Their new school was a stone building with a huge glass turret-thing that she had to admit looked pretty cool. Kids were bunched up in cliques on the blacktop next to the school while an older woman in khaki and a safari helmet studied a clipboard cradled in her arm.

"That woman looks like she's in charge." Mom took off, leaving her and Robbie to catch up. "Good morning." Mom sounded as perky as a cheerleader at a school assembly.

"And a fine one it is," the woman said with a deep voice and a dentured grin.

"I'm Mrs. Ferguson, and you must be the Finlays."

"We are," Mom said, "and we so appreciate you including Caitie and Robbie today."

Caitie shot Mom a sideways glance.

"With your boots and packed lunches, you both look ready for the off. But first, I'd like to introduce you to two of your classmates." She cupped her hand to her mouth and shouted like a marine sergeant. "Bonnie. Duncan."

A pretty girl turned her head in response. She swung her long brown hair and backed away from her group. In an instant, Caitie could see she had all the guys whipped and the other girls in awe.

A boy, a lot bigger than Robbie, also sauntered over.

"Duncan, I'd like you to meet Robbie Finlay. Robbie, this is Duncan Mackenzie," Mrs. Ferguson said.

"Hi," Robbie said.

"Want to come meet my mates?" the freckle-faced boy asked.

Clearly the kid had been told what to do ahead of time.

Robbie drew a deep breath. "Sure." He smiled, but Caitie knew Robbie was faking it and didn't want to go anywhere with Duncan. The only place she knew he wanted to go less was back to the farm to face the backside of heifer #42. The two walked over to a group of boys who all looked huge compared to Robbie.

"Bonnie McLaren, this is Caitie," Mrs. Ferguson said.

"Welcome to Drum." Bonnie had the confidence of a class president.

"Thanks."

"I'll be leaving then," Mom said. "See you at 4:00."

Bonnie waved a finger for Caitie to follow. "I heard you're from California. Did you live near Hollywood?"

"No, but I've been there once," Caitie said as they walked toward Bonnie's friends.

"Ever meet a movie star?"

"Nope. Never have," Caitie said with a chuckle. "What's the best part about living here?"

Bonnie shrugged her shoulders "Oh, I don't know. Maybe the guys." Bonnie raised her brows and flashed a practiced grin.

"Who's your friend, Bonnie?" a guy in a flannel shirt asked.

"Caitie from California." Bonnie pointed to a shoulder length blonde with blue eyes. "This is Aileen. And that's Maggie." A short girl standing with her hip popped to the side waved.

After that, the names all came so fast Caitie wasn't sure if she got any of them straight before Willie, the cute guy from the hotel, showed up.

"Hi, Caitie."

He knew her name. "Hi," she said, beaming.

Bonnie raised one eyebrow and crossed her arms. "When did you two meet?"

He didn't look at Bonnie when he answered. He just kept those warm brown eyes focused on Caitie's. "Well, we haven't met proper, but she was at the hotel on Monday." He had a slightly crooked smile that showed off nice teeth. "I'm Willie Matheson."

"I know," Caitie said. That smile of his got even bigger. She liked his dark auburn hair. It went great with his eyes.

"Bonnie, can you please bring me the megaphone?" Mrs. Ferguson called. "Miss Bowers has it, near the bus."

"I really do wish she'd ask someone else to do her bidding once in a while," Bonnie said under her breath.

"Do you want me to go?" Aileen asked.

"No, I'll do it." Bonnie rolled her eyes. "Aye, Mrs. Ferguson," she called cheerfully.

"So you're coming with us today?" Willie looked pleased.

Caitie liked the dimple on his chin too. "Yeah." The day was definitely looking better.

Bonnie tugged Caitie's arm. "You need to meet Miss Bowers. She's the P.E. teacher."

Caitie didn't want to leave. She was plenty happy to hang out with Willie, but she didn't want to tick off Bonnie either, not if she wanted to make new friends. "Okay."

They strolled toward Miss Bowers, who looked liked she did triathlons every weekend.

"We're here for the megaphone," Bonnie said. "Mrs. Ferguson wants it. Oh, and this is Caitie Finlay. She just moved here."

"Welcome, Caitie."

"Thanks."

They delivered the megaphone, and Mrs. Ferguson gave the order to load the bus. Willie sat ahead of her and Bonnie. Robbie and Duncan were in seats a couple of rows behind. The driver shut the door, and the bus rolled forward. It stopped again, the door swung open, and Rose, the waitress from the hotel, climbed aboard, looking like she'd woken up about five minutes earlier. There was a seat between her and Bonnie, so Caitie raised her hand to flag Rose over. Bonnie just barely shook her head and put her backpack in the empty spot.

Caitie felt bad but didn't argue. "Hey, Rose."

"Hi, Caitie." Rose acted shy compared to the day they met.

Bonnie chatted with the guy across the aisle, never pausing as Rose passed by. Caitie watched Rose take an empty seat at the rear of the bus with girls close to Robbie's age.

MRS. FERGUSON STOOD UP AND STEPPED INTO THE NARROW AISLE, smooshing her big hips between the seatbacks in the first row. "Wheesht! I have a few announcements before we're off. We've a short nature walk to the spot where we'll be weaselling. Take your packed lunches as we won't be coming back for them. Once you get off the bus, go to the van and pick up your weaselling gear. You'll each need overtrousers, a cagoule, and a helmet," she said, marking them off with three fingers. "You're all responsible for making sure that every bit of your gear is returned to our guide, Craig, when we return. Once you have everything you need, come to the start of the path." Mrs. Ferguson waddled a pirouette and got off the bus.

"Did you get all that?" Bonnie asked.

"I don't know what a cagoule is."

"A pullover waterproof," Bonnie said, like that was obvious.

They lined up at the side of a beat-up VW van where a tall guy in his twenties, with light brown hair in a curly ponytail, passed out their gear. Miss Bowers stood beside him handing out helmets. Caitie watched Robbie a few feet ahead reach the front of the line.

"I think I need a small pair of pants," Robbie said.

Duncan and the others burst out laughing. Robbie turned to Duncan, clearly not getting what he'd said wrong.

Their guide grinned. "We're hoping you're wearing your own."

"Well, sure," Robbie said defensively. "But Mrs. Ferguson said we each have to have a pair of pants."

Duncan laughed so hard he had to hold his stomach.

"That's not quite what Mrs. Ferguson said, Robbie. She used the word overtrousers." Miss Bowers smiled and handed him a helmet. "Here in Scotland, when you speak of pants you're referring to..."

"Underwear!" Duncan shrieked. "I think that's what you Yanks call it." He and his friends howled with laughter.

"Oh." Robbie's face turned bright red.

"Here you go." Craig handed him a pair of blue overtrousers. "They look a wee bit big, but it's the best I can do for you."

Caitie couldn't help but feel a little sorry for Robbie. She got her gear and walked with Bonnie over to Mrs. Ferguson. A few minutes later, the van door slammed shut, and she spotted Rose talking to Miss Bowers at the back of the crowd. Craig met up with Mrs. Ferguson, and the two led the group on the wide, wooded path.

After hiking into the boulder-strewn hills for maybe twenty minutes, they came to a clearing with a cave in the massive gray rock.

"Time to get your gear on," Craig announced.

Mrs. Ferguson spread out a small blanket under a tree and half-sat, half-fell onto it. Everyone else set their lunch sacks down and started getting ready.

Caitie took her boots off before putting on her overtrousers. The last thing she wanted was to fall down around people she didn't know. While she sat on the ground, re-tying her boot laces, Willie walked over. He reached out a hand to help her up and she took it.

"It's your lucky day, Caitie Finlay."

"It is?"

"For one thing, you met me."

Her cheeks warmed. She bent down to pick up her jacket, hoping he hadn't notice her blush, then slipped it over her head and pushed her arms through the sleeves. Her hair went all static, and she tried to smooth it down. She was sure she looked like she had stuck her finger in an electrical socket.

"And because I'm giving you a four-leaf clover." He handed her the delicate surprise.

Her mouth dropped, and she counted the four tiny heart-shaped leaves joined to the thin stem. "I've never seen a real one before. Where'd you find it?"

"Over there." Willie pointed to a spot near a rock where he'd set down his lunch.

"Thanks." She looked around trying to find some place safe to keep it. "Where should I put it, so it won't get lost?"

"In your pocket?"

"It'll get wrecked there."

Willie reached for her helmet lying on the ground. "How about in here between the strips of padding?"

Caitie gently laid the four-leaf clover between the thick foam pads and leaned forward to put the helmet on so the clover wouldn't fall out. She straightened up and tightened the chin strap.

Willie nodded. "That should work."

"I hope so." Caitie picked up her camera and slid the strap over her wrist, cinched it up, and slipped the Lumix up the sleeve of her jacket to give it more protection.

"Help, Willie! I'm stuck!" Bonnie balanced on one foot while trying to get her other boot through her overtrousers.

He grabbed Bonnie's arm to steady her. *She was good.*

Once everyone was ready, they all crowded around the opening in the boulders.

Craig held up his hands. "Listen up," he shouted and everyone got quiet. "A long time ago, glaciers moved through this area, and as they did, they broke up the granite rock that formed these mountains. With the movement of the glaciers, the boulders tumbled down, creating the spaces we'll explore today. We'll start in this large opening," Craig pointed to the cave, "and follow a system of tunnels and gaps in the boulders. You'll be popping in and out of the holes just as a weasel would, hence the name. We won't go too deep into the hillside though as we don't wish to disturb the wee folk." He winked.

Caitie remembered Miss Moncrieff, the funny old lady on the train, and her crazy ideas about magical Scotland. At least this guy didn't take it seriously.

"Some of the spaces get a bit snug," Craig went on, "so if you start to feel as though you're getting stuck, just stop and relax. Your body size actually grows when you're stressed. That's why it's important to stay calm and patiently wriggle through. If there are no questions, follow me."

The large group headed single file into the hillside. Caitie looked for Robbie and saw him walking toward Mrs. Ferguson. She knew what was up.

"You coming, Caitie?" Willie asked.

She wanted to say yes but shook her head. "Go ahead. I'll catch up with you later." She walked toward Mrs. Ferguson coming close enough behind Robbie to hear him.

"Mrs. Ferguson, I don't feel so good," he said. "Sort of like I might throw up."

Caitie shook her head. *Yeah, right.*

"Oh, no." Mrs. Ferguson's forehead wrinkled with sympathy. "Then perhaps you should stay here and rest."

"Okay." Robbie sounded pathetic.

Rose came up to her. "Is everything all right?"

"Yeah, I think so. It's just my little brother wimping out."

"Do you want me to stay here with you?" Rose asked.

"No, that's all right. Thanks for offering though." Caitie followed Robbie as he walked to the spot where he'd left his lunch. "What's the matter with you?" she asked in a whisper.

"I don't feel good." Robbie sat down on the ground and took off his helmet.

"You don't look sick to me. I think you're too scared to go inside that mountain."

"So what if I am?" he snapped at her.

"Look, I know you hate the dark. But you're not sleepwalking now, and chances are you're not going to get hurt in there. You're not four years old anymore. You gotta grow up and get over that night, Robbie. That's what Dad would want, and you know it." She left him to join Miss Bowers and the last kids heading into the cave.

"Caitie, wait up."

She turned around and saw Robbie grab his helmet. Caitie sighed. She'd done her big sister duty, and as a reward she got to go weaselling with him instead of Willie. Life wasn't fair.

15 *the path was chosen*

· the exile ·

LEANNAN CLOSED THE CUPBOARD IN THE PREPARATION alcove, wishing she could turn back time. If Tianna were still alive, she would be on her way to retrieve the queen's breakfast tray. Tianna would welcome her into the royal chambers and chat about the day ahead. Leannan swallowed hard to fight off the rising lump in her throat.

Lileas, with a smile so broad and bright it almost reached her pointy ears, grabbed Leannan's hand.

"Come, my friend, for ye have a grand surprise." Lileas bubbled with excitement like a mountain burn in the spring. "Your three hundredth birthday will be one ye shall ne'er forget."

"My heart is still so sore with grief, I did not remember," Leannan said as her dearest friend guided her down the Corridor of Wares.

Lileas squeezed her hand. "'Tis why I am so pleased for ye." She swung the double doors to the Clothiers' Shoppe open and waltzed in. Lileas curtseyed and flourished an arm in Leannan's direction."The fair maiden has arrived," she trumpeted in a tone befitting a royal announcement.

Leannan flushed and hoped no one else was in the passageway to hear.

Pàislig and the other seamstress Ùna embraced her.

"We have a gift for ye on this very special day," Pàislig said, offering up her willowy hands.

"Aye." Ùna raised a pair of squat fingers. "And it took us two days to make it."

Pàislig pursed her thin lips and quirked her brows. "It took us two days to agree on the style, Ùna, but just a wee while to fashion it."

"An eternity for ye to work on one dress," Leannan said. "I deserve not such an effort."

"Aye, but ye do." Pàislig's aging face beamed. "Now close your eyes."

Leannan obeyed.

"Be careful! Ye are going to step upon it," Ùna whispered.

"I shan't," Pàislig spoke softly.

"Are we ready yet?" Sweetness and impatience mixed perfectly in Lileas's voice.

"Aye," the seamstresses answered in unison.

Leannan opened her eyes wide, drew a hand to her mouth, and gasped at the shimmering gown held out before her. She touched the iridescent gossamer skirting and admired the crystal-beaded hearts adorning the waist. "'Tis exquisite!" she whispered. Her eyes brimmed with tears.

"Put it on, dear." Pàislig's laugh lines crinkled deep around her merry eyes.

"Do not forget these as well." Lileas scooped up a pair of pearl satin slippers embellished with crystal Celtic knots.

Leannan entered the door to the circular changing chamber in the middle of the shoppe. She removed her apron and simple dress, hung them on a silver hook, and donned the satin slippers. She slipped into the pearl-white gown and stepped outside to find Lileas and the seamstresses gathered at the open end of the horseshoe looking glass, their eyelids closed tight. Leannan tiptoed onto the marble platform and drew the feather curtain closed. A swirl of stardust enveloped her. The transformation chamber, Pàislig's inspiration and one of Earnan's most appreciated gifts to the Daoine Shi maidens, always made one look and feel as polished as the looking glass. Each hair magically fell into place. Her face tingled to a brighter shine. Her lips glistened as if kissed with dew drops, and her cheeks blushed the soft pink of a summer rose. Leannan opened the curtain.

"Ahh." A mixture of pride and delight radiated from Ùna's round face.

Pàislig clasped her hands and brought them to her chest as she let out a deep sigh. "It frames your figure perfectly."

Lileas's eyes glistened. "Ye are a princess in that gown."

If only Mungan would think so. "How can I express my gratitude for this extraordinary gift?"

"No need," Pàislig said. "But ye must know 'twas Queen Tianna who asked us to create the gown a few days before she...." The eldest seamstress's smile quivered. "She wanted the day marking your coming of age to be most memorable."

Leannan bit her lip and a tear spilled onto her cheek.

In an instant, Lileas pulled a hankie from her abundant cleavage, stepped onto the platform, and gently wiped away the tear. "Do not open the spigots for I fear my hankie shan't be able to sop up our puddles."

"I only wish she was here," Leannan said, in a voice not more than a whisper.

Lileas grasped her shoulders. "I know…." Her lips, as red and plump as cherries, trembled. "I know, but Queen Tianna would want ye to be happy this day."

The peach flames in the crystal cauldron suspended above the platform shifted to the golden yellow of the morning torchlights and beamed down on Leannan like a ray from heaven. The strands of crystals draped below her bare shoulders, along the heart shaped neckline, and at the empire waist twinkled as the light shifted to bright yellow, then rosy pink, royal blue and finally moonlight silver.

"It looks stunning on ye, Leannan, at any time of day," Ùna said.

"Ye shall certainly turn heads at the Midsummer's Eve banquet," Lileas said. "Being of marriageable age now, I wonder how many proposals ye will receive before the main course."

"We have another surprise." Pàislig's eyes sparkled.

Leannan looked down at her dress. "This magnificent gown is far more than enough."

"We are closing the shoppe a little early today," Ùna announced, "for we shall be serving the banquet in your place." The short seamstress swept her arms toward them both.

Lileas's eyes grew wide and several chins appeared as she dropped her generous jaw. "But 'tis not your role."

Pàislig grinned. "King Oseron approved the exception so Leannan could celebrate with her bosom friend."

Lileas hunched her shoulders in delight. "Oh my, and that I too should profit from your birthday, Leannan. I must go and find a gown to wear. I shall meet ye in the Great Hall," she called as she bustled from the shoppe.

"Your kindness is much appreciated." Leannan gave both seamstresses a warm embrace and then entered the passageway feeling brighter than she had in days.

Mungan came round the corner and halted at the sight of her. He gazed at her as if 'twere the first time they had ever met. "Leannan, ye have stolen my breath away."

"Queen Tianna asked the seamstresses to sew a new gown for me," Leannan said. "She arranged it some time ago as a wee gift for my birthday."

"'Tis more than a wee gift," Nuala groused as she stepped from the Cobblers' Shoppe with a new pair of slippers. "And most inappropriate for passing out plates." The dancer crossed her arms and sidled up to Mungan.

He glanced at Nuala with disapproval.

"The queen wanted it to be special as I have come of age today," Leannan said.

A smile spread across Mungan's face. "'Tis a stunning gown. Oh, that I could be so fortunate as to have ye accompany me to the Midsummer's Eve banquet."

Leannan bowed her head. "With the king's approval, the seamstresses are serving in place of Lileas and me."

"Then will ye do me the honour of sitting at my side?"

Leannan's knees went weak. "Of course."

"Give me a few moments, and I shall be back to escort ye into the Great Hall." Mungan bowed his head in farewell and strode down the corridor.

The dancer bristled. "If the king knew what ye did, he would ne'er allow ye to receive this gift, nor Mungan, clearly beguiled by that gown, have extended that invitation."

Leannan's joy vanished as fast as a candle's flame in the wind. What did the dancer know? "Nuala, I…I know not what ye mean."

"Then ye shall stew o'er my words as I must dance at the banquet in a wee while."

"'Tis true, I am most anxious to understand why ye would say such a thing, but I shan't stew long, for in a short while, I shall be seated with Mungan, enjoying the festivities." As soon as the words left her lips, she wished they had not.

"Listen carefully, Leannan. With perhaps the exception of the triplets, ye are the lowliest in this kingdom. The mountain shall fall down before ye will ever be considered worthy of Mungan." The dancer's green eyes blazed with danger. "I have my eyes on our esteemed Searsanach. I am the logical choice for him. And ye can be certain, I will do anything to convince him and the king of it."

"If ye have your eyes set on Mungan, then why were ye with Ballard in the Crystal Garden till the wee hours of the morning the night of the chess match?"

"Ballard meant nothing to me," Nuala said. "We talked the night away. That is all."

"Then why not clear his name of the queen's murder?" Leannan clasped her hands tight so as not to wring them.

"The king declared Ballard guilty of the offense. Who am I to question His Majesty? What is of more importance, Leannan, is that ye left the mountain the morning the queen was found dead. Ye carried a satchel out into the mortal realm. Did it hold something ye felt compelled to dispose of?"

Leannan had to choose her words carefully or bring condemnation upon herself. 'Twas true that her satchel held her beloved brushes which she would never discard. "I cannot fathom that of which ye speak." Leannan hoped she sounded convincing, though she feared her shaking hands would betray her.

"I think ye do, Leannan. And that dress shan't stay pretty very long in the dungeon."

Leannan's heart pounded so fast and hard she felt sure 'twould burst through her chest. "'Twas a bag of brushes and a canvas ye saw me with. I went to the other realm to paint."

"So the lowly maidservant aspires to be an artist. 'Tis another impossible desire, only this one will be your undoing. Tell me, did Mungan like your painting?"

Leannan swallowed hard.

"He must have, as I saw him enter the passageway to the portal and a short while later return carrying your canvas. It appears our Searsanach shared not this little tidbit with the king."

"Please, Nuala, I can explain."

"No need. I believe I understand quite well. Leaving the mountain and directly defying the king's orders." Nuala held her palm out as if it were weighed down with the words. "Or murdering the queen." She dropped her other palm lower like a merchant's scale out of balance. "In either case, the lowly maidservant pays dearly."

"I did not kill Queen Tianna."

"The queen was poisoned and ye brought her the cup. If 'twas not Ballard as ye say, than who do ye suppose looks most suspicious?" Nuala looked down her nose at Leannan. "If ye say a word to Mungan or the king regarding Ballard, I shall find the words to deny it. And ye will find yourself locked away for either one of your transgressions."

Nuala flipped her long black locks. "'Twould be best for all of us, Leannan, if ye were to quietly slip from our mountain before I find it impossible to contain your secret from the king."

Leannan bristled. "I would not want ye to burst from the strain, Nuala. My leaving the mountain was wrong. I am willing to pay for my indiscretion."

"But are ye willing for Mungan to pay as well?"

"Mungan did nothing wrong. He has merely been gracious in keeping silent about my venture as no harm was done. Besides, 'twould not serve your desires to have him punished."

"Aye, but if I cannot have him, no one will." The dancer narrowed her viridian eyes. "The price for my silence regarding both Mungan and ye is your exile."

'Twas as though Nuala dealt a mighty blow to Leannan's stomach. "Will ye vow so?"

"Aye." The dancer turned her head toward the closest painting on the wall of the passageway. "It appears to be a fine day for your departure. There is not a cloud in the sky." Nuala glowered at Leannan once more with eyes as cold as a frozen loch. "Have a pleasant birthday."

Leannan watched the dancer strut down the corridor. 'Twas hard to believe Nuala would betray Mungan to the king. Nevertheless, 'twas not a risk she was willing to take. She had caused him enough trouble already. Her heart ached and her whole being shook.

With leaden footsteps, Leannan too walked through the Corridor of Wares. How could this day, one she had dreamed of for the last one hundred and fifty years, have taken such a cruel turn in mere moments? Her knees grew weak and her chest weighed heavy with despair. She fought to clear the cloud of sorrow and shame that enveloped her. Leannan stood tall and gulped deep breaths. To save Mungan, she would leave the Daoine Shi and the only home she had ever known.

But where in the other realm could she go? She would make herself wee and try to find the Asrai. Perhaps the delicate female fae would take her in as a servant. She turned into the passageway bordering the Great Hall. Plates clattered in the kitchen. Instinctively, Leannan quickened her pace. Lileas! She had completely forgotten about meeting Lileas. Peering into the Great Hall, she realized her dearest friend had not yet arrived. Nuala, flitting from table to table, glanced at her with vicious eyes and a slight nod of the head toward the portal.

Several steps more and she could sit at Mungan's side in the Great Hall with Lileas, a nigh impossible dream. 'Twould be grand until Nuala announced to King Oseron, or perhaps to one and all, that she had left the mountain, and Mungan had kept it secret. Or, she could pass the archway and slip out the portal, insulting the one who ruled her heart and deeply hurting her closest friend.

The turmoil in Leannan's mind made her feel as though she were being rent in two. Her heart willed her to wait for Mungan and Lileas while her mind told her feet to flee. She passed the archway of the Great Hall and kept walking.

If anyone approached as she reached the end of the corridor, Leannan would turn into the passageway branching off to her chamber. If not, she would disappear into the tunnel leading out of the mountain. She glimpsed into the preparation alcove. 'Twas empty. In the Great Hall, the Daoine Shi laughed and clinked their chalices. The king spoke with Cormag, their backs to her. No one would notice. Leannan ducked into the portal's dim tunnel and did not look back.

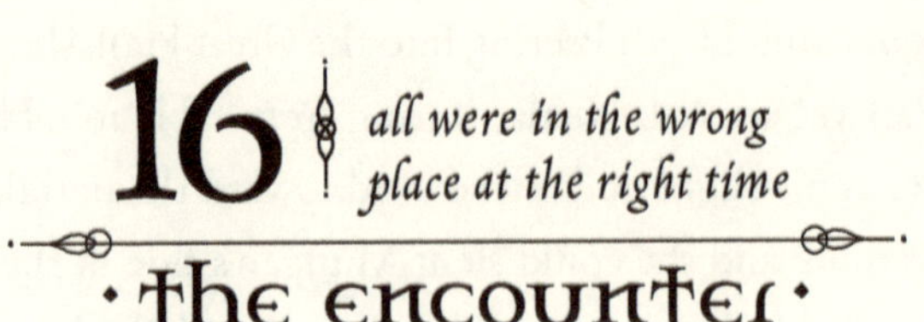

16 *all were in the wrong place at the right time*

· the encounter ·

11:03 AM
JUNE 24TH

ROBBIE'S STOMACH CHURNED WITH EACH STEP CLOSER TO the black hole in the hillside. Last in the long line of kids, he trudged after Caitie into the giant stone mouth. Swallowed in darkness, he shivered. Miss Bowers's footsteps echoed behind him, but they didn't make him feel any better. One look at his face, and she'd see how freaked out he was.

What was hiding in there—bats, spiders, snakes? Or maybe like Craig said, there were wee folk just waiting to pop out at him. He flashed back to the night on the train when he had seen their lights on the hillside. Now he imagined hundreds of them with tiny torches chasing him through the cave.

Around a massive boulder, a shaft of sunlight poured through a gap onto a pile of stones. Caitie scrambled up them and disappeared through the hole. He scampered after her, his nylon clothes whistling and whining as they scraped against the granite. By the time he squeezed through the opening in the hillside, he was breathing hard. The bright sunshine made him squint, but he was glad to be outside again. It only lasted a minute though before he went feet first through a hole not much wider than his shoulders, carefully feeling for the ground below. In and out of the darkness, the group slowly made their way higher. His shoulders ached, his legs shook, and his hands tingled from rock burns.

He wiggled out into the fresh air and found Caitie snapping a picture of the countryside.

"Wish we were down there instead of here," he muttered.

"And I wish I was up with Bonnie and Willie instead of babysitting you." She tucked the camera back up her shirtsleeve before scaling two huge rocks and disappearing back into the hillside.

Robbie's fingers slipped on the stone as he went up after her. His body slid down the face of the rock until his boot found a ledge to stop him. He hated this. Stretching for a handhold, his fingers caught a small ridge, and he used it to drag himself up the boulder.

"Check this out, Robbie," Caitie said. "The girl ahead of me called it the cheese press." She turned her head to the side and inched through the gap between two parallel boulders.

Once she was through, he grabbed the top edge of the rock with his fingertips and found a toehold. He pushed up with his leg, keeping the inside of his thigh against the stone so his body stayed flat. His helmet scraped and banged against the boulder above him.

Caitie laughed. "I hope there's not an earthquake while we're in here. We'll all be squished."

Robbie squirmed through the slot as fast as he could and entered a big cave. He gave Caitie the evil eye. "Thanks! That makes me feel real good."

"Well done, Robbie!" Miss Bowers called from below.

Caitie pulled out her camera. "I want a picture to show Mom. She won't believe this."

Miss Bowers cleared the opening. "Would you like me to take it? That way you both can be in the photo."

"Sure." Caitie handed Miss Bowers the Lumix.

The teacher studied the camera while he and Caitie crammed close on either side of the gap they'd wriggled through.

"Just press the smaller silver button on top," Caitie said.

The bright light from the camera flash blinded him for a second.

Miss Bowers's face took on a creepy gray glow as she looked at the picture on the camera display. "It turned out great." She turned the camera around for Caitie and him to see. With their scarred helmets, they looked like under-aged miners. It wasn't that great a photo.

"Yeah. Thanks." Caitie grinned.

"Help!" a girl up ahead cried.

The teacher jerked her head in the direction of the terrified voice.

"Miss Bowers! Help!" A silhouette appeared against the bright light of the cave entrance. It stumbled forward, and a girl close to his age bent over with her hands on her knees, gasping for breath.

"What is it, Annabel?" Miss Bowers's forehead wrinkled with panic.

"Elsie's stuck!" the girl yelled. "She went the wrong way and can't get herself out."

Miss Bowers practically threw the Lumix at Caitie. "You two, stay here. I'll be right back. I promise."

"Don't worry. We're fine." Caitie shot him a *Don't argue* look.

Just once, Robbie wished Caitie didn't open her mouth and talk for him like she knew better than he did what was going on in his head.

"Lead the way, Annabel." Miss Bowers sprinted out of the cave following the girl.

He fought the urge to take off after them. "How long do you think she'll be?"

"Not long," Caitie said.

"What time is it?"

"Mom's got my cell."

"Look at your camera!" His voice echoed off the cave walls.

"Why do you care what time it is anyway?"

"We should keep track of it, in case Miss Bowers forgets about us."

"Get real, Robbie. She's not gonna do that. It's almost noon."

Robbie looked for a place to sit and wait. A chin-high boulder against the cave wall looked nice and flat. He crawled up smaller rocks beside it to reach the ledge. In the dim light, he could see there was nothing creeping around up there. He hoisted himself onto the rock, leaned back against the wall, and hugged his knees, feeling better that nothing could sneak up behind him.

Caitie walked toward the cave entrance.

"Where are you going? We're supposed to wait here!"

"I'm not leaving. I'm just going to check out the view."

How long ago did Miss Bowers leave? Three minutes, maybe? She should be back soon. It was so quiet he could hear his pulse pounding in his ears.

I MINUTE BEFORE NOON

HER MIND MADE UP, LEANNAN TOOK A STEADYING breath in front of the portal while the music and laughter in the Great Hall echoed down the long tunnel as compelling as an old friend coaxing her to stay. *"Fosgail an dorus drùidheil,"* she whispered. The mystical door flew inward. A lad wearing a strange red ball of a cap fell backwards at her feet. His head hit the tunnel floor with a loud crack. Leannan jumped backwards.

"Ouch!" the lad cried.

"Shhh!" She looked back down the passageway in fear. Had anyone in the Great Hall heard?

"Who said that?" He jumped to his feet and spun in the direction of her voice.

"I did," Leannan whispered. "Now, not another word!"

"Where am I? What's happening?" The lad's eyes frantically searched the surroundings, staring right through her as he trembled in the golden glow of the torchlight.

Thankfully, he possessed not "the gift" for he could not see her.

"Ye have to be quiet," Leannan whispered.

He stood frozen with fear. "Caitie!" he sobbed. "Come back!"

She had to remove him from their tunnel and close the portal. "Run from here. Please!" Leannan begged. She placed her hands on his shoulders, turned him in the direction of the portal, and lightly pushed him away. The lad bristled at her touch and stumbled toward the stone ledge. She stepped round him and glided down to the cavern floor. With him out of the way, she commanded, *"Dùin an dorus drùidheil."* The portal to the fae world closed, and she drew a calming breath. She turned to make her escape and jumped at the sight of a lass barreling in her direction.

12:03 PM

ROBBIE'S WHOLE BODY QUIVERED AS THE ROCK PRESSED against his back and nudged him forward a step.

Caitie raced toward him, then skidded to a stop. Her jawed dropped and her eyes narrowed. "Who are you? How'd you get here?" she asked, but she wasn't looking at him.

"Who are you talking to?" Robbie cried.

"You can't see her?" Caitie asked like it was impossible for him not to.

"No! But I heard someone. And then somebody touched me. Where are they?"

"She's right in front of you!" Caitie's finger shot straight out, pointed in his direction.

He plastered his back against the cave wall and thrust his arms out to keep the thing away.

"She's not that close, Robbie."

"Do ye have 'the gift'?" The voice asked, this time sounding scared.

"What gift?" Caitie stared at the invisible whatever.

"The ability to set your eyes into the other world," the voice said.

Caitie shook her head. "No."

"Is she a ghost? How come I can't see her, and you can?"

"I am no ghost." Whoever it was sounded ticked. "And I have not revealed myself to either of ye."

With her fists planted on her hips, Caitie took a step toward it. "Well, I can see you just fine."

"Come no closer." Miss Invisible sounded as freaked as he was. "Did ye drink a potion of thyme or calendula today?"

"What?" Caitie blurted. "I don't drink potions. Nobody I know drinks potions."

"Then ye must have a four-leaf clover in your cap," the voice accused.

Caitie brought both hands to her head. "I do."

Robbie's heart banged inside his chest. He couldn't stand being blind another second. "Give me your helmet, Caitie. I want to see."

"I must go," the voice said.

Caitie stretched her arms out like she was gonna stop whoever it was from going around her. "No." She sounded way more brave than he could believe. "Robbie, come here."

He didn't know what to do, even if Caitie seemed like she did.

"Now, Robbie! And stick your arms out."

He jumped off the rock and did what she said, staring hard at the same spot his sister was.

"You're not going until you show yourself to Robbie. You're gonna prove I'm not crazy and seeing things. And if you don't, I'm gonna scream real loud. There are a lot of people close by, and they'll come running. And we'll trap you in here, and I'll let everyone of them see you with my clover."

"Do ye vow to keep silent if I reveal myself to the lad?"

"Yeah, I promise."

Suddenly, a tall, wispy woman materialized right in front of him. Robbie's knees went weak, and his vision started whiting out. He tottered back and shook his head to clear the fog closing in. She looked misty, like he could throw a rock right through her. A few seconds later, she wasn't transparent but almost human, except for a dazzling aura that pulsed all around her.

She looked at him with amazing eyes, the deep, dark blue-green of a peacock's head. The highlights in her auburn hair danced the way sunlight reflects off a goldfish, and her brilliant white dress shimmered like a million tiny prisms. She was so beautiful he couldn't take his eyes off her. All his fear melted away. "Are you an angel?"

"No," she said gently.

"Robbie, you don't see angels with four-leaf clovers," Caitie said.

And then his memory clicked. The old lady on the train must have had a four-leaf clover inside her tam. That's how he'd seen the lights out the train window. "Caitie, remember Miss Moncrieff? You see fairies!"

She couldn't be one of the wee folk Miss Moncrieff and Craig talked about though. She had to be close to six feet tall. "But you can't be one. You're not little."

Her aura faded, leaving her skin glowing softly. "I am a Daoine Shi."

"What's that?" Caitie asked.

She closed her eyes for a second and bit her lip. "The Daoine Shi are mountain fae."

"So what's your name?" Robbie took a step closer.

"Leannan." She looked at Caitie. "I have done what ye asked of me, now let me pass."

Caitie crossed her arms. "Not so fast. If you're a fairy, where's you magic wand?"

"Only wizards possess wands. I am no wizard, thus I have no wand." Leannan said it like he and Caitie were already supposed to have that figured out.

Robbie tilted his head. "Wizards aren't the only ones who use wands. Fairies are supposed to. Tinker Bell, the three fat fairies from Sleeping Beauty, and Cinderella's fairy godmother, they all had wands. I saw it on DVD when I was little."

Leannan scrunched her eyebrows, totally clueless. "DVD?"

"They're movies for your TV," Robbie said before realizing she probably didn't know what a TV was either.

"You don't have wings," Caitie said. "All the fairies in the books I've read have wings."

"None of the Daoine Shi have wings," Leannan said.

"Where are the rest of them?" Caitie asked.

Leannan didn't answer.

Robbie looked back at the boulder he'd sat on, remembering how the cave wall had given way before he hit his head. "They're behind some kind of trap door up there." He pointed to the wall above the rock. "There was a torch. And I remember hearing voices and music."

Caitie's eyes went wide. "You were in there?"

"Well, sort of. I didn't know it, but I was leaning against their door, and when it opened, I fell in and hit my head," he said. "She pushed me out, said some weird stuff, and the door shut again."

Leannan pulled her hair back and started pacing in front of them.

"Look, Caitie." Robbie pointed at Leannan's head. "She's got pointy ears."

"Elves have pointy ears," Caitie said.

Leannan stared at Caitie like she'd given her the ultimate diss. "I am not an elf."

"And you're way too tall to be a dwarf," he added.

"Why certainly."

"If you're really a fairy, you can do magic," Caitie said.

Leannan sighed and closed her eyes. "I can."

"Then prove it," Caitie dared.

The fairy pursed her lips and stared at her. "I must leave."

"Turn my brother into Lonnie Moore, the lead singer for Hooked, and we'll let you go, I promise."

"No! Turn her," he pointed to his sister, "into Chica Chic and make it rain money."

"Chica Chic! Seriously? Is that the best you can come up with?" Caitie wrinkled her nose in disgust. "She's so dim. It's a miracle she can find the runway at a fashion show."

"But she's hot," Robbie said.

Leannan studied his sister and then him. "I know not of whom ye speak." Her eyes flashed with anger like she'd had enough, "but feast your eyes on this."

17 *the deed was done*

·capturing magic·

MUNGAN AMBLED THROUGH THE CORRIDOR TO THE archway into the Great Hall, pleased at the prospect of the lovely Leannan as his escort to the Midsummer's Eve festivities. Instead Lileas stood there in a bright orange gown looking remarkably like a pumpkin, her thick neck craned as she roamed the banquet hall with her eyes.

"Have ye spied Leannan amongst the crowd?" he asked.

"No," Lileas answered. "We are to attend the celebration together. And I cannot imagine why she is not here."

Nuala ascended the stage. He had left Leannan in the passageway with the dancer only minutes earlier. Perhaps she knew of the maiden's whereabouts. Nuala gave him a coy smile and flicked her long locks as he sauntered over.

"Do ye know where Leannan is?"

The dancer breezed across the stage and extended her hand for him to help her down. Mungan clasped it, and with the lightness of a butterfly, she fluttered off the platform.

"It seems the ungrateful maidservant changed her mind about accompanying ye to the banquet." Nuala fingered the collar on his shirt. "I would gladly take her place though."

"Why would Leannan do so?" he asked.

Nuala's brows arched in disapproval. "It seems she prefers the outside world."

Mungan could not believe it. He turned in pursuit.

The dancer clutched his arm. "Mungan, let her go. 'Tis what the chambermaid desires."

"I cannot allow it."

"'Tis too late. She has made her choice." Nuala pleaded with her hypnotic eyes. "Leannan has likely left by now. 'Twould be unwise to chase after her. Ye know the king's decree."

He tore his arm from the dancer's grip and strode from the Great Hall, passing Lileas without a word. Racing up the passageway, he hoped he was not too late. The portal was empty. He had to find her before something terrible happened. *"Fosgail an dorus drùidheil."*

The portal inched open in silence. Voices streamed through the gap from the other realm. Mungan pressed against the granite door to stop it from moving any further. Instantly, he recognized Leannan speaking. Then two mortals replied. He ran his hands through his curly hair. Crivvens!

MESMERIZED, CAITIE WATCHED THE FAIRY CLOSE HER EYES and stretch her long neck, her head held high. Leannan turned up her delicate nose, pursed her rosy lips, and started to spin slowly. Robbie edged nearer to Caitie.

No one would believe this. Caitie didn't believe it herself. But maybe she could capture it all on her camera. It was worth a try. With her arms behind her back, she carefully retrieved the Lumix from inside her shirtsleeve. Running her pointer finger along the top of the camera, she slid the power switch to "ON." She kept the Lumix behind her back, with her finger poised on the shutter button, ready to bring the camera to her face and take a picture at the perfect moment.

As Leannan turned, she blew out a sparkling rainbow vapor that transformed everything it touched before vanishing. The fairy's first pirouette changed the rocky ground to a shiny marble floor. The lower third of the rough cave walls became smooth. The boulders scattered around turned to chairs and polished tables.

Caitie gasped. She wanted to stoop down and touch the floor to see if it was real but froze at the last second. *What if that changes me?* Leannan started a second pirouette, building on what she'd just created the way a Dairy Queen waitress swirls a soft serve cone. The shadowy cave changed from the ground up into a room you'd find in a castle. Leannan's rainbow breath now landed on the middle of the walls and created statues on the tables. Paintings and tapestries appeared.

Caitie pulled the camera from behind her back and raised it to her face. She centered the fairy in the display, pressed the shutter button half-way down to focus, and waited for Leannan to turn toward her. The second Leannan did, Caitie pressed the shutter button all the way down. In an instant, the flash went off, and sparkling rainbow stuff hit the camera and Caitie's face and hair. Leannan's eyes popped open.

The transformation of the cave stopped and undid the way twisted ropes on a swing twirl when let go. The statues, paintings, and tapestries melted away in a whirl. The cave's rugged walls and boulders returned, and the shiny marble floor disappeared.

Leannan's wide eyes filled with terror, and a cry escaped her lips. Caitie dropped the camera, letting it dangle from the wrist strap. The fairy convulsed and choked. The cloud of rainbow vapor that spewed out of her mouth enveloped her and Robbie. Caitie wiped her face, trying to get rid of the sparkling mist or whatever it was that stung her eyes. She could make out Robbie doing the same thing. She prayed they wouldn't go blind.

Leannan's shimmering thick auburn hair dissolved into a few coarse strands. Her perfect complexion dulled to gray green. Her cheeks sunk in, and her skin sagged like the jowls on one of those super-wrinkled Chinese dogs. Dark circles framed her blue-green eyes. Then the whites became glow-in-the-dark green and her irises turned coal black. The fairy's delicate nose ballooned like a zucchini. Several decayed stumps took the place of her perfect teeth. Her tall graceful figure sank, her shoulders stooped, her back hunched. The shimmering dress vanished, replaced with rags. Her legs and feet flipped backwards.

Caitie screamed. It was worse than any scary movie she'd ever seen. Robbie threw his arms around her, nearly knocking her over.

What little life that was left in Leannan's horrifying eyes focused on Caitie. "What have ye done to me?" she asked in a raspy voice.

"I didn't do anything!" Caitie cried. Every part of her body shook.

Leannan waddled toward the stair-step rocks. She half-loped, half-crawled up the boulders and disappeared, slipping through an opening in the cave wall, outlined in golden light.

17 MINUTES
PAST 12 PM

MUNGAN GASPED AS GNARLED GREY GREEN FINGERS curled around the edge of the door and pushed the portal wide open. He watched in horror as an unrecognizable hag slipped inside the mountain.

"Leannan?" he asked, appalled at the possibility that the figure before him could be her.

"Aye," she croaked.

Unable to bear the sight of her, Mungan turned away and recited the incantation to seal out the mortals. He steeled himself and faced her once more in the golden torchlight. Ale rose in his throat and he swallowed hard to push it back down. "How did this happen to ye?"

Leannan sobbed. "That lass stole my magic."

"She shall pay for this." He took off his dress cloak and covered her with it. "Go straight to your chamber and wait till I return."

"But the king…"

"Leannan, ye must do as I say. I only hope that the Daoine Shi are too full of drink and mirth to notice ye steal past them."

She nodded obediently.

"Do not answer the door for anyone but me."

"I shan't, I promise. Mungan, I am so ashamed and so very sorry. I deserve what has become of me."

"No one deserves this." He looked into her monstrous eyes. "I know not how long it shall be before I return, but stay guarded and patient."

"What do ye plan to do?"

"To follow the mortals. I must find out where they live, if we hope to retrieve your magic."

"Mungan, I beg of ye, do not pursue them. I alone must pay the price for my decision. The humans are more wicked and clever than I ever suspected."

"There is no time to argue, Leannan. Now be off."

She clutched his arm with her gnarled and bony hand. "The lad, Robbie, will not be able to see ye, but the lass, Caitie, has a four-leaf clover in her strange cap. Be cautious, for ye shan't be invisible to her."

"I shall be careful." His mind raced as he watched Leannan turn and waddle down the tunnel in the direction of her chamber. A few short days ago, he had admonished Leannan for leaving their mountain, and now he planned to commit the same crime. But there was no time to seek King Oseron's approval. 'Twas not only his responsibility as Searsanach but his duty as her friend. If he knew where the mortals lived, he could plot his course to right this terrible wrong.

"Beagaich!" In an instant, Mungan stood only a foot tall. Resting his hands along the edge of the portal, he commanded, *"Fosgail an dorus drùidheil"* and cautiously slipped through the crack as the door opened to the mortal realm.

CAITIE STOOD STUNNED, HER ARMS WRAPPED AROUND Robbie. He looked up in her face.

"How'd you do that to her?"

"I didn't do anything but take her picture." The accusation and look on the fairy's face haunted Caitie though. The thought that this was somehow her fault made her whole body tremble. "Robbie, if I did do that to Leannan, I've gotta fix it somehow."

Robbie pulled away. "You can't. She ran back inside the mountain."

"I don't get this. Not any of it." Caitie stripped the camera from her wrist. "It's like a super bad dream, only I can feel things."

"It's not a freakin' nightmare. It's real. We gotta get out of here, Caitie. Before the others see her and come after us!"

The camera looked normal. Did the picture turn out? Caitie's hands shook so hard that she couldn't get her Lumix into review mode.

"C'mon, Caitie, we gotta find Miss Bowers and tell her what happened."

"Are you kidding? We can't tell her or anybody."

"Why not?" Robbie asked.

"'Cause nobody will believe it. They'll think you're crazy. Just as nuts as people who say they've been abducted by aliens."

"But you've got the picture."

"We don't know that yet," she said, still fumbling with the camera.

Miss Bowers appeared through the cave entrance and rushed toward them.

"Are you all right? I heard a scream."

Caitie pressed the off button on the Lumix and slipped it up her shirtsleeve. "We're fine, Miss Bowers. Robbie just played a little trick on me, and I fell for it."

"Well, I'm glad everything's okay. Let's catch up with the others," the P.E. teacher said.

"Sounds good to me." Robbie took a deep breath and exhaled so loud it echoed in the cave.

It wasn't okay. She'd just turned a mountain fairy, which really couldn't exist, into a monster. Her conscience was in overdrive hurtling down a highway of guilt. But they were with an adult now who would lead them back to normality, at least that's what she hoped.

18 *the world had changed*

· the trip home ·

HALF~PAST 12 IN THE AFTERNOON
JUNE 24TH

MUNGAN SCRAMBLED NOISELESSLY OFF THE ROCK NEAR the portal. At his normal size, 'twas a mere step down from each boulder, but at a foot high, he slid off two cliffs. The witch that stole Leannan's magic, the lad, and a woman Leannan failed to mention strode toward the cave entrance. He ran to keep from falling too far behind them. The heartless lass looked back before heading outside. He dove behind a rock. Did she sense him, feel his ire?

Moments later, Mungan stepped into the blinding sunlight. He followed as the three wove in and out of the hillside. They caught up with a large troupe of mortals. He checked his pocket watch. 'Twas not long past noon on Midsummer's Eve, a Friday no less, and with most of the horde being young, he was more vulnerable to discovery. With care, he shadowed them as a tall man led the troupe's descent single-file to the base of the mountain.

Mungan hid behind a birch tree at the edge of the clearing where the witch and the lad walked amongst the troupe, stripping off their helmets and outer garments. The lad handed her something dark blue, a cap perhaps?

Bending down on one knee, the witch placed the cap on the ground and removed the red helmet. She retrieved the four-leaf clover and showed it to her companion. The other lass's smile quickly faded. The witch placed the four-leaf clover in the blue cap and took off her outer garments.

Reaching up her sleeve, the witch retrieved an object that glinted in the sunlight and slipped it into a front pocket on her odd sweater. She picked up the cap, bent over, and set it atop her head. Mungan sighed. He had to be diligent, lest she spy him.

After their meal, a portly woman rose from a tartan blanket and drew a strange yellow trumpet to her mouth. "It's time to gather our belongings and head for the bus," boomed the woman's voice. Within a few minutes the leader guided the troupe out of the clearing, leaving behind only trampled grass. They moved swiftly on the wide path.

Mungan dodged one obstacle after another to ensure no one witnessed a disturbance of the brush created by his invisible passage through it. Were he his true size, the tall weeds and stones would not slow him a bit. But now he struggled through and round them, fighting to match the mortals' pace.

Before long, the troupe arrived at a lane where a monstrous white box with windows and bold stripes and a much smaller blue box rested on wheels under a canopy of trees. The strange contraptions had to be some type of carriages or the bus the portly woman referred to. Mungan watched from the weeds as the young ones filed past the man. One by one, they handed him their garments and helmets, and he tossed it all inside the blue carriage. In small groups of two or three, the noisy scoundrels then strode to the gigantic bus and disappeared inside.

The mortals' departure was imminent. Mungan knew he could never keep up with a carriage this size while on foot, and looking round, no other fleeter options appeared available. He had to ride in their bus. Mungan searched its darkened windows for the witch. If he could spot her, perhaps he could time his move to avoid her gaze. He found her six windows from the front, still wearing the cap. She turned her head away, and Mungan darted across the gravel lane beneath the coach, re-emerging at the wheel well near the door.

With the two women and the troupe's leader still engaged in conversation, Mungan stepped away from the protection of the undercarriage and peered through the open doorway at an older man seated in the lone chair in front, reading large papers. Thankful for this distraction, Mungan planted his palms flat on the first step. He thrust upward, and in one smooth motion swung his right leg onto the stair, and hoisted himself up. He scaled the second step and prepared to mount the third.

"Thank you again, Craig," the trim woman from the cave called. Mungan turned to see her with one foot on the bottom step, waving farewell. He braced himself against the wall of the short stairway. She looked right in his direction, completely unaware of him. Holding her knapsack by the top strap, the woman hopped up the second and third steps, her right hand low at her side.

Mungan watched in horror as the massive knapsack loomed toward him and knocked him off his feet, slamming him into the stair.

He stood up dazed and pulled himself atop the last step, next to the woman's boot heels. She stepped into the front row and sat down. Mungan followed and stole under the grey bench. Hunched over and gasping for breath, the knapsack shoved Mungan from behind and threw him into the wall as the woman stowed it beneath the seat.

Once the second woman boarded, the carriage thrummed to life. Mungan's whole body shook with the vibrating floor. The doors shut, the coach lurched, and Mungan crashed onto the knapsack. He clung to it as the carriage rattled down the gravel lane. The ride smoothed out, and after what seemed an eternity, the coach rolled to a stop.

The doors swung open, and the young mortals poured off the bus, prattling incessantly.

Mungan recognized the voice of the lad from the cave coming up the long aisle. He crouched down behind the knapsack.

"Do you see the car, Caitie?" the lad asked.

"I think it's parked over there near the back of the lot."

Mungan watched the lad's blue breeches and boots disappear.

"Bye, Bonnie. Thanks for today," the witch said.

"Sure. Hey, are you going to the ceilidh tomorrow night?" her companion asked.

The witch started down the carriage steps. "What's a ceilidh?"

"A dance. Your grandparents never miss them."

"Then I guess we'll be there."

Many more young ones followed, blocking Mungan's escape. He grew uneasy as the seconds ticked by. Finally, the bus grew quiet, and the portly woman stood up. The sound of air rushed back into the seat cushion.

The younger woman yanked her knapsack away and stepped toward the carriage driver.

Mungan slipped into the aisle behind her, staying as close as he dared. Planting a hand on the floor, he jumped off each stair. The driver's chair creaked as Mungan reached the last step. He turned his head in the old man's direction. The coachman reached for the lever attached to the carriage doors, and Mungan flung himself through the opening. The doors slapped shut behind him. After tumbling onto the ground, Mungan sprang to his feet and rushed under the front of the carriage.

Hunched over, so as not to hit his head, Mungan watched the witch and lad approach another small coach. What had the lad called it? A…car. A lovely woman, as humans go, emerged from it. She embraced them both. The resemblance between them was strong. The woman had to be their mother. There was no time to catch up to them. He had to devise a plan to intercept them instead.

He studied the line of carriages stopping frequently as they slowly rolled past the bus. He would dash to the witch's car as they paraded by and stow away somewhere in the undercarriage. The trio climbed inside their white coach. The young woman from the cave strode to her red one and tossed her knapsack inside.

The witch's car rumbled to a stop between Mungan and the young woman.

"Thank you for letting my kids join your outing today."

Mungan raced across the gravel and ducked beneath the coach, moving toward the rear as he searched for a place to secure himself for what would surely be another rough ride.

As the two women spoke, he crawled up the black wheel. Filthy as it was, he was grateful 'twas not iron, for he had no protection from the searing heat that would bring. He pulled himself up to a much larger pipe spanning the width of the car between the two rear wheels. He dropped to his stomach and circled his arms and legs round it, ready to grab the pipe tight.

From his perch, Mungan heard the young woman's footsteps fade. The car rolled forward and turned. With nary a hint of warning, the coach bolted forward at the speed of a gallop.

The wind roared in his ears and whipped his hair across his face. Stones pinged against the metal underside of the car. A rock struck his shin. The sharp pain made him flinch. He drew his face close to the pipe to shield himself from a stone's blow to his head.

After a much shorter ride than the one on the bus, the carriage again rolled to a stop. A dog's bark grew louder. The trio emerged and shut their doors one after another, shaking the car. Mungan could see four huge paws next to the lad's boots.

"Hi Balfour. How are you, boy?" the lad asked.

Two paws disappeared from Mungan's line of sight, and a wagging tail came into view as the dog jumped up on the lad. A moment later the paws were back on the ground, and the three humans strode away, the mongrel following behind.

"I see you both survived," came the distant voice of an old man.

"Yeah," the lad shouted back with little enthusiasm.

The voices faded and a door closed. Mungan released his grip on the shaft and dropped to the ground. He crept toward the other end of the car as the dog trotted to the dock, where an old man worked in the back of a tawny red boat. The mongrel lay down on the end of the pier, facing the dwelling.

As if his journey had not been difficult enough already, he now had to contend with a large dog. Mungan sighed. He hated the beasts. Their vision unhindered, they took pleasure in chasing the fae. As soon as he left the safety of the carriage, the mongrel would likely notice him and start a chase from which there was no good means of escape. He could run to a tree and climb it to get away from the dog. But if the mongrel sat at the base of it barking, 'twould draw the attention of the family, and they could very well come outside to see what was disturbing the animal. If the lass were still wearing her cap, he could be spotted. No, he needed to figure out a way to leave quickly, get his bearings to the location of this croft, and return to the mountain.

Mungan surveyed the grounds and spied a garden. *Of course! Every good farmer's wife grew cabbage.* The distance to the garden appeared to be half what it was to the dock. If he could make it to the garden, he had a fine chance of locating a tool of escape.

He searched the windows of the dwelling for the lass with no success. Deciding there was no benefit in delaying any further, Mungan stepped away from the protection of the carriage. He stole toward the garden. Encouraged that the dog did not detect his movement the first quarter-length, he pressed onward.

Two steps more and Mungan saw one ear of the dog shoot straight up. A split second later, the second ear followed. The black and white beast rose on his haunches. A low growl rose from its wretched throat. It snarled, baring its teeth. The old man looked up from his work at the dog and then in Mungan's direction.

Knowing the blasted dog had discovered him, Mungan sprinted toward the garden. The beast bolted after him. Mungan's short legs were no match for the mongrel's galloping stride. He barreled into the large vegetable patch hurdling radishes and carrots before finding the cabbage. Thankfully there were a few plants with flower stalks. The nasty beast breeched the perimeter of the garden as Mungan broke off a light green stalk. He mounted it like a horse as the dog bounded into the vegetables. The towering beast lunged at him as he cried, *"Gabh air iteig!"*

19 *a picture was worth a thousand doubts*

· the photo ·

4:15 PM
JUNE 24TH

THE LONG BUS RIDE BACK TO DRUM HAD GIVEN CAITIE plenty of time to obsess over what she and Robbie thought they'd seen in the cave. She had to be crazy. Fairies didn't exist, but her camera held the proof she wasn't.

She had wanted to show Bonnie the picture, but then everyone would find out, and somebody would go back to the mountain and investigate. Then those Daoine, whatever they were, could try and get even for what had happened to Leannan, and she'd be responsible for starting some kind of human-fairy war. So instead she'd kept her cool, smiling and responding with "uh-huh" and "yeah" as Bonnie talked about all the new clothes she was going to get for her vacation in the south of France. When the itch to turn the camera on got too strong, she'd crossed her arms and dug her nails into her hoodie, thinking it wouldn't be long before she'd be in her own room where no one but her could see the photo.

Caitie'd been just as stressed on the short ride home, but at least Robbie didn't say anything when Mom asked about their day. Thankfully, the bribe for his silence in the car had only cost her the promise of another king-size candy bar.

A tea kettle whistled on the stove as the three of them walked through the backdoor.

"Sounds like we got home at the perfect time." Mom hung her purse on a kitchen chair. "Wash up quick, you two."

Grandma MacGregor flipped a super thick cookie out of a mold onto a big plate. It smelled so good that Caitie's mouth watered. She was starving and guessed the camera could wait.

Robbie eyed the mega-cookie. "What's that?"

"Shortbread." Grandma MacGregor sliced it into wedges like a pie while they scrubbed their gritty hands at the sink.

"Can I have mine with milk?" he asked.

Grandma's blue eyes twinkled. "Of course, Robbie." She brought the plate to the table and set it between a bowl of fresh raspberries and a quart of vanilla ice cream.

"Did you get any good pictures?" Mom asked as she poured him a glass.

"Boy, did she!" Robbie said.

Caitie shot him a look that warned, "Keep your mouth shut."

"I'd like to see them after we eat," Mom said.

Caitie's chest caved in as dread sucked the air from her lungs. This couldn't possibly end well. She had to keep the last photo a secret until she could figure out what to do about this whole mess. "Probably only a couple are any good."

Outside, the dog went totally schizo.

"What's wrong with Balfour?" Mom asked.

"I don't know." Robbie pressed his nose against the window pane while ice cream dripped off the spoon in his hand. "He's standing in the garden barking at the vegetables."

"Likely he spied a rabbit." Grandma MacGregor wiped up Robbie's mess on the table. "Now tell me of your adventure."

Caitie ladled a spoonful of sugar from the bowl and stirred it into her tea. "I've never done anything like that before. Some spots were so narrow you could only turn your head a certain way to get through, otherwise you'd get stuck between the boulders."

"My goodness," Grandma MacGregor said. "What did you think of it, Robbie?"

He dumped raspberries all over his mound of ice cream. "It was pretty scary. We got to this cave, and Miss Bowers just left me and Caitie there."

"She did what?" Mom sounded horrified.

Caitie slid her arm under the table and squeezed his knee as hard as she could. "A girl ahead of us got stuck. Miss Bowers went to help her. She came back for us a little while later. It was no big deal."

He glared at her and shoved a forkful of dessert in his mouth.

Mom shook her head. "She should never have left you. Something could have happened."

Robbie's eyes got huge. "It—"

Caitie smashed his foot with the heel of her boot and gave Mom her best *You're overreacting* look. "But nothing did, Mom."

"Did you get to know any of the other students?" Grandma MacGregor asked.

"Duncan Mackenzie," Robbie answered. "He's pretty nice."

"We'll likely see the Mackenzie's tomorrow night at the ceilidh," Grandma said.

Caitie smirked, anticipating her brother's reaction. "That's a dance, Robbie." His face scrunched up with disgust right on cue.

Mom's eyebrows crinkled in surprise. "How do you know that?"

"Bonnie McLaren asked me if I was gonna go," Caitie said.

Mom stopped with a spoonful of raspberries half-way to her mouth. "That's not Doug McLaren's daughter, is it, Mum?"

"Aye. He was a few years older than you, wasn't he, Maisie?"

"Mm-hmm. I remember him though. Everyone knew and liked Doug."

"He went off to University and met a striking lass from Edinburgh. They say he's a very important man at a medical company in Inverness. I think his wife would rather live up there, but Doug built her a lovely home up the glen instead."

Pretty and rich that explained why Bonnie had everyone twirled so tight around her pinkie.

"So we have to go?" Robbie whined.

Mom tilted her chin and raised her eyebrows. "I'm sure you'll enjoy it, Robbie." End of discussion.

"Did Alicia call?" Caitie asked.

Mom nodded. "I explained where you were and she understood."

"Yeah, right. She's probably ticked."

"She didn't seem to be."

Caitie set aside her fork and plate. "Alicia's not going to sound that way to you."

Grandma MacGregor inhaled sharply. "So Caitie, can you show us your pictures?"

No, I don't want to. But Caitie retrieved the Lumix from her hoodie anyway, turned it on, and flipped the switch to review mode. She tilted the camera so no one could see the display and pushed the button to cycle the photos backwards since the last one she took would come up first.

Clink. Robbie's glass tipped over as he leaned across the table to look at her camera.

"Oh, Robbie." Mom stood and mopped up the spilled milk with her napkin.

Caitie looked back down at the image on the camera. The Lumix had already passed the cave photo. She kept clicking backward until she reached the first picture of the day.

Grandma MacGregor propped the reading glasses, hanging from a pearl chain around her neck, onto her nose.

Caitie held the display so they could all see it. The first picture was of the trail they'd hiked at the base of the steep hills. The second showed a violet framed by Caitie's boots, heels together at a 45° angle.

"I like that one," Mom said.

The next few were of them weaselling. Grandma studied the one with the loch. "Did Mrs. Ferguson happen to tell you where they took you today?"

Caitie shook her head.

Grandma squinted. "I believe your picture is of Loch Ness. And I suspect your mountain is northeast, across the water from us.

"Really?" Robbie sounded panicky like the big, bad fairies were near enough to burst through the door any minute and get him.

"Look at the hills on the opposite side of the water. That's Urquhart Castle and over here is our farm," Grandma said.

"Let me see." Mom leaned closer. "I think you're right, Mum."

Caitie clicked to the next photo, the one of the two of them together.

"You two look so cute in your helmets and weaselling outfits," Mom said.

Robbie shifted from wimp to Mr. Annoyed at being called cute.

"That's it," Caitie said.

"Is not," Robbie argued. "You took one more in that cave."

"Come on, Caitie. Show us," Mom said.

Thanks, Robbie! The shortbread tumbled inside Caitie's stomach. If she argued, Mom would know something was up, and Robbie would spill it all anyway. Her little brother had hosed her good this time. Caitie swallowed hard. A quick press on the tiny silver button, and the image came up. Robbie was on the left, looking freaked. The fairy, in her shimmering white dress, was to his right. Her curly, auburn hair framed her pretty face. She stood with her arms straight at her sides, palms facing back, neck stretched long, face uplifted, eyes closed, and lips pursed. A stream of rainbow whatever-it-was came from her mouth. Behind Robbie were the chairs, tables, tapestries, and paintings they'd seen Leannan create. The smooth stone walls faded into a wispy blur and above them the rough rock of the cave remained untouched. It was just as Caitie remembered it. If it wasn't so unbelievable, this photo would win a contest. Caitie looked up, bracing herself for Mom and Grandma's reaction.

"Robbie, you certainly looked scared." Mom wore a *my poor baby* expression on her face as she wrapped her arm around his shoulder.

"I think I would have been more troubled by the tighter spaces than the cave." Grandma sat back in her chair and crossed her arms over her stomach. "At least you didn't have to worry about getting stuck in there."

What? Caitie's gaze flitted back and forth between Mom and Grandma, clueless as to why they'd said what they did. Her stomach dropped with a sudden realization. They couldn't see the fairy! None of this was making any sense.

"Can't you see it?" Robbie asked.

"See what, honey?"

She and Robbie were certifiable! And no one was gonna figure it out. Not if she could help it. "How spooky the cave is." Caitie kicked Robbie in the shin. He flinched. "You can't really tell how dark it was 'cause of the flash. And you know how he gets about the dark."

"I still don't think Miss Bowers was right in leaving you. You could have gotten impatient and wandered off. And then lost. But look at the picture, Robbie. There's nothing there to see, but rocks. You can't let that vivid imagination of yours get the best of you." Mom tousled the hair on the back of his head.

She wanted to believe Mom was right and that the whole thing had been bad cave air messing with their heads. But that stupid fairy kept staring back at her from the camera. Caitie turned off the Lumix and slipped it into the pocket of her hoodie.

Grandma MacGregor wrapped an arm around her. "Thank you for sharing your pictures."

"You're welcome," Caitie said on polite autopilot. She stood up from the table and started to leave.

So did Robbie.

"What are you two forgetting?" Mom asked.

"Sorry." Robbie picked up his plate and glass.

Caitie set her dishes in the sink and headed to the backyard to sort things out.

"Off with you, Balfour!" Grandpa shouted from the dock. He raised his hands and shooed the dog away. Balfour galloped toward them as the backdoor slammed shut behind Robbie.

"You didn't have to pinch and kick me," Robbie said.

"And let you blab what happened? The only thing either of us can do now is try to forget today!"

Caitie plopped down in the velvety grass facing the Loch. "I'm deleting that picture."

"No, you can't!"

Balfour circled them, barking.

Caitie pulled the camera out of the pocket of her hoodie. "We haven't got proof that anybody but us can see. If somebody told me a story like ours, I'd say they were nuts. And when Grandpa MacGregor finds out..." Caitie shook her head. "It won't be pretty. I can tell you that much. He'll probably want to ship us off to some creepy Scottish asylum. Then it's only a matter of time 'til the lady at the bank knows along with everyone else. News goes viral in a place this size. And we'll be the local crazies."

Balfour pawed at Robbie and then ran into the garden.

"But..."

"I'm telling you, that's what's gonna happen if you say a word to anyone."

Robbie chewed his nails. "How come only you and me can see her?"

The dog trotted back to them, still barking. He wedged his snout under Robbie's arm, danced in front of his face, and barked some more.

"Maybe the fairy put some kind of spell on us." Caitie couldn't believe she even said that.

"You think?" Robbie petted the dog, but Balfour wouldn't settle down.

"I don't know. Maybe it was that rainbow stuff she spewed that got in our eyes."

"What's gotten into you, boy?" Robbie asked.

Caitie didn't care why the dog was acting goofy. There was way bigger stuff to worry about. "Who knows?" She turned on the camera and studied the cave photo—fascinated by it. But it had to go.

Robbie stood up. "Don't delete it, Caitie! You took that picture and something horrible happened to her. Don't do anything else you can't undo." He followed Balfour to the garden. "Come here." Robbie called, sounding even more scared.

"What now?" She hurried over to him, her finger still poised over the delete button on the Lumix.

Something had trampled Grandma MacGregor's tidy rows of radishes and carrots.

Robbie squatted by a cabbage plant. "Look at this."

Caitie gingerly stepped along the furrows. In the black soil next to the cabbage mound was a tiny set of tracks. The shape of each imprint was long and narrow.

His eyes were as big as the cabbages. "Those look like tiny footprints."

Why wouldn't all this weirdness stop? Caitie pulled her finger off the delete button, afraid Robbie was right.

20 *beauty was in the eye of the beholder*

· beauty & a beast ·

4:30 IN THE AFTERNOON
JUNE 24TH

ON MUNGAN'S COMMAND TO FLY, THE CABBAGE stalk steed lifted him from the ground and away from the snap of the dog's strong jaws by no more than the depth of his shadow. He pulled back hard on the stalk to increase his ascent and put more distance between himself and the beast on the ground. Beanstalks and sunflower leaves lashed his arms, legs, and face as he veered wildly through them, soaring at last out of the mortals' garden. He steered west, barely clearing the roofline of the dwelling.

The dog chased after him in vain, trampling the plants and barking furiously.

Mungan flew higher and circled their croft, tormenting the mongrel and trying to get his bearings. He studied the vaguely familiar shoreline. Of course! 'Twas the Great Loch below. He set his course flying northeast and began to work out his plan.

BACK INSIDE THE MOUNTAIN, MUNGAN GLANCED BY ROSY torchlight at the scripted plaque bearing Leannan's name above her door. He took a deep breath and braced himself for her ghastly visage, and then rapped quietly on the birch teardrop. "'Tis me, Mungan."

Leannan opened the door just enough for him to slip inside her simple chamber. Concealed in her own hooded cape, she waddled to the foot of her bed. Her gnarled fingers picked up his dress cloak and offered it up to him. "I am most grateful for your kindness, Mungan." Leannan hung her head, hiding her face.

He reached for the garment, avoiding her decrepit hand. "I followed them, Leannan. I know where the mortals live."

She turned away from him.

"Their croft is just across the Great Loch." He tenderly grasped her shoulders and turned her round.

She buried her face in her hands and sobbed. "I am truly sorry for leaving. And even more ashamed that ye risked your life on my behalf to follow them." She took a deep breath and raised her head to look up at him. The hood slipped off.

Mungan recoiled at her grey green face with its flaking, blackened blotches. He fought to hide his revulsion; reminding himself that trapped inside this hideous form was the Leannan he cared for. Pitying her, he forced a faint smile.

"'Twill be best for ye, Mungan, to go back to the banquet hall and enjoy the celebration before anyone finds out what ye have done. I must go to the king and confess my foolish actions. I deserve whatever punishment King Oseron deems fit."

"No, Leannan, there is another way. But ye must tell me what possessed ye to leave."

She hesitated before answering, her eyes filled with the strain of a secret burden. "Ballard did not murder your sister."

Her words stirred up his unsettled intuition about his only suspect. "How do ye know?"

"After I took Queen Tianna the wine and cheese, I went to the artists' studio for a new brush to take with me the next morning. On my return, I recognized Nuala's coy laugh as I passed the entrance to the Crystal Garden. 'Twas nosy of me, but I wondered who she was with at such a late hour, so I crept in, peered round the great column and spied her on the bridge in Ballard's arms."

"Then what did ye do?"

"I left for my chamber and went to bed. I awoke as the torchlights shifted to peach and gathered my canvas and brushes. I cracked open my door to depart and heard whispering in the hall. I peeked through the slivered opening and saw Ballard and Nuala in a passionate embrace. She retired to her chamber, and he strode off to his. From what I saw then and earlier, murder was not on his mind."

"But what does this have to do with ye running away?"

"Nuala witnessed me leave the mountain that morning, Mungan. I recall her wearing Ballard's cloak when he kissed her. 'Tis likely she left her chamber to return it and spied me then." Leannan lowered her head. "Nuala despises me. She threatened to tell the king I ventured from the mountain or spread suspicion that I murdered Queen Tianna."

Mungan steeled himself and raised her warted chin with the tip of his finger. "I know ye did not do it, Leannan."

"When word gets out that Ballard is not the murderer, someone else will be accused. This lowly servant brought Queen Tianna the wine with which she was poisoned. If someone must pay, I feared 'twould be easy for one and all to accuse me. I wanted to take my chances in the other realm rather than be imprisoned."

"I fear ye shall be anyway, if anyone sees ye like this. Tonight, I will bring back that witch and make her undo this evil spell. In the meantime, I shall tell Lileas that ye are here in your chamber, feeling..." He sought a truthful word to describe her condition—wretched.

"No, 'tis wrong for me to allow ye to take another risk and suffer for my folly."

"Leannan, I act on my own decisions."

A sharp knock at the door drew their attention. Neither said a word or moved.

Lileas burst through the teardrop. "Leannan, I have been searching all over for ye, trying to understand how ye...." Her eyes grew as large as banquet chalice rims, contorting her face into a swirl of deep wrinkles. Lileas screamed, her head lolled back, and she fainted.

Corc, passing through the corridor, rushed in at the shriek, catching Lileas on her way down to the marble floor. The wiry cobbler collapsed under the load of her substantial frame. Both landed on the stone floor with Corc laid out beneath Lileas and buried in the mounds of her orange gown. Corc thrashed and squirmed to extricate himself. Once free, he rose, gawked at Leannan, and gasped.

"Who are ye?" Corc sputtered his eyes wide with fear and disbelief.

"'Tis me, Leannan," she rasped.

"What in all the fae realm has happened to ye?" Corc asked.

Cormag, the surly guard stormed into Leannan's chamber. "Who is shrieking?" His jaw dropped at the sight of her. "Crivvens! Who is this hag, and how did she get here?"

Any thought of restoring Leannan's magic without King Oseron's knowledge was lost. Mungan shot Corc a glance. The cobbler's eyes reflected his own worry. Cormag sneered at Corc and turned his beady eyes to Mungan. No one answered the guard.

Lileas came to and groaned as she rolled over on her stomach. Bracing her palms against the floor, she pushed herself up on her hands and knees. She tried to stand up amidst the billowing cloud of her gown but trapped the hem beneath her foot. The snared fabric did not give way, catapulting her toward Cormag. She flattened him from the front with the skill of a wrestler's lunge, pinning down the unsuspecting guard.

"Get off me!" Cormag shouted.

Mungan reached for Lileas's hand. "Help me, Corc." Together they hoisted her up while Cormag crawled from beneath her bountiful skirt.

The guard rose and pointed an accusing finger. "Is this shriveled hag Leannan?"

Again, no one spoke. A pit grew in Mungan's stomach as he felt her fate being pulled from his control while Cormag solved the puzzle before him.

"The only place this could have happened is outside the mountain," the surly guard declared in triumph. Cormag seized Leannan's arm. His face twisted as if he were disposing of a mouldering mutton leg. "King Oseron must see what has become of ye."

"Let her go," Mungan ordered, not about to let him parade her before the king.

"She has disobeyed King's Oseron's orders and must be brought before His Majesty."

"I am the Searsanach, not ye."

"Then act as such. Ye should have delivered her to King Oseron, the moment she was discovered." Cormag sneered. "If ye refuse to do so, Mungan, I will."

"Only a fool rushes to speak of that he does not know or understand. I wanted to interrogate Leannan first."

"There is nothing to understand. She must be presented for sentencing."

"Step back. I shall deliver her," Mungan declared, angry that the guard was right.

Cormag's lips curled, and he looked like a cat that had trapped a plump and juicy rat.

"Come, Leannan," Mungan said in a quiet voice. He clasped the back of her arm and gently led her to the festivities in the Great Hall. Though he knew what punishment King Oseron could rightly mete out, His Majesty had always been reasonable and, for that matter, liked Leannan. Once reminded of her many years of devoted service, surely the king would be lenient.

Mungan, Leannan, and Cormag stepped through the marble archway into the Great Hall, and the fae at the banquet tables took notice. The jabs to the ribs, pointing, stares, and murmuring spread like a mighty rolling wave as they approached the royal platform. The musicians ceased playing their tune and the dancers halted.

King Oseron sobered as they drew closer to the throne. "What is this horrid creature ye bring before me, spoiling our day of merriment?"

"'Tis Leannan, Your Majesty," Mungan said with a slight bow.

The attentive crowd gasped before falling silent.

The king's eyes narrowed with doubt. "This horrid creature cannot be the fair Leannan."

"'Tis true," she whispered.

"Who or what has done this to ye?"

Mungan had to convince the king, her transformation was the unfortunate outcome of a small indiscretion. "Your Majesty,—"

"Silence, Mungan." King Oseron said, his eyes keenly focused on Leannan.

Mungan's ears grew hot.

"I foolishly passed through the portal to the other realm…" Leannan hung her head.

"Ye have broken our code," King Oseron interrupted.

She nodded and answered in a quiet voice, "Aye."

"Why did ye do so?" The king leaned forward, his arms resting on the gilded throne.

"The outside world calls to me. My heart yearned to go and this day I could not resist the temptation. There, I encountered two young mortals and one stole my magic."

For the moment, Mungan breathed easier at the skillful choice of Leannan's words.

King Oseron raised his hands. "Earnan, how could a young mortal steal her magic?"

The wizard stood, his glowing robes undulating more red-violet than blue. He approached the royal platform. "She has to be some kind of witch." The wizard curled the silky silver ends of his long beard between his fingers. "What did the witch do, Leannan?"

"She held something to her face. It flashed as bright as lightning and turned me into this."

"What was in her grasp?" Earnan asked.

"I only caught a glimpse of it. 'Twas silver, or white perhaps, and about this size." Leannan touched the tips of her thumbs to her pointer fingers. "'Twas a small box of sorts."

"Where did ye encounter this witch?" King Oseron demanded.

"Near the portal."

Fury and fear flashed in King Oseron's eyes. "So they know where to find us. Do ye realize what your disobedience has done?"

Leannan did not answer.

"Ye have placed our kingdom in great jeopardy. If their weapon has the power to turn ye into this, perhaps they can enter the portal and harm us all." The king sat up straight. His hands clenched the carved ends of the throne's armrests. "Your actions, Leannan, are worthy of death."

The whispers of the crowd sizzled like water on a hot pan.

Mungan swallowed hard. "I know where the witch lives, Your Majesty."

"And ye were a partner in this folly?" the king roared.

"I came upon the scene and witnessed Leannan's transformation. She returned to the mountain, and I entered the other realm to follow the miscreants."

"Were ye seen?"

"No, I was not. But at your command, King Oseron, I will go forth again to retrieve the box from the witch. If I can bring it back, perhaps Earnan can restore Leannan's magic."

"'Tis too dangerous."

"King Oseron, if the witch can steal Leannan's magic with this box, all the other Daoine Shi are likely in peril," Earnan said.

Again, the crowd broke out in a storm of whispers.

The king squirmed on the throne. "If we stay inside, we shall be safe!" King Oseron pronounced for all to hear.

Earnan furrowed his bushy brows till they touched to form a huntsman's bow.

"Your Majesty, if the box has the power to steal fae magic, perhaps it has the power to open the portal as well."

"Aye, ye may be right." The king's eyes took on a calculating glint as he studied Leannan. "It must be a powerful box indeed. And far better off in my hands than in the other realm as a threat to us."

Mungan was taken aback by the king's desire to possess the cursed box but pounced at the opportunity to spare Leannan. "Your Majesty, I scouted their croft and know they shall be away on the evening hence."

"And how are ye privy of their departure?"

"I heard the witch who stole Leannan's magic say so."

"If Mungan can retrieve the box, all will be well, of that I am sure," Earnan said.

"Then the course will be as ye proposed, and Leannan shall remain in the dungeon that she may contemplate the error of her disobedient and reckless ways."

"'Tis most gracious of ye, Your Majesty." Mungan bowed deeply.

"Cormag, off to the dungeon with her," the king commanded.

The surly guard scowled at Mungan as he clenched Leannan's arm. She winced as he led her through the archway and off to the dungeon in the dank depths of the mountain. Mungan's heart went out to her, but at least she had been spared.

MUNGAN SAT ON A BENCH IN THE GREAT HALL WITH HIS ELBOWS ON the banquet table and his jaw cupped in the palm of his left hand. He studied Nuala as she danced on the stage. His mind drifted to the irony of the moment. Only a few hours earlier, he aided in putting a hag with the purest of hearts in the dungeon, and now he gazed upon a beauty with the heart of a wretch. If this was the natural order of their kingdom, it seemed neither just nor right. The task of setting things straight fell only to him.

He could not fend off the notion that all of these troubles led back to Tianna's death and the one responsible. His sister had summoned him to the portal that day to share some troubling information. And it was there he caught Leannan returning from her foray to the other realm. Tianna was dead, and he had to find her murderer. Ballard was dead and accused of a murder that according to Leannan, he could not have committed. Leannan's awful fate had been tied to these events as well.

Somehow he would untangle this web, and the thread he suspected would be the web's undoing, danced before him.

At every opportunity, Nuala glanced at him with those alluring viridian eyes. He would have to outplay a master at her own game to get the information he wanted.

"It cannot be denied. Nuala is a beauty." Corc took a swig from his chalice.

She moved on the stage with more grace than a gliding swan. A dip and coy turn of her leg, the slow arching of her back, the fluidity of her inviting arms, and swirl of her locks were mesmerizing. As the final note played, Mungan found her almond-shaped eyes piercing his. "She is a fine rose, Corc. But every rose has wicked thorns." Mungan stood up from the table.

"Then ye best be careful."

"I plan to." He sauntered up to the stage and raised his hand. She grasped it and hopped down to the marble floor. Another dancer graced the platform and a new tune began.

"Did I please ye this evening?" Nuala entwined her arm in his.

"Ye are quite beguiling."

"Then let us go to the garden where I can dance for ye alone."

"'Tis an intriguing invitation to be sure, but my mind is troubled, and I seek the truth."

"I can soothe your troubled mind. Let us steal far away from all the others."

"I am afraid 'twould be unwise, for I must have my wits about me."

"Och, Mungan," Nuala extended a pouty, ruby-red lip.

"Would ye like a drink?" He ushered her to an empty table.

"Aye." She sat on the bench and pulled her long locks off her neck, piling them on her head and holding them there with one hand. Wisps of her shiny black hair fell loose and carefree. With elegant fingers, she fanned her face and neck.

He spotted Pàislig and waved her over. The seamstress turned barmaid for the day nodded in understanding. He sat down on the opposite bench. "Nuala, 'tis important ye twist your words no more."

She batted her long eyelashes. "Mungan, I…"

"Please, merely listen."

She let her hair fall and placed her elbow on the table, resting her chin on her balled fist.

Unpracticed, he tried to look and sound jealous like the broken-hearted lover he needed to be to get Nuala to tell him what he desired to know. "Someone saw ye in the garden with Ballard after the chess match."

Her brow furrowed. "Who said such a thing? Leannan?"

"'Tis not important who told me. What is, Nuala, is that ye were with him."

She crossed her arms. "I did not want to be. Ye had left for the night, and Ballard asked me to stroll with him. I tried to decline, but he absolutely refused to take no for an answer."

Pàislig appeared carrying a tray with two goblets and a pitcher. She filled each chalice to the brim with heather ale.

Nuala took a long drink. "We stayed only a wee while."

"Ballard bid ye goodnight at dawn."

"Mungan!" She tilted her head in indignation.

"Ye were seen, Nuala."

"Or so that hag, Leannan, claims. I do not trust her. And neither should ye. Think of what she has done." She bit her lip.

"We cannot lie, Nuala." He reached for her hand and looked deeply into her eyes. "'Tis important to me, to us, for ye to tell me what ye and Ballard were doing until dawn."

"We…we were talking."

Trying to sound relieved, he sighed and smiled broadly. "What was so very interesting it took most of the night to discuss?"

Nuala swirled her pointer finger in her ale, drew it to her mouth, and sucked the droplets off. "Mungan, your questions are so tedious." Her narrow foot caressed his leg.

"They are most important. If ye cannot tell me, I can only assume ye were preoccupied."

She looked at him with eyes as innocent as a wee bairn's. "Ballard spoke of golden treasure. That 'twould not be long before he had some of his own."

Gold! Not a single Daoine Shi possessed any. Mungan fought to keep his voice calm. "And how was he going to come by it?"

"He would not say. Only that once he had it in his possession, he wished to share it with me, for he found my dancing captivating."

"Did Ballard say if Tianna knew of his plans?"

She tilted her head. "Is this all about Queen Tianna's murder?"

"If he was with ye all night, he could not have been the one to kill her."

Nuala stiffened and looked round, agitated. He needed her on his side and for her to keep silent about Ballard's innocence until he could find Tianna's murderer.

"Ballard's gone, Nuala." Mungan clasped her hand in both of his. "Ye are right. I did want to speak with ye about that night, for the one who is responsible for my sister's murder must pay." He raised his gaze and fixed it upon her. "But most of all, I wanted to know for myself that Ballard had not captured your heart ahead of me."

The dancer relaxed and flashed a flirtatious smile.

"Nuala, ye must help me free my heart from the burden of my sister's death. I cannot rest until the blaggard that has done this terrible deed receives the justice he deserves. Please tell me, can ye think of anyone who had reason to kill Queen Tianna?"

"Leannan is, of course, the most logical one. She brought Her Majesty the cup with which she was poisoned." Nuala moved in close. "And I saw *her*," the dancer gave him a knowing glance, "leave the mountain the morning Queen Tianna was found dead."

His heart raced, wondering if Nuala had seen him at the portal when Leannan returned. "But Leannan and Tianna were so close."

"Do not forget, a kitten will nip the mother who suckles her."

"Is there anyone else ye believe who had cause to do it?"

"I have caught Lileas dancing behind the *Faerie Forest of Roles* painting when she thought no one was watching. The Daoine Shi standards for dancers are high, and your sister would never allow one as rotund as Lileas on the stage. The barmaid knows that."

"That is not worthy of murder, Nuala."

"Think again, Mungan. Dreams drive desperate measures."

21 *there were more questions than answers*

·searching·

HALF-PAST II IN THE MORN JUNE 25TH

MUNGAN STRODE DOWN THE GOLDEN LIT CORRIDOR of the maidens' chambers, troubled with the task before him. After Nuala's suggestion that Lileas had a motive for murdering Tianna, he had no choice but to question her about the night of his sister's death. Guilt as persistent and painful as a canker sore on his conscience would drive him down any path, however obscure, to find the one responsible for the vile deed.

Lileas stopped her rolling cart in front of Ùna's door. The hefty maidservant panted as she lifted the cage of cheeping chicks.

"Pleasant day, Lileas."

"And to ye as well," she said with a slight bow of her head. Her cheeks were flushed and wisps of her tight brown curls were damp with perspiration.

"Are ye all right?"

"No, I am not. My heart aches sorely, for my dearest friend chose to abandon me on the most special occasion. And then for Leannan to leave the mountain when she knew what the consequences would be." Lileas shook her head, and her voice rose. "And now, as angry as I am at her, I am distraught over the awful transformation she has suffered, where she is, and what she is enduring!"

He wrestled with the same maddening frustration. "I understand."

"Not to mention that I now have twice as much work to do. But I am sure ye did not come down the passageway to hear me rant."

"I was hoping to have a word with ye."

"Be quiet!" she scolded the chicks. Their beaks snapped shut. "Of course, Mungan, only I beg of ye to let me tidy while we talk."

"Certainly." He followed her into Ùna's chamber.

She opened the door on the gilded cage, and six enchanted chicks flew out.

Alighting on the headboard, chest of drawers, and bedside table, they began to dust the furniture with their fluffy feathered bottoms. She placed the cage on the floor at the foot of the bed.

"Lileas, what did ye do after the chess match?" Mungan studied her expression to see if he could sense a tension in the way she answered that might betray a twisting of her words.

She looked him straight in the eye and blew the wisps off her brow. "Serving, of course, until the king fell and I helped him to his chambers." Bustling out into the passageway, she retrieved the broom from the cart where 'twas locked in place. It swung excitedly in her hand, batting at her knees. "Not yet!" she said to the broom in a brusque voice. "Why do ye ask?"

"'Tis important for me as Searsanach to know where everyone was that night."

Her eyes went wide. "Do ye not believe that Ballard, now mouldering in the dungeon, murdered the queen?" She carried the broom to the other side of the seamstress's chamber and released it. "Make sure ye sweep every nook and cranny this time." The broom flew to the corner and whisked the floor with ferocity.

"Those are your words regarding Ballard. Not mine." He had feared his questions would prompt Lileas to think such thoughts, but they had to be asked. And though he did not want her spreading rumors of his doubts about Ballard's guilt, 'twas likely a vain desire and a sure outcome if he asked her to stay quiet about it. "After the king fell, and ye escorted him to his chambers, did ye remain at his side?"

Her eyes narrowed. "Mungan, I was in the royal chambers the entire night."

He stepped out of the way of the enchanted broom as it swept across the floor. "I assume King Oseron fell asleep at some point."

The maidservant stiffened her bulky frame. "Naturally. Earnan's potion acted swiftly as was intended."

Then she could have slipped through the private passage between the king and queen's chambers while His Majesty slept. "Lileas, did Tianna know of your desire to dance?"

She flushed beet red. "I am not so foolish, Mungan, as to think I could ever dance upon the stage." Her neck grew taut as she hammered out the words. "Nor so oblivious as to where these questions are leading. After all the years we have known each other, how could ye even contemplate such a thing?" The creases on her brow and the hurt in her voice convicted him of betrayal.

Yet his sister was dead, and Lileas not only had access to Tianna's chambers, but to the queen's chalices as well. No one would ever take note of her opening the royal cupboard or even waltzing down the passageways, cup in hand. But then again, she could not have known King Oseron would injure himself and require her service, providing the perfect opportunity, yet little time for her to devise and orchestrate such a plot. "Before King Oseron fell, do ye recall who was in the Great Hall and when they departed?"

"No, Mungan, I cannot give ye a full list of one and all. And I cannot be sure as to when they left, for I only know time by the color of the torchlights. I was not paying close attention, for I did not know a murderer was in our midst." She went to the bed and straightened the sheets. "I do remember Corc and Earnan were still there in the silvery-blue hours, for Earnan came to assist with the king. The triplets were bellowing off-key." She plumped a pillow, and a smile crossed her generous lips. "The seamstresses were winning handily at sparc, which had the cobblers and masons down to their skivvies and in a most foul mood. And then, of course, the musicians and dancers were on their stages."

"All of the dancers?"

"Och, Mungan, I cannot speak with complete certainty." She crossed to the other side of the bed, fluffed the other pillow, and smoothed the sunny yellow covering.

"Did ye see Leannan after she brought the queen her tray?"

"Aye, she returned and tidied up the alcove with me. With the crowd dwindling in the Great Hall, I told her she need not stay."

Mungan wondered if that was when Leannan left to get a paintbrush and spied Nuala with Ballard.

Lileas opened the door to the cage. The chicks flew back to their perches, and she shut them up tight. "Is that all?" Her voice was as frosty as a December morn. She grabbed the broom stick in one hand and scooped up the handle to the birdcage in her other.

"Aye, Lileas."

She left in a huff. Mungan retreated from the maidens' corridor intent on revisiting Ballard's chamber. Lileas could have twisted her words. She did have a motive, as weak as it was, to kill Tianna, as well as the perfect chance. And if that was not enough, she entered Earnan's chambers daily where should could tidy a bottle of St John's wort right into her apron pocket. Perhaps Nuala had some credibility after all. But when had he become such a poor judge of character?

Earnan ambled down the passageway in Mungan's direction, his robe undulating between deep purple and cobalt blue. "Ye appear puzzled, my friend."

"I am baffled."

"Then let us stroll, and perhaps, we can together reason out that which perplexes ye."

Mungan looked up and down the corridor to ensure they were alone. "Earnan, can I trust ye to keep what I am about to tell in the strictest confidence?"

"Of course." The wizard's amethyst eyes studied him with concern as they ambled down the hall.

"I do not believe Ballard stole Tianna's life."

The wizard froze with surprise. "What has convinced ye of this?"

"He was in the garden with Nuala all night."

Earnan raised his bushy white brows. "And how do ye know?"

"There was a witness who heard and saw them. I confronted Nuala and she admitted 'twas true."

"Does the king know?"

"Not yet. 'Twould be best if I could deliver Tianna's murderer to him before stating he has declared the wrong one guilty."

Earnan nodded and they started off once more. "There is wisdom in your words."

"I have also learned that Lileas has a desire to dance."

Earnan sighed. "Poor Lileas. A sunflower that will ne'er a violet be."

"Exactly," Mungan said. "Tianna would never have allowed that. Lileas was also in the king's chambers while he slept soundly under the influence of your potion. She could have stolen into Tianna's chambers through the king's private passage, and no one would ever have been the wiser."

Earnan cocked his head with doubt. "But Mungan—"

"I know, it sounds absurd, but who else pray tell, rummages through the royal cupboard in the alcove where the foxglove chalice was kept, or for that matter, comes and goes freely into your study from where the St. John's wort was taken?"

"Leannan," Earnan said softly.

"But she did not murder my sister. I read it in her eyes and know it in my heart."

"I too think not. But why would Leannan not have done the deed?" Earnan asked the question with the patience of a master waiting for his pupil to offer up the only logical answer.

"For she was devoted to Tianna."

"Aye, Leannan was. Tianna's loss has been devastating to the poor maid. And who is Lileas's dearest friend?"

"Leannan, of course."

"Mungan, I cannot believe that Lileas would cause her bosom friend such pain in order to dance upon the stage. It makes no more sense than Leannan or King Oseron himself taking Tianna's life."

He had never really considered His Majesty as a suspect. The king went to the treasure room before Mungan left the Great Hall that night and was escorted after his fall to his chambers, leaving him no time alone to commit the murder. "Then I remain befuddled, Earnan. Was anything else missing besides the St. John's wort?"

The wizard scissored his snowy beard. "I did not notice. But would ye like to join me for another look?"

"Indeed, I would. Perhaps, the one who stole the St. John's wort left a telltale sign behind."

They reached Earnan's door, and the wizard gestured for Mungan to step inside. Earnan raised his wand as they drew near the shoreline mural painted on the heavy curtains at the far side of his chambers. The scene with its roaring waves and cawing gulls parted in the middle. On the right side of the alcove were shelves with ancient books of spells and wizardry. On the back wall, smaller racks held potions, herbs, scrolls, and more ingredients of the wizard's trade. A writing desk to the left provided a place for Earnan to work.

"I kept the St. John's wort here." Earnan pointed to an open spot on the rack of vials neatly labeled and alphabetized.

Mungan scoured the shelves but found nothing unusual. "Do ye keep any iron as well?"

"No, I do not relish having the nasty substance at hand. If I need it, I go to the masons or carpenters for they have a small stash of iron nails. The cobblers and artists may as well." The wizard's eyes scanned the small chamber. He walked to the bookshelf, raised his pointer finger, and scanned the volumes. "My *Sorcerer's Compendium* is missing." Earnan pivoted and strode to his desk. With both hands, he gently opened the hinged lid on a carved wooden box. He fingered the wands inside and looked up, his eyes wide with surprise. "One of my wands is gone as well."

"Are ye sure?" Mungan asked.

"Aye. I do not lose track of my wands, not even the poorest performers." Earnan folded his hands and brought them to his face. "Mungan, I feel foolish as I should have realized the possible significance of something that transpired several days before Queen Tianna was murdered."

"Go on."

"The queen came to me with a strange query."

"And what was that?" Mungan's pulse quickened.

"She asked me if I had chosen a successor."

"And what did ye tell her?"

"No, for I have not yet found an apprentice with the magical gifts and skills required."

"I see," Mungan said. What did Tianna know that prompted such a question? "Did she say anything more?"

Earnan shook his head. "No, but I read worry in her eyes. When I probed further, Queen Tianna would share no more."

"Nuala told me that Ballard spoke of coming into golden treasure of his own. Do ye suppose 'twas he who stole your wand, intending to use magic to get the Daoine Shi gold?"

"Perhaps." Earnan sighed. "'Tis most unfortunate a spider bite has sealed Ballard's secrets."

"Most unfortunate indeed and quite suspicious."

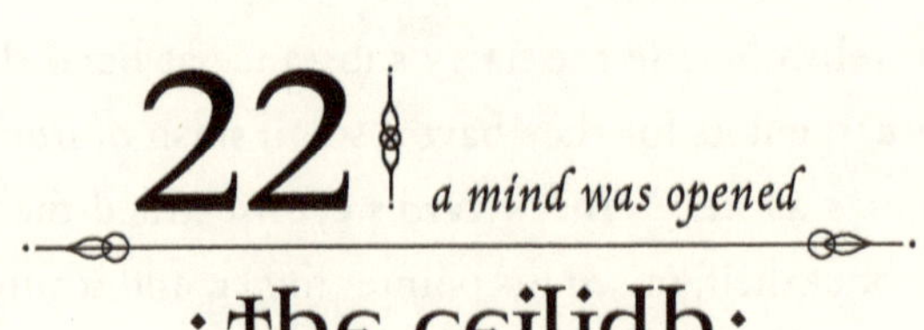

22 *a mind was opened*

· the ceilidh ·

8:30 PM
JUNE 25TH

ROBBIE SCOOPED CAITIE'S PHONE OFF THE BATHROOM counter and clunked down the stairs, just waiting for her to figure out she didn't have it. He dropped hard on the old beige couch facing the fireplace, settled into the cushions, and propped his skate shoes on the coffee table, knowing he shouldn't. He scrolled through the phone's options to find the games. Caitie would be ticked when she found him playing with it, but that wasn't any reason to stop. If he was stuck going to a dance tonight, then spreading his misery was all right with him. It didn't help that Mom forced him to wear a collared shirt and khakis either. At least he'd won the battle over the dress shoes.

Ross came in and sat on a recliner, the leather swooshing under his weight. Robbie hadn't seen him this dressed up before. There wasn't a wrinkle in his white shirt or his dark blue slacks, and his black shoes gleamed in the sunlight pouring through the bay window.

"You look awfully fancy," Robbie said with attitude.

"And why are you in such a foul mood, my little friend?"

Robbie shot him a dirty look. "I'm not little. I'm fun-sized."

"Excuse me."

Mom's heels clicked on the hardwood floor, and her perfume that made him hungry for raspberries wafted into the room. "Get your feet off the coffee table, young man."

"You look very nice, Maisie," Ross said as she walked around the back of the couch.

Mom was in the sleeveless peach dress she'd worn to his 6th grade graduation. She did look pretty in it, but he didn't like Ross noticing.

"So do you." She sat down next to Robbie.

He didn't like Mom complimenting Ross any better.

Slow footsteps creaked the stairs. Over his shoulder, he saw Caitie and Grandma MacGregor linked arm in arm on their way down. Grandma looked like any other old lady in her red skirt and lacy white blouse except for the red, green, and white plaid scarf tied into a flower and pinned near her shoulder. It trailed down her back like a kite's tail.

Caitie's face was as bright as her sundress until she saw what he was holding. "Who said you could play with my phone?" She escorted Grandma MacGregor to the other recliner. "Mom, my battery's already low, and he's going to use it all."

The screen went dark. Robbie shrugged his shoulders. "It's dead."

"Robbie!" Caitie raised a fist.

The washing machine buzzed, calling an end to Round One.

"You didn't need it tonight, anyway," Mom said. "Robbie, put her phone back on its charger. Caitie, you can toss your towels in the dryer and throw in that other load quick before we leave."

Caitie glared at him as she headed for the laundry room. "Get my camera while you're at it. It's on my vanity next to the charger."

"I'm not your slave."

Mom sighed. "Please, Robbie."

The old man started down the staircase as Robbie headed up. He wore a skirt out of the same plaid as Grandma's with a white shirt, black bow tie, and a short black jacket with silver buttons on the front and sleeves. A brown leather purse with tassels hung from a chain around his waist. He had on red knee highs with green patches on the sides and a knife sticking out of one of his socks.

Robbie cringed. He didn't want to go out in public with the old man dressed like this.

"Good evening," his grandfather said, his chest all puffed up like a rooster's.

"Wow," was all Robbie could manage to say.

"You like it? It's the MacGregor tartan. It will look fine on you too."

"Red's not my color," Robbie said as they passed each other on the stairs.

"Nonsense. It's your heritage, lad. Next time we're in Inverness, we'll stop at Ben Wyvis' and pick up a kilt for you."

Robbie rolled his eyes and plodded the rest of the way to Caitie's room. He plugged her phone into the charger, picked up her camera, and trudged back downstairs. Everyone but Ross had left the living room. "My grandfather's wearing a skirt."

"It's a kilt, and he looks grand in it." Ross raised his eyebrows. "Don't you agree?"

Robbie got the message he shouldn't have said what he did. "It's just that none of the guys I know wear them or carry a purse."

"We call the bag a sporran. The Highlanders of old were fierce warriors, wearing kilts made of a single piece of cloth. At night they used them as a cloak or blanket to keep warm. And since their kilts didn't have pockets for carrying things, they made themselves sporrans. So you see, Robbie, what your granddad is wearing represents his very manly heritage."

"Hmm." Then the whole kilt thing was sort of like Dad's dress uniform. "Well, what's with the knife in his sock?"

"It's a *sgian dubh*. The Highlanders, as a courtesy and show of trust, would turn over their weapons when they entered a home, but left their knife in their hose so it could be seen by their host yet still be handy." Ross nodded toward the backdoor. "Shall we be off?"

"Okay." The knife thing was pretty cool, but no way he'd be caught dead in a kilt.

CELTIC MUSIC PLAYED AS THEY WALKED INTO THE STUFFY AND LOUD Glenurquhart Public Hall. Everyone in the whole village had to be there. On the stage at the end of the room, the bass player called into his mic while a short guy played a fiddle and a fat one danced with his accordion. The drummer worked at looking cool in the back and another guy with a red face played an instrument like the recorder Robbie learned in his 5th grade music class, only this one was metal.

Tables and chairs lined the sides of the hall, and a bunch of people danced in the middle. Grandma MacGregor led them to the table where the woman who'd bought the eggs the day they arrived sat.

"Good evening, Fiona," Grandma MacGregor said. "May we join you?"

"Certainly," the old woman said. "Oh Maisie, it's good to see you again. You're coming over with your Mum tomorrow to quilt and have a good blether, I hope."

"I'd love too," Mom said.

Robbie took the chair next to Mom. "What's a blether?" he whispered in her ear.

"A gossipy visit," she whispered back.

"Ina, they're playing *St. Bernard's Waltz.*" His grandfather reached for Grandma's hand and they joined the others in the circle. He twirled her way faster than the guys half his age.

Caitie snapped their picture. "They're pretty good."

"They love to dance, especially your granddad," Mom said.

The waltz ended and Grandma MacGregor came back while their grandfather found a new partner that looked younger than Mom.

"Why aren't you still out there dancing, Grandma?" Caitie asked.

"Your granddad has much more stamina than I. He'll be out there most of the night with one lass or another."

"Doesn't that bother you?" Caitie asked.

"Heavens no, for I'm the lucky lass he comes home with at the end of the night." Grandma flashed a smile at the egg lady, Fiona.

A tap on Robbie's shoulder made him jump. He whipped his head around and saw Duncan Mackenzie.

"I didn't know you'd be here," the boy from school said.

"It's not 'cause I want to be," Robbie said.

Duncan waved his hand. "Let's go get something to drink."

Robbie followed him out to the concessions. He ordered a Coke while Duncan asked for an Irn Bru. "What's that stuff?"

Duncan handed him the bottle of bright orange soda. "Try it."

It tasted sort of like ginger ale with bubble gum. "Not bad. Hey Duncan, you don't dance at these things, do you?"

"If my gran is in a mood, she'll make me. She pinches my cheeks if I don't. And tonight, she's got that look in her eyes, so I'm trying to stay clear of her."

They went back to the main hall and sat with some of the boys Robbie'd met weaselling.

"Uh-oh." Duncan jabbed Robbie in the ribs with an elbow. "This isn't a good sign."

"What are you talking about?"

"My gran's over at your gran's table. That means trouble. They'll be over here in a second. I just know it."

Mom and Ross headed to the dance floor, and sure enough Grandma MacGregor and Duncan's grandmother with hair the most ridiculous shade of blue strolled towards them. Duncan's grandma smelled just like the lavender soap Mom used to keep in the guest bathroom at the house in San Diego. "Will my favorite grandson give this old woman the pleasure of the next dance?" she asked.

"Oh Gran, do I have to?" Duncan couldn't have looked more miserable if she'd asked him to eat haggis.

"Aye. You need to be a fine example for your American friend."

Grandma MacGregor whispered in Robbie's ear. "I believe Mrs. Mackenzie suspects you can't turn a jig. Would you like to prove her wrong?"

He shook his head no.

Grandma begged him with her blue eyes. "I'll take you to Inverness and buy you one of those video games, if you'll do this for me. But it must be our wee secret."

The offer was way tempting. "I've only square danced, Grandma. And it was for Heritage Day two years ago."

"You have?" A smile brightened her face. "The *Circassian Circle* is not so different."

Robbie watched Duncan follow his grandma to the circle of dancers. Mrs. Mackenzie smirked at them like Duncan was the greatest kid in the world and she was sorry Grandma MacGregor had a loser for a grandson. "Okay, Grandma." He stuck out his arm to escort her, the way the other men had for their partners. "Just tell me what to do out there."

Robbie's eyes narrowed as Ross clasped Mom's right hand. He winked at her, and she laughed.

Robbie hadn't seen Mom look so happy in a long time. How could she do this to Dad?

CAITIE SCOURED THE CROWDED HALL LOOKING for Bonnie or any of the other kids she'd met weaselling while Fiona gave her an earful about blood pressure medicine and arthritic knees. Bonnie's followers, Aileen and Maggie, flirted with two guys at a table near the front. The idea of joining them was out as she'd probably be as welcome as a fifth player at four-man beach volleyball. Rose sat at a table close to the stage. "I see one of my friends. If you don't mind…"

Fiona nodded in understanding.

Caitie picked up her camera and skirted the dance floor to get to Rose's table. "Hi," Caitie said. "I feel bad about yesterday. I didn't get much of a chance to talk to you."

"That's okay." Rose flashed a forgiving smile and turned to her friends. "This is Caitie Finlay. She's Angus and Ina's granddaughter."

Caitie nodded to the older girls Rose sat with.

"That's Rhona, Jaimie, and Heather." Rose pointed to a girl with a stud on her nose, a chubby blonde, and a waitress with a shock of fuchsia hair Caitie remembered from the cafe. "They work at the hotel too. Do you want to join us?"

"Sure." Caitie pulled out a black plastic chair from the table. Just as she sat down, a fight broke out in the back of the hall. Shouting and a scuffle sent a buzz through the crowd. A drunk stumbled toward the dance floor, shoving off the smaller guy trying to drag him back out.

"I'm fine. Can't a bloke have a good time in this one-horse village?" the guy bellowed, slurring his words. He staggered around the dance floor and ran into an old woman dancing with Robbie's friend Duncan. "Pardon me." The guy wobbled like a spinning top just before it falls.

Caitie shook her head. "He's a mess."

Rose sank in her chair with her head down.

"Do you know him?"

"Aye." Rose sighed, burying her face in her hands. The drunken party crasher stumbled off the dance floor and staggered his way from table to table.

Rose's uncle entered the hall, walking fast toward the drunk who tottered in their direction. It was a slow motion race with the drunk reaching the finish line first. "There you are, Rosie," he shouted as the hall fell silent. "I've been looking all over for you!"

Rose glanced at him, squeezed her eyes shut tight, and put her hands together raising them to her lips as if praying to disappear. Caitie could see the tears leaking from the corners of her eyes.

"Let's go home, Payton." Rose's uncle put a hand on the guy's shoulder.

The drunk tried to brush off her uncle's grip and swayed. "I'm here to see my girl." His speech was thick and slow.

Rose stood. "C'mon, Dad." Her head hung low as she took the guy's arm. Her uncle grabbed his other.

The guy tried to shake them off. "It's still early, and I'm ready to dance."

"Not tonight, Dad."

Caitie's heart ached for her friend as she watched them escort Rose's father out. The awkward scene left Caitie with little to say to the others. She got up to leave. "Nice meeting you."

"You too, Caitie," Jaimie said. Rhona and Heather nodded with sad smiles.

Caitie turned around to find Bonnie in her face.

"You need to stay away from Rose Matheson," Bonnie said in a hushed tone. "Her Dad's blootered most of the time. And you don't want to be associated with her."

"But Rose is—"

"I'm telling you for your own good." Bonnie pulled her away from the hotel staff.

"Okay." It didn't feel right not standing up for the first friend she'd made in Drum, but she didn't want to argue with Bonnie and wind up stuck with the old folks all night either. Besides, she couldn't do anything to fix what had happened to Rose.

They joined the Aileen and Maggie foursome, and Caitie laid her camera on the table.

"Can you take our picture?" blonde and blue-eyed Aileen asked. "It's Maggie's birthday."

"Sure," Caitie said.

"Bonnie, come over here." Maggie flipped her long side bangs."We want you in it too."

The three girls latched on to one another and smiled like the photo was for a full-page spread in the school yearbook. Bonnie broke free and waved to someone. Caitie turned to see Willie strolling toward them. He stopped next to her and bent so close to her ear that Caitie smelled his freshly shampooed hair.

"Would you like to dance?" Willie asked.

Her heart skipped a beat. Of course, she wanted to, but not to this Scottish do-si-do stuff. She turned her head to him. "I don't know how to dance to this kind of music."

"It's not so hard. The caller will tell you what to do, and I'll help."

She gazed into his warm brown eyes and melted faster than a Hershey's chocolate kiss in a hot car.

"Okay, but I'm going to suck at this."

Willie gave her that great crooked smile. His hand light on her back sent a tingle down her spine as he guided her to the dance floor near Robbie and Grandma as the last dance ended.

"I must say, Ina, you have a respectable partner on your hands." The old lady with Duncan nodded in approval.

"I have to agree," Grandma MacGregor said.

Grandpa walked up and slapped Robbie on the back. "You did me proud, lad."

"All right now, let's have the men lined up on my right," ordered the caller, "and the women on my left in groups of eight for *Strip the Willow*."

Everyone on the floor scrambled into position. Willie took her to the end of a group of eight headed up by Grandpa MacGregor.

What was I thinking? I'm going to make a fool of myself. She looked at Willie, biting her lip.

"Don't worry. This one's easy." He winked.

Suddenly Scotland didn't seem so bad.

The band started to play. Caitie watched Grandpa MacGregor and a young woman at the end of the line meet in the middle and spin to the right. They separated. She went to the second guy in line and spun him around the other way before meeting Grandpa again in the middle. Down the line they went, and then it was Grandpa MacGregor's turn to twirl each girl in line, starting with Caitie. He skipped and spun her way faster than she expected. Grandpa MacGregor and his partner went up and down the line one more time before a new couple started the dance. Caitie and Willie were last.

At first, she struggled to remember which direction to spin, but got the hang of it. Half way down the line though, she got dizzy and collided with Willie.

"You're doing great," he assured her.

"It doesn't feel like it!" Caitie laughed her way down the rest of the line. The music ended, and she rested her hands on her thighs, gasping for breath.

Grandpa MacGregor swaggered over and wrapped an arm around her shoulder. "You look puggled, Caitie."

"What?" she asked, her chest heaving.

"He's thinks you look tired," Willie said. "You want to sit down for a minute?"

"Yeah, I would!" Willie escorted her back to the table where Bonnie, Aileen, and Maggie were laughing at a picture on Caitie's camera.

"You gotta see Caitie's pictures, Willie," Bonnie said. "They're great."

Could they see the fairy?

"Looks like she's got a boyfriend back in San Diego." Bonnie turned the display so Willie could see the one with Santi's arm around her at the beach.

Caitie reached for her camera.

Bonnie pulled it back out of her grasp. "What's the matter, Caitie? You want to keep your big hunk a little secret?"

"Santi's not my boyfriend." Caitie fought the swell of anger at Bonnie for both touching her camera and looking through her pictures without asking.

"Sure doesn't look that way." Bonnie gave her a sickening sweet smile as she clicked the camera forward a few pics. "Check out this one, Willie." She turned the display toward him. This time it showed the photo of Caitie dancing in her underwear with her hair in a crazy ponytail on the side of her head and her face smeared with a green masque.

Why hadn't she deleted that stupid picture Sara had taken the last night they'd spent together at her old house? She'd never dreamed it would be used against her. Boiling inside, Caitie reached for her camera, but Bonnie switched it to her other hand. Willie chuckled at the image. Caitie wanted to crawl under the floor.

"You'd better watch out for her, Willie. You wouldn't want to risk your reputation spending too much time with a wild one like Caitie."

"Oh, Bonnie, don't be daft," Willie said.

"I'm not. I'm just looking out for you. C'mon, let's dance." She tossed Caitie the camera and wormed her arm around Willie's, dragging him out to the floor. Aileen and Maggie giggled.

Caitie took aim at Bonnie's back with her eyes like she had a table full of Scottish sock knives just begging to be hurled at that witch.

23 *a secret hunt for treasure*

· the quest ·

HALF-PAST 9 IN THE EVENING
JUNE 25TH

KEEN TO THE DANGER OF THE MISSION AHEAD, MUNGAN circled high above the mortals' croft on a ragwort stem, scouting the grounds for a sign of the dreaded witch and their savage dog. The carriage he had clung to for life the day before was nowhere to be found. Unfortunately, though not unexpected, the mongrel lay asleep on the grass facing the Loch, a guard who could all too easily be aroused. Mungan descended as silent as the setting sun, touching softly on the roof.

He dismounted the stem and crept close to the edge of the sloping grey slate tiles on the inland-side of the dwelling. Studying the ground far below, he pressed on till he stood over the entrance. Aiming his ragwort stem so 'twould land on the front step and await his departure, he released the stalk and hit his mark.

Mungan scaled the roof and climbed atop the stone chimney. He pulled the rope and grappling hook out of his pack and fastened them to his belt. Gathering the bottom of the sack in one hand and the top in his other, Mungan raised his arms over his head and jumped down the chimney. The sack billowed with air, breaking his fall just enough to keep him from crashing onto the hearth. A cloud of ash enveloped him as his feet hit the grate. He slipped, and his hand landed on the ironwork, sending a searing wave of pain up his arm. Mungan jumped to his feet and edged to the mesh screen. As agonizing as iron was to the touch, he could not imagine how excruciating it must have been for Tianna to have swallowed it with her wine.

A low rumble and rhythmic clink issued from somewhere to his right. So he was not alone and would have to proceed with utmost caution. Mungan wrapped his hand and arm in the sack for protection and pushed through the opening in the iron mesh curtain. He stripped the sack from his arm and spread it on the brick hearth to wipe the soot off the soles of his boots. 'Twould be foolish to leave footprints.

The shadows of nightfall shrouded the dwelling as the last rays of sunlight streamed low through the windows. Mungan glanced round at the furnishings. The spinning wheel near the fireplace caught his eye as did a large box with a grey glass front, but nothing he saw in the drawing room looked like the object Leannan had described.

He stole past a stairway toward the clinking sound. The sudden whoosh of running water startled him as he rounded the corner. He dashed across the corridor. With his back against the wall, he peeked round the doorframe into the noisy chamber. An empty basket sat on the floor in front of two large white boxes. The contraption on the right made most of the racket. Just as suddenly as the sound of pouring water started, it stopped. Mungan's eyes widened as a knob on the box to the left spun slowly. Was it enchanted or the invention of a clever mortal's mind? There was no time to find out.

The corridor led to a tidy bedchamber. A picture too real to be a painting sat on the wooden chest next to the bed. 'Twas a portrait of the mother he had seen the day before in the arms of a man. Another image rising from the bottom of the frame replaced it. 'Twas of the same man, only now he was dwarfed by a massive metal bird. This had to be the mother's chamber. Searching here would waste precious time. He scurried back down the corridor, pondering the clarity of the images and how they changed from one to the next.

To his right, he found an alcove with a table, chairs, wooden cupboards, a short and another tall white cabinet, likely their kitchen. He spied no small silver box here nor in the banquet room beyond. The witch's chamber had to be on the floor above. He had no choice but to scale the stairs.

Winded, he reached a landing leading to four open doors. To his left, a man's shirt hung on a doorknob. A second door led to a small alcove with a long white trough set on clawed feet and a shiny white throne. Peering through the third doorway, he spied a small pair of boots half-hidden beneath the bed. They must be the lad's. He would return here if his search of the witch's chamber proved fruitless.

The strange hooded sweater he had seen her wear the day before lay on the floor just inside the fourth doorway. At last! The box he sought was likely close at hand. The witch's chamber was woefully unkempt with piles of garments strewn everywhere. From his low vantage point, he could not see what lay atop the furnishings. He tossed the grappling hook onto the blue cushioned bench in front of the dressing table and shimmied up the rope. As he pulled himself atop the cushion, he spied a tall white stick with a round cover on top of the chest next to the bed. Perhaps the odd toadstool was a strange lantern of sorts. At the base of it was a silver egg-shaped object with a flat panel, 10:15 glowed red on the black face. 'Twas too large and the wrong shape to be the box he sought. The number changed before his eyes to 10:16. The meaning of the numbers became clear. 'Twas a clock of some sort. He fought the urge to steal it, for 'twas too large to fit in his tiny pack, and his mission did not concern another timepiece.

Mungan turned and spotted a thin silver box amongst scraps of paper, open bottles of potions, and rectangular boxes of colored powder scattered about the dressing table. He pulled the hook out of the seat cushion and tossed it across the wood. Pulling the line taut, he secured the hook on the back edge of the tabletop and climbed the rope. He rushed over to the metal box. It appeared to match Leannan's description for size, but 'twas tethered by a black rope-like line attached to the wall.

He tugged on the black line, but 'twould not come free. Perhaps if he braced his feet against the box, he could wrench it out. If it suddenly gave way though, the box would likely fly o'er the edge of the dressing table. At his true size, this task would be trivial. Mungan sighed. 'Twas not worth the risk with all the enchanted objects in the dwelling. He sat down instead and straddled the box, his legs gripping it tight. The silver box vibrated wildly and blared, "Answer Me! Answer Me!" He thrust the fetish from him and skittered away like a crab. His heart nigh leapt through his throat. The mysterious voice continued its chant, and the box danced in a circle, buzzing like an angry bee.

In an instant, the fetish lay still. Mungan's inner voice shouted at him to flee, but the vision of poor Leannan steeled him to capture it. Her only hope for restoration depended upon him. With caution he approached the object, crouched down, and reached out to try to remove the line again. The box came to life, vibrating briefly. A short ring burst forth. A tiny blue light flashed repeatedly on the glass atop the silver box. The soft indigo shadows of dusk filled the chamber, and he knew he must not dally. He lifted the box on one end and mounted it like a steed. Yanking on the black rope with all his strength, the line broke free. He lurched backwards, crashing his back and head onto the tabletop. Dazed, he stood, opened his pack, and stuffed the fetish inside. As much trouble as the object was, it had to be the right box. Now to return safely to the mountain with it and restore Leannan.

THE MOMENT MUNGAN APPEARED IN THE GREAT HALL, THE MUSICIANS ceased playing, the dancers stood still as statues, and all bantering amongst the Daoine Shi fell to a hushed murmur.

The king sat forward on his throne. "Did ye find the box?"

"I believe so." Mungan opened the sack and reached deep to extract the now small object. He held the fetish high in the palm of his hand for the king's inspection.

King Oseron's eyes roved the Great Hall. "Come, Earnan. Your assistance is needed."

The old wizard rose from a banquet table and strode toward the throne, his robes undulating more purple than blue.

"Cormag, bring Leannan from the dungeon," King Oseron commanded.

"Aye, Your Majesty." The guard bowed low and disappeared through an archway.

The silver object glinted in the candlelight as Mungan offered it to Earnan. "I must warn ye, the object shook and chanted when I first touched it in the mortals' dwelling."

Earnan took the box and turned it over in his hands, studying it through his crescent spectacles. On the side of the silver box with black glass, the tiny blue light still flashed with persistence. "So this is the fetish that stole Leannan's magic."

"'Twas the only silver box I found in the witch's chambers."

"Can ye retrieve Leannan's magic from it, Earnan?" King Oseron asked.

"The answer may very well lie in the strength of our magic against that of the witch, Your Majesty."

The crowd grew silent and still.

Cradling the box in one hand, Earnan pressed on it with his pointer finger, and it lit up his face with a strange blue glow. He drew in a sharp breath.

The king craned his neck like a great heron's. "What is it?"

"It appears the fetish contains the essence of two mortals."

"Crivvens!" King Oseron exclaimed.

The wizard's eyes narrowed and his pursed lips protruded from his bearded face like a rosebud from a blanket of snow. "Is one of these the witch Leannan encountered?" Earnan turned the glowing glass toward Mungan.

Drawing close, Mungan swallowed hard at the sight of the lass he had followed to the croft. The other he did not recognize. The image was akin to the one in the mortal's dwelling. 'Twas perfectly clear and captured behind a glass window. Mungan's fear that the witch's powers exceeded theirs was reflected in Earnan's eyes.

"The one with blonde-streaked hair, not the dark curls, is indeed her," Mungan said.

Earnan pressed the glass and a faint sound issued from the box. The wizard's bushy brows flew upward, he drew the case lid to his ear, and his mouth gaped open.

"What is it?" King Oseron asked.

"There is a voice!" Earnan said.

"What does it say?" the king demanded.

Earnan tapped the box with his wand. *"Fàs nas fuaimnich!"*

"Where are you?" roared a female voice. "OMG. You're impossible to get a hold of. A bunch of us are together and wanted to talk to you. If you keep this up, we're gonna fly all the way over there, kidnap you, and bring you back. Okay, bye."

Mungan's stomach clenched. Was the message for him? Or perhaps for Leannan?

"And who do ye suppose this voice speaks of?" King Oseron's eyes drilled into Mungan's.

He refused to flinch. "'Tis difficult to say, Your Majesty."

"Well, I know." The king narrowed his eyes. "The witch has left this message for *me.* 'Twas no random encounter in the cave. 'Twas an attack against the Daoine Shi." He pounded his fist on the arm of his throne. "I shan't be trifled with!"

A shuffle behind Mungan drew his attention. Cormag dragged Leannan toward the throne; her wretched face grimaced in pain, though she uttered not a word of complaint. Mungan thought she seemed to have grown more grotesque than the day before, her flaking skin a deeper grey green and her face even more disfigured by warts.

With her head hung low, Leannan raised her eyes to King Oseron who glowered back. She turned to Mungan, and though fighting revulsion, he tried to send a silent message of hope and reassurance with his gaze. She drew a deep breath and looked away to Earnan whose amethyst eyes were filled with uncertainty.

"Are ye ready, Leannan?" Earnan asked.

She nodded and Cormag backed away. The wizard extended the case toward her. He tapped the silver box with his wand twice. *"Thig a mach agus till innte a rithist!"*

A silence that could be broken by a butterfly's beating wing filled the Great Hall. Mungan waited and longed for a vapor, a sparkle of light, something to come forth from the box and find its way back to Leannan. With no change to her gruesome visage, sorrow suffocated his hope.

"Could it have been a different box?" Earnan asked.

"Perhaps," Leannan rasped.

"This has to be the one," Mungan said. "It holds the essence of the mortals. Leannan's magic must be in there too."

"Come, Leannan," Earnan said. "Look closely, and tell us if this is the silver box ye recall."

She hesitated before inching toward the wizard on her backward feet. Her splotchy brow wrinkled. "It seems a wee bit larger than I remember."

"Are ye certain, Leannan?" Mungan pleaded with his eyes.

"Not entirely. But the box that captured my magic flashed bright as lightning."

"May I have the fetish, Earnan?" Mungan asked.

The wizard handed it to him. Mungan studied the tiny squares at the base of the image of the witch.

The square with a flower had "Gallery" written beneath it. Perhaps Leannan's magic was trapped inside the gallery. He pressed the square and a new image appeared. "Look, Earnan."

The wizard drew close.

"What is it doing now?" King Oseron asked.

"It shows the sun sinking into the sea," Mungan said.

The king thrust forward on the throne. "The witch has captured the sun too?"

"No, I think not, as I saw it set this night. Perhaps 'tis a memory of it." Mungan pressed an arrow on the side of the image and his eyes grew wide.

"Tell me what ye see?" King Oseron demanded.

"Scantily clad mortals frolicking on sand. And three more of them standing precariously on ocean waves."

King Oseron looked to Earnan. "What magic allows mortals to stand on water?"

The wizard twirled the end of his long beard. "Powerful magic, Your Majesty."

"Now, I see the lad from the cave hunched low, yet hovering in the air above a strange board with wheels beneath."

"They can fly as well?" King Oseron's voice wavered.

"It appears so." Mungan's shoulders slumped as the first image he had seen, that of the witch and the other mortal appeared at the next press of the arrow.

"Did ye find any trace of Leannan's magic?" the king pressed.

"No," Mungan answered quietly.

Earnan shook his head slowly. "I do not believe this to be the silver box we seek, Your Majesty."

The wizard's words wrenched the air from Mungan's chest. He had failed again.

"I must agree." King Oseron's nostrils flared. "'Tis merely a coward's tool to deliver threats. It appears your folly has cost ye dearly, Leannan." He nodded at Cormag. "Return her to the dungeon."

"Let me go back once more, King Oseron," Mungan pleaded. "I am sure I can find the true box if given a second chance."

"And why pray tell should I grant this request? I need ye here as Searsanach. Another fruitless venture in the mortal realm in search of the witch's fetish is not worth the risk." King Oseron shook his head. "No more I say. 'Tis obvious that fate has seen to punish the maidservant for her disobedience. Ye gave it a worthy try, Mungan. 'Tis time to commence with what I should have commanded in the first place."

"And what is that, Your Majesty?" Mungan asked.

"To mete out the one sentence that will punish Leannan for sedition as well as avenge the deed the witch has done. The mortal knows not whom she is dealing with."

Leannan stood stoic as the weight of the king's words fell upon her. The crowd murmured, and the marble floor seemed to drop beneath Mungan.

King Oseron closed his eyes. "I take no pleasure in this judgment, but the use of a *Tàcharan* is a just penalty for both."

Leannan shuddered and terror filled her eyes.

Mungan's mind raced. He could hear the whisperings behind him as the crowd recalled the last time the *Tàcharan* punishment had been meted out four hundred years earlier. Retrieving the true silver box was the only way to save her and quiet his conscience. "When do ye desire the sentence be carried out?"

"After sunset on the morrow."

"Your Majesty, may I respectfully urge ye to reconsider."

"Reconsider?" the king shouted. "Leannan's fate as well as that of the witch is set."

"Our code must be respected to be sure, but if we can resolve this dilemma by disarming the witch of her fetish and Earnan returning Leannan's magic, then no lasting harm has come to the Daoine Shi. Leannan has already paid a terrible price for her disobedience. The witch will no doubt be thwarted with the loss of such a valuable weapon and will realize 'tis unwise to provoke ye further."

King Oseron crossed his arms and sat back on his throne.

Mungan bowed slightly. "Your Majesty, I humbly ask that ye permit me one last venture on the morrow to seek the silver box. The mortal realm is indeed far more perilous than it used to be, and though retribution is warranted, I fear ye may invite a grave consequence upon the Daoine Shi."

The king studied Mungan. "I am leery of another venture."

"Ye have my word as Searsanach that I shall return safely as I have done so before."

With his elbow on the arm of the throne, King Oseron stroked his chin. "Mungan, ye have my permission for one more attempt, but if ye are unsuccessful, the night will surely end with Daoine Shi justice for Leannan and the witch."

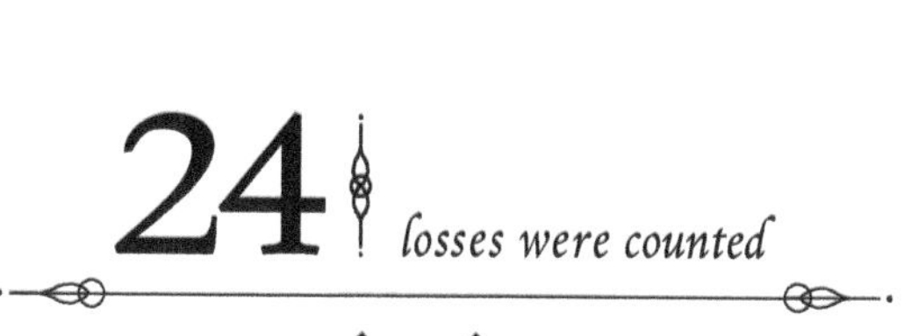

24 *losses were counted*

·missing·

ROBBIE STARED OUT HIS BEDROOM WINDOW AT THE Loch sparkling in the moonlight. Could Dad look down at him from heaven? Did he know what had happened in the cave or at the ceilidh?

"What are you thinking about?" Mom asked as she walked into his room.

"Have you forgotten about Dad?" He turned his head to see her answer.

"Of course not. Why would you even ask such a thing?"

"'Cause you and Ross were spending an awful lot of time dancing tonight."

"Oh, Robbie." Her eyes glistened. "I'll never forget your father. I loved him with all my heart. Ross was being kind, and I enjoyed dancing with him. But no one can ever take your Dad's place."

"It looked like you might want Ross to," Robbie said.

"That's not the case. Ross has been very good to all of us, and I am grateful for his kindness."

"Are you sure that's all it is?" he persisted.

Mom sat down on the bed and patted the quilt. The bedsprings squeaked when he sat on the mattress next to her.

"You know, Robbie, it's only been six months since we lost Dad, and the three of us are all still a little broken. Ross, your gran, and granddad understand that and are trying to help us heal."

"Grandma's great. But tonight, Ross was trying way too hard. And Grandpa? C'mon, Mom."

"He's getting better, honey."

"You call wanting me to look ridiculous wearing a kilt and playing the bagpipes, helping me? He wants me to play shinty with kids twice my size that will more than likely kill me. And what about asking me to stick my arm all the way up a cow's you know what? That old man just wants to turn me into somebody else he'd like better."

She shifted on the bed and looked out the window. "You know that's not true."

"It sure seems like it."

"Your granddad's a little rough around the edges, but he means well."

"Yeah, right."

She wrapped her arms around Robbie.

"I miss Dad," he whispered. He could feel his mom's uneven breathing.

"I know, honey. I miss him too. He wants us to go on though. Do you think Dad wouldn't want you to laugh anymore? Or not to have fun?"

"No, but I feel bad when I do."

"Robbie, it would make Dad awfully sad to hear you say that. He loved you and Caitie and me so very much. You need to understand and know that he wouldn't want you to feel guilty about enjoying your life. The best way to honour your dad is to remember him with joy and love and to live in a way that would make him proud."

"I guess."

Mom pulled back a little and combed his bangs out of his eyes with her fingers.

"Robbie!" Caitie shouted before storming into his room. "Where's my phone?"

"It's on your vanity, plugged into your charger, 'cause that's where I put it before we left for the ceilidh."

"Well, it's not there now," she said, hands on her hips.

Robbie glowered at her. "Try looking a little harder."

"I did. I looked all around the vanity for it, and it's not there! The cord's still plugged into the outlet, but the phone's gone."

"Not my problem. When I left your room earlier tonight, it was there."

"Mom!" Caitie said, begging for her to take her side.

"Look, it's late, and we're all tired. Let's not worry about it tonight. I'm sure you'll find it in the morning."

"But Mom…"

"I mean it, Caitie, I don't want to discuss this any further. Now off to bed."

Mom stood up to leave. Caitie stomped back to her room, slamming her bedroom door behind her.

Robbie got off the bed too, turned the covers down and crawled inside. "You and Grandma are going over to the egg lady's tomorrow, right?"

Mom tucked the covers up over his shoulders. "You mean to Mrs. Chattan's, and yes, that's the plan."

"What are Caitie and I supposed to do?"

"Your granddad and Ross have something special in mind for the two of you."

"What is it?" he asked, suspicious of anything the old man could be planning. Somehow he was sure it would be some Scottish stuff he wanted no part of. "Grandpa's not thinking of driving us to that place in Inverness to go kilt shopping, is he?"

The stairs creaked.

"No, not yet. But I don't want to spoil the surprise." Mom bent down and kissed his forehead. He looked past her and saw the silhouette of the old man filling the doorframe.

"Maisie, he's not a bairn that needs tucking in."

"Oh, Dad. Not tonight."

"Sleep fast and hard, Robbie. We've a big day ahead."

"Great," Robbie muttered. He'd give anything if he could be with Dad instead.

25 *one thing sought and another gained*

·strange behavior·

HALF-PAST 10 IN THE MORN JUNE 26TH

MUNGAN WRESTLED WITH HIS WORRIES THROUGH THE WEE hours of the morning until the peach torchlight of dawn brought blissful sleep at last. Lileas's cheeping chicks stirred him awake as her cart trundled through the corridor. He stretched and yawned like a lazy cat and slowly opened his eyes, focusing on the mantel clock. Half past ten! He bolted upright. 'Twas a poor reflection on him as Searsanach to be late and foolish to miss breakfast with all that the day held. He intended to visit the shoppes after the morning meal as he knew they would be empty of their labourers. Now there was little morning left, and his plans to fly to the croft in the early afternoon could not keep.

He went to the dresser and tipped the suspended pitcher. A cascade of opalescent vapors danced into the silver basin beneath. He dipped his hands into the bowl and wafted the vapors toward his face. The sparkling fog enveloped his head, untangled his hair, freshened his face, and brightened his smile. He tapped the curved blade of purple moor grass lying next to the basin, and it whirled to life. Tipping his head back, the spinning blade soared upward, curved round his throat, and trimmed the stubble of a days' beard from his neck and face before sailing back to its resting place. He drew his hand across his smooth skin. *Much better.*

Mungan donned his breeches, slipped a rust colored shirt over his head, and tucked it in. He scooped the pocket watch off the table next to his bed and slid its chain through the custom loops on his breeches so the treasure dangled just below his waist. The gnawing in his stomach was fierce as he tugged on his boots. Only food would likely not abate the discomfort. 'Twas dread of the day ahead that caused the pain. Hopefully, time in the shoppes searching for iron nails, something he knew he could identify, would distract his troubled mind.

The artists' studio yielded only silver nails. A search of the masons and carpenters tools produced bronze nails in a variety of sizes but no iron. He would come back though on the morrow to question them about a possible stash.

Mungan hoped his luck would change in the Cobblers' Shoppe. He opened the door and found Corc working at his bench.

"Why, my friend, are ye toiling on your day of leisure?" Mungan asked.

"My own boot heel is in need of repair. And where were ye this morning at the breakfast hour?"

"Asleep. 'Twas a most unpleasant night."

"How unfortunate for ye. Lileas served a tasty moss gruel."

"Corc, do ye ever use iron nails on the shoes or boots?"

"No 'twould be too dangerous. We only use brass." The cobbler's face clouded. "Was iron responsible for stealing Queen Tianna's life?"

"Earnan suspects 'twas St. John's wort and iron combined."

Corc shuddered. "Did ye find some in Ballard's room?"

"No, nothing. I have reason to believe Ballard is not the one who did the deed."

"But the king..."

"I know. However, justice demands the true culprit be held accountable."

"Ye must be careful, Mungan, for to contradict the king—"

"'Twould be dishonouring. Only presenting King Oseron with indisputable evidence would lessen the sting. So I search, but I do not know what for."

"I yearn to help ye, Mungan, but am befuddled as to how."

"Are ye aware of anything peculiar in the days leading to Tianna's death?"

Corc rubbed his jaw. "'Tis likely nothing, but three nights before the queen left us, I came back to the shoppe very late. A musician alerted me to the flopping sole of his boot. It hampered his ability to keep time to his tunes. So, he asked me to bring him a spare. When I stepped through the door, Cormag was standing there with his back to me." Corc hesitated.

"Go on."

"He had a row of boots facing him, and I could have sworn he was speaking to them."

Mungan's mind whirled as he tried to make sense of the scene he envisioned. Were there too many pairs for Cormag to choose from? If the guard had been trying them on, they would have been facing away from him. Why talk to the boots? Unless....Could Cormag have been trying to make the boots dance? Earnan's missing wand and Tianna's query regarding the wizard's successor. Perhaps 'twas all tied together. "Did Cormag have a wand in his hand?"

Corc could not have looked more shocked if he had dropped a hammer on his own toe. "Mungan, ye know that Earnan is the only one amongst us who possesses a wand."

"Aye, 'tis true. And ye must not breathe a word of this, but one of Earnan's wands is missing."

Corc shut his eyes. "I cannot recall seeing a wand. But I do remember thinking the scene very odd indeed."

"What did ye say to him?"

"I asked what he was doing in the shoppe. He said his boots were pinching his toes, and he could not wait till morning for a new pair."

"So what happened next?" Mungan asked.

"He took a pair and left."

"And what did ye do?"

"I cursed Cormag for the mess and on account of his general disposition, lined the boots up proper where they belonged, and picked up a spare for the musician."

"Hmm." Mungan combed back the hair from his brow with his fingers.

"Do ye suppose it means anything other than that Cormag may be daft as well as unpleasant?"

"Perhaps, Corc." Mungan checked the time on his pocket watch. Half-past twelve. "I must be going."

"For the mid-day meal?"

"No, I am afraid there is no time for that." He hurried back to his chamber for his sack and the tools he would need on his foray to the croft.

What if Cormag truly desired to be Earnan's successor? He would be a poor choice indeed. Perhaps Tianna had caught him stealing Earnan's wand. Was that worth her life in Cormag's eyes? He would search the guard's room for Earnan's wand, if not this evening, then on the morrow.

26 *the proving was in the finishing*

·fishing·

SUNDAY AFTERNOON, ROBBIE SAT ON THE LIVING ROOM floor, fighting for his survival against endless hordes of zombies on his Xbox.

"Caitie! Robbie! It's time to go fishing," boomed the old man.

Robbie zapped a glowing orange-eyed zombie on the TV screen. "But Grandpa…"

"No buts. Now move. And dress warm as it's a touch cool on the water."

Robbie saved his game and went upstairs for his boots and jacket. After what he'd seen in the mountain, Nessie was probably real too and with his luck, just waiting for him out on the Loch.

Caitie clicked away on the computer keyboard. "Tell Grandpa, I'm busy."

"I don't want to go either, but we don't get a choice."

"This sucks!" Caitie cracked her knuckles and stood. "Can I borrow your iTouch?"

"And let you drop it off the boat? No way! Bring your iPod."

"Battery's dead."

"Too bad," he said.

She glared at him. "You owe me after losing my phone."

"And I'm telling you for the last time, I didn't lose it."

"What about your nano? I can't spend hours on a boat without some music at least."

Robbie pulled his nano out of the nightstand drawer and handed it to her. "If anything happens to it, your life is over."

"It pretty much is anyway." She left with a pained sigh.

Robbie grabbed his boots and put them on. Trudging down the stairs, he wondered how he could get out of this.

The old man stood by the backdoor in a navy wool coat, coveralls, and galoshes.

"I really don't feel good," Robbie said.

"That's no surprise." The old man crossed his arms. "Your muscles have likely atrophied, sitting in front of the telly for so long. There's nothin' wrong with you, lad, that a good dose of fresh air won't cure."

Caitie walked up, putting the earbuds in, and stuffing the nano and her camera into the pockets of her hoodie.

As they headed out the backdoor, the old man asked, "Do you like to fish, Caitie?"

She scrunched her nose. "I hate putting the worms on the hook. They wiggle,and the whole stabbing thing is just gross."

Grandpa chuckled. "We won't be baiting hooks today."

"That's good," she said.

The wind gusted, flapping Robbie's jacket and pushing the waves over into white caps. The wooden dock groaned as they strode to the bigger fishing boat with Balfour. Ross was already at the stern bent over a rusty tackle box. The old man boarded the boat, grunting as he stepped down onto the deck. Balfour jumped on after him. "Here, you two." He handed them each an orange life jacket.

Caitie hopped onto the boat.

Robbie clicked together the buckles on the life jacket and scanned the endless Loch wondering where Nessie was hiding. "You got a fish finder on there?"

"No need for one," the old man answered. "I know this loch as well my own name and the best places to drop the lines."

"You could probably find them faster or see other stuff down there with one."

"What else would we be looking for? Are you fretting about Nessie?" The old man shook his head. "Get in the boat."

Robbie climbed aboard and followed Caitie inside the small cabin. The musty smell reminded him of the Star of India back in San Diego. The old sailing ship was haunted by a kid who'd fallen from the main mast over a hundred years ago which made standing watch in the middle of the night on Robbie's class sleepover mega creepy. He was sure he'd felt a cold spot and smelled fresh baked bread in the galley too and no one had been cooking in there for years. Robbie shuddered just thinking about it. He stepped out for some fresh air. "What are you doing?"

he asked the old man.

"Checking the lights and radio to make sure everything works properly. Better safe than sorry. I think we're ready now." The old man started the motor, the engine gurgled, and the smell of gas stung Robbie's nose. "Grab the pier tire, Robbie. We don't want to drift away and leave Ross behind."

Ross untied the dock line at the stern.

Robbie kneeled on the bench that ran along the side of the boat and wrapped his arms around the tire, sucking in his stomach to keep from touching a lacy cobweb strung across the inside. The old man, spiders—how many more of his un-favorite things would he have to deal with?

With the boat free, Ross jumped back on board.

"Push us away, Robbie," the old man said.

He gladly let go of the spider-tire and shoved them off. The old man spun the boat's wheel and turned the craft out into Loch Ness at a slow speed.

Caitie emerged from the cabin and crossed the deck. She sat on a bench close to the stern. "How deep is the Loch?"

"About seven hundred and fifty feet." Ross cast a line with a red minnow lure off the stern. "Here, Robbie." He handed over the fishing rod and put out a second line for Caitie.

"I'm not very good at this," she said.

"The fish don't know that," Ross said. "Give it a go. You may surprise yourself."

The tip of Robbie's rod jerked down. "I've got one!" He spun the reel with the rod lying flat against the stern.

"Stop reeling so fast! Give it some slack to run, and slowly raise the rod!" the old man shouted.

Before he could do any of those things, the pull on the rod disappeared and slack line lay on the water. Robbie reeled it in, but the red minnow was gone.

"You should've done what I told you," the old man nagged.

"It happened so fast. I tried, but the fish snapped the line."

"It wouldn't have if you'd kept the rod up and been ready."

"I was ready!" How was he supposed to know that stuff?

The old man turned back to the wheel, gunned the motor, and followed the shoreline. Robbie fumed over the old man's fit. Ross fixed his line and handed it back.

Caitie watched the scenery more than her rod as they neared a crumbling building. "What's that, Grandpa?"

"What's left of Urquhart Castle."

"What happened to it?" she asked.

"A lot of people fought over the place. It was abandoned in the 1600's, and villagers took some of the stones from it to build their own homes. A war left it in worse condition, and finally, a bad wind brought down one of the tower walls."

"Must have been some wind." She held the fishing rod between her knees, wriggled her hand under her life jacket to get her camera, and aimed it for a picture. Just as the camera clicked, her fishing rod jerked downward. "Ahh!" Caitie laid the camera on the seat bench and grabbed the rod with both hands. Its tip bent over like an upside down 'U.' It had to be a big fish to pull that hard. The old man cut the engine.

"It looks like you got something, Caitie," Ross said.

The line swayed left and right through the choppy water as the fish shot back and forth on the end, thrashing to get away. "I don't know what I'm doing!" she cried.

"Let it run for a bit to tire him out. Then slowly bring in the line Caitie, nice and smooth." The old man smiled so wide you'd have thought it was his fish.

Caitie tilted the rod up and down while struggling with the crank as the fish fought to free itself. In a few minutes, she'd reeled it in close to the boat. Half out of the water, the fish lashed its tail wildly as Ross leaned over the side and netted it. Balfour jumped onto the bench with his paws on the side of the boat and barked.

"What kind is it?" Caitie called, all excited.

"It's a brownie. I'm guessing it's close to 3 lbs," Ross said.

"Well done, Caitie." The old man beamed and nodded his head. "Too bad you let that one get away, Robbie. Now your sister's officially beaten you at bringing in the day's first catch."

Well, the old man finally got the grandson he always wanted. Too bad it was his sister.

"Take a picture for me, Robbie. I want to send it to everyone back home. They'll never believe I caught one this big."

"This is your home now, Caitie," the old man said.

Robbie rolled his eyes. Holding his rod with one hand, he crossed the deck and pulled the camera from the bench.

"Hurry, Robbie."

Ross pulled the fish off the hook and then gripped its underbelly with one hand near the head and the other close to the tail. It had to be a foot and a half long. "Hold it sideways like this."

Caitie shook her head in disgust. "No thanks."

"Your friends will be much more impressed if you do."

She scrunched her face and barely grasped the fish with her fingertips. "He's slimy!" The golden-brown skin with red and black spots gleamed, and its white mouth gaped open. The gills moved slowly in and out.

"You'll need a better grip than that, Caitie. Squeeze harder or he'll get away from you," Ross said, still holding on.

The corners of her mouth practically dropped level with her chin as she clenched the fish in her grip and held it as far from her body as she could. The trout twitched, Caitie screamed, and Robbie snapped the photo.

"Do it again, Robbie. I wasn't ready."

He checked out the camera display. "Why? That one was really good. You should see your face. I'm gonna post it on Facebook."

"Just take it again," she yelled with a forced smile. The limp fish looked dead.

He snapped another picture.

The gills suddenly moved. Caitie squealed and flinched, losing her grip on the slimy trophy. She bounced it toward Ross like a volleyball save. He caught it and laughed. "What's the matter, Caitie?"

"Nothing. I've just held him long enough."

Ross stowed the fish in an ice chest and then cast Caitie's line back in the water. The old man pushed the throttle and the boat sped up again.

Cold spray stung Robbie's face as they cut through the waves. The whipping wind and icy water soaking his clothes made him shiver. He stared at the Loch, and from the corner of his eye, he'd think he spotted movement, but whenever he turned to look, there was nothing but more whitecaps.

This is stupid. I gotta stop being paranoid. People had been searching for years and spending lots of money on fancy equipment trying to find Nessie. What made him think on his first afternoon fishing, he'd see the thing? Chances of that would be like one in a zillion. But then again, he'd seen and talked to a fairy. Maybe he should be worried.

His line yanked the rod, bending the tip down. "I got something!" Robbie shouted. His arms shook from the adrenaline rush. He pulled up on the rod. This one wasn't gonna get away.

Ross grinned. "Aye, you've hooked a big one."

The old man cut the engine's power. "Hold on, Robbie."

"I'm trying." The harder he strained to keep the rod up, the more the fish fought back. Whenever Robbie would reel in some line, whatever was on the end of it would zip off that much and more, making him work harder to get back what he'd lost.

"Hold the rod tip higher. Ease it down as you reel in some line, stop, and bring it back up again. Slowly lad, slowly!" the old man yelled.

He felt like he had a whale on his hook, or worse. After what seemed like hours of pulling on the rod and cranking the reel, his arms and shoulders ached like they were on fire. He turned to Ross for help. "I can't do this anymore!"

"Yes, you can, Robbie. You're stronger than that fish for sure."

"You've got to stay with it and wear him down," the old man ordered.

Balfour pawed the deck excitedly.

"But he's too strong!"

"Take a deep breath, relax your arms a bit, and wind him in a little. Keep working it, and you'll tire him out," Ross said.

"Be persistent, lad. Don't give in to him," the old man added.

Robbie tried to relax. He gave a little line, and then when he felt it slacken some, he slowly reeled in what he could.

"You're doing it, Robbie. You've got him!" Caitie yelled.

Robbie worked to breathe and leaned forward a little to ease the ache in his stomach. The line stayed taut as he kept working the rod and the crank, bringing the huge silver fish to the surface.

"Steady, Robbie! You're almost there!" Ross leaned over the side of the boat with the net.

Robbie's arms and shoulders were all but gone.

"You've a beauty of a salmon here." Ross netted the fighting fish. With the line slack and the struggle over, Robbie's arms and shoulders went limp. He slumped over barely hanging on to the rod, wheezing for breath. The old man killed the engine and crossed the deck. Balfour followed.

"Aye, it's a fine specimen!" The old man squeezed his shoulders. "I'm proud of you. You hung on there and fought to the finish like a true Scot." The old man wore the biggest smile Robbie'd seen all day.

Ross worked to get the hook out and then passed the slippery salmon to Robbie. It was ice cold. He gripped the fish just like Caitie had, only he held his prize close to his chest. Caitie took his picture.

"Put that on Facebook!" Robbie shouted. "How much do you suppose it weighs?"

"He's a big one. Somewhere around twelve pounds." Ross took the salmon and put it on the ice with Caitie's trout. Grandpa MacGregor started up the engine.

Ross picked up the rod to cast it.

"That's okay, Ross. I'm worn out." He collapsed on the bench and leaned back against the side of the boat, feeling shaky all over.

"I'm done too." Caitie reeled in her line and propped the rod on the edge of the bench. Grandpa MacGregor, still grinning, circled the boat back toward the farm. Caitie pulled the nano out of her hoodie and headed for the cabin.

"What's that in your hand?" Grandpa MacGregor asked.

She looked like she couldn't believe he didn't know. "It's an iPod Grandpa. Haven't you ever seen one before?"

"No. What does it do?"

"It plays music." She took the earbud from her ear and put it close to his for him to hear.

"That sounds terrible!" he cried.

Caitie chuckled. She slipped the earbud back in and ducked into the cabin.

Robbie wasn't surprised Grandpa MacGregor didn't like his music, but it didn't matter. He'd caught his fish, landed it, and proved to the old man he wasn't a wimp after all. And for the first time, in a long time, he began to believe it too until he looked up at the mountains on the other side of the Loch and remembered the cave.

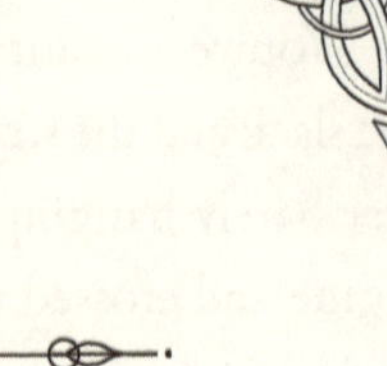

27 *the unintended game of cat & mouse*

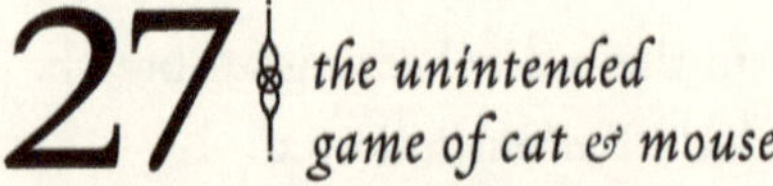

· the second chance ·

3:45 IN THE AFTERNOON JUNE 26TH

FIGHTING A GUSTY HEADWIND, MUNGAN FLEW O'ER THE loch on his ragwort stem and surveyed the shoreline in search of the mortals' croft. He spotted the small white dinghy tied to the dock and soared toward it as straight as an archer's arrow. The tawny red boat was gone, a good sign that the mortals were away.

As he passed above the stone shed, the white carriage rolled onto the gravel lane. He darted left and rose higher in the sky, circling round to avoid being seen and then dove into the bushes that bordered the side of the dwelling as the coach rolled to a stop. With the ragwort stem tucked under his arm, he raced to reach the entrance before the mortals did.

"Fiona hasn't changed a bit," the mother said.

"You mean she's still the best source of gossip in the village?" the old woman asked.

"Aye." The mother chuckled. "Go inside, Mum. I'll get your quilting basket."

"Thank you, dear." The old woman strolled up the flagstone path.

Mungan crouched, waiting to steal inside.

Grasping the tarnished knob with a wrinkled hand, the old woman opened the door and tarried, her eyes focused on her daughter.

'Tis child's play. He propped the stem against the bush and quietly slipped past her. Through the short corridor and into the drawing room he sprinted, arriving at the stairwell before the mortals' footsteps tapped across the wooden floor.

"Where do you keep the basket, Mum?"

"In the cupboard under the stairs."

Mungan vaulted the steps at a furious pace. A door creaked open beneath his spot on the stairway.

He paused.

"When do you think our fishermen will return?" the mother asked.

"Very soon I expect, this being their first venture on the Loch," the old woman said.

"I think I'll do some straightening upstairs and one last load of laundry while we wait."

Rummaging below followed by a thud drew Mungan's attention. He peered through the railing's balusters and spied a strange contraption below with a squat, beige block at its base and a long thin stick attached to the back of it. A cord was looped round protrusions on one side of the stick and a slender maroon bag hung off the other with white letters that spelled HOOVER. It bore a mild resemblance to bagpipes but had only one drone. And with no blowpipe or chanter stock 'twould be nigh impossible to play. The mother closed the closet and walked back toward the entryway. Though his curiosity was piqued by the odd contrivance, there was no time to waste. He climbed the remaining stairs.

Atop the landing, Mungan ran to the witch's bedchamber as slow footsteps creaked up the stairwell. He leaned against the doorframe with one eye toward the stairs, waiting to see where the mortal would go. If she came his direction, he would take refuge under the bed. The mother carried the strange contraption in one hand and a large wicker basket in the other. To his relief, she turned into the lad's bedchamber.

Mungan raced to the bench, hurled the grappling hook atop the cushion, and inch-wormed up the line. A thin white box with silver sides and cords lay on the cluttered tabletop at the base of the looking glass. At the ends of each thin string was a small white bulb, like a flower with no petals and a dull grey center. He searched his memory, not sure whether the object the witch slipped into her pocket on Midsummer's Eve was white or silver. Nor could he recall any cords attached to the magic box. But with one last chance, he would pilfer this and any other boxes with at least some silver that were close in size to what Leannan had described.

A whirring sound startled him. Was it the bagpipe contraption? Though unsettling, as long as the noise persisted, the mother was likely occupied in the other chamber.

He pulled himself onto the dressing table, crouched next to the box and touched the white ring. The black rectangle on top turned grey and what appeared to be a keg lying on its side filled with green light, emptied and refilled again, over and over. A lightning bolt was inscribed on the tiny keg.

Leannan spoke of a lightning flash! After pulling, twisting, and at last, squeezing he disconnected the cord, and stuffed the thin box with its denuded flowers into his sack.

The whirring stopped.

Shouldering his pack, he leapt from the tabletop to the bench cushion.

The mother's footsteps grew louder as did the sound of something being dragged across the floor.

He tossed the rope and grappling hook onto the rug below. Hanging over the edge of the bench, Mungan lowered the sack as far as he could before dropping it. He jumped down and grabbed the pack as the bag/stick contraption and two enormous feet thundered towards him. The hook was too far away to reach. He had to take cover.

Mungan dove under the bench, leaving the tool out in the open. Hiding behind the wooden leg, he held his breath and watched the mother retrieve the witch's clothes from the rug just beyond him.

He remained poised to dash for the door should he be discovered. With her backside toward him, she tossed the clothing on the bed. Mungan stretched forward in a half-crawl for the rope and tried to gather it up, but one of the three points on his hook dug into the rug. He glommed onto the middle of the rope and retreated to his hiding place, pulling the free end until the mother stepped on it with her massive shoe. Unless she had "the gift," the hook and rope would not be visible to her as long as he held onto some portion of it.

The mother turned and planted her feet facing him. She slid the bench under the dressing table. Mungan scooped up his pack and moved as well to remain hidden underneath the seat. He held his breath as she bent down to pick a braided loop off the rug very near his hook. She did not notice it, a sure sign she was an ordinary mortal. The tension binding his chest eased.

The mother reached for the strange contraption, and the whirring started again, only this time, painfully loud. The bag swelled much like a bagpipe. But this was no bagpipe indeed, and certainly not melodic in any measure of the term. He had to get out and soon but would not leave his grappling hook behind. Hugging the wooden bench leg, he watched the mother push and pull the sticked beast back and forth, timing his move.

He sprinted to his hook and tugged the bronze point free from the rug. As he rose to dash back to his pack, the other end of the rope was drawn into the square bottom of the whirring contraption. The slack in the rope disappeared in a snap. Mungan fought to hold on to the hook, planting his heels in the rug. But the strength of the woman drawing the stick backwards lifted him off his feet like a fish pulled from the water on the end of a line. He crashed hard on the rug, and the block sucked more of the rope into its mouth. Mungan clung to the hook as the voracious monster dragged him closer.

Oblivious to his presence or predicament, the woman reversed her direction and pushed the contraption toward him. Even more of his rope was devoured and the base crashed into his body, sending him flying onto the block. Dazed and sprawled on the vibrating beast, he held fast to the grappling hook as she jerked him forward and back across the woven rug. 'Twas worse than the pitching of a ship on a stormy sea.

The whirring stopped, and she leaned the stick against the bed. The swollen bag deflated. Mungan pulled on the rope, and the dead stick yielded it slowly. He looped the rope as the woman stepped toward him. She organized the bottles and small cases on the tabletop. He ran round her legs, dove under the bench to snatch his pack, and raced from the witch's chamber.

Mungan dashed across the landing, passing the wicker basket he had seen in the mother's arm. Now 'twas filled with garments. He stepped round it and inside the lad's chamber to look for more boxes to plunder. A silver line just above the edge of the table next to the lad's bed caught his eye. He slipped his head and shoulder through the drawstring of his pack to free up his hands. With the help of the grappling hook, he scaled the bed, nimble as a spider.

Hastening to the table, he saw a thin box outlined in silver. This had a grey face with black bands on two ends. He picked it up and turned it over. 'Twas bigger in size, more like what Leannan had described and the back was silver. An apple was inscribed in the center of the box with a bite taken out of it and below the fruit—"iPod" just like the box he had stolen from the witch's chamber. There were no lines attached to this one, so he easily stuffed it into his sack. Surely one of these two had to be the wicked fetish.

As he rushed back across the lad's bed, Mungan glanced out the window and saw the tawny red boat approaching from the south. With the drawstring of his pack looped onto his hook, Mungan lowered his loot to the floor. He scrambled off the bedcover onto the rug, stuffed his tools into the weighty sack, and ran toward the doorway.

The mother stood at the railing. "Mum, do you have any laundry you'd like me to do?"

"There might be a few things in the hamper," the old woman called.

"I'll check." The mother entered the chamber across the hallway. Having no desire to negotiate the stairs as she came down them with either the basket, the whirring bag-beast, or both, he ran toward the laundry, slid the sack off his back, and flung it into the clothes. He dove in after it, tunneling through the smelly garments and dragging his pack down with him. He finished burying himself and his booty as the mother dumped more clothing on top.

The woman hummed a tune, picked up the basket, and descended the stairs, bouncing him with her triplet cadence. She dropped him hard on floor, bashing his head against the bottom of the basket.

Afraid of ruffling the clothes and drawing attention to himself, he lay still as a cupboard door squeaked opened, and something that sounded like grains of sand was poured. He heard a click and the burbling of running water.

Suddenly, the basket lifted from the floor. He tumbled with the clothes into a metal tub with a barkless, white tree trunk in the center. A waterfall cascaded on the opposite side of the tub from where he'd landed on his bottom. He lifted the pack to keep it from getting wet. The rising water reached his waist. The mother's large hand came into view for a moment before a lid clunked shut above the tub, sealing him in darkness deeper than the night.

He scrambled to his feet. If only he could say the spell and return to his true size. But at the speed that would happen, he'd likely knock himself out on the metal lid and tear it off its hinges. 'Twould be difficult for the mortals not to notice that. The sudsy water reached his knees.

The fetish! He eased the smaller of the two boxes half out of the sack and touched the white ring. The black panel cast a soft grey light on the tub wall. He aimed it up toward the lid and looked at the periphery of the square opening. A white lip curved the corner near the free end of the lid. He waded through clothing to stand beneath it.

Mungan shoved the fetish back in the sack, and the tub grew dark once more. The warm water reached his thighs as he fumbled to stick his head and a shoulder through the drawstring. With the pack secure, he jumped in the blackness, stretching for the lip. He missed and landed just as the base of the barkless tree twisted violently one direction and just as fast, back the other. He was thrown into the wall as the clothes he stood on swished beneath him. A dozen times he jumped from the water in the dark amidst the swirling clothes desperately clawing the air for the lip, until at last one hand found it and then the other. With every ounce of strength he could muster, he pulled himself up, his head banging on the lid and lifting it. He dropped his elbows into a slippery dish smelling vaguely of spring rain and inched his chest and then his torso up over the lip. With a final surge of strength, he swung his legs up and out of the tub and collapsed exhausted and sandwiched between the lid and the top of the big white box.

He shimmied out and eased the lid down so as not to make a sound. The top of the box was too far from the floor for leaping. Next to the box was a towel ring. He retrieved his grappling hook, tied it round his waist, and threaded the free end through the ring. Grabbing the rope, he swung toward the wall, and slowly lowered himself by loosening his grip on the free end a wee bit at a time. The rope was not quite long enough, leaving him to drop more than his height to the ground. The free end flew through the loop and landed on top of him.

The stairs creaked.

"It looks like our fishermen are returning," the mother called.

"I'll put the kettle on and set out some biscuits. I'm sure they'll be famished," the old woman said.

Mungan grabbed his pack and stole to the doorway, dripping along the way.

"I'm going to meet them," the mother replied.

He flung the pack over his shoulder and stole along the wall to the kitchen, hoping to dart out the door as the woman opened it. As he turned the corner in the hallway, the door slammed shut. He sighed and took refuge under the sideboard, waiting for the next opportunity to escape.

The old woman ambled across the kitchen after her daughter, opened the door, and stepped outside. She waved with one hand and cupped the other near her mouth. "Any luck?"

He could see the mother halfway to the dock. He scuttled out from under the server and passed through the door. He froze at the sight of the witch on the boat and the mongrel trotting toward the mother. The lass appeared to be holding something silver up to her face. No, it couldn't be. The black and white beast barked and bounded toward him.

"Och, not again," Mungan muttered. He ducked into the bushes and seized the ragwort stem. Struggling with his pack, he broke into a frantic dash, dodging and flailing at the low hanging branches that blocked his path while trying to keep his balance. The vicious dog thrust his head through the line of shrubs, sniffing furiously to find his prey. Picking up his scent, the mongrel charged through the bushes, snarling and baring large white teeth. Staying a hair's breadth ahead, Mungan broke free of the bushes at the front corner of the house, mounted his flying stem, and shouted, *"Gabh air iteig!"* Taking flight, he wobbled under the weight of his pack as he gained speed and height away from the snapping dog, who leapt madly to catch him.

"In your eye, ye mongrel!" Mungan yelled, shaking a fist and nearly tipping off his stem. The satisfaction of his narrow escape was tempered by his glimpse of the witch. Had she foiled him once again?

28 *it added up all wrong*

· the discovery ·

CAITIE STOOD ON THE SEAT BENCH OVERLOOKING THE BOAT cabin and snapped the picture of Mom and Grandma waving to them as Grandpa finished pulling the boat up to the dock. Balfour had jumped off and was trotting up to Mom when Caitie framed the picture. It would have been a good one if he had just stopped to greet her, but he bolted toward the house instead, barking like crazy. Caitie glanced at the display. Sure enough, Balfour was blurred. She turned the camera off and slipped it back into the pocket of her hoodie.

Robbie scrambled out to meet Mom while Ross secured the dock lines.

She swung one leg over the side and onto the pier. "That was pretty fun, Grandpa."

"Do you suppose there's bagpipe music for an iPod?" he asked her, looking totally serious.

He couldn't be expecting her or Robbie to listen to that stuff. "Why?"

"It might be enjoyable to have when you're out for a full day fishing."

"For you?" She couldn't believe what she was hearing. "You'd better watch out, Grandpa. First, it'll be an iPod, next a laptop, and before you know it, you'll be putting in a home theater. If you're not careful, you'll turn into a techno-geek," she half-teased.

He rubbed his chin. "Perhaps you're right. I'd best give it a wee bit more thought."

Caitie couldn't shake the chill of the loch and went to her room to curl up under a blanket and listen to her own music for a while. She took the camera and Robbie's iPod out of her pocket and set them on her chest of drawers before stripping off her hoodie and dropping it on the floor. She sauntered over to the vanity to get her iPod. It wasn't there.

She didn't want to believe her eyes. The charger was plugged into the outlet, but the iPod was gone. Her make-up was organized, and her clothes were off the floor. Mom must have been in her room. Maybe she'd taken it, but that didn't make much sense. Caitie marched downstairs to the kitchen where Grandma and Mom were doing dishes.

"Mom, where did you put my iPod?"

"I didn't take it," Mom said.

"You were in my room and now it's gone." She didn't even try hiding her frustration.

"I was in there straightening up, but I didn't take your iPod. In fact, I didn't see it."

"Well, when I left to go fishing, it was on the vanity plugged into the charger." She hurled the words at Mom.

"Just like your phone?"

She was ready to explode. "Yeah!"

"Caitie, do you see a pattern here? Because I do, and I don't like it."

"What?" Caitie lashed out.

"First, you misplace your brand new phone and accuse your brother. Now your iPod vanishes, and you want to blame me. Perhaps if you weren't so messy and took better care of your things, you wouldn't be losing them." Mom crossed her arms. Her eyes bored into Caitie's.

"I didn't lose it!" Caitie stomped out of the kitchen and up the stairs, slammed the door to her room, and threw herself on the bed. It squeaked in defiance.

Was she going nuts? No. She wasn't crazy, only mad, real mad. Maybe Robbie punked her with one of his stupid practical jokes. She'd kill him. That's what she'd do. She rolled off the bed and stormed into his room.

"What died in here?" She raised her hand to cover her nose.

"Nothing," Robbie said. "I just took off my boots. Where's my iTouch? I want that and my nano back now."

"I'll get you your nano, but I didn't take your iTouch."

"Well, it was on my nightstand, and now it's gone."

"Are you sure? Cause my iPod is missing too."

"What?" His blue eyes clouded with confusion.

"Robbie, somebody's stealing our stuff."

"Who? Why?" he asked with a half-laugh.

She didn't answer.

"Caitie?"

"I don't know, but in the last 24 hours, my cell phone and iPod and now your iTouch have disappeared." A thought as chilling as an ice bath made her shiver. "I'll be back."

She hurried to her bedroom, picked up the nano as well as her camera, paused for a moment, and studied the two boxes in her hand. She wheeled around and dashed back to his room. She plopped down on the bed and sat Indian style, facing him. "Robbie, could they be after my camera?" She handed him his nano.

"Who?" he asked.

"Hellllloooo! The fairy or one of her friends." She looked Robbie square in the eyes. "I bet they've figured out she changed when I took her picture. They're after the camera so they can change her back."

"But how are they gonna do that?" he asked.

"I don't know. But if my Lumix did that to her, maybe they know how to reverse it with their magic or something."

"If they want the camera, why take the other stuff?"

"Think about it. I had my camera with me when the other things were taken. I took it to the ceilidh last night when my cell phone disappeared, and I had it today when we went fishing. All three things are kind of close to a camera in size."

"No way, Caitie. They're all super skinny compared to your camera. Nobody would be that dumb."

"She didn't know what a DVD was, Robbie. They wouldn't know the difference between that stuff and a camera. I bet they're not really sure what they're even looking for."

Caitie turned her Lumix on and put it into review mode so she could go back to the fairy's photo.

The most recent picture she had taken filled the LCD screen. Mom stood closest in the picture waving from the backyard. Balfour was the blur between her and the house. She remembered how he bolted, barking real loud at Grandma MacGregor. Grandma was in the background, standing by the door. There was a dark spot near Grandma's feet.

"OMG!" She zoomed in on Grandma MacGregor. "No way!" She couldn't believe what she saw.

"What? What is it?"

"Look." She pointed a trembling finger at the screen.

Robbie scooted over on the bed, twisting around and leaning his face near hers to see the picture right-side up. Her hand was shaking so badly that Robbie cupped both of his around the camera to steady it.

"Whoa," Robbie said, his voice wavering.

Clearly to the right of Grandma's feet was a super tiny man dressed in a rust shirt with puffy sleeves and what looked like khakis tucked into high boots. He carried a pack kind of like Santa Claus. She and Robbie turned and looked at each other for a long while without saying a word.

"So that little guy took my iTouch?" Robbie asked.

"I bet he did," Caitie whispered.

"Why didn't Grandma see him? He was right next to her."

"They're invisible. Remember? You have to have a four-leaf clover or drink potions or get that rainbow junk in your eyes."

"But he's like the size of a Barbie doll. Leannan was a giant compared to him."

"I know. But they've got to be connected somehow, Robbie. That's our stuff in his sack."

Robbie looked toward the window. "So those were his footprints in the garden."

"He must have followed us home from the mountain."

"If you showed Mom and Grandma, they wouldn't be able to see him either, would they?"

"I doubt it, since they couldn't see Leannan."

"So what do we do now?"

"I'm not sure what we can do." She laid the camera on her lap. With her elbows on her knees, she folded her hands and rested her chin on her thumbs, pressing her clasped fingers to her mouth.

"Caitie, do you remember what Grandma MacGregor said on the way home from the train station our first day here?"

"She said a lot of things. Which one are you talking about?"

"That we should ask Ross if we want to find out about creepy Scottish stuff."

"What good will that do?"

"Maybe he knows about fairies and he can tell us what to do."

"If Mom or Grandma couldn't see her in the pictures, I doubt Ross will be able to either. How much of our story can we tell before he thinks we should be locked away?"

"Well, I want my iTouch. And if you're right, that fairy-midget in the picture took it. Maybe Ross can help us capture this guy. He doesn't look very scary, and we're a lot bigger than he is. If we catch him, we can hold him ransom 'til they give us back our stuff."

She shook her head. "You catch one fish, and you think you're some superhero. Listen to what you're saying. Look, I'm not very happy about my stuff disappearing either. And I definitely don't want my camera stolen. But I don't think your ransom plan is gonna work."

"Why not? That guy's been here twice. I bet he'll be back again, once he figures out the iTouch and nano aren't your camera either."

"Robbie, they use real magic! I don't think we want to mess with these guys."

"Let's just talk to Ross and see what he knows."

"It's a bad idea."

"You haven't come up with anything better."

She wished she had a snappy comeback for him, but she didn't. "All right." Scooping up her camera, she went to the window. Ross and Grandpa MacGregor were by the shed. Grandpa took the filleted fish from him and headed toward the house with Balfour tagging alongside. "Well, if you want to talk to Ross, now's your chance. He's alone."

"Okay." Robbie slipped into his skate shoes, and the two left for the backyard, Caitie carrying her camera and Robbie leading the way.

"Where'd you disappear to, lad?" Grandpa asked as they passed each other going through the backdoor. "You should have cleaned your own fish."

"Sorry." Robbie kept walking.

Caitie shrugged her shoulders.

They found Ross wiping up an old stainless table on the side of the shed close to the Loch. The smell of dead fish and the site of their guts and blood made her want to heave. The heads and bones were in a bucket on the ground. She couldn't ralph in there, for sure.

"We'll be having a fine dinner tonight thanks to you two."

"Yup." Robbie puffed up his small chest.

"I guess," Caitie added trying not to think about the knotting sensation in her stomach. She gave Robbie her *well, say something* look.

"Ross..."

"Aye, Robbie."

"When we first got here, Grandma MacGregor said you know about Nessie and things like that."

"And what, my friend, is stirring your curiosity?"

"We're just wondering." Caitie realized she'd answered way too fast to be believable.

"Oh, I see," Ross said. "Well, the Scots are very superstitious going back hundreds of years. And many have said they've seen Nessie in the Loch as I'm sure you know, and then the stories go round and get passed down from one generation to the next."

"Yeah, we've heard about Nessie, but what about the other creatures?" Robbie asked.

"You mean the fae, selkies, banshees, ghosts and such?

"Yeah," Robbie said. "We know about ghosts, but what are those other things?"

"Banshees are mystical green women that wail down by the water when someone is about to die. Selkies are creatures that live off the islands. They can shed their seal skin becoming beautiful women and then lure men in boats to their death on the rocky shores. And, of course, there are many, many kinds of fae."

"Do *you* believe in them?" Caitie looked straight into his eyes.

"I think I'm finished here. Let's go inside the shed for a bit. I suspect this discussion may take a while."

Ross led her and Robbie through the weathered door into the ancient one-room house, smelling of wood smoke and new paint. Ross crossed the room to a tiny kitchen and washed his hands at the sink. "Have a seat."

They sat at the table beneath the window, facing each other.

"Now where do I begin?" Ross collapsed on the chair between them. "There are some people that can see things that others don't. Here in Scotland we call that ability 'the gift.' My mum was one of those people."

Caitie's heart started pounding. The fairy had asked her if she had "the gift."

"What did she see?" Robbie asked.

"She would never tell me. Having 'the gift' is troublesome, and something many don't care to confess. But I've heard many stories of those with 'the gift' who were able to see into the faerie realm."

"Is that the only way a person can see fairies?" Caitie asked, already knowing the answer to her question.

"No, they can make themselves visible to people if they choose to."

Robbie kicked her under the table.

She glared at her little brother. "Any other way?"

"Perhaps." He scooted his chair back and crossed to the nightstand. "I have something of my mum's that might give us the answer." Crouching down, he pulled a worn leather-bound book from the bottom shelf and brought it back to the table, gently opening the gold-gilded binding.

"It looks old," Robbie said.

"It is. This book has been in my family for generations." Ross turned the yellowed pages with care.

The binding crackled as he searched the calligraphy finally stopping at a hand-painted picture of a four-leaf clover.

"Aye, here it is. Be patient as I try to translate the Gaelic. 'One who desires to observe the world of faerie can do so by placing a four-leaf clover in their cap. If one cannot be found, concoct a potion of calendula, which when swallowed will enable one to view the fae. Thyme works as well and also protects against faerie mischief.'"

Leannan had asked her about all that stuff.

Ross tilted his chin and folded his arms. "I can't help but suspect there's a stronger reason for your questions than mere curiosity."

"You're gonna think we're insane," Caitie said.

"If you explain to me what this is all about, I might be able to help make sense of it."

"We met a fairy while we were weaselling," Robbie blurted.

Ross sat up straight and bit his lower lip. His eyes filled with concern flashed between her and Robbie. "Tell me, did the fairy appear to the whole group?"

"Huh-uh. We got left in this cave for a while 'cause some girl was stuck ahead of us. I was sitting on a rock, leaning against the cave wall. And then it went out behind me. I fell backwards and hit my head. And someone started whispering, telling me to get up."

"Robbie, do you suppose the bang on your head could have made you think you were hearing something?" Ross asked.

"I saw her," Caitie said. "She was surprised I could and started asking me if I had 'the gift' or if I'd drunk a potion of the stuff in your book."

"And you hadn't, right?" Ross's eyebrows crinkled with the question.

"I didn't drink any potion," she said indignantly. "But Willie Matheson gave me a four-leaf clover before we went weaselling, and I put it in my helmet so I wouldn't lose it."

Ross closed his eyes like that was the last thing he wanted to hear. "Oh, Caitie."

"But I never heard of fairies living in caves," Robbie said.

"Here in Scotland, different kinds of fae live in different places. Some in the forests, but many are said to occupy fairy hills, living underground. The Daoine Shi are known for that."

"That's them!" Robbie cried. "Our fairy Leannan said she was a Daoine Shi."

"She was pretty at first, Ross," Caitie said. "And then tried to prove she was a fairy by doing magic."

"What did she do?"

Robbie brought his hands to his face. "Leannan started breathing out this sparkly stuff," he said, talking with his fingers, "and when it hit the walls and floor, the cave started changing into a room like you'd see in a castle."

"Some of that sparkly stuff got in our eyes and hit the camera. And the second I took her picture, she turned into this ugly, old witch and ran through a secret door in the cave wall."

"And the cave went back to looking like it did before the sparkly stuff landed on it," Robbie added.

Ross sat back in his chair as he listened, one arm lying across his stomach, his other hand stroking his chin.

"It's like the sparkly stuff touched the lens when the shutter opened, and her magic got sucked inside my camera. Robbie and I are the only ones who can see

Leannan and the fancy furniture in the picture. Mom and Grandma just see Robbie in the cave."

She turned the camera on and scrolled to the photo of the fairy before passing it to Ross. He looked at the screen. His brow twitched and for a moment, a hint of a frown crossed his face.

"You can see her Ross! I saw it on your face. You have 'the gift,'" Caitie said.

He looked her in the eyes. "Aye."

"And now our stuff is disappearing," Robbie added. "First, Caitie's cell phone vanished while we were at the ceilidh, and now, my iTouch and her iPod are gone."

"We're pretty sure it's because of Leannan," Caitie said. "We think they're after my camera, and I've got another picture to prove it. Let me show you."

Ross gave her back the Lumix, and she pulled up the picture of the little guy and zoomed in. She handed him the camera.

"Oh my. This is indeed a problem." Ross stared out the window. "Caitie, if they've come for it twice, you need to leave the camera out for them."

"No way! It's from my Dad."

"I wouldn't tell you to if I didn't think it was best. I understand the camera means a lot to you, but I'm afraid you'll be in danger if you don't give it up. They say the fae can be mean and nasty. They're known for thieving, which you've obviously discovered yourselves. For pinching sleeping humans until they're black and blue, destroying herds, and even stealing babies."

"But Ross..."

"You've been lucky so far, Caitie. And I'm afraid they..."

Her heart hammered loud in her ears. "I don't care what they do to me. I'm not gonna let them have it."

"I'll get you a new camera," Ross offered.

"I don't want a different one!" Her cheeks burned with rage.

Robbie looked panicky. "You got to give it to them. They're gonna hurt us."

"I won't do it!" Caitie shook her head. "You wouldn't let them take away the knife Dad gave you. And I wouldn't ask you to either."

There had to be another way!

29 *plans were made*

· the plot ·

HALF-PAST 5 IN THE AFTERNOON
JUNE 26TH

LEANNAN HUDDLED ON THE FLOOR OF THE DANK DUNGEON, her back to the five coffins stacked against the far wall. A single candle outside her cell sent its faint light filtering through the narrow slots of the door's iron bars. The dim illumination could not hide her grotesque hands and the rags that covered her. Her stomach ached with hunger from two days of missed meals. She willed her essence to melt into the blackness in hopes of ending her misery, but her spirit would not comply. Clicking heels and jangling keys broke the silence. Stiff from sitting too long on the cold stone floor, she moaned as she stood to see who approached.

Cormag strode into the dungeon and scowled as he inserted the ancient brass key into the lock.

"Your Mungan is returning."

"He is not *my* Mungan," she rasped.

"Suit yourself. But he is a fool to risk his life trying to help ye." The door groaned as Cormag opened it with gloved hands.

Leannan chose not to reply. He clutched her arm and steered her back up the long passageway to the banquet hall lit by the rosy torch glow of twilight. She shuffled awkwardly as he paraded her before the gathering crowd toward King Oseron's throne. Her shame weighed so heavy she could not look into any of the surrounding faces, especially not the king's.

"Leannan, Your Majesty," Cormag announced.

"And where is Mungan?" King Oseron asked.

"I am here." He stepped through the crowd and approached the throne. Mungan swung his large pack from his back, loosened the drawstring, and dug deep to pull out two thin boxes—one black and silver, the other white with a split string dangling from it. He smiled at her with pity in his eyes. 'Twas almost more than she could bear; yet a smidgen of hope welled deep within, for he had not returned from the mortals' croft empty-handed.

"I see ye have managed to bring back more than one item on your venture," the king said.

"Aye, Your Majesty."

"Leannan, are either of these the culprit box?"

She wished she could be sure. "I cannot say, Your Majesty."

Earnan drew close to Mungan. "May I see them?"

Mungan handed him the larger black and silver box.

The wizard studied the silver side, flipped it over, and held the fetish in the palm of his hand. He pressed a round button at the bottom of the black face with a tentative finger. Leannan watched the box come to life with a myriad of colors. Earnan smiled triumphantly for a moment. He then drew a deep breath and pursed his lips. "It is advising me to *Slide to unlock*."

"Then do as it says, but be careful," King Oseron admonished.

The wizard slid his pointed boot across the floor, and the box went black.

"What happened?" the king asked.

"Nothing." Earnan touched the box a second time and slid his finger across the black face.

"Well?" King Oseron asked impatiently.

"Small squares with images have appeared."

"What of?" Mungan asked.

"Some I do not recognize. But there is a water droplet, a snowflake, a ghoulish face, and a picture of a warrior's head."

"Does the box give any further instruction?" King Oseron asked.

"No," Earnan said.

"Then press upon the warrior," King Oseron ordered.

The wizard nodded, touching the helmet with his pointer finger. His eyes widened.

"What is it?" King Oseron demanded.

"Moving pictures have appeared of warriors running on a wooded path. Strange carriages with shells that resemble turtles are chasing after them. The men are attacking with bizarre weapons." Earnan's voice grew more concerned with each description of the scene playing out on the box. "A carriage just exploded in a flash."

"A flash burst forth from the box that stole Leannan's magic," Mungan said.

Leannan wanted to believe this could be the box, but she remembered no images of battle, only the intense flash of light.

"This could be the one, Your Majesty," Mungan said.

"But the flash Leannan described was bright," the king countered.

"'Tis true," Earnan said. "However, just now, the box was not breeched by magic as was the case with Leannan back in the cave."

King Oseron, his face knotted with frustration, waved off Earnan. "Then cast a spell."

Earnan turned to Leannan and held the box with the moving pictures facing her. He drew his wand from a deep pocket in his robe. Tapping the silver box with it he commanded, *"Thig a mach agus till innte a rithist!"*

Heart pounding, she watched a warrior run and the land around him explode. The moving picture went black. She felt no different. The warrior reappeared in the woods just as dead as the hope within her.

"What, do tell, is the point of that contraption?" the king demanded. "Are we to feel threatened by this wee display of war?"

"I know not." Earnan shook his head bewildered. "May I examine the other box?"

Mungan exchanged the larger box in Earnan's palm with the smaller white one.

The wizard slipped the length of the cord through his fingers until he reached the two hard white bulbs with the grey circles. "Mungan, do ye know what these strange looking eyes are for?"

"I cannot imagine."

"Come close, Leannan," Earnan said.

She hobbled over to him, her bare feet soaking in the cold from the marble floor. He pressed the white circle inside a grey ring on the box, and musical notes appeared with words beneath.

"What is it?" King Oseron asked.

"It brings a message," the wizard answered.

The king sat forward on his throne. "What does it say?"

Earnan looked at the king in alarm. "'You're Busted.'"

"Busted?"

The wise wizard appeared perplexed. "Perhaps it means burst or broken."

"This impudent witch does not know whom she goads!" King Oseron's voice rose in anger.

"I do not believe the message is from her."

"Then who pray tell sent it?" the king demanded.

"It says, 'I Yo King' and below that 'Warned.'"

"They informed their ruler of the incident with Leannan?"

"I cannot be sure. Perhaps there is more." Earnan pressed the center button a few times, but nothing happened.

"Is there anything else of significance on the box?" King Oseron asked agitated.

"There are symbols resembling arrows, two opposing double arrows, and a single larger one."

The king drummed his fingers on the arm of the throne. "Arrows are weapons of war."

"Perhaps the witch pressed the arrow to steal Leannan's magic," Mungan said.

"Then do not aim that box at anyone else and do likewise, Earnan!" King Oseron shifted on his throne.

"Aye, Your Majesty, but perhaps if I press the arrow and cast a spell I can draw her magic out of the box and send it back to the maid."

The king sighed. "Ye have my permission to try."

"Leannan, do ye remember these strange eyes?" Earnan pointed to two white bulbs.

She strained to recall the encounter in the cave, but it happened in the flutter of a butterfly's wing. "No, I do not. But I caught only a glimpse of the box."

The wizard pursed his lips; his eyes shifted from her to the strange object and back. "Then hold the eyes so they are facing ye." Earnan gave her the two hard pieces at the end of the split cord.

With shaking hands, she did what Earnan told her too.

Holding the tip of his wand poised on the arrow, he said in a commanding voice, *"Thig a mach agus till innte a rithist!"* Pressing the arrow with the wand at the end of the incantation, a tinny tune burst from the white bulbs, taking her by surprise. She dropped the singing eyes. They swung down bouncing off Earnan's glowing purple robe while she remained a hag.

"What is that noise coming forth?" King Oseron asked.

"'Tis a strange melody, Your Majesty." The wizard tapped his wand thrice on the box. *"Fàs nas fuaimnich!"*

A peculiar drumbeat thundered in the hall, and a voice spoke in a sing-song rhythm.

"You got a dark little secret you been trying hard to keep.
It's a dirty little scheme – ain't no way you gonna sleep.
You been busted – now I'm after you,
You been busted – don't think I got no clue,
You been busted – don't deny it's true,
You been busted; busted, busted, busted."

The dulcimer player tapped his toe while the piper flexed his knees. King Oseron sat up straight on his throne.

"I know what you are, don't hide it anymore,
Saw a window to your world, now I'm standin' at your door,
To bust you, I ain't no helpless fool,
Gonna' bust you, Don't care if it be cruel,
Gonna bust you; bust you, bust you, bust you."

"Silence!" King Oseron cried. "Do they believe we can be intimidated by such a ridiculous battle cry?"

Earnan tapped the box with the wand, and it fell silent. "Perhaps 'tis merely a tune and not a threat, Your Majesty." The wizard's voice was as calm and cool as a pond on a still afternoon.

"No! This I Yo King delivers a declaration of war upon us! They plan to attack the mountain." King Oseron pounded his fist on the arm of the throne.

"I believe not, Your Majesty. If the mortals planned to declare war on the Daoine Shi, I cannot help but believe they would not leave the means of delivering the message on a lass's dressing table," Mungan said.

"I must agree." Earnan held out the white box with its promise of violence to Mungan.

The king tugged at his lip in silence. "Fate has thwarted your efforts a second time, Mungan." King Oseron paused. "I have no choice but to impose the penalty of the Tàcharan."

Mungan looked into Leannan's eyes with an apology so profound her heart ached more for his anguish than her own plight.

"Ye tried," Earnan said.

Mungan scooped the sack holding his tools off the floor and dropped the mortals' belongings inside.

He stood beside her and faced the king.

"How old are the mortals?" King Oseron asked.

"The witch is a young woman, and the lad is several years younger, perhaps eleven or twelve," Mungan answered.

The king sat back in his throne and crossed his arms. "Leannan, I believe ye said the witch is solely responsible for stealing your magic. Is that so?"

"Aye," she answered in a quiet rasp.

"Your sentence then for the act of sedition is to become a changeling for the witch. Cormag, ye will deliver Leannan to the mortals' home."

A heartless smile curled the guard's lips. "Of course."

"Earnan, ye will perform the transformation," King Oseron commanded.

The wizard nodded, resignation in his eyes.

"Mungan, ye will lead the expedition, for ye alone know the location of the croft."

"Aye, Your Majesty." Mungan dropped his head.

"Ye will bring the witch here to answer for her actions."

The crowd murmured. There had not been a kidnapping in over four hundred years. Leannan had only heard stories of the last troublesome Daoine Shi who had become a changeling. He never returned. The old ones said he withered away, and the baby stolen in his place had been raised as a Daoine Shi. Their identity was still a guarded secret amongst the elders. Now she would know the same fate for the trouble she had wrought.

"As for the lad…" King Oseron continued.

"He is innocent," Leannan croaked.

"He saw ye, did he not?" the king asked.

"Aye, he did," she answered, "But 'twas I who revealed myself to him. He did not try to intrude upon our world."

"The code demands that he be blinded. Earnan, ye will see to that as well."

The crowd gasped.

"Blind an innocent lad?" Elvy boomed.

"Aye, a wee lad?" Alvy and Ulvy echoed in horror.

"No, please, Your Majesty," Leannan begged.

"Your Highness, may I speak?" Mungan asked.

"Not if it is to request a delay in Leannan's sentence."

"'Tis not."

"Then proceed."

"May I suggest we carefully consider our options that we may pursue a more amiable resolution with the mortals?"

"The code is very clear, Mungan," King Oseron said.

"Aye, but I have seen firsthand what dangerous means they have at their disposal. I fear for the safety of us all should we start a war with them. Perhaps we can implore the witch once she is here to tell us where the fetish is that stole Leannan's magic. Then it can be retrieved and peace maybe maintained."

"And who pray tell would go after the box?" King Oseron asked, tilting his head with mock curiosity and twisting his wrist as he extended his fingers in Mungan's direction.

"I would be willing to bring back both the box and Leannan if the witch complies. 'Twould have to be done in the wee hours, so as not to alert the other mortals in the house. Once Leannan's magic is restored, the witch can be returned."

"And ye are willing to let a young lass roam the Highlands sharing her knowledge of our mountain with whomever she pleases?"

"Earnan can help us with a spell to cloud her memory."

"That can be done," the wizard offered.

The king let out a deep sigh. "What do ye propose to do if the witch will not cooperate?"

"Then she will remain a captive."

King Oseron rubbed his jaw as he pondered Mungan's suggestion. "Agreed."

"And if Leannan finds the box on her own?" Mungan queried.

"She has three days or she too will pay the price."

Mungan looked to her.

"I understand," she rasped.

"That leaves the lad," Mungan said. "He may be more helpful to Leannan with eyes that can see."

The king looked up at the wheel-spoke chandelier and sighed. "All right."

Leannan was grateful for Mungan's quick thinking. She could certainly use all the assistance she could muster, for if the lass did not cooperate, she had only three days to find the magic box or die.

30 *from one realm to another*

· the intruders ·

NEAR MIDNIGHT
JUNE 26TH

LEANNAN CRINGED AS SHE PASSED THROUGH THE PORTAL, re-living the encounter with the witch and lad that had sparked the dreadful catastrophe leading to this moment. Humiliated by the trouble she had caused, Leannan remained silent as they left the black cave behind.

The full moon shone through wispy clouds of silvery white, illuminating the mountain path with a beauty she could never capture on canvas. The air smelled sweet from the summer wildflowers, and she welcomed the soft breeze coming across the Loch. It gently ruffled what was left of her once lovely hair. Had the circumstances been different and her heart not full of fear and remorse, she would have savored every moment of this venture outside the mountain.

Mungan brought them to a ragwort patch and broke off three stout stalks, handing one each to Earnan and Cormag. Their Searsanach spoke the spell, and in the swish of a horse's tail, his height was well below her knee.

"Do not tarry, Earnan. I will not change until ye have turned Leannan into a wee one," the guard said.

"What is the matter Cormag? Afraid Leannan may step on ye if she has the chance?" Mungan asked.

The guard looked at him with contempt and muttered, "'Twould please me to mash ye both like tatties."

"Are ye ready, Leannan?" Earnan asked.

"Aye, I am," she replied.

"Beagaich!" Earnan commanded as he circled his blackthorn wand round her head and dropped it low in a flamboyant gesture. From the look on the wizard's face, she feared she looked more shriveled and repulsive than she had the instant before.

The old wizard diminished his size with the same flair he had used to alter her. Once Cormag saw no one else could be a threat to him, he shrunk himself as well.

"Let us waste no more time as the summer night will be short," Mungan said.

Cormag climbed onto his stem with the flower in the front. "Come, Leannan." She hesitated, knowing not where to sit.

Mungan shook his head in disgust. "Ye will have a splendid view of where ye have been, Cormag, unless ye reverse yourself for in case ye have not noticed, your mount is backwards."

"I was merely… looking to see that the stem had the proper droop," the guard said, defiance in his voice.

"I would sooner believe our mountain capable of crossing the Loch than that excuse," Mungan said.

A smile crept across her face.

Cormag sneered. "Grin like that again, Leannan, and ye will find yourself plunging to the ground far below."

She bit her lip to prevent aggravating the guard further as he turned round. Then she climbed on behind him and wrapped her arms about his waist.

"Not so tight," he complained.

"I do not wish to tumble and take ye with me," she answered.

Earnan tucked his wand into his belt and mounted his stem.

"There is a wee problem at the mortals' croft," Mungan said.

"Do tell!" The wizard's forehead wrinkled with concern.

"There is a snarling mongrel of substantial size with a vicious bent toward us fae. He has a loud and persistent bark, and escaping his notice is nigh impossible."

"When we draw near, let us circle high till ye spot him. Then lead me by him low, and I will do the rest."

"Very well." Mungan aimed his stem away from the mountain and cried, *"Gabh air iteig!"* He shot off the boulder-strewn hillside.

Earnan gave the same command and rose into the air.

Cormag repeated the magical charge and took off wobbling. Leannan's bare feet painfully scraped the rocks below. She gripped him tighter.

"Ugh," Cormag grunted.

They set off across the Loch, Mungan glancing back on occasion to ensure that Cormag and Earnan were still following. His mahogany curls and cloak ruffled in the wind. She dearly wished it were Mungan's stem she shared instead of the surly guard's. But given her condition, 'twas better that she ride with Cormag, for they made a truly repulsive pair; him inside and her out. If misfortune befell them on this journey, the Daoine Shi would indeed be better off with the loss of both.

Leannan watched Earnan take in the beautiful scene, first eyeing the delicate clouds and then peering down at the Loch shimmering like thousands of diamonds on black velvet. His long silver hair fluttered in the breeze. It had been a very long time since any of them, but Mungan, had been out flying. Leannan could not help but enjoy the light wind on her face. It was damp and cool, and unlike the still dungeon air, gloriously fresh. Her heart beat faster as they approached the other side of the Great Loch. 'Twould not be long now before they would be in the witch's chambers.

Cormag followed as Mungan circled high above the croft and pointed to the dog below, asleep near the barn door. The wizard nodded and whipped his wand from his belt. With it poised in his hand, Earnan plunged after Mungan, swept past the dog, and cast a spell to keep the beast quiet.

Soaring to the rooftop, Mungan and Earnan landed smoothly on the slate tiles. Cormag aimed the stem downward, and Leannan braced herself as they barreled toward the looming chimney. Turning too late, they collided with the corner of the stone column, knocking her off the stem.

"Ahh!" she cried as she slipped and rolled down the tiles toward the edge of the roof. Mungan raced to her rescue, grabbed her hand, and held fast as her legs flew over the edge, dangling dangerously. He pulled her to safety and glowered at the guard. "Do ye think it possible for ye to be any more careless?"

Cormag ripped her from Mungan's grasp. "'Twas all her fault. She held so tight I could not steer properly."

Mungan shook his head and sighed. "The witch will be upstairs, along with the lad. There is a third bedchamber up there and one on the floor below. I suspect all will be occupied."

"Shall we use the chimney for an entrance?" Earnan asked.

"Aye, I was hoping you could assist us with a bit of magic."

"Of course," Earnan's eyes glistened in the moonlight.

Mungan climbed atop the chimney and reached down to help Leannan up. Cormag grumbled at giving her a boost before shimmying up himself.

Earnan flew to the top of the chimney on his stem. Pointing his wand at Mungan, he commanded *"Tuit gu slaodach!"* Mungan stepped off the stone, grinning at her and Earnan as he floated down the black flue like a marble sinking in heavy oil. Cormag edged over to the hole, his hand once again fiercely gripping her arm.

"No tricks, Earnan. I drop down slow just as Mungan did."

"Ye should have more faith in your fellow Daoine Shi, Cormag. I am not here to bring trouble or harm to ye just for the amusement of it."

Cormag scowled at Earnan who cast the spell again as she and the guard stepped off the chimney stone, sinking into the darkness. Her stomach rose ever so gently as they descended, more out of fear than speed. They landed unharmed on the sooty fireplace grate. Mungan held back the metal curtain for her with his boot. Cormag pushed on the iron mesh with his hand and winced. "Move," he said, shoving her onto the hearth. Raucous snoring upstairs disturbed the dwelling's peace.

Earnan fluttered down, holding up his glowing robe to avoid the ash. He swished his wand, the curtain parted, and he high-stepped out from behind the mesh screen on the balls of his pointed silver boots. With a flick of his wand and a quiet *"Sguab sùithe"* the fireplace brush swept away their sooty footprints, and the mesh closed once more.

"Follow me," Mungan whispered.

Her heart pounded, and her arm ached under Cormag's crushing grip as she crossed the drawing room floor to the rug at the base of the stairway. Leannan looked to the top of the daunting steps uncertain as to how she could make it all the way up with her hobbled feet.

"Steady yourselves, and I shall make this ascent much more pleasant," Earnan said in a hushed tone.

"'Twould be most appreciated." Leannan shook from her head to her backward toes with the prospect of what awaited her at the top of the stairs.

Earnan pointed his wand at the rug beneath their feet. *"Gabh air iteig!"* the wizard commanded.

The rug took flight over the stairs up to the landing.

Cormag yanked her off of it as soon as it settled on the floor.

"There's no need to be so harsh," Mungan scolded.

Cormag scowled. "I am the one in charge of the prisoner."

Bedsprings squeaked and a light went on in the closest bedchamber. Mungan put his finger to his lips to silence the guard. The lad sat up and padded out of his room yawning. He stopped short and his mouth froze, hanging wide open.

Leannan looked up at the giant of a lad and knew he could see them. Mungan must have too for he ordered Earnan, "Make him wee!"

"Beagaich!" Earnan pointed his wand toward Robbie and swirled it in a circular motion before dropping it low to the floor.

31 *a tiny nightmare*

petrified

HALF-AWAKE AND TRUDGING TO THE BATHROOM, ROBBIE stopped short as a miniature old man in a robe glowing like Fierce Grape Gatorade in sunlight swirled a small stick at him. Two other Barbie-sized guys close by held the arms of a third that looked like a Halloween mini-monster come to life.

Robbie's jaw hung open. His brain fought to wake up and make sense of what he was seeing. He balled his fists and rubbed his eyes, hoping they'd be gone when he looked again. They were still there.

The purple-robed old guy dropped his stick low to the ground, and Robbie's stomach jumped to his throat the way it did on Supreme Scream at Knott's Berry Farm when he and Dad free fell for what felt like a billion feet. The skin all over his body smooshed like he'd been shrink-wrapped by those decorative bands that tighten around Easter eggs in boiling water. His eyelids slammed shut. Just as fast as it started, the squishing stopped.

He opened his eyes. The banister looked like a skyscraper. The little guys and mini-monster were all now taller than him. He knew that monster. "Leannan!" Robbie cried. The fairies were here. They'd shrunk him. And the guy in the rust shirt had to be the one Caitie had taken a picture of.

The four started walking toward him real slow. He scooted back.

"How is he able to see us?" the old guy in the purple robe asked.

"He must have 'the gift,'" the guy in the rust shirt said.

Leannan turned to the wizard. "Perhaps the glamour got in his eyes when they captured my magic."

"Caitie! Mom!" he shouted as loud as he could.

"They cannot hear ye," the guy in the rust shirt said.

"Who are you? What'd you do to me?" Robbie asked.

"I am Mungan. And we have made the playing field fair."

"I'm not playing any games. Make me big again."

Mungan shook his head. "'Twould not be to our advantage to do so. Ye have taken something of Leannan's, and we want it back."

Robbie's heart pounded so hard he thought it was gonna burst. "I never took a thing from you."

"But the witch ye were with did. She stole Leannan's magic with a silver box," Mungan said.

"Caitie's not a witch. All she did was take Leannan's picture. She didn't know she was gonna screw up her magic." Robbie glared at the guy from Caitie's picture. "You're the only ones stealing stuff."

"Give us the silver box and we shall leave," Mungan said.

"It's a camera. And I don't know where it is!"

"I do not believe ye. Now where is this camera contraption? Give it to us and I will return your other things."

"The king gave us orders and negotiating with the lad was not one of them, Mungan," the guy in the black shirt said.

What was that supposed to mean? I gotta get away from these guys. Robbie turned around and bolted toward his room as fast as his miniature legs would go.

"Get him!" Black Shirt shouted.

Robbie glanced back to see Mungan and Black Shirt running after him. *Where can I hide?* Maybe behind the books on the bottom shelf of the nightstand, but there wasn't time to climb over and down behind them.

The lower shelf of his bookcase next to the window held his RC truck. He raced around the corner of the bed and over to it. He climbed into the driver's seat of the monster truck, shut the door, and laid down, hanging off the passenger's seat as the remote control box took up most of the rest of it. With his chest heaving, he lay still on the hard plastic, straining to hear them.

"Did ye see where he went?" Black Shirt asked.

"No, but he has to be in here somewhere. Search under the bed," Mungan ordered.

He heard them rustling the bedspread.

"He is not there," Black Shirt said.

"Could he be in the wardrobe?" the old guy with the glowing robe asked.

"Dean mise nas àirde!"

The door to the wardrobe creaked softly.

"Leannan, come here." The old guy's voice was now raspy like a whisper only it was way louder. *"Fàs thusa nas àirde!"*

"Dean mise nas àirde!" Mungan commanded.

His voice was close, too close. He cautiously peeked up over the dashboard and saw a gigantic pair of polished black boots in front of the bookcase. One boot went back and the column turned from black leather to khaki fabric as Mungan dropped on one knee.

Robbie bolted upright in the driver's seat and turned on the RC box. The truck headlights came on and the motor whirred. He slammed the joystick forward. The truck flew off the bookcase.

Mungan's giant boots were square in the middle of the truck's light beams. Robbie ran the vehicle up and over them. He pushed the stick to the right, and the truck turned just in time to miss his bed. The desk was straight ahead. A hard left and he could head out the door of his room.

A pair of mega hands clamped onto the sides of the vehicle and lifted it off the floor, the wheels spinning in the air. Mungan's hands turned the truck around. Terror cinched Robbie's chest so tight he couldn't breathe as the leather cord lacing on the fairy's shirt appeared in the windshield, then strong neck muscles, a dimpled chin, smiling mouth, and finally piercing copper eyes.

"I have ye now, lad," Mungan's whisper reverberated in Robbie's ears.

The guy in the glowing purple robe touched a wand to the truck, and it went dead. The giant opened the driver's door. Robbie dove for the other side. He hooked his fingers over the open window frame on the passenger door. Mungan pulled on his legs. Robbie clung to the door frame his grip giving a little with each of Mungan's tugs. One hand broke free, and the other couldn't hold on any longer. His chest crashed on the hard plastic. He scraped and clawed at the seat as Mungan pulled him from the truck, the palm of the big fairy's hand wrapped around his legs. He was way too high to try to get free. If he did, the fall would kill him. Mungan stooped and the air whooshed past Robbie. The giant fairy set the truck back on the shelf, and Robbie wriggled to get free. Mungan only tightened his grip.

"Stop fighting, lad." Mungan stood again, and Robbie's stomach felt like he was on the Superman Roller Coaster at Six Flags as he was swooped up high above the bed and bookcase.

"Dean mise nas àirde!" Black Shirt said.

Robbie whipped his head around toward the wardrobe in time to see Black Shirt shoot up to the size of Leannan and the old guy in the glowing robe.

"Where is the camera contraption?" Mungan asked.

"I don't know!" Robbie sobbed. "Caitie hid it! She said it would be safer if only she knew where it was."

"I believe him," Leannan whispered.

"Then we carry out the plan just as the king ordered," Black Shirt said.

The old guy nodded his bearded head. "I must agree with Cormag."

"What about the lad?" Mungan asked.

"Leave it to me," the old guy raised his stick.

Mungan nodded and stepped next to the bed, thrusting Robbie toward the old guy's ski slope of a beard.

"Cadail gu trom!"

Instantly, Robbie's eyelids got heavy, and everything went black.

32 *it was one life for another*

· the exchange ·

LEANNAN'S BODY SHOOK FROM THE POINTS OF HER EARS to her backward toes, frightened by Robbie and his resourcefulness. Somehow even the Daoine dungeon seemed less formidable than this dwelling and its occupants.

Earnan cast the spell and the lad fell asleep in Mungan's grip. His wee head flopped down with his chin on his chest. "He shall believe it all a dream."

The terror etched on Robbie's face disappeared, just as it did on the day in the cavern when he had been so frightened.

Mungan laid him down on the mattress with his tiny head on the edge of the pillow. "Will he wake from the change?"

"No, for he is in the deepest of sleeps. *Fàs thusa nas àirde!"* Earnan swept the wand from the lad's head down to his feet with panache, stretching Robbie to his true size. His eyelids grew taut for a moment as though he were trying to open his eyes but then relaxed. Robbie shifted to his side, curled up like a wee bairn, and drew his arm beneath the pillow. Leannan pulled the tartan duvet up round the lad's shoulder to tuck him in.

Cormag's fingers dug into Leannan's arm tighter than a falcon's clutch on its prey. "There is no time for such dallying." She hid a smile as the surly guard tried repeatedly to blow out the mushroom-shaped lantern. It shined steadfast in defiance.

"Step aside, Cormag." Earnan doused the light with his wand, leaving the chamber illuminated only by the soft amethyst glow of his robe and moonlight spilling through the large window.

"I say we wake the witch and compel her to give us the camera contraption," Mungan said.

Cormag scowled. "Are ye daft? We could all end up as hideous as Leannan or worse."

His words stung Leannan as fierce as iron.

"But if there is a chance that we could bring this camera back now and end the trouble—" Mungan said.

"Ye are bound to execute the king's orders, or in your arrogance, have ye forgotten who rules in our mountain?" the guard said.

"I know my place, Cormag. I am merely thinking of how to best protect the Daoine Shi, as is my role."

Earnan scissored his beard. "I am afraid 'tis best to do as King Oseron has commanded."

Mungan opened the door and led them from the lad's chamber into the witch's. The wizard walked toward the head of the bed. Leannan hobbled after him and looked down at the lass sleeping soundly on her side, her mouth half-open and her hair strewn across the pillow.

Cormag bumped into the dresser. The brass drawer pull clacked lightly against its back plate. The lass stirred at the sound. She rolled on to her back yet remained asleep; the sound of her breath steady and even.

Earnan raised his wand over the lass's head and whispered, *"Cadail gu trom agus na dùisg gus an ruig sinn a bheinn!"* He swept his hand over her eyes. "She will not wake till we reach the mountain." With pursed lips, the wizard studied Caitie's face then pulled back the bedcover. "'Tis time," he said without looking at Leannan."

"Aye." A whirlpool of emotions swirled in Leannan's head—fear at what she was about to do, regret over what she had done, and joy in anticipation of shedding her wretched appearance.

Earnan outlined Caitie's body with his wand, creating a shimmering blue aura deeper than the clearest sky. *"Bi 'nad thacharan!"* he whispered and shifted the wand immediately from the lass to Leannan. With a flick of his wrist, the aura engulfed Leannan, transforming her. Her feet flipped round, revealing strangely colored toe nails. Her sagging body and flaky skin filled out to Caitie's shorter physique. Leannan ran her fingers through long, wavy hair and then pressed her new firm cheeks and soft lips. She ran her tongue over a full set of teeth and her spirit soared. Leannan felt strong and young once more.

"There." A satisfied smile crossed the wizard's face as he put his wand back in his belt.

Mungan's eyes shifted between Leannan and Caitie. "She's the witch's perfect twin."

Leannan turned to face the looking glass, and in the shadowy room she saw the lass's likeness in the reflection gazing back. Gone were her pointy ears; rounded ones took their place with hoops piercing her lobes. She was dressed in the same strange bedclothes as Caitie, a sleeveless undergarment with a deep scooped neck and soft dark trews that fit most poorly. Although the fabric felt comfortable on her skin, she felt self-conscious under Mungan's gaze.

"Ye must be careful, Leannan, and do not be so graceful or they will suspect something," he whispered.

"Aye." She smiled up at him. Her voice had changed as well to match Caitie's.

Mungan grasped her bare shoulders, and she tingled at his touch. "Leannan, ye must work quickly to find the silver box. Remember ye only have three days."

"I know," she whispered, "but I look and feel so much better than I did mere moments ago. May I not enjoy it for just a wee while?"

"No, there is no time for that. Ye must not let this world distract ye from your purpose here," his voice barely audible.

She lowered her head. "Ye are right, Mungan. I beg your forgiveness."

He smiled and gently squeezed her shoulders before turning to the bed.

With a flourish of Earnan's wand, the sleeping lass became wee. Mungan scooped Caitie up in his palms and rested her on his shoulder with one forearm. He led them from her chamber, across the landing where he retrieved the rug and returned it to its spot at the base of the stairs, before ushering them from the dwelling.

Leannan eased the backdoor closed.

"The ragwort stems are on the roof," Cormag said. "Earnan, can ye get them?"

"We need them not," Mungan said. "'Twould be too dangerous to fly with the sleeping witch." He looked at Cormag. "Balancing on a stem appeared difficult enough with two who were awake."

"Then how do ye plan to get back to the mountain?" the guard asked.

"We shall cross the Loch by skiff and carry her back the rest of the way."

"A fine idea," Earnan said.

"Ye should go back inside now, Leannan." Mungan nodded toward the door.

"Not just yet for I desire to see ye off." She reveled in the cool night air under the canopy of countless stars.

They stole past the sleeping dog, the stone shed, and out onto the pier. Mungan rested the wee lass against his shoulder and stepped into the white boat.

"I have not been on the water for a very long time," Earnan said as he lifted his glowing robe and climbed on board. "'Tis lovely to see the light of the moon dancing on the Loch, to hear the sound of the waves lapping against the boat, and to smell the water."

"'Tis likely dead fish," the sour guard said, dropping into the stern.

"No, 'tis life, Cormag," Mungan said. "Ye have lost the joy in yours, hence ye cannot sense it in the world around ye. Now get the oars out."

"No need," Earnan replied. "I shall sail us across."

"Farewell, Leannan," Mungan whispered. "I will come for ye in three days, if not sooner."

"I would not place a wager on that," Cormag said.

"And I promise I will find the camera in the meantime. Be careful," she said.

"And ye as well. Do not give yourself away," Mungan warned.

Earnan turned the skiff around with a swish of his wand and sent it gliding toward the opposite shore.

As she stood on the pier watching them sail away, her heart weighed heavy. She looked and sounded like Caitie, but she knew nothing of the lass. How could she fool Robbie and the rest of the family? Her life, however, depended on doing so and also on finding that camera.

33 *waking up on the wrong side of the Loch*

·kidnapped·

7:30 AM
JUNE 27TH

CAITIE DREAMED SHE WAS BEING STRETCHED LIKE A rubber band, fast and far, and it hurt so bad she woke up. An old man in a glowing violet robe bent over her. With crescent spectacles, long white hair, and a beard and mustache, it was the best Merlin costume she'd ever seen. What little she saw of his cheeks were rosy, and peering from under bushy brows were eyes the color of her birthstone amethyst. This had to be part of the same weird dream. She shut her eyes again and counted to three. She peeked with her left eye, then her right. Each time he was there. With both eyes open wide, she screamed as loud and as long as she could. He didn't go away, just covered his ears.

"Silence!" came a shout from somewhere behind her.

She bolted upright and twisted around to see steps leading to a king seated on a gold throne. It was like she'd been dropped into a movie set for King Arthur, only the make-up was weird, 'cause the actors and actresses all seemed to glow. That adrenaline rush that sets everything into slow motion took over as she started sorting out the bizarre nightmare. "Who are you and where am I?" Caitie already suspected the answer.

"I am King Oseron. And I will ask the questions."

She stood up and looked around the hall for a way to escape but found a whole crowd staring at her like she was from another planet.

"What is your name?" the king asked.

Somehow it didn't seem like a good idea to tell him. "Why do you want to know?" she asked.

The king's eyes narrowed, and he gripped the armrests on the throne, his knuckles going white. "I told ye I will ask the questions. Now give me an answer."

She steeled her eyes against the king's and said nothing.

"Ye have troubled us, and now ye shall pay."

"Troubled you?" she asked. "Look, I went to bed last night in my Grandma and Grandpa's house, and the next thing I know, I wake up here—wherever here is—and now I'm being accused of something I don't even know about. If this is some kind of a joke, it isn't funny, and I want outta here right now!" It wasn't exactly the truth. She figured this had to be tied to Leannan, but Dad always said, "Don't let a bully think you're scared."

The crowd gasped, and the king sat silent for a moment.

"Lassie," he said, syrupy sweet, "ye have been brought here by the three behind ye. And I am King Oseron of the Daoine Shi."

"Am I inside a mountain?" she asked.

"Aye, ye are," he answered. "Our mountain to be specific. Ye have done a terrible thing to one of our own."

"Oh." She lowered her eyes.

"Do ye know now what I am referring to?" he asked.

"I have a better idea." She looked up at the king. "I didn't mean to hurt her though. You gotta believe me."

"What did ye mean to do then?" The king thrust his hands in the air.

"Just to take her picture. I wanted proof she was real."

"Then ye admit ye wanted to steal something from her."

"What are you talking about?" Caitie asked.

"Ye just said ye wanted to take something of hers. And ye did! And now we want it back."

"When you take someone's picture, you freeze—"

The king shook his head. "She was not frozen."

"Okay, maybe frozen isn't a good word. It's like you capture their image."

"Did ye 'capture' her image with a box?"

"A box?" Caitie asked.

"Aye, a small silver box."

"Oh, you mean my camera. Yeah, I used my Lumix."

"Your camera Lumix captured more than Leannan's image. It stole her magic, and we want it back."

"I'm really sorry about that."

"Ye should be. Now where is this camera Lumix?"

"It's a Lumix camera, and it's not here. It's..." She decided maybe it wasn't such a good idea to tell him. "Have you been stealing stuff from me?"

"No, I have not taken anything from ye," the king answered like she'd majorly dissed him.

"Then who took my phone and iPod, and my brother's iTouch?"

His Royal Highness sat back on the throne. "If ye give me the Lumix camera, perhaps I can have the other items returned to ye."

"That camera was a gift to me from my Dad. I am not giving it to anybody!"

The king waved her off with his hand. "I am weary of this discussion. Cormag, when we are through here, take her to the dungeon where she can reconsider her words."

"Aye, Your Majesty." He grabbed her roughly by the arm.

"Stop it! You're hurting me, you big jerk!"

The guard eased the pressure on her arm.

"Where are Durell and Hefeydd?" the king called.

"I am here, Your Majesty." A tall guy in a green tunic, plaid Capri pants and boots broke through the crowd.

"And I as well, King Oseron," The crowd parted for another big guy wearing more medieval clothes.

The king nodded, and the two came alongside the cute guy in the rust shirt that had kidnapped her.

They each grabbed one of his arms like he'd just won a trip to the dungeon too.

"What is the meaning of this, King Oseron?" the cute guy asked.

"Mungan, it is with great regret that I report ye have betrayed each and every one of the Daoine Shi."

"What?" Mungan sounded clueless.

The king craned his neck like he was looking for someone. "Lileas, give an account of what ye discovered while tidying up Leannan's room."

A fat fairy standing near an arch came forward, her chin trembling. "A sack with paintbrushes and a gallery's worth of paintings in her wardrobe."

"'Tis not a crime for Leannan to paint," Mungan said.

"No, 'tis not. But to leave the mountain without my permission is," the king said. "What did ye find on the sack of brushes, Lileas?"

"Bits of grass and dirt." Her voice wavered.

"So Leannan's foray the other day into the mortal realm where she encountered this witch," King Oseron pointed to Caitie, "was not her first. And the many paintings of Highland scenery suggest she has committed this act of sedition on numerous occasions."

Caitie strained to get away from the guard's hold. "Hey, wait a minute, I'm not a witch!"

"Mungan, your relentless desire to help one who has broken the code, and ye, our Searsanach, has struck me as strange." The king sat forward on the throne, a hand on each knee. His expression changed like he'd just been backstabbed by his best friend. "Such behavior would only make sense if ye were in love with Leannan."

From all the whispering, Caitie figured this was some big shock.

"I—" the cute guy said, obviously trying to deny it, but the king wouldn't let him.

"And if ye knew of her secret journeys into the mortal realm."

"But—"

"Someone else found out about them too and confronted ye. That someone was your sister, my queen."

"I loved Tianna. I could never harm her."

"I want to believe ye, Mungan. But your behavior has been so determined in regard to Leannan. Lileas was distraught over what she found. Naturally, I convinced her to share what was troubling her. When I saw the evidence on Leannan's bag of brushes, I had no choice but to see if the suspicions haunting me were valid. The only way was to have her search your chamber. If ye were innocent, there would be nothing for ye to hide." The king looked to the fat fairy. "What did ye find there, Lileas?"

"A note from Queen Tianna." The fairy's eyes never left the marble floor.

"And what was written in the note?" King Oseron asked.

"That she was troubled, and she wanted Mungan to meet her at the portal before anyone was awake."

"Is that all ye found in Mungan's chamber?"

"No." The fat fairy bit her lip.

"Tell us, Lileas," the king demanded.

"I found...." She drew a shaky breath. "I found a wee trunk under Mungan's bed."

"And what was inside the trunk?"

"Queen Tianna's goblet with the bluebells." Her voice broke again. "Inside it were iron nails along with a vial of St. John's wort."

The crowd gasped in horror. Caitie had no idea what was going on, but this Mungan guy was in trouble. Big, big trouble, maybe worse than the mess she was in.

The king's fingers clenched his knees. "Ye killed Tianna so Leannan's secret would not get out. The life of my beloved queen was taken to protect the secret of a rebellious chambermaid. Take Mungan to the dungeon that he may rot in the bowels of the mountain for the treacherous deed he has done!" the king cried.

"But Your Majesty—"

"Silence!"

Two large guards jerked Mungan toward an archway. The bearded old man in the dark violet robe looked so shocked she probably could have knocked him over with a puff from Robbie's inhaler.

The king's henchman held Caitie's arm by a death grip as he dragged her from the large hall. They followed Mungan and the two guards down a dim passageway lit with torches that had peach flames. The cold marble floor on her bare feet made the goosebumps all over her ten times worse. The guard led her down a spiraling passageway deeper into the mountain until they arrived in the dungeon.

Her jailer opened one iron-barred door that was ajar using the toe of his boot and pushed her inside, slamming the entrance shut with a swift kick. He locked it with a huge curlicued key. She was surrounded by cold, black stone on the ceiling, walls, and floor. Five long wooden boxes were stacked against the back wall. A single metal ring, the size of her fist, hung on one of the cell walls. She remembered seeing prisoners or skeletons shackled to rings like that in the movies. It was hard to breathe the dank air.

An iron door close by banged shut, and she heard the clink of the keys as Mungan was locked in. She looked through the slits from the very narrow bars of her cell door more scared than she'd ever been in her whole life and watched the three guards swagger away.

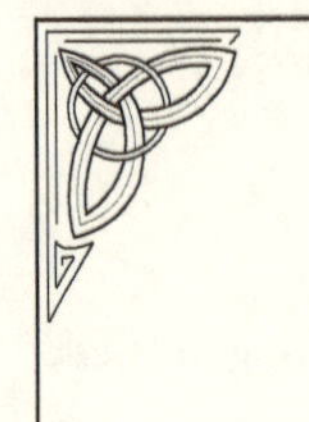

34 *the ruse began*

· the changeling ·

3:00 IN THE MORN
JUNE 27TH

LEANNAN RUMMAGED THE REST OF THE NIGHT AWAY IN Caitie's bedchamber, searching for the silver box but to no avail. If the lass was unwilling to tell even her brother where the camera contraption was hidden, her chances of finding it seemed dismal.

Glorious light filtered through the window with the rising sun, and as the night's shadows disappeared, her mood brightened. Sometime later the mortals stirred, yet she could not bring herself to join them down below. She tidied the bed and picked Caitie's clothing up off the floor. Should she dress first? Perhaps Robbie could help her without him even knowing it. She drew a deep breath and went to awaken him. Wrapped up in the bedcover, Robbie looked like a large, tartan caterpillar.

She laid a hand on his shoulder. "Robbie, the sun rose long ago and ye must as well."

There was no response from the lump on the bed.

"Robbie," Leannan shook him, "'tis time for ye to arise."

"Huh?" came his muffled reply. "What's gotten into you, Caitie? It's way too early to get up."

Leannan was careful to listen to his reply. "It's" for "'tis," "you" for "ye," "get up" for "arise."

"Come now. It's time for you to get up." She hoped that sounded better.

"Since when do you care?"

"I thought we could have breakfast together this fine morning."

"Who are you?" He pulled the tartan bedcover back from his head and looked into her face. "You never come get me for breakfast." He yawned. "Not on a 'fine' morning or any other."

In the briefest of moments, she had proven the folly of this ruse. He knew she was not Caitie, and now she was doomed. Still, she had no choice but to play the part to its bitter conclusion. The lass had been feisty in the cave. "I am fine, Robbie. Now come on." She yanked the duvet off of him.

"I guess it really is you. Only my sister is this mean." He pulled the bedcover back over his head.

She had done well and smiled. "Robbie, get up!"

"Leave me alone. I'm too tired. I didn't sleep so good. I had a bad nightmare."

She sat down on the edge of the bed already sure of what he was going to say. "What was it about?"

"Leannan came here. The ugly version of her, along with a wizard in a glowing robe and two other guys."

She cringed at his description of her.

"I caught them coming up the stairs. They were all small, and then they made me small too. They wanted your camera, and I tried to get away by hiding in my monster truck. But they found me. They made themselves big, and one of them lifted me out of the truck, and they were gonna do something to me."

"What?"

"I don't remember anymore."

"'Tw…It was just a dream, Robbie. Dwell on it no more."

He looked puzzled by her words, though she knew not why.

"It was creepy. And it seemed so real. Think they'll come here like that while we're sleeping?"

Without my magic, can I lie? "I hope not." The words slipped with ease off her tongue. Yet, she wanted this conversation to go no further. "Are you hungry?"

"Yeah." He stretched his arms wide, thrusting out his small chest and yawned.

"Good. Shall we go down then?"

He threw off the bedcover and plodded down the stairs. Bedclothes must be proper attire for breakfast in the mortal realm. She followed close behind.

"Good morning," an old woman said as they entered the kitchen.

"Morning, Grandma. Morning, Mom." Robbie padded over to a younger woman sitting at a small table holding a large paper covered with black print. He kissed her on the cheek, walked to the other side of the table, and plopped down on a chair.

"Morning, Grandma." Leannan mimicked him. "Morning, Mom." She kissed the young woman as well though 'twas most uncomfortable.

The grandma pulled several bowls out of an upper cabinet, and Leannan went to help her.

"You must be very hungry, Caitie," the grandma said.

"I am famished," Leannan said, unsure as to how the grandma knew.

The older woman dished out a large helping of porridge into a bowl and gave it to her.

"How kind of you, Grandma." Leannan waited for the woman to fill the other two bowls and carried the three large dishes to the table, one in the crook of her arm, and one in each hand. She served the mom and Robbie before herself.

"Thank you, Caitie." The mom cocked her head and gave Leannan a quizzical smile.

"You are most welcome." Leannan went back for the two stemless goblets of milk the grandma poured. Since the mom had a tiny tankard of sorts with steaming liquid, Leannan assumed the milk was meant for her and Robbie and passed him the beverage before sitting down next to him.

"Ross has graciously agreed to take me into town to go car shopping. Would you two like to go along?"

Leannan squirmed in her chair. What was car shopping?

"What kind do you want to get?" Robbie asked.

"I don't know. Something practical."

"Then never mind," Robbie replied.

"What about you, Caitie? Would you like come with us and do a little shopping afterwards?"

She did not want to go anywhere without the lad. "I don't think so. I thought Robbie and I could spend the day together enjoying the sunshine."

With those words, the mother set the paper down and looked her directly in the eyes. "Are you all right, Caitie?"

"Why, of course." Leannan hoped she sounded convincing.

"Turning down shopping to spend the day outside with your brother does not sound like the Caitie Anne Finlay I know and love."

"It does not?"

The mother squinted and crossed her arms. "No, it doesn't."

Leannan made another quick note of "doesn't" instead of "does not" and gave the woman a reassuring smile. "I…I'm fine, Mom."

The door opened, and a handsome man stuck his head inside. "Can you tell me where the binoculars are, Ina?" the tension evident in his voice.

"They're in the sideboard," the grandma said.

"What's wrong, Ross?" the mom asked.

The man shook his head, looking most perplexed. "The dinghy's gone, Maisie."

"What?" The mom's brow furrowed, and her pretty face grew serious.

"It's strange, isn't it?" He stepped through the doorway and over to the oak sideboard.

Leannan tried not to choke on her spoonful of porridge.

Ross opened and closed each of the drawers. "There appears to be a small white dinghy on the other side of the Loch, but before I take the fishing boat out, I thought I'd try to look at it through the binoculars. Ahh, here they are. Thanks." Ross scooped two black spyglasses joined together at the middle from the drawer and went back outside.

Robbie gulped down the rest of his porridge, handed his dishes to the grandma, and ran after him.

Moments later, Robbie raced back inside and shouted on his way up the stairs, "Hey, Caitie, Ross thinks it's our dinghy. We're going over to get it and tow it back. Want to come?"

"Certainly." Leannan picked up her bowl and odd goblet. "Are you finished, Mom?"

"Not quite, Caitie. But it was awfully nice of you to ask. My little girl is growing up."

If ye only knew. Leannan went over to the sink. "May I give these dishes a quick wash?"

The grandma was up to her elbow in clouds of bubbles. "No, you go ahead, Caitie. But thank you for the offer and for being so helpful this morning."

"You are most welcome," she said with a confident grin. Water trickled in the small alcove atop the stairs. Inside, Robbie scrubbed his teeth with a wee brush that had a very long handle. He had changed into blue trews and a tunic with sleeves that only partially covered his arms.

"Is it cold outside? For I know not what to wear."

Robbie spit blue froth in the sink. The sight turned her stomach. He rinsed the brush in the stream of water and shook it out. Droplets spattered everywhere. Several landed on her bedclothes, leaving tiny holes in the fabric. The breach in the material expanded. Why had Earnan not warned her? The clothes he conjured were melting. She had to change quickly or soon she would be naked.

"You'll be okay in jeans and a T-shirt." He studied her in the looking glass. "And maybe a sweatshirt." His brow wrinkled and he tilted his head. "How'd you get those holes in your tank top?"

She gathered the disintegrating fabric. "A wee mishap."

Robbie gave her the same baffled look often afforded the triplets back in the mountain.

"Whatever. Just hurry up and change if you want to go." Robbie dashed into his bedchamber, and she rushed into Caitie's, anxious to get out of the delicate replica of the lass's real clothes. She yanked open drawers in the chest until she found trews out of the same material as Robbie's, which had to be the jeans he spoke of. Throwing open the wardrobe doors, she sorted through Caitie's tunics, choosing one similar to his. Leannan hastily changed into one the bright yellow of buttercups. She took off the baggy trews and put the jeans on. They came nowhere near her waist and hugged her bottom. Despite buttoning them, an obscene hole gaped wide between two strips of metal sewn to the fabric. Desperate, she pulled up the metal tab at the bottom of the hole, and the jeans mended themselves. *Amazing!* The trews were most uncomfortable though compared to her flowing skirts.

Robbie crouched by the stairs, wearing a coat over his tunic and tying his shoes. He looked at her bare feet. "Aren't you forgetting something?"

"Aye, I am." Leannan returned to Caitie's chamber where she found a pair of shoes without sides. She slipped her feet under the straps with the shank on each shoe between her garish teal-painted toes and then retrieved the soft hooded shirt she had hung in the wardrobe. With the noisy shoes thwapping against the soles of her feet, she followed Robbie down the stairs and out the door to the garden. Robbie ran to the pier so she did too. Free in broad daylight, she yearned to dance, to sing, and capture the scene on a canvas—all at the same instant.

"Morning, Caitie." Ross shouted over a powerful clamor coming from the back of the craft. An acrid smell filled the air on the pier.

"Morning, Ross," she yelled back, having no idea who the handsome man was in this family.

"Can one of you release the hawsers for me?" Ross asked, pointing to the ropes.

"I will." Robbie freed the rope holding the front of the craft to the pier.

Leannan twirled in a slow pirouette, drinking in the beauty of the woods, hills and vast loch. "The cat's paws on the water are lovely."

"What cat's paws?" Robbie asked.

"That's what we Scots call white caps," Ross said. "Your sister's certainly starting to sound as though she's from here."

Leannan tried to appear as if grateful for a compliment. *I shan't make it through the day.*

"Come on, Caitie, time is wasting away," Ross said.

Leannan hesitated as she had never been in a boat before. He extended a hand to her, and she carefully stepped onto the side bench and then onto the floor of the craft. Ross passed her a padded orange vest.

"Am I improperly attired?"

He stared at her suspiciously. "Not once you get the life jacket on."

A jacket that gives life. What could that possibly mean?

Robbie jumped on board, picked up the other life jacket lying on the bench, and put it on.

Leannan put hers on and clicked together the strange clasp on the jacket's black belt just the way he did.

Ross moved a lever, and the craft magically floated backwards away from the dock. He turned the ship's wheel and pushed the lever in the opposite direction. The contraption hanging off the back roared, the boat took off, and Leannan fell backward.

"What happened, Caitie?" Ross asked.

Leannan pulled herself back up. "I'm afraid I'm just clumsy."

They flew across the water like a gull skimming o'er the sea, her long hair flying wildly in the breeze. The spray on her face thrilled her. If this was the beginning of her end, she would relish each moment of the adventure. All too soon, they reached the other side of the Great Loch. The boat slowed as they approached the skiff Mungan had taken.

"That's our dinghy," Robbie said. "It has the same blue trim."

"Aye," Ross answered. "But how did it get free from the dock and make it all the way over here?" He drew the fishing boat close to the bow of the skiff adrift near the shore. "Robbie, I need you to grab the rope off the bow."

"Okay." Robbie leaned over the side, but the waves rocking the crafts kept the rope just out of his grasp. He leaned out further.

"Caitie, help steady him," Ross ordered.

Leannan held his waist and braced herself against the bench. The instant the side of their boat dipped down and the skiff came up, Robbie grasped the rope and slid it through his hand until the free end came up out of the water.

"Good. Now come hold the wheel, Caitie, so I can secure the dinghy for the tow home."

"All right." She held the spindles, wondering how the journey back to the mountain went for Mungan and the lass.

Ross took the rope from Robbie, tied it to the back of their boat, and returned to the wheel. "Thanks."

"You are most welcome," she answered.

Ross studied her face for a moment, and she knew that if she still had her magic, he would see she was fae. Her knees went weak. "What is it?" she asked.

"Nothing," he replied. He moved the lever, and the contraption at the back of the boat roared, speeding the craft homeward with the dinghy in tow. "You two missing anything new this morning?"

"I'm not," Robbie answered, "What about you, Caitie?"

"Not a thing." She tried to flash a serene smile.

Ross eyed her. "Nothing's been returned then either, I suppose."

"No." Her stomach churned like the water off the back of the boat.

"Nope. My iTouch is still gone. And Mom's gonna be ticked when she finds out. She just gave it to me for Christmas."

Leannan's pulse raced. She focused her eyes on the shore, not wanting Ross to catch her gaze.

Before long, they were back at the dock.

"I promised to take your mum to Inverness to look for a car," Ross said. "Do you two want to come along?"

"Huh-uh. Caitie wants to hang out here."

He looked over at her. "Why? To message your friends back home?" He half-chuckled.

Did he *know* she was not Caitie? If so, how did he think she would get a message to the mountain? "No, it's so lovely I thought we could walk in the woods."

Ross's smile faded. "You surprise me, Caitie. I somehow thought you were more of a city girl. Just be careful. And don't get lost."

"Don't worry, we shan't."

Ross chewed his upper lip, and his brown eyes reflected concern.

She turned away, anxious to leave the boat.

Robbie grabbed her arm as she stepped on to the dock. "Stop trying to sound like you're from here. It doesn't work. It just sounds creepy."

"All right." She started for the woods.

"We'd better let Mom know where we're going," Robbie said.

"Fine. Go inside and tell her."

"I'll be right back." He ran to the house.

Leannan looked around the farm. 'Twas beautiful here. Robbie rejoined her, and they started off once more.

"Hey wait. Aren't you forgetting something?" he asked.

"What would that be?" Leannan replied.

"Your camera. You never go anywhere without it." His soft blue eyes looked at her incredulously.

She knew not how to respond and feared 'twas evident on her face.

"What's the matter, Caitie? Did you forget where you put it?"

Perhaps she could trick him into helping her find the camera. Surely, he would know better than she where to look. "No, I didn't forget." 'Twas not a lie as she could not forget where she put something she never hid. "Where do *you* suppose it's hidden?"

"No clue. So are you gonna get it or not?"

"I think not."

"Caitie, what's wrong with you today?" Robbie asked.

"Nothing," she said, knowing she was in trouble.

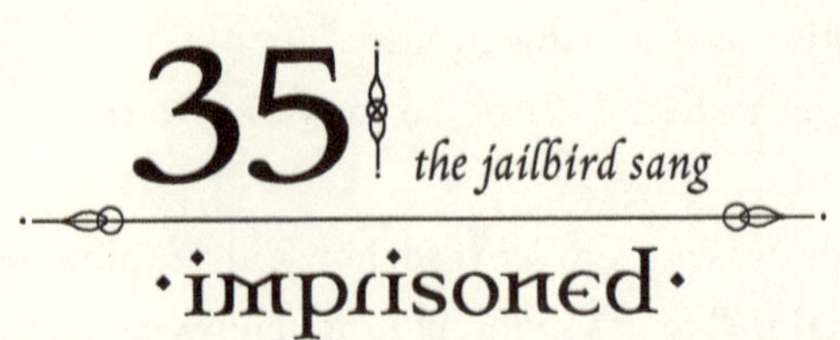

35 *the jailbird sang*

· imprisoned ·

HUDDLED IN THE MIDDLE OF THE DUNGEON'S COLD FLOOR, Caitie cried her eyes dry and wretched 'til the sobs were too excruciating. She sniffled and rubbed her arms covered in goosebumps. All she wanted was to get out of this mess, but she didn't have a clue how.

"Are ye finally done?" came the voice of the other prisoner.

She was too tired and miserable to think of a snappy comeback and the dirtiest look she could give him wouldn't pierce the stone wall between their cells either. "That was a rotten thing to say," was all she could manage.

"It has not been pleasant to sit and listen to ye wail for so long either."

"Look, I don't deserve to be here." She spat out the words.

"Clearly, King Oseron disagrees."

"It seems to me, Leannan is the one who's caused all the trouble. And I don't see her down here!" Every joint in her body was stiff so it took way longer than it should to get on her feet.

"Ye had no right to do what ye did to her."

"Well, if she hadn't opened that rock, none of this would have happened." Caitie plodded over to the cell door and wiggled her fingers through the thin spaces between the iron bars. How weird was that. Every jail cell she'd ever seen before on TV, prisoners could stick their hands through.

"Leannan only left the mountain as she feared she would be accused of killing the queen. The vile blaggard who murdered Tianna is truly the one responsible for this nightmare."

"Seems to me, your king's pretty sure you're the one who's guilty." She tried shaking the bars. They creaked, but held firm.

"I did not murder my sister. I loved her. The only thing I am guilty of is trying to help Leannan get her magic back."

"So you're the one that stole our stuff because you don't know what my camera looks like."

"'Twas not me who started the stealing, lassie. It seems ye initiated all of the thieving here."

"I didn't mean to though, and that's the difference." She stooped down and studied the lock. She'd never picked one before, but if she could get some kind of tool, it was worth a try.

"Whether or not ye intended to, ye stole what was not yours," he added.

"So why did you kidnap me?"

"I was not able to find your camera, and the king grew impatient."

"I don't like him." Caitie pulled out her hoop earring, worked it through the bars, and tried to stick it into the lock. It didn't budge.

"I do not believe he cares for you either."

"I've got to get out of here and get home. My mom and brother are going to freak when they realize I'm not there."

"They will know not that ye are gone," Mungan said.

She wriggled the hoop back through the narrow bars, wiped it off on her tank top, and stuck it back in her ear. "How can you say that? When I don't come down for breakfast, they'll come up to my room and look for me."

"And they will find ye."

"You're not making any sense. They won't find me if I'm stuck in here." Caitie inspected the door hinges, wondering if she could somehow take them off.

"Aye, they will as Earnan has made Leannan a changeling who looks just like ye."

His words were like a punch to her gut. "He couldn't."

"He did."

"So what do I do?"

"There is not much ye can do for now, only wait to see what the king has planned for ye."

Caitie stepped away from the cell door and began to whimper.

"Please do not start that again. I cannot get away from ye," Mungan said.

"I'm cold and I'm hungry and I want to go home!"

"Ye are no good to yourself or anyone else as long as ye are locked in this dungeon."

"But there's no way out of here, is there?" Her eyes roved the rough stone walls and rested on the five boxes. "Hey, what's in the boxes? Is there anything in there I could use to bust out with?"

"Only dead Daoine Shi."

She screamed. "Get me outta here now!"

"I cannot. But think it through, lass."

Caitie tried to clear her head. The guy was right. Feeling sorry for herself wasn't going to get her free. She needed an escape plan. The king threw her in this dungeon because she wouldn't say she'd give him her camera. So she just needed to be a little more cooperative and then maybe she'd get an opportunity to hightail it out of this place. "I'm Caitie. What's your name again?"

"Mungan."

"You think they'll come back down here for me, don't you?"

"I believe they will, which is more than can be said of me."

Caitie didn't know much about Mungan, but he obviously cared a lot about Leannan if he was willing to break into her grandparent's house twice trying to find her camera. He sure didn't seem the type to murder somebody, but on the other hand, she didn't know what type would. "Help me understand. King Oseron had you kidnap me, so I would tell him where my camera is, right?"

"Aye."

"So if I do that, who will they send to go and get it?"

"Likely Cormag will be the one to retrieve it."

"What will happen to Leannan?"

"The king has given her three days to find the camera herself."

"What happens after three days?"

"Leannan has no magic to help her return. She cannot stay in the mortal realm permanently as a changeling. She will wither and die."

Caitie's conscience screamed this was all her fault. "So she has three days for me to tell them where my camera is or for her to find it before she withers away?"

"Aye."

"And Cormag will bring her back along with my camera if I tell him where it is."

"Perhaps."

"But Oseron will definitely let me go if I give him what he wants, right?"

Caitie heard the faint clinking of keys and approaching footsteps. In the dim light of the corridor, she could make out the growing silhouette of a man. Was she about to be taken back to the king?

Most of the time it was easy for her to make friends, and she was pretty good at getting what she wanted except for this whole move to Scotland thing. Still, she didn't think her skills were up to negotiating with a fairy king.

Caitie heard Mungan whisper, "Be wise Caitie, and please remember Leannan. Her life may very well depend on ye. Oh, and do not..."

She couldn't make out his last words as the figure drawing near started whistling an eerie tune.

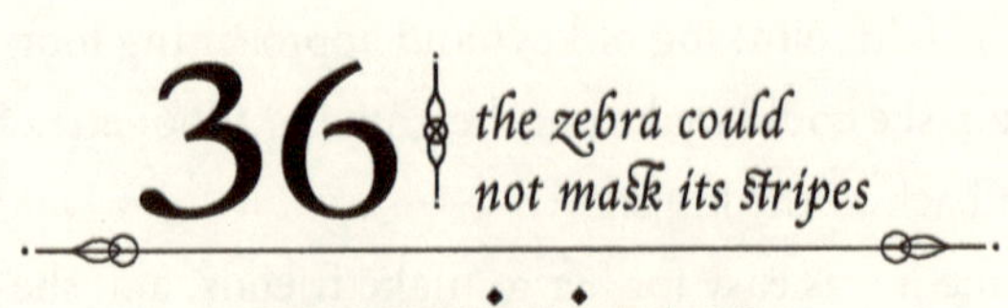

36 *the zebra could not mask its stripes*

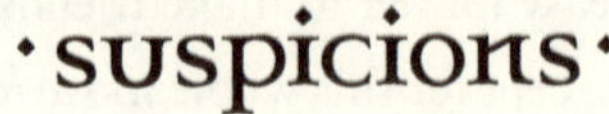

·suspicions·

GIDDY WITH JOY, LEANNAN LED ROBBIE THROUGH THE BIRCH trees skipping or running. She spied a patch of forget-me-nots, raced to it, and dropped to her knees burying her face in them and drinking in their light fragrance. The flowers on this side of the Loch were just as blue, and she longed for her brushes and the chance to paint them. A burn in the hollow called to her, and she rushed to find its bank. Dare she? No longer in the fragile clothing crafted by Earnan, she tossed the flapping shoes from her feet, rolled up the strange trews, and squished her toes in the mud before wading far into the frigid water. Leannan squealed in delight.

"Caitie, what has gotten into you today?" Robbie kicked off his shoes and tip-toed in after her. "Ahh! The river's like ice."

"I know. Is it not wonderful?" She splashed him, and they chased each other till each was breathless.

"I can't feel my toes anymore!" Robbie traipsed out of the water and collapsed on the grass near the brook in a puddle of sunlight.

Leannan collected their shoes and lay down next to him. With her arm behind her head, she watched the puffy clouds drift lazily. "Oh, that I could sail upon that ship," she said, pointing to a long cloud shaped like a mighty vessel floating across the sky.

"That one looks like a big dog," Robbie said, pointing upward. "Remember when we used to do this with Dad?" He looked over at her and bit his lip.

She sensed his deep sadness and nodded. A light breeze blew. Leannan sat up, closed her eyes, and inclined her ear.

"What is it?" Robbie asked.

"Did you hear them?"

"The birds?" he asked.

Leannan caught herself and replied, "It's nothing." She stood up trying to control her feet as her toes started twitching.

"C'mon, Caitie, tell me."

"I thought I heard bluebells ringing." The twitch moved from her toes to the balls of her feet, which started tapping. It spread to her ankles, and she bounced lightly, shifting her weight from one heel to the other.

He gave her a suspicious look.

"Let's dance, Robbie," she said, unable to control her response to the bluebell's melody any longer.

She grabbed Robbie's hands and dragged him round and round in time with the music in her soul.

"Stop, Caitie!" he cried.

"Come on, Robbie."

"You're scaring me."

"How? We're only dancing."

"But you don't dance like this. And not when there's no music."

Leannan stopped immediately, creating a war within her fragile changeling being. The faerie part of her nature willed her to dance to the tinkling music of the floral bells, yet the fear of discovery fought fiercely to keep her still. The turmoil took a toll on her very essence. "You're right, Robbie. I got carried away." No sooner had she spoken the words, her legs went out from under her, and she dropped to the ground.

"What happened?" Robbie asked.

"I don't know." She looked up into Robbie's face. "Perhaps I need to rest for just a moment."

Robbie's bright blue eyes were wide with worry. "Are you feeling okay?"

"I am wispy in the head."

"Wispy? I'm gonna go get help." Robbie's voice shook.

"No, give me a wee moment." The air had grown still once more, and thankfully the music faded away. "We should go." 'Twould be best to leave before the breeze picked up again. She still felt strange but steady enough to walk. She raised her hand and Robbie pulled her up. The exuberance that had overwhelmed her at the beginning of their woodland adventure was lost.

They strolled back to the croft. They found the grandpa and the large black and white dog leaving the barn. The dog caught sight of her, hunched down, and hung his head low.

Leannan started to tremble. Would he attack?

"You two certainly have been gone a good long while," the grandpa called.

The closer Leannan and Robbie got to the old man, the more threatening the dog became. The black hair on his back raised, and a low growl came from deep in his throat, making its way through clenched jaws, teeth bared.

"What's the matter with you, Balfour?" the grandpa asked. "It's only Caitie and Robbie." He leaned sideways to pat the dog on his shoulder. "The old boy's acting strange today. I had to wake him up this morning. He slept so soundly he never even heard my footsteps. I don't recall that happening before. And now this with you two, I almost wonder if I shouldn't call the vet."

"He looks fine to me." She had to get away from the dog. "I think I'll go into the house." She turned her back to Balfour. He barked his disapproval of her. *I don't like you either.*

AFTER DINNER LEANNAN CLEARED THE TABLE, ROBBIE HEADED UPSTAIRS, and the mom and grandma washed the dishes. Leannan found Ross sitting on the sofa in the drawing room, reading large papers just like Robbie's mother had at breakfast. The grandpa pressed a button on a black box on top of a cabinet by the fireplace. Suddenly a fiddler played, though not as well as any of the Daoine Shi. Mystified, Leannan wondered where was the musician making the melody.

The grandpa sat down on an overstuffed chair, picked up a book resting on the small table beside him, and started to read.

Leannan looked round the chamber for the silver box. She opened the cabinet and found a chess set on one of the shelves. She fingered the pieces and thought of Mungan.

"Do you know how to play, Caitie?" the old man asked.

"Yes, but—"

"Bring it out then, and let's see if you can beat your granddad." The old man set the book down in his lap. "Black or white?"

Leannan carried the board to the table and settled on the overstuffed chair across from the grandfather. "White." Leannan moved her first pawn. The granddad countered. She wished Mungan was there to advise her as they battled for quite a long while.

Robbie stopped half-way down the stairs. "Since when do you know how to play chess?" Robbie asked, his tone unpleasant.

"I've known for a long time, Robbie," Leannan bantered back.

"But we don't have a chess set," he answered.

Her heart skipped a beat. "My friends taught me," she said as she fought her mounting panic.

"I didn't think they were that smart."

"That wasn't very nice. Now apologize, Robbie." The mom sauntered over to watch.

"But it's true," Robbie said.

Leannan made her next move. "Check."

"I think you'd better take back that last remark, Robbie," the granddad said.

Ross set down the paper. Leannan felt his penetrating gaze. Her opponent moved his queen after much deliberation.

Leannan quickly took his queen with her rook. "Checkmate."

"That was a fine game, Caitie."

"I am glad you enjoyed it, Grandpa."

"Aye, that was quite an accomplishment." Ross stroked his chin.

Robbie looked at her with one eyebrow cocked and shook his head.

The joy of a well-fought match vanished, and dread that Robbie saw through her ruse took its place.

37 *the bait was taken*

·tricked & trapped·

4:15 PM
JUNE 27TH

CAITIE STEPPED AWAY FROM THE CELL DOOR AS THE eerie whistler in the corridor drew close, hoping she'd somehow get a chance to speak again with the king and talk her way out of the mountain.

"King Oseron requests your presence." The creepy guard wiggled his gloved hand through a slot between the bars to grasp the door.

The prospect of leaving the holding tank of fairy corpses and meeting with the guy who stuck her down there to begin with sent adrenaline surging through her.

Cormag fiddled with the curlicue key, cursing at the lock before it finally released with a clunk. The door groaned as he pulled it open. With his hand stuck between the bars, Caitie considered bolting, but she had no idea how to find her way out. Before she could think it through, the guard freed his hand and seized her by the arm, pinching her tight.

Caitie glared at him with narrowed eyes. "Stop squeezing so hard. You keep hurting me, and I'm getting ticked."

"What do I care?" The jerk dragged her up the passageway lit by bright yellow torches. She could have sworn the torch flames were peach when he took her down earlier, but that didn't make any sense. The crowd gathered and circled behind her, making Caitie feel like a fairy magnet as the jerk pulled her through the archway toward the throne.

With his chin resting on his folded hands, the king studied her so hard, it freaked her out. "Our first meeting was most unpleasant. I believe we should try again."

Caitie didn't trust him, but she didn't want to go back to the dungeon either. She'd play along to see where the king was going to go with this. "You're right. I'm just not a morning person. I guess I overreacted when I woke up here. Sorry, I was kind of rude."

"Your apology is accepted." The king's lips curved in a smug smile.

She faked a pleasant "thanks."

He closed his eyes like she'd totally said the wrong thing and was struggling to overlook it. "Cormag, I want ye to release her in good faith."

The guard let Caitie go, and she rubbed her arm to work out the soreness.

"Let us try once again with introductions." He pointed to himself. "I am King Oseron of the Daoine Shi. And ye are?"

It couldn't hurt to give him just her first name. "I'm Caitie."

"Welcome to our mountain, Caitie." The king looked down at her feet. "Ye must be hungry and perhaps a little cold."

"Yeah, my feet are freezing."

"Then I insist we find ye more suitable attire and that ye join me for the evening banquet." The king grinned like he expected her to grovel at his kindness. "Lileas."

The fat fairy with tight dark curls that had sold Mungan out approached the throne. "Aye, Your Majesty." She curtsied deep and her shimmering copper skirt ballooned around her like a bell.

"Take Caitie to the seamstresses and cobblers that she may enjoy some of our finery."

"Aye, Your Highness." Lileas turned to her. "This way."

The fairy had seemed pretty shook up about getting Mungan in trouble, but still Caitie decided she'd have to be careful around this one. The two of them left the main hall and strolled down the surrounding corridor as the flames on the torches turned rosy pink. She wasn't crazy. The fire did change colors here. The large paintings hanging in the corridor seemed normal enough until the sun disappeared behind a puffy cloud drifting across the sky. Her jaw dropped. "Lileas, the cloud in that painting moved."

"Of course, it did." Lileas sounded polite, but not super-friendly. "These paintings are our windows to your realm."

"Whoa."

They reached the entrance to a passageway with "Workshoppes and Wares" carved on a fancy sign.

On each side of the hallway were double doors that curved into points at the top like big teardrops.

Above each doorway hung a different sign—Candlemakers, Woodcarvers, Silversmiths, Spinners, and Weavers.

Lileas threw open the doors beneath the sign for the Clothiers' Shoppe and ushered Caitie into a clothing store like she'd never seen. An L-shaped rack on the left revolved with long dresses, and its mirror image on the right side turned with men's outfits. The clothing seemed to come alive like it was worn by invisible people. Reaching the center of the room on either side of the double doors, the outfits spun, curtsied or bowed to each other before circling back on the rack. A short fairy draped fabric over a life-like dress form. A tall one admired the sketch of a dress with a feather pen tucked behind her pointy ear. Both seamstresses stopped their work when she and Lileas entered the shop.

"This is Caitie, and we are here to find her some suitable clothes," Lileas announced.

"So she can turn another gown to rags as she did Leannan's?" Anger flashed in the tall one's eyes.

"Look, that was an accident. I don't even know how that happened to her," Caitie said.

Lileas raised her hands like she was just doing what she was told. "Caitie is to dine at the king's table tonight."

The two seamstresses shifted their eyes to one another.

The short one put her hands on her hips. "Perhaps a gown of black will do. Though 'tis a shame, we have no pointy hat to go with it."

"I'm not a witch." Caitie looked at both revolving racks and headed for the men's clothing. She wasn't a prom dress kind of girl, and if she couldn't talk her way out and needed to escape, these funny Capri pants would be more practical.

"Oh no, lass, trews are for the menfolk. Ye need to come to this side and choose a lovely gown." Lileas turned Caitie's shoulders toward the women's clothing.

Caitie slipped out of her grasp. "But I'd feel much more comfortable in these." She pulled out a pair of dark blue trews, buttoned beneath the knee, before the rack could sweep them away.

"Ye cannot wear a pair of trews." Lileas sounded shocked like Caitie had just announced she was gonna go naked.

"But I'm not a Daoine Shi." Caitie picked a cream-colored man's shirt with long puffy sleeves and a deep open collar with crisscrossed leather cords. "Can

I try this on?"

Lileas shook her curly head. "There will surely be trouble if that is your choice."

Caitie stepped into the round dressing room, closed the door, and changed into the trews. They fit perfectly, better than anything ever did back at the mall in Fashion Valley. She wouldn't want any of her friends to see her in them, but they'd work for now. The shirt fit too like it was made for her. All she needed was a red bandana and a pair of boots, and she'd look like a pirate.

Caitie left the dressing room and spied a mirror behind Lileas then stepped onto the platform to check out the clothes. Lileas drew the feathered curtain closed. Sparkling flecks swirled throughout the small space like snow devils on a ski slope, only way prettier. "What the…" Caitie whispered.

Invisible hands brushed her hair, massaged her face, and rolled super-sweet gloss on her lips. The sparkles settled and Caitie pulled the curtain back. "That's so cool." Her face tingled.

"The chamber helped some, but those clothes are most unflattering." Lileas clasped her hands and rested her chin on them, a worried look in her cocoa eyes.

Even though the mirror was curved like a horseshoe, Caitie wasn't all distorted like in the weird ones at the science museum. This one made her look great. Her skinned glowed, and her hair looked better tossed than when she spent hours doing it herself. And the lighting was awesome too, shifting from peach to gold, yellow, rose, blue, and then silver.

Lileas held up a sheer green dress embroidered with delicate blue flowers that shimmered. It had cap sleeves, a scoop neck, and deep blue crystals that lined the empire waist. "Please consider this gown. 'Twill look lovely on ye."

"I'd better stick with what I've got on. I'd trip and fall in that."

"King Oseron shan't be pleased, and I shall be blamed." Worry lines creased Lileas's forehead. "Please, Caitie."

The fat fairy was the only one who didn't seem to hate her here. And maybe having a friend could help her get out of this place. "Okay, I'll try it on." Caitie took the gown from the seamstress back to the dressing room and slipped it on over the trews. It really was pretty, but the long skirt would slow her down if she had to run for it. She stepped out to show the others. "Do you suppose we could just cut the bottom off to about here?" Caitie held her hands flat, palm-side up just below her hips.

A look of horror spread across all three fairy faces.

"Oh, I'll still wear these." Caitie tugged on the trews.

"I think it not a wise idea," Lileas said.

"Never mind. I'll stick with the man's shirt," Caitie said.

Lileas cupped her large rosy cheek in her hand, "Let us shorten the gown."

The look in the tall one's eyes was as lethal as the pointy scissors she used to cut the dress. The short one then hemmed it in about a second.

"Thank…" Caitie swallowed the "you" as all three Daoine Shi grimaced. "Did I say something wrong?"

"Ye offend us with the phrase," Lileas explained.

"Why?"

"Mortals use those words far too freely, making their sincerity dubious," the tall one said.

"Okay. Will I offend you if I say it looks really nice?"

The short one let a smile cross her lips. "No, I suppose not."

"And now, we must be off to the cobblers for a pair of slippers." Lileas opened the door and led Caitie from the room.

The cobbler's workshop was one door down on the opposite side of the rosy corridor.

"Good day. King Oseron has sent us for a pair of slippers to shod the lass." Lileas pointed to Caitie's bare feet.

The three cobblers looked up from their workbenches. A younger one was bending the cuff on the tops of a pair of black boots. The second hammered soles on some brown ones, and the third traced a pattern. The two old guys' faces looked as worn as the leather they used for the boots.

One by one, they set down their tools. The youngest one scowled at her. "I shall be back in a wee while," he said to the older two. He marched toward the door, coming so close and fast toward Caitie, she backed out of his way. He slammed his hand onto the wood, throwing the door open.

The two old Daoine Shi studied Caitie for a minute without saying a word. They tugged on their generous beards and shifted their eyes from her to one another and back to her again.

"I know," Lileas said. "Her fate is out of my hands."

"And what colour slippers would ye like?" the cobbler who had been tracing asked.

"Can I try a pair of black boots like the ones that other guy is making?" she asked.

Their eyes shifted nervously to Lileas.

"I'll tell the king I picked them out and that it wasn't your fault," Caitie said.

"But King Oseron will still be displeased," Brown Boot said.

"Aye, he will," the tracing cobbler added.

"Please?" Caitie begged, using her big green eyes to soften the old guys up.

A few moments later, she and Lileas left the Cobblers' Shoppe with her feet toasty warm in a pair of tall black boots.

"Corc, I need ye for a wee while," Lileas called to the younger cobbler sitting at a table in the banquet hall. He was talking to a couple of other Daoine Shi playing a game of chess.

"What for?" he asked.

"I must prepare for dinner. Please, Corc, keep Caitie company until the king arrives."

"Lileas—" The cobbler eyed Caitie like she was carrying some horrible disease.

He was so rude, and Caitie didn't get why.

"'Twill not be long," Lileas led her over to him and left before Corc could refuse.

"Look, I'll go sit at a table by myself." Caitie turned toward the massive painting running the width of the Great Hall.

"No. If Lileas wants me to keep ye company, I shan't disappoint her." He got up from the table and joined her.

Caitie stepped closer to the canvas forest. "Why do I get the feeling you hate me?" she asked.

"Ye have troubled my friends," he answered.

"I honestly didn't mean to." She wished she could just fix this mess.

"Ye have done so just the same."

The banquet hall began to fill quickly with Daoine Shi. The musicians took to a platform on one side of the throne, and several dancers climbed a stage on the other. King Oseron came in last. He sat at a small table close to the front. Corc walked Caitie over to the king's table.

"I am pleased that ye have joined me although your attire is unbecoming a young lass." King Oseron looked her over. "Lileas advised ye poorly."

"It's not her fault, or the seamstresses, or the cobblers. I picked this out on my own." She sat down across from him on a velvet-cushioned chair. The plate in front of her held cakes and cheeses, and a silver goblet was filled to the brim with honey gold liquid.

King Oseron raised his chalice and held it out to her. Caitie did the same.

"To your health and a very long life." He smiled.

Caitie didn't know what to say so she clinked his chalice with hers and took a sip of the drink. It tasted delicate and sweet, the way wild flowers smell. She hadn't had anything to drink or eat all day. She gulped it down.

"Try the saffron cakes. I am sure that ye will find them most pleasing," King Oseron said.

Caitie took a bite of one of the golden cakes. "They're really good."

"Then eat heartily," he replied.

Starved, Caitie finished them off as she tried to figure out how to negotiate her way out of there.

"King Oseron, I've changed my mind. If you'll let me go, I'm willing to get you my camera so that your wizard can try to get Leannan her magic back."

"That shan't be necessary."

"I don't understand."

"Leannan was foolish and is no longer welcome here. But we have another to take her place."

"Who?" Caitie asked.

"'Tis ye."

"No, I won't do it. I want to go home. And I want to go now!"

"I am afraid that is not possible, Caitie, for ye have partaken of our food and drink, thus ye are bound to the Daoine Shi. 'Tis true, Leannan has broken our code, but ye are guilty as well. Ye have wronged one of my people, and ye must pay for your actions. Justice demands it." King Oseron placed his napkin on the plate, scooted his chair back from the table, and stood up. "Pleasant Evening."

Caitie looked at her empty plate, stunned.

38 *pieces fell in place*

· the revelation ·

8:00 AM
JUNE 28TH

THUNDER RUMBLED, WAKING ROBBIE AND SHAKING the house the way a low-flying FA-18 Hornet would at their old place in San Diego. The wind howled, lightning flashed, and rain pounded the roof. They never had storms like this in California. He dashed into Caitie's room, crawled under her covers, and scunched his sister over.

"What are ye doing in my bed?" Caitie's voice was weak.

A crack of thunder sent him scrambling deeper between the sheets.

"Leave me be. I don't feel good, Robbie." She pushed him toward the edge of the mattress.

"C'mon, Caitie."

"You cannot stay."

She'd never kicked him out before if he'd had a nightmare and was scared. What had gotten into her?

Raindrops as big as quarters splat on the window, making it impossible to see through the panes.

Robbie hurried from her room and down the stairs, taking two at a time and jumping off the last four. He found Mom in the kitchen with Ross, Grandma, and Grandpa, finishing breakfast.

"This storm's gonna flatten the house!" Robbie pressed his nose against the backdoor window, watching the wind blow the rain sideways and white caps roll across the loch.

"Welcome to the Highlands," Ross said with a chuckle.

Grandma MacGregor rose to clear the dishes. "Aye, you've been blessed with good weather since arriving, but today Mother Nature is making up for it."

Grandpa got up from the table. "I'm off for my wellies and waterproof jacket."

"Where are you going?" Robbie asked.

"Out to the barn to muck stalls. Why don't you come and help after you've finished your breakfast?"

"I wouldn't want to get in the way or do it wrong."

Grandpa MacGregor crossed his arms and nodded his head. "I'll teach you how it's done. Dish him up plenty of black pudding, beans, and eggs, Ina."

Ross pulled his yellow jacket off the back of the kitchen chair. "Where's your sister?"

"She's still in bed. She said she wasn't feeling good."

"I wonder what's wrong," Mom said. "I think I'll go up and check on her."

"What's black pudding, Grandma?"

"Blood sausage."

"I think I'll pass." Why couldn't he just have a bowl of cereal like he used to?

ROBBIE TRUDGED UPSTAIRS TO BRUSH HIS TEETH AND FOUND CAITIE in his room pulling a T-shirt off the floor. "What are you doing?"

"Tidying up a bit." She added it to a small pile of dirty clothes she'd gathered and started making his bed.

Her not touching the computer for over 24 hours was weird enough, but the way she was acting now wasn't right. Her dancing in the woods and playing chess were spooky, but this—wanting to "tidy" his room—it was all wrong! He had to talk to Ross. He snagged his jacket and shoes.

Caitie stopped plumping the pillow. "Where are you going?"

He didn't want her tagging after him. "To muck stalls with Grandpa."

"That will sprout the hair on your chest."

The cold stung Robbie's cheeks, and the blasting wind drove the drops through his clothes as he sprinted across the yard. He opened the barn door and poked his head inside. Grandpa's back was to him as he scraped dirty shavings off the floor and shoveled them into the wheelbarrow. Inside a stall closer to the door, Ross jerked his head back in surprise with a big grin on his face. Robbie brought his pointer finger to his lips, hoping Ross wouldn't give him away. Then he waved Ross over.

"I'll be back in a minute, Angus," Ross said.

Robbie eased the door shut and waited in the rain for Ross. "We've gotta talk."

"Not out here!" Ross ran to the shed and opened the weathered door.

Robbie followed him inside.

A charred log smoked in the fireplace.

"Now what is this all about?" Ross hung his jacket on a coat hook near the door.

"I'm scared. Something's wrong with Caitie, and I don't know what it is." Robbie plopped down on the hard chair at the table in front of the window.

"Is she feeling worse?" Ross asked.

"No, that's not it. It's how she's acting and the way she's talking."

Ross pulled out a chair from the table and sat down, leaning forward, his elbows on his knees and his hands clasped. "What's she done?"

"She danced in the woods."

"But Robbie, I saw how much Caitie enjoyed dancing at the ceilidh."

"Okay, you're right. She likes to dance. But yesterday, it was weird. I've never seen her move that way."

"Hmm."

"And the whole chess thing came out of nowhere. But you want to know what's the scariest part of all?"

"Tell me."

"My sister is up there 'tidying' my room! Not texting—not on Facebook—she's cleaning!" Robbie shook his head. "It's like she's been abducted by aliens or something."

Ross sat up straight. "Robbie, I've had suspicions myself." He laid his palm on the cover of the Scottish Folklore book still lying on the table. "There's an old Scottish belief that the Daoine Shi would steal human babies, young women, or nursing mothers. The book says they did it to bring in new blood for the perpetuation of their race."

"They couldn't have stolen Caitie. She's still here," Robbie reasoned.

"Well, there was more to it than just kidnapping. They would leave a changeling which is a fake baby in the real baby's place."

"What do you mean by fake?"

"The changeling looked like the real thing, but could be made of wood. Other times they would leave a troublesome fairy in the baby's place."

"But if they left a fairy, did it grow up like a regular person?"

"No, they would die shortly thereafter. Now people believe all that old talk of babies being stolen and replaced with changelings was really cot death. I think you'd call it crib death though. Either way, I'm not so sure anymore."

"Then that's not Caitie upstairs?"

"I'm afraid it isn't."

"Well, if it's not her, who is—" Suddenly it all clicked. "That's Leannan. It wasn't a dream then. It really happened!"

"What are you talking about?"

"Sunday night, I dreamed Leannan and three other fairies were on our stairway." Ross listened to every word as Robbie explained all he could remember. "When I told Caitie or Leannan about it yesterday, she blew it off."

"It's possible they cast a spell on you to make you think it was a dream."

"Why would they take Caitie when they could have just woken her and made her give them the camera?"

"Revenge, maybe?" Ross rested his elbow on the table and leaned his forehead on the palm of his hand.

It suddenly felt like it was 120 degrees in the shed, and Robbie was sure he was gonna black out. Caitie and he didn't always get along, but he still loved her. He took a deep breath. "And they made Leannan the changeling because she was troublesome?"

"Could be, or maybe they thought Leannan could find the camera herself."

"Ross, we've gotta get Caitie back."

"I know."

"How?"

"We'll need Leannan's help."

39 *a ray of hope appeared*

maid to the fae

THE KNOCK ON THE DOOR JOLTED CAITIE AWAKE FROM A short and restless night. The torchlight bathed the unfamiliar room in a golden glow, and for a groggy moment, she didn't know where she was.

"Caitie?" came a muffled call from the other side of the door.

The lilting voice grounded her, and the nightmare of the day before crashed her back to reality.

"Go away." The latch clicked and the door opened. She peeked over the puffy comforter. Lileas filled the doorway.

"Ye must accept it, Caitie. Ye will be happier when ye do."

Caitie rolled over and buried her face in the feather pillow. The mattress gave under Lileas's weight.

"'Tis not a bad sort of life. There is music and merriment in the mountain. I admit there is less these days, but feeling sorry for yourself is not the answer." Lileas gently rubbed Caitie's back the way Mom used to.

Caitie turned over and propped herself up on her elbows. "I don't belong here. I have a family that loves me, and I love them. I want to go home!"

"Arise, Caitie. Some breakfast will make ye feel better."

"I'm not eating another thing!" she snapped.

"Suit yourself. But ye need your strength as we have tidying to do."

"What does that mean?"

"We shall straighten up the bedchambers, starting with your own." Lileas rolled her toward the edge of the bed and plumped a pillow.

"It's not my room," Caitie replied.

"'Tis for now." Lileas glided toward the door. "I shall await ye in the passageway."

Caitie changed out of Leannan's nightgown into her new clothes, determined she'd find a way out.

PUSHING A CART WITH A CAGE OF CHEEPING CHICKS DOWN THE passageway, Caitie followed Lileas.

"I will tidy up the bedchambers on this side of the corridor, and ye shall take the other." The fairy opened the door beneath a wooden plaque with "Corc" written in calligraphy. She nodded for Caitie to enter. Lileas handed her a box and the broom from Leannan's cart and then passed her the cage of chicks.

"What am I supposed to do with these guys?"

"Just shut the cage door when they are finished." Lileas opened the latch. The chicks flew out and dusted the furniture with their fluffy bottoms. Caitie's jaw dropped, and her eyes grew wide. "And have the broom start in the back corner."

Caitie set the box on the dresser and started toward the back of the room.

"No, Caitie, your words will suffice." Lileas took the broom from her hand and released the handle. "To the corner and be swift." The broom whisked away and swept briskly. "Now I must be off."

Caitie stood speechless as Lileas bustled toward the door. "Wait! What's in the box?"

With her hand on the doorknob, Lileas turned and smiled. "A wee gift from Earnan. He thought you could use the assistance." She shut the door quietly on the way out.

Caitie looked at the unmade bed and clothes on the floor. The room looked perfectly fine to her.

She walked over to the box and lifted the lid. A pair of white gloves popped out as full of life as if there were hands inside. They clapped. She screamed. The left glove wagged a finger at her.

Lileas poked her head inside with a broad grin.

"This isn't funny!" Caitie's heart pounded like it was trying to escape through her throat.

"I know not whether Earnan meant it to be. But if I were ye, I'd be grateful for an extra pair of hands." Lileas shut the door again. The gloves spread apart, palms up like they were asking, "What now?"

"Just stay away from me!" Caitie yelled at the hands as the straw on the broom brushed her boot.

She jumped and turned to see the chicks lined up on the dresser staring at her like *she* was crazy.

Caitie crawled on the bed to get out of the broom's way while the hands twiddled their thumbs in the corner. "All right," she said to the hands, "you two can help me out."

The pair of gloves flew over, picked her up under her armpits, and carried her toward the door.

"Hey, let go of me!"

The hands dropped her and she landed on her butt. "Ouch!" She got up, rubbing her backside. "I meant for you to help straighten up in here." The hands dipped to the floor and picked up Corc's shirt. If this was home and she was stuck cleaning her room, she'd probably think the dusting birds, auto-broom, and magic hands were way cool. But she was "maid to the fairies" now and so mad she wanted to smash their fingers in the door and bat the birds to oblivion with the broom before breaking it in two. She didn't deserve this.

One hand opened the wardrobe and got out a hanger, and the other hung the shirt. "Drop it," Caitie ordered. "Corc can hang up his own stuff." The hand released the hanger, and the shirt crumpled on the floor. Both palms faced her like she'd said "Stick 'em up." But what if Corc complained to Lileas later that she hadn't done a good job? What would they do? Throw her back in the dungeon? "Never mind. Go ahead and put the shirt away." The hands obeyed. She wasn't going back to the dungeon if she could help it.

She needed to find a way out, but she was always with Lileas. If she had her phone, she could call Robbie and he could bring back help. But her phone was here, somewhere! Oseron had said he could get it for her. Maybe it was in his chambers.

Corc's door opened as Caitie and the hands, working on opposite sides, made the bed.

"Ye must be very thorough at your task as I have tidied up a dozen chambers and ye are still here in Corc's."

"I'm trying," she said with faked enthusiasm. "Lileas, I want to ask you something. The king wasn't too happy 'cause of the clothes I picked out, so I want to make it up by doing a really good job cleaning his room. Can I?" Caitie shut the cage door with the chicks perched inside.

"Oh, I think not," Lileas said, "But perhaps we can work together."

Arguing didn't seem like a good idea. "Okay."

Lileas led her through a connecting passageway to the end of the corridor, stopping at an intricately carved door. King Oseron's name was inlaid with emeralds on the gold plaque above.

Lileas ushered her inside the large room. The alcove at one end looked like a gazebo with a huge stormy mural in the background. Wind whipped the trees and flashes of lightning appeared in the scene. Caitie swore she even heard faint thunder.

A pretty Daoine Shi barged into the room. "Lileas, the pitcher of cleansing vapors above my dressing table crashed. 'Tis a frightful mess. Ye must come and tidy it at once."

"I cannot now, Nuala. I shall come as soon as we have finished here."

The dark haired Daoine Shi shook her finger at Lileas. "Do not argue with me, ye sow. If ye are not in my chamber before I reach my door, I shall report your negligence to the king."

"I will return shortly, Caitie."

Nuala sneered at them both. "Do not count on that!" She left in a huff with Lileas at her heels.

And they think I'm the witch. Caitie freed the chicks, broom, and gloves. "You know the drill. And do a really good job. I've got to look for something." Against one wall was a canopied bed covered in red silk. She'd search there before the hands straightened it up.

None of her and Robbie's stuff was under the pillows, mattress, or the bed. It wasn't on top of the nightstands, dressers, or tables either. She went to both chests of drawers and rifled through his clothing. Her conscience bothered her some, but then again, Oseron hadn't played fair with her. She'd been honest, willing to negotiate, and all he wanted to do was be a jerk. She rummaged through the giant wardrobe and lifted seat cushions. No luck.

She searched every trunk, decorative box, and vase. The only things left in the room were two statues—a small one of a pretty fairy wearing a crown and a big one of King Oseron mounted on a prancing horse with bells woven into its mane. The king's statue stood in the corner as tall as she was. Caitie checked the round base holding the tiny fairy, but there was no hidden drawer. She lifted it up to look underneath. In the center, a four-leaf clover hung down like a key on a music box. She twisted it, but there was no winding sound. The base and statue were all one piece, so the fairy couldn't spin. She twisted the clover a little more, and it dropped from the base into her hand. The other end of the clover was a key. Caitie gasped. There had to be a safe or something that the key went to.

She looked behind every painting, but only found more wood paneling. "Be quiet!" she told the chicks perched on the king's crown. "I've gotta think."

The little statue must have been of the queen. And kings and queens go together. She raced over to the big statue, and the chicks took flight. She combed every inch on the horse and the king, looking for a place to insert the key, but there wasn't any. Caitie sighed.

It had made so much sense. She'd twisted the key to get it out of the little statue. Maybe something on the big one could be moved, and she'd find where the key fit. She pushed on the statue, but it wouldn't give. She searched for a seam near his hands, neck, and shoulders, but it was all solid brass. Running her fingers through her hair, she finally saw it. There was a ring at the base of the crown.

With a twist, the crown came off, revealing a key slot in the top of the king's head. Caitie took a deep breath, inserted the key, and turned it. Hinges creaked. A panel behind her swung inward, revealing a secret passageway.

This kind of thing only happened in the movies, not in her life. Should she go in? What if she did, and the door was timed or something, and she got stuck? She waited, counting to 60 three times to see if the door would close. It didn't. She turned the key, and the door groaned shut. The passage could be her way out. She turned the key, and the panel opened once more.

Caitie picked up the ringed candleholder on the nightstand and shielded the flickering flame with her hand. Entering the passageway, she wished she wasn't alone. She walked for several minutes through the narrow corridor gradually climbing up hill. Parked up ahead close to the tunnel wall, was a beat-up wheelbarrow with a hooked pole attached to the front and a large trunk set inside. Rounding the curve and reaching the wheelbarrow, she spied a sliver of light, outlining a door.

Her heart raced. She'd found her way out of the mountain. Caitie moved as fast as she could without letting the candle go out. She reached a wooden door. A twig at the threshold left it slightly ajar. There was no knob to pull or hinges to hold it in place. She set the candleholder on the ground and pried the door inward with her fingernails. Its exterior was a stone face, camouflaging the entrance. She squealed at the sight of the stormy sky and the hillside. There was no real trail from the door, but that didn't matter, she'd figure out her way down the mountain and home.

Adrenaline surged through her body. Caitie took a deep breath along with her next step to freedom. Her toe, chest, and nose smashed into something, repelling her backward. Stunned, Caitie shook her head. She couldn't see what she had run into. With her hands up and out in front of her, she tried to cross the mountain threshold a second time, but again she bumped into something invisible. Panic set in. Caitie moved her hands and stretched her arms, testing the transparent barrier only to discover it was as wide and tall as the doorway. She kicked and pounded the invisible wall with her fists until her feet hurt and hands ached. Half-crying, Caitie mustered all her strength and hurled the side of her body against the barrier. It didn't budge. Her back against the wall, Caitie pushed until her feet went out from under her, and she slumped to the floor.

"How can this be happening to me?" she whimpered. A replay of dinner flashed through her mind with Oseron smugly telling her she was bound to the Daoine Shi.

40 *the curtain came down*

· the allegation ·

ROBBIE'S INSIDES FELT AS STORMY AS THE WEATHER. ANGER and fear swirled up from the pit of his stomach and whirled through his brain 'til his head ached. Was Caitie okay? What if their plan to trick his pretend sister didn't work? He couldn't think like that. It had to work. He'd make it work!

The rain poured down like water wrung from a washrag as Robbie ran from the shed to the chicken yard. He opened the gate and slogged through the mud to the reach the stone henhouse. The stink of chicken manure blasted his nose as he stepped through the open doorway. He backed out, gulped a deep breath, and pinched his nose before charging back inside.

Two bare bulbs lit the old building packed with more hens than Robbie could count. They clucked and bobbed about the floor. A few roosters perched on stair-stepped poles along one side of the henhouse stared at him with black beady eyes. They creeped him out. He tried to ignore them while he dodged the noisy chickens to get to the wooden boxes that lined the back wall.

A rose colored egg rested on the hay in the first box he checked. What was wrong with these chickens? Eggs were supposed to be white. Robbie scooped it up anyway and stashed the egg in his jacket pocket. A huge hen, a few feet from him, flitted away, uncovering a white one. He snatched up the warm egg and stuffed it in his other pocket. Unable to hold his breath a second longer, Robbie gasped and gagged and searched furiously for one more. A box in the corner held a cream one. He grabbed it, raced outside, and filled his lungs with soggy air before he dashed back to the shed.

"Were you able to find some?" Ross asked.

"Yeah. But I like pulling eggs from a carton way better!"

"Well, hand me what you've got and go get 'Caitie.'"

"Okay." Robbie's stomach tensed, knowing he had to convince Leannan to come with him without her figuring something was up.

The wind had died down, but the rain poured as he ran back to the house. He found "Caitie" on her hands and knees peering under his bed.

"What are you doing?" he asked.

She stood up real slow, breathing hard from the effort. "I was looking to see if the floor beneath was dusty."

"My room's just fine." It was hard to believe by looking at her that this wasn't Caitie—the sun-streaked hair, the freckles on her nose in exactly the right places, the scar on her wrist from surgery after a volleyball accident.

"Your wardrobe certainly was not." Leannan sighed.

"Look, I didn't give you permission to go through my stuff."

"I had to go through your stuff to tidy your room!" Leannan lay on his bed.

She must not have found Caitie's camera yet. "Ross wants us to come to the shed."

"Why?"

"It's some kind of surprise."

"All right. I'll go get my slippers and don something warm." Leannan wobbled a little as she stood.

She left the room and met him at the top of the stairs, carrying Caitie's tie-dyed sweatshirt with a peace sign.

"You're gonna get soaked," Robbie said.

"We have not far to go."

"Whatever." Robbie headed down the stairs and out the door. They were back at the shed less than ten minutes after he'd left it.

The hinges squeaked as Ross opened the door. "Come in."

"So what's up?" Robbie tried hard to sound like he didn't have a clue.

"I thought I'd invite you over for a special cup of tea, seeing as it's such a blustery day." Ross walked over to the stove. "The kettle's almost boiled."

Robbie hoped and prayed she'd fall for the trick they'd gotten from Ross's old book. Craning her neck, "Caitie" watched Ross fiddle with the tiny pot. Robbie followed her over to the stove.

Steam rose from the six half-eggshells emptied of the yolks and whites and wedged together in the kettle. The jagged eggshells themselves looked like tiny colored pots filled with boiling water. She crinkled her nose for a second and tilted her head. With her eyes fixed on the kettle like she was in some kind of trance, she half-sang, half-laughed a weird chant:

"I seen the acorn afore the oak, the egg afore the hen,
But ne'er in all my many years beheld such in any glen."

Any doubt Robbie might have had trying to convince himself that she was somehow his real sister vanished. For the first time, Robbie could see the fairy in her and not just hear it. Caitie was really gone.

Leannan drew a hand to her mouth and fear exploded across her face. "Ye tricked me!"

Ross crossed his arms and looked her square in the eyes. "Aye, we did. And I don't suppose you have seen anything like that in your hundreds of years, Leannan. Now tell us what's happened to Caitie."

Leannan's gaze darted back and forth between him and Ross.

"Yeah. Where's my sister?" Robbie planted clenched fists on his waist and moved toward her.

Leannan backed into the cabinet next to the stove. "She is…." Leannan swallowed, "in our mountain."

"We gotta get her back." Robbie mustered his courage and hoped he sound tough. "And you gotta help us."

"I have no magic. And what is more, I fear I shan't last much longer myself."

"How much time do we have to work with?" Ross asked.

"I must return by tomorrow night and bring Caitie's camera with me."

"Or what?" Robbie asked.

Leannan bit her lip and dropped her head. "I am doomed."

Was Caitie too?

"You'll die?" Ross asked.

"The withering has already begun."

Robbie had seen it in the woods yesterday and a few minutes ago when she lay down on his bed.

"My only hope is to atone for the wrong I have done by retrieving the camera in the allotted time," Leannan said. "Then I shall plead for mercy from King Oseron, and perhaps, he will allow our wizard to change me back before it is too late."

Robbie couldn't help but feel scared for her. "Okay. We'll just have to get you home in time."

"Do you know where Caitie's camera is?" Ross asked.

Robbie shook his head. "She wouldn't tell me. Leannan, what if we just go buy another camera?"

Leannan turned pale and terrified. "There is more than one camera in your world?"

"Millions," Ross said.

"I must find Caitie's for that is the one with my magic. Not only that, King Oseron believes 'tis a threat to the Daoine Shi as long as ye mortals possess it."

Ross raised his hands. "We don't want to harm you or the Daoine Shi. We just need to have Caitie returned. The Lumix and you, Leannan, are an even exchange for her." He looked at Robbie, "We'll get a new camera for your sister once she's home."

"I have searched high and low for that contraption." Leannan clasped her hands and drew them to her face. "'Tis nowhere to be found."

"It's got to be here somewhere," Ross said.

"We'll find it today," Robbie said, trying to convince himself. "So can we take her back tonight, Ross?"

"Without my magic, 'twill be more difficult to enter the mountain." Leannan shifted her weight, bracing herself with her hands cupped on the edge of the counter behind her. "There are things we will need for the journey, which will take us time to gather."

"Like what?" Robbie asked.

"Primroses and a ravenstone," Leannan said.

"What's that stuff?"

"The primroses will open the portal to my world. And the ravenstone—"

"Makes one invisible," Ross interrupted.

Leannan quirked her brows. "Ye know of that?"

"I've read it in a very old book. But you need to steal a raven's egg to get one, and the ravens' chicks have already hatched by now."

"Aye, 'tis true, but perhaps a raven could be tricked."

"So if they find an egg now, they'll think it should have hatched already—" Ross said.

"And be more prompt in retrieving the magical pebble." Leannan smiled.

"I still don't get it," Robbie said.

"A ravenstone brings to life a chick that has not hatched," Leannan said. "So if ye desire a ravenstone, ye rob the raven eggs before they hatch, hard-boil them so they never can, and then return them to the nest. The mother raven realizes something is wrong with her babies and brings a ravenstone to save them. Then ye steal the magical pebble."

"So where do we get a raven's egg if they've all hatched already?" Robbie asked.

"My guess is another trip to the henhouse," Ross said.

Leannan nodded in agreement. "And we shall need a little paint."

"What color is a raven's egg?" Robbie asked.

"'Tis greenish and speckled with brown."

"The Araucana hens lay greenish-blue eggs. Perhaps we can find a couple of small ones," Ross said.

"I think Caitie has some paint. I'd rather go find that." Robbie crossed his arms. "I've already been to the henhouse."

"All right. I'll go this time," Ross said.

"I think I shall lie down for a wee bit." Leannan took one step forward and fainted.

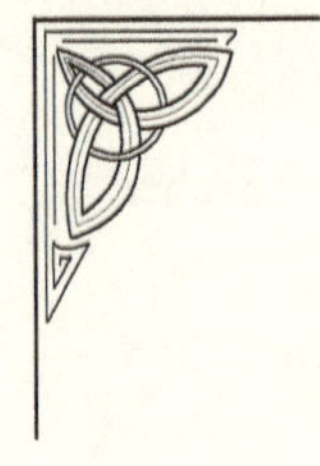

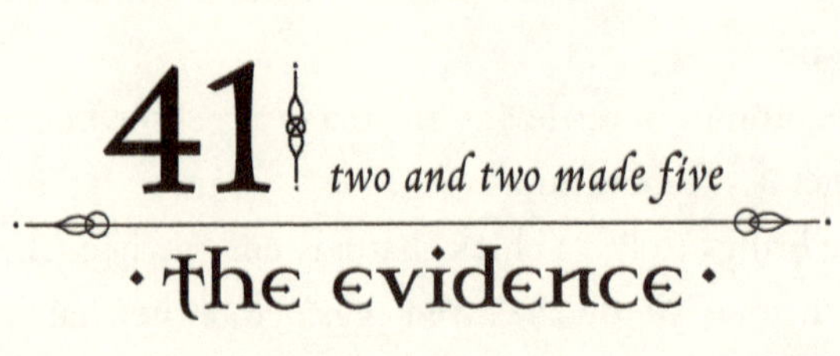

41 *two and two made five*

· the evidence ·

EVEN MORE SCARED THAN MAD, CAITIE PRESSED AGAINST the invisible barrier at the tunnel opening and got to her feet. Lileas would be coming back to Oseron's room soon, and if she didn't want the chambermaid to find out what she'd discovered, she had to get back. It wasn't fair she could see her way out and not be able to escape. But even worse was the fact that she didn't know how to break the spell or whatever it was that kept her captive. If she couldn't figure it out, she'd be stuck here forever. She'd never see Mom or Robbie or her grandparents ever again. Her chin trembled and eyes blurred. She couldn't think like that. She wouldn't think like that! Caitie closed the strange door, leaving it open just a crack, the way she'd found it.

Stooping down, she picked up the candleholder and plodded back down the passageway. Maybe that trunk in the wheelbarrow had something she could use to poke through the barrier. Or maybe that's where the king hid her phone. Its brass latch gleamed in the candlelight. With trembling fingers, Caitie twisted the barrel-shaped piece ninety degrees to align it with the slot. The stubborn hasp couldn't be budged with her one free hand.

Caitie set the candleholder on the ground next to the ancient wheelbarrow. She released the latch on the large trunk using both hands, retrieved her light, and eased the heavy lid open a third of the way. In the dim candlelight, a crumpled body popped up, bobbing like a buoy in the ocean. King Oseron's vacant, bulging eyes stared through her inches from her face, and his blue lips gaped wide. She wretched from the body's sickening sweet smell, and bile seared the back of her throat. She jerked her hand from the trunk lid. It slammed shut.

Shaking uncontrollably, she set the candleholder back down on the ground, the liquid wax burning as it dribbled down her hand. She wriggled her finger free from the candleholder's ring. She pressed her cupped hands hard against her mouth to stifle a scream. Had she really seen what she thought she did?

This time, pinching the ring on the candleholder, she raised the light, lifted the lid only four inches, and took a second look. The floating face was still there. It was King Oseron, no doubt about it.

She released the lid and walked back to the king's room as fast as the flickering flame would allow. Once inside, she removed the key from the slot in the statue's head, shutting the secret passageway's entrance. She returned the key to the base of the small statue of the queen and the candleholder to the nightstand. With shaky hands, she shut the cage door on the chicks that cheeped cheerfully on their perches. Lileas waltzed through the door.

"I must apologize for leaving all this for ye to do. I knew not how difficult Nuala was going to be," Lileas said.

"It's okay." Caitie felt light-headed.

"Ye look so pale."

"I don't feel so good. I need to lie down."

"All right. But ye must recover soon, for King Oseron expects ye to do all of Leannan's work."

He doesn't anymore.

Lileas led the way back to Leannan's room.

"Have you seen King Oseron today?" Caitie asked as casual as she could.

"Aye, I served him breakfast this morning before he went to the treasure room, and I went to wake ye."

"Oh." *Then he wasn't killed last night.*

Lileas opened Leannan's door. "I will come for ye in a wee while."

Caitie collapsed on the bed trying to sort out what she'd seen and what to do next.

THE KNOCK AT THE DOOR, THOUGH EXPECTED, STILL STARTLED CAITIE. She opened it by the light of the rose colored torch in her room.

Lileas filled the doorway and looked Caitie over, concern in her warm brown eyes. "Are ye feeling better?"

"Much," she lied.

"Then let us go prepare for dinner."

Once in the alcove off the main hall, Lileas showed her how to fix a plate, filling it with toadstools, cheeses, beans, and seaweed all arranged to create a food picture.

"Look, I'm not that artistic," Caitie said. "It'll take me all night to get one ready."

Lileas let out a sigh that jiggled the tight curls on her forehead. She grabbed a plate and in two seconds arranged the seaweed into a stem, the cheese slices into petals and the beans into the flower's center. "Then do this or lump it all into a bird." Lileas went to work on another one. "This morning at breakfast King Oseron requested ye be the one to serve him the evening meal."

Caitie wanted to tell her it didn't matter now anyway, but she wasn't going to be the one to say the king was stuffed in a trunk. "What did you say to him?"

"That I was sure ye would serve him well," Lileas cocked her head with an *And you'd better too* look.

"I don't know how to be a waitress."

Lileas looked confused with her eyebrows squished together and her lips shut tight.

"You know, the whole serving thing."

"I believe ye can, Caitie, and ye will. There are only a few things for ye to remember." The fairy clasped her hands together. "King Oseron is always served first. Ye start by filling his chalice with mead as soon as he arrives. Ye must remain attentive, while never hovering. 'Tis a challenge to keep the proper balance."

"Okay," Caitie said, just to humor her.

"Ahh, here he comes. Now go. And be pleasant!" Lileas shoved a pitcher into Caitie's hands.

Caitie turned her head to see Oseron take the seat at his table. Her mouth hung open and her feet froze in place.

"What is wrong, Caitie?"

"Oh, nothing." She'd been sure it was him in the trunk. The body, or what she thought was one, had been bobbing in the trunk like a balloon though. But it too gross and real to be fake. And that sickening smell.

"Then go," Lileas urged.

Caitie walked over to the king's table. "Good evening." She bent down near him and sniffed. No sweet smell.

"Pleasant evening, Caitie. Lileas has reported what a fine maidservant ye shall make."

"Thanks." She picked up his chalice and poured, only she was studying him so hard the mead flowed over the brim onto the table.

"Perhaps Lileas was mistaken," he said, nodding to her mess. "And mind your words. 'Tis not how we express gratitude here."

"Oh yeah. Sorry."

"Ye are a bonnie lass, Caitie, but I have the power to make your life here better or worse. Think about that. By the way, 'twould please me to see ye in a fine dress on the morrow instead of trews."

Just what was that supposed to mean? Did he plan for her to end up in a trunk too? "I'll be back with your dinner." She gave him a super sugary smile, her mind reeling.

If Oseron was still alive, which he sure seemed to be, the poor guy in the trunk had to be his twin, one the king didn't want around. Or maybe the guy in the trunk was the real king and the brother was impersonating him.

42 *the decoys were set*

·running out of time·

3:30 PM
JUNE 28TH

THE PATTER OF RAIN ON THE SHED ROOF STOPPED, drawing Robbie to the window. The fuzzy gray blanket of sky was way lighter now, a good sign for their plan with the hard-boiled, blue-green eggs Leannan had speckled with burnt umber watercolor. Those stupid eggs had to look real if they wanted any chance of fooling a raven, and the rain wasn't going to help.

"Do you think they're small enough?" Robbie asked, worried their plan wouldn't work.

"The only way to truly know will be to place them in the nests." Leannan's voice was soft as velvet.

Robbie stuffed a towel in an old coffee can and gently buried the eggs inside, covering them so they wouldn't get wet. "Are you feeling better?"

"A wee bit," she answered.

"I'm gonna put two in the nest out back." He picked up the can and left Leannan resting on Ross's bed with her eyes closed and hands folded on her stomach. It was weird to see her like that. Caitie always curled up on her side when she didn't feel good.

He set the can beneath the eaves and picked up the rickety ladder leaning against the shed. Ross had pointed out a ravens' nest in an old tree by the henhouse before going back to work in the barn with Grandpa MacGregor. Robbie propped the ladder against the tree trunk and retrieved two eggs. He gingerly crawled up the groaning rungs. At least, the view of the tree was blocked from the house windows by the barn and shed. Mom probably wouldn't be happy if she could see what he was doing. The twig nest was within reach but empty. He nestled one egg inside on the dirty sheep's wool lining it.

Bummed, Robbie returned to the shed and set the can on the table. "That nest looks abandoned."

Leannan sat up slowly. "We shall find another."

"Can you even go for a walk?"

"I must. We have this one chance, and we cannot waste it." She stood, took a deep breath, and stepped toward the door.

He wasn't sure the next nest would be any more promising. "We'd better tell Mom, I mean, my mom we're going." Robbie set the coffee can under the bushes by the back door so no one would see it and stepped inside. "Mom?"

"Gran and I are in the living room, looking at old photos of you two."

"We're gonna go for a hike."

"Again? You just went yesterday."

"We want to see if the burn rose," Leannan said.

Mom leaned back on the couch and looked down the hallway at them. "I didn't know you knew a river was a burn, Caitie. I'm impressed. Well, be careful. And put your boots on."

He and Leannan passed behind Mom and Grandma, who were pouring over an album from his pre-school days. He steadied Leannan as she climbed the stairs real slow. She went to look for Caitie's boots while he searched for his. He found them on the other side of his wardrobe and sat on the carpet to put them on. Leannan came in as he finished tying the laces of the first boot. He shoved the second one on, but his toes ran into something hard. "What the…?" He pulled the boot off, stuck his hand in, and pulled out Caitie's camera. "I found it!"

Leannan went pale. "The silver box!"

"I guess Caitie figured nobody would search here. My boots smell pretty bad."

"I must sit down." Leannan's eyes didn't leave Caitie's Lumix. "I am more weary than I thought, Robbie."

"Are you strong enough to go to the woods?"

"'Tis my hope that I am."

He got on his knees and gazed up into the face of his sister. "Then stay, Leannan. I can go alone."

"Ye know not what ye seek. I must accompany ye."

She was right. "Okay. We'll just take it real easy." He stashed the camera inside the nightstand.

Leannan gave him a puzzled look.

"I just want to make sure it doesn't disappear."

They strolled toward the woods in silence. The wet grasses soaked his jeans, and occasionally, a huge water droplet fell from a tree and landed on his head. The river was way louder, running faster and higher after the storm. They came to a spot where a fallen tree made a bridge to a small island. A bunch of ravens roosted on the trunk not far from a mud spattered nest camouflaged by branches.

"Do ye spy their nest, Robbie?" Leannan asked.

"Yeah." He pulled two of the painted eggs from the coffee can and slipped one in each of his jacket pockets. He crawled onto the tree near the upturned roots and moved like a monkey along the narrow trunk.

The baby ravens and their parents took flight. Robbie's heart whomped in his chest as he crossed over the rushing river. He straddled the trunk and deposited the eggs into the nest as the seat of his jeans got wetter with each second.

With no idea where the birds had gone, it didn't seem smart to shout over the raging water, so he nodded to Leannan instead to signal he'd done it. She smiled weakly in return, worry wrinkling her brow. His clunky boots slipped on the smooth bark, making it hard to keep his balance on the skinny log.

"I'm glad that's over with." He jumped down to the ground.

"Well done, Robbie."

They left the river and followed the squishy path through the woods. The rain made everything smell so fresh, and a thousand different birds called out to one another. He watched Leannan as she studied the trees.

"There Robbie, do ye see the raven up in that oak?" Leannan pointed up.

"No," he answered.

"There on the fourth branch of the tree with the large knot. A mother is on her nest."

"I see her." He wished Ross were there to do this. The little finches in the backyard in San Diego were bad enough when they guarded their nests. This one looked mean and way bigger. He handed Leannan the coffee can and jumped, stretching for the lowest limb. He didn't come close. With his arms wrapped most of the way around the trunk, he tried shimmying up, but he didn't get far, only sore hands.

The raven stayed put, glaring at him.

He needed a rope to swing over a branch to help him climb up, but they didn't have one. He scanned the ground and saw a fallen limb. "There's a big branch over there. Maybe I can use that."

"Try to urge her out of her nest with it. Perhaps I can fool her as well."

"How?" Robbie asked.

"Ye shall see."

Robbie lugged the heavy limb over, but Leannan had disappeared. He stood it upright and waved it near the raven's nest. The bird cawed and swooped down to attack him. He tried swinging the branch at her. A bush nearby rustled and a loud, "OooOoooo. OooOoooo," came from somewhere inside, freaking him out even more.

The raven took off.

Leannan crawled out from beneath the bush and collapsed on the ground. "Hurry, Robbie, she shan't be gone long."

"That was good. What kind of call was it?" He propped the lighter end of the branch against the oak so it nestled into the 'Y' of the main trunk.

"An eagle owl. They are one of the raven's few enemies."

Robbie half-crawled, half-shimmied three quarters of the way up the wobbly limb before stopping.

"I forgot the eggs," he said. "Can you hand them to me?"

Groaning, she stood, picked up the can, and held it up to him.

Robbie leaned over as far as he dared to take it. He slipped the last two eggs into his pockets and tossed the container to the ground before making his way up the rest of the branch and into the oak tree.

He duck-walked across the limb toward the nest, steadying himself with the branches above. Inside were four scruffy black babies, squawking for their mother. Robbie pulled out the first egg and deposited it in the nest, being careful not to touch any of the baby birds. He dropped in the second egg, scooted back to the trunk, and was half-way down his branch ladder when the mother came flying back. The raven screeched and dive bombed him. He dropped to the ground, and she rejoined her babies.

"She is none too happy with ye, Robbie."

"I kinda got that feeling. Let's get outta here."

They followed a fork in the trail that circled back toward the farm. Leannan reached for his hand and led him to a patch of yellow flowers. "Remember this spot, Robbie, as these are primroses, and we must come back for them on the morrow."

"Can't we just pick 'em now?" he asked.

"I am afraid they will be dead by then," she said sadly. She stumbled, and he caught her before she went down.

"Do you need me to carry you?" he asked.

"Not yet. I want to feel the earth beneath me for as long as I can."

43 the lights came on

·'Twas Murder·

11:59 PM
JUNE 28TH

CAITIE TRIED TUGGING THE PURPLE BERRY JUG FROM ITS cubbyhole in the tree painted on the cask room wall, but it wouldn't come out. Her life was so screwed up. Here she was barmaid to fairies when it was illegal for her to go into a pub this late at night.

The latch on the door clicked closed, startling her. She whipped around to find Cormag leering at her and swaying like he'd drunk a keg of ale all by himself.

"Hellooo there, lassie." He stumbled toward her.

Her heart raced. "I gotta go."

"I think not." The drunken guard chuckled and flopped his head from side to side.

She tried to scoot around him, but he grabbed her arm and pushed her against the giant keg of heather ale on the opposite wall. He reeked of the stuff, and she wondered which one of them was gonna puke first.

Cormag thrust his glowing hand around her throat. His steamy breath burned her ear. "Now why did ye try to run away from me?"

"Cormag!" Lileas boomed.

Thank you!

The guard didn't move. "Go away."

"Leave her be." Lileas approached as calm and controlled as any officer on the TV show *Cops*.

"Ye have no place giving me orders. Go out to the Hall where ye belong. All that should be concerning ye is keeping the tankards full." His black eyes bore into Caitie's, and the hair on the back of her neck rose. "I told ye to leave, Lileas."

"And ye must know that King Oseron has taken a keen interest in Caitie. For your sake and hers, go to bed."

Cormag loosened his grip on her throat. He ran his fingers through his oily black hair and staggered away.

Caitie shivered and rubbed her neck. "Am I glad to see you!"

Lileas gently pried her away from the wall. "'Tis over, Caitie. Ye are fine. And Cormag shan't remember a thing come morning."

"He's horrible."

"Aye. That he is." Lileas nodded. "I think ye have had quite enough for one day." She walked Caitie through the corridors bathed in blue torchlight.

"Don't you ever get tired of waiting on everyone? Especially jerks like Cormag?"

"No." The chambermaid looked surprised. "'Tis my duty."

"That doesn't mean you don't get sick of it."

Lileas stopped at Leannan's door. "My friends depend on me. I do my duties the best I can, and there is honour in that, even if my role is lowly." She swung the door open and ushered Caitie inside.

"Well, what if someone said you could be anything you wanted to be. What would you choose?"

"To be one of the dancers," she said without hesitation.

"Why don't you some night?"

"Look at me, Caitie." Lileas spread her arms wide. "They would laugh at me if I tried."

"Well, if it's your dream, you should go for it."

"The dancers are long, lean, and graceful. I am none of that." Her brown eyes looked sadder than a Basset Hound's.

"You work hard every day 'cause your friends depend on you, and you want to make them happy, right?"

"Aye."

"Well, if they're real friends, and they know what it means to you, they won't laugh," she said, shaking her head.

"Your words are most kind, but I know my place and 'twill never be on the dance floor. Now I must return to the Hall. Pleasant evening." Lileas waltzed from the room.

I guess I'm not the only one getting a raw deal here. She didn't know how she could help Lileas, but she had to get out of the mountain before things got any worse for herself.

Arms wrapped around her knees, Caitie rocked on Leannan's bed biding her time until there was finally an end to the footsteps and the conversations outside her door, well past the change in the torchlight from royal to silvery blue. Caitie eased open Leannan's door, leaned her head out into the hallway, and glanced in both directions. It was empty. She slipped into the passageway and shut the door. Staying in the shadows as best she could, she tiptoed toward the Great Hall. She paused near the main corridor to see if she could sense anyone there. It was silent. She stole past the banquet room and into the tunnel leading to the dungeon. The deeper she went, the colder and danker the air got.

Reaching the cell doors, she quietly whispered, "Mungan?"

No reply.

"Mungan, wake up!"

The dark lump in the corner stirred. "Aye." He ambled to the door.

"Look, I've been thinking. You want to help Leannan, right?"

"Of course."

"Well, I'll help you get out of here, if you'll help me."

"How?"

"I'm somehow 'bound' to this place. I need to know what to do to break the spell."

"Caitie, did ye partake of our food and drink?" He sounded like she couldn't have done anything more stupid in the whole world.

"Yeah. I was starving."

"But I warned ye not to."

"Well, I missed it if you did. The point is, there's got to be something I can do to fix this. I found a way out, but this invisible wall kept me from leaving."

"How did ye get to our portal without anyone noticing?"

"I found a secret passage."

"Where?" His eyes glinted in the dim candlelight.

"I'll tell you in a minute after you tell me how I can get free."

"There is only one way, and that is for a free mortal to throw a knife above your head at dawn on the third day after the binding."

She had to have misunderstood. "What?"

Mungan repeated it way slower.

She'd heard him right the first time. "So where am I gonna find a free mortal?"

"Not inside the mountain."

She spread her hands high on the iron barred door and dropped her head. *Could this nightmare possibly get any worse?*

Mungan's boots scuffed on the floor as he came closer. "Now tell me, Caitie, where is this secret passage?"

"In Oseron's room."

He drew back in surprise. "How did ye find it?"

"By accident, but there's something horrible in there."

"What is it?"

"Does Oseron have a twin brother?"

"No. Why?"

"Because there's a body in a trunk in that passageway, and it looks exactly like the king. At first, I thought it was the king 'cause I hadn't seen him this morning. But when he showed up for dinner, I realized it couldn't be him."

"Was it dark in the passage? Could ye have been mistaken?"

"The only light was from my candle. But I'm telling you it was bright enough for me to know what I saw. The weird thing though was he floated like a balloon."

"Dead fae do that over time." Mungan knocked his forehead with his clenched fist. "Leannan's mysterious mouse the night of the chess match and Ballard's spider. 'Tis finally making sense."

"Well, I'm glad it does for somebody."

"I did not kill my sister, Caitie, but ye revealed to me who did and found the proof of my innocence."

"I have?" She didn't understand how.

"Ye are a brave and resourceful lass." He smiled and even in the dim light she could see that he looked at her with new respect in his eyes.

"That's kind, but I'm desperate to get out of here! I miss my family and I want to go home."

"Fate has thrust us together through an unfortunate turn of events. It appears we need each other to make things right for us all. Time is frittering away as is Leannan's life. If ye will help me to escape and tell me where the camera is, I will bring your brother back to the mountain along with Leannan. And he can be the one to unbind ye."

Robbie wasn't the greatest with a baseball. She doubted she'd survive him pitching a knife in her direction. "My camera's in Robbie's room. It's in his hiking boot. But you gotta bring Ross back instead. He knows about you guys, but he's cool. And I trust him way more with a knife than Robbie." Mungan didn't argue. "That guy on the throne isn't the king then."

"No. He is not."

"Who is he?"

"Someone most dangerous indeed. So ye must be very careful."

"I need to get going, but I'll come back tomorrow night. Will that give you enough time to get Leannan and Ross here?"

"The sooner ye free me, the better. Do ye have a plan for my escape?"

"I'm still working on that, but I've got an idea."

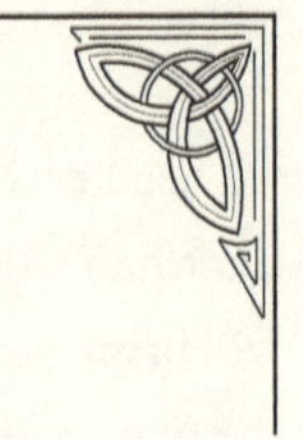

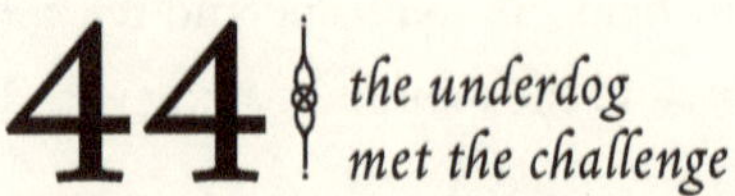

·seeking the advantage·

GUSTY WINDS WHISTLING THROUGH THE ATTIC WOKE Robbie. He sat up in bed and looked out the window at Loch Ness covered in white caps. Robbie wished the day was already over with Caitie back home and Leannan in her mountain.

Too nervous to go back to sleep, he threw the covers off and got out of bed. He padded down the hallway into Caitie's room. His foot froze mid-step.

Leannan slept curled up on her side with her head and upper body hovering a couple of inches above the mattress. The quilt and sheets pinned her legs to the bed. "Leannan," he whispered.

She didn't stir.

"Wake up."

The changeling opened her eyes, just barely. "Is it morning already?"

"Yeah and you're floating. What do we do?"

"Nothing can be done for there is not much left of me."

"We gotta get you home."

"The best thing to do is for ye to check the nests for ravenstones that we may leave tonight when the others in the house are asleep."

"Okay. Can you come down for breakfast?"

"If I am floating, they will suspect something is amiss."

"And if you stay in bed all day, they'll *know* something's wrong."

Robbie went to the chest of drawers and pulled out a pair of Caitie's jeans and the heaviest long sleeve sweater he could find. "Put these on. Maybe that'll help. I'll be back in a minute." He left to get dressed and returned to find Leannan in a sitting position hovering a couple of inches above the end of Caitie's bed. "If my mom sees you like this, she'll freak."

Leannan squinched her eyebrows in confusion.

"She'll be super worried. I'll just have to hold you down. C'mon, let's try and practice."

Leannan wobbled into a standing position and tried to walk. She floated like an old helium balloon just above the floor. Robbie grabbed the belt loop on the back of her jeans and pushed down lightly.

"Now walk." She took a few steps. "This'll work as long as I don't let go."

The two left Caitie's room and tottered down the stairs. By the time they reached the kitchen, Robbie had figured out the pace and how close he had to be to Leannan without them looking goofy.

Mom sat at the kitchen table reading the want ads. "Good morning, you two."

Grandma MacGregor dished up bowls of porridge for them.

Robbie pulled out the chair for Leannan and pressed down on her neck as she sat down. She gripped the side of the seat as he pushed her under the table. He grabbed their breakfast.

"It's a blustery day out there, so I made the porridge extra thick," Grandma said.

"Thanks." Robbie was more than happy to offer his to Leannan if it would help weigh her down. He was sick of porridge but couldn't come up with a way to tell Grandma without hurting her feelings and getting into trouble.

He sat down and crossed his right leg with his left, resting his foot on Leannan's knee to keep her on the chair. They both stirred the porridge around in their bowls but didn't eat much.

Mom lowered the newspaper. "I was wondering, would you two like to invite a couple of friends over this afternoon? I could take you into Inverness to the indoor pool, and afterwards, we could grab a pizza or something. You could even ask if they wanted to spend the night."

Why did Mom have to pick today? "Could we do it tomorrow?"

"Why wait? It's so miserable out. Seems like a good day to have some inside-fun planned. Go ahead, call Duncan and see if he can come. And Caitie, what about Bonnie? Or Rose?"

"I don't feel too well, Mom," Leannan said. "Perhaps tomorrow?"

"Yeah, I don't want to if Caitie's not up for it."

"Do you suppose Caitie should be seen by Doctor McTavish, Maisie?" Grandma asked.

"It might be a good idea."

Robbie cleared the dishes and rinsed half the porridge down the sink.

"I will be fit as a fiddle tomorrow, Mom. You will see."

"I certainly hope so. You don't even sound like yourself, honey."

They left the kitchen the same way they came in without Mom or Grandma noticing anything else funny about "Caitie."

"Robbie, I have no strength," Leannan whispered.

"Then I'll carry you up the stairs." He lifted Leannan on to the back of the couch and turned away from her. "Put your arms around my neck, and I'll give you a piggyback ride."

"Piggyback? 'Tis an odd expression."

She was so light like she wasn't there. He set her on his bed.

"Robbie, I fear ye must go to the woods alone today."

"I figured as much. Will you be okay here?"

"Perhaps I will lie down."

"I don't think that's such a good idea. You heard my mom. She's threatening to take you to the doctor. That's the last thing we need."

"But, Robbie, I have so little strength."

"I got an idea. I'll sit you in front of the computer and pull up You-Tube. That'll keep you busy for hours, and Mom won't suspect a thing."

He pulled out his desk chair and lifted her onto it. Then he brought over his pillow and tucked it under the desk so it rested on the top of her legs, holding her in place. He logged on. "You use the mouse to pick what you want to see. Like this."

"What mouse?"

"It's this thing." He tapped on the computer mouse. She looked at him like he'd lost his mind.

"Robbie, there are peculiar fae caged in this computer box."

"Those aren't fairies. They're people."

She looked up at him with Caitie's big green eyes, totally clueless. "They are too tiny to be people."

"They're not real people in the box. They're movies of people. Cameras like Caitie's sort of capture memories of people doing stuff. And when they're downloaded on a computer, they replay what the people did. It's kind of complicated."

"Robbie, it frightens me."

"It's not gonna hurt you." But he knew she wasn't getting any of what he said. "I gotta go."

"Do ye remember how to find the nests?"

"Yeah." He wasn't about to tell her he didn't want to go to the woods by himself. She had enough of her own problems to worry about. "I'll be back soon." He snuck out of the house through the front door.

THE WIND BLASTED ROBBIE AS HE JOGGED TOWARD THE WOODS, whipping the brush and stirring his imagination. Any movement out of the corner of his eye or strange sounds spooked him. He felt sure invisible eyes were watching, maybe even hunting him. After all, he had a changeling in his own bedroom. What else was out there he didn't know about?

Robbie found the right path and hurried to the river. The ravens were gone, but he scurried across the tree bridge anyway. The speckled eggs were in the nest just as he left them. But there was no ravenstone.

He rushed to the tree in the woods. The mama raven was on her nest. He wished Leannan was there. Hiding behind a bush, he rustled it and tried to hoot like an owl the way she did. The bird didn't flinch. No reason to. His imitation was lame. The tree limb up the old oak was still in place. *I can do this.* He took a deep breath and crawled up it. The raven screeched as soon as he climbed into the tree. He was sure his heart was beating as fast as the raven's. He flailed his arms, tried his pathetic owl call again, and edged toward her nest. The closer he got, the louder she squawked. He brought his arm close to his face to shield against an attack and inched within a foot of the nest. The raven spread her wings and lunged at him, tearing gashes in his sleeve and arm with her claws and ripping the flesh on his head with her beak.

"Stop it! Stop it!" he screamed.

She battered him with her flapping wings, knocking him off balance. He latched onto a branch, catching himself.

Robbie waved the raven away with his battered arm and glanced inside the nest. The babies were huddled together and squeaking. The two eggs had been rolled to one side. Resting on top of them was a small black pebble. Robbie couldn't believe his eyes. He scooped up the rock. "Got it!" He pivoted on the branch to make his way back down. The raven attacked him again, gouging the flesh on the back of his neck with her beak.

Clutching the pebble tight in his hand, he watched where he put his feet on the branch, afraid that with one wrong step he'd tumble out of the tree. But his boots started turning transparent, revealing the branch supporting him. He freaked. His jeans were disappearing too along with the rest of his body. Robbie stopped when he reached the tree trunk. The raven was back on her nest and seemed to be looking for him. He scrambled down the tree holding the pebble in his clenched fist.

Back on the ground, he slid the pebble into his jeans pocket. As soon as the rock was away from his skin, he was visible. He raced over the trail he and Leannan had taken the day before, stopping only long enough to pick a dozen primroses and then ran back to the farm. At the edge of the woods, he pulled out the pebble and held it tightly. Within a few seconds his body, shredded jacket, jeans, boots, and the flowers he held were completely invisible. This could probably come in handy and not just today.

Robbie marched straight across the lawn to the shed and slipped through the door. He set the ravenstone on the table, and his body slowly reappeared. The flowers needed a vase. He pulled a glass from a shelf, filled it at the sink, and stuck the primrose stems in the water. He snuck out back and carried the ladder over to check the other nest near the henhouse. The egg was there but no ravenstone.

Still, he couldn't help but smile from the inside out. He'd done it! He got a ravenstone and it worked. Only problem though was that there were three of them and only one ravenstone.

45 *the fox set out to trap the hound*

the set-up

CAITIE TOSSED AND TURNED THE REST OF THE NIGHT, trying to remember every jailbreak scene she'd ever watched on TV. The torchlights changed from silvery blue to peach while she finalized her plan to free Mungan. With no cell phone or watch, all she could do was wait and guess when it was about time to get up. This no-clock business was making her nuts. She dressed, left Leannan's room, and strode toward Lileas's, stopping at the corridor paintings to check the weather. The landscape skies were dark, and the tree tops whipped in the wind. She hoped for Mungan's sake it would clear up later in the day.

Knock. Knock-knock.

Lileas answered, stifling a yawn. "Ye certainly are the early bird today." The maidservant stretched her stocky arms and quadrupled her chin.

"I can't tell time by torchlight very well. Besides, I got a new attitude and can't wait to start the day."

THE BANQUET TABLES IN THE ALCOVE WERE PILED WITH PLATES each holding a bird whose body was sculpted from cheese slices with berries she didn't recognize for eyes and sitting on a nest of weird, lacy things that had to be roots. Caitie picked up a plate in each hand and plastered a broad smile on her face. Deciding it might help her plan if she could win over the Daoine Shi, Caitie bubbled with friendliness as she set their breakfast before them. Most of the men reciprocated with admiring eyes and appreciation. The women, however, glanced at her sideways with distrust and tight lips. At first, it was a total act to be so perky while serving. But as she made her way around the Hall, the conversation she had with Lileas about the job re-played like a CD track in Caitie's head, and it didn't seem so bad. Or maybe it was the possibility that she could be out of this place by the next day that lifted her spirits.

Cormag and Oseron entered the Great Hall later than most. King Oseron went to his table, and Cormag left him to find a seat at one of the banquet tables. Caitie wanted to dump a plate over Cormag's head but that would only get her in trouble and she had big enough problems as it was.

Lileas bustled over to King Oseron with his breakfast, but she returned just as fast with his plate still in her hands, chewing her lower lip. The maidservant's eyes brimmed and tears spilled over.

Caitie took the tea towel and wiped Lileas's generous cheeks. "What's the matter? What did he say to you?"

Lileas handed her the king's plate. "King Oseron prefers for ye to serve him from now on."

"What?" She didn't like where this was headed.

"I cannot understand as I have waited on the king for more than a hundred and fifty years." Lileas swallowed hard and shooed Caitie away with her large hands. "Now go. Ye must not keep him waiting."

Caitie wanted to tell Lileas that King Oseron was a fake, but she couldn't risk the news getting out. Mungan's warning about the imposter being dangerous rang in her ears, and she sure didn't want anything wrecking her plan. She strode to King Oseron's table and plastered on a mask of calm to hide how disgusted she was with and by him. "Would you like some breakfast, King Oseron?"

"Now that's better." The king's lip curled. "It pleases me no end that my prize aptly does my bidding."

Caitie fought the temptation to mash the bird on his plate all over his face. She set his breakfast on the table instead. "Where I come from, we wish an actor well by saying 'Break a leg' and address a king such as you, Your Majesty, by saying 'Choke on it.'"

Oseron got a stupid look on his face like a cartoon character with gears turning in a bubble over his head, trying to figure out if he'd been insulted. Caitie gave him a prom queen smile. She curtseyed and rushed back to Lileas, who was throwing the food on the plates. Her birds now looked like Picasso paintings with extra eyes and upside down wings.

"He's such a jerk!" Caitie said quietly.

"Ye misunderstand him." Lileas took a shuddering breath and put on a brave but totally fake smile. "King Oseron has been a good and faithful ruler for longer than I have been alive."

"I don't like seeing my friend hurt by someone who thinks they can get away with it. It's not right. A good king wouldn't do that. No one should act like that."

"Ye are still naïve but a dear."

"Not always."

"TODAY CAITIE, WE SHALL CHANGE THE LINENS." LILEAS OPENED THE SET of double doors to the laundry.

There were no washing machines and dryers. Instead the small room was filled with a large vat and a gigantic press made of twirling rollers attached to a folding table. One laundress swished a stick in the vat and tossed a sheet from the frothy water effortlessly into the air. Another caught it and whisked the fabric through the press that rolled it flat and folded it perfectly. The last laundress smoothed out any wrinkles with the touch of her pointer finger and placed the sheet onto a cart. Mom would love this set-up on laundry day. Lonesomeness for her and Robbie gripped Caitie even stronger than what she had felt when she left her friends in San Diego. If she could make it home, she'd be more helpful to Mom and not give Robbie such a hard time.

Lileas steered the cart of fresh linens toward the door. "Caitie, bring that one along for the soiled sheets."

The wheels in Caitie's brain took off like a sprint car at a race track. This will work perfectly. She followed Lileas into the corridor pushing the empty linen cart, thrilled that its wheels spun silently.

"Since we're here, can I visit the seamstresses for a second?"

"All right. I shall get started on the bedchambers." Lileas pushed her cart down the hall.

Caitie popped her head through the next doorway. "I don't suppose you have any of the fabric left from my top, do you?" She tugged on her shirt when the seamstresses looked confused.

"Oh." Ùna went to one of the cabinets and pulled the fabric out. "I saved it as 'twas so lovely. I thought I would fashion a tiny dress for one of the wee ones with the remnant."

"Could I possibly have a long strip to tie back my hair?" Caitie gathered her hair for a ponytail. "It gets in the way when I'm serving."

"Just give me a wee moment," the short seamstress said.

Caitie let her hair down and watched the moving rack model the gowns while she waited. A soft pink dress with long sleeves and a simple square neckline caught her eye. She touched the dress, and the rack stopped moving.

"That one is not your size," Pàislig said.

"I know. I was thinking it would look really nice on Lileas." She had other plans for it first, but eventually, she'd give it to her friend. Caitie looked at the friendship ring on her finger from Sara and reluctantly pulled it off. "I don't have any money to pay for the dress, but can I give you this ring for it?"

Pàislig cocked her head and studied Caitie. "No, ye cannot." The seamstress glided over to the rack and slipped the pink dress from the hanger. She smiled. "But ye can have the gown all the same."

The tall seamstress's eyes twinkled as she presented it to Caitie.

"That's so generous of you. She's gonna love it." Caitie draped the dress over her arm and slipped Sara's ring back on her finger.

Ùna glided over and handed Caitie the scarf.

"This is perfect!" She tied it around her head like a headband. "I'm really grateful." Caitie never realized how casually and often she used the word "thanks" 'til now. Maybe there was something to the Daoine Shi's dislike for the phrase. It took more effort to find other ways to express her thankfulness and that definitely made it more sincere.

CAITIE SAW HER OPPORTUNITY TO SNEAK AWAY AFTER SERVING LUNCH as the Daoine Shi stayed in the Great Hall laughing and talking or scattered to their chambers for a fae version of an afternoon siesta.

"Do you think it will be all right if I go back to my room for a few minutes?" she asked Lileas. "I want to rest for a little bit. We've worked really hard this morning."

Lileas gathered the used forks and spoons. "As ye wish."

Caitie hustled to her cleaning cart stowed in an alcove off the passageway leading to all the bedchambers. She grabbed the box with the gloves from the cart and headed back toward the Great Hall. Careful not to be seen, she casually peeked around a column in the main corridor opposite the preparation alcove, searching for Lileas. The maidservant was still busy cleaning with her back toward the banquet hall. Caitie strolled past and entered the hallway leading to the workshops.

She knocked on the wooden door of the Cobblers' Shoppe, expecting it to be empty. When no one answered, she slipped inside. She opened the gloves' box, and they popped out. "I need you to hold the door shut," she told them. "And if someone tries to come in, only let go when I nod. Then put yourselves back in the box." The gloves gave her the thumbs up sign and flew to the doorway, bracing the teardrop shut.

Caitie set their open box on a display rack next to the door and went over to the workbenches. They were covered with boots and shoes in various stages of completion. She plucked a small wooden hammer from the tools hanging on the wall. Next she searched for shoelaces and borrowed several long pairs.

The door handle turned and the gloves held it closed. Her heart raced. She shoved the shoelaces in the top of her trews underneath her shirt. The handle jiggled repeatedly and angry voices rose on the other side of the door, but the gloves held them back. Caitie yanked off her boot and pulled a wedge from the rack above the workbench. The cobblers pounded on the door. With shaking hands, she worked the heel of her boot free, hammering the wedge between the sole and heel. She slipped the small hammer into her trews beside the laces and exchanged the wedge for another hammer. Swallowing hard, she nodded to the gloves. They released their grip on the door and sailed into the box, pulling the lid down with their fingertips.

The cobblers burst inside. "What are ye doing in here?"Corc demanded.

Caitie's stomach somersaulted.

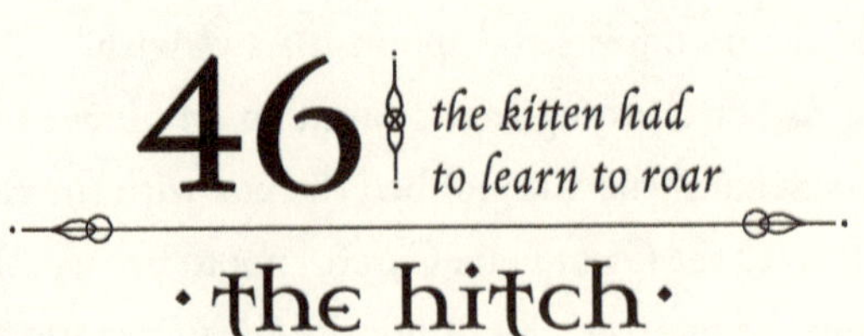

46 *the kitten had to learn to roar*

· the hitch ·

11:31 AM
JUNE 29TH

ROBBIE STOOD AT THE SINK IN THE SHED, GENTLY dabbing the blood off the scratches on his hands, arms, and face, and the gouges on his neck from the raven's attack. No way Mom wasn't going to notice he'd ended up on the wrong side of a fight. And no way could he explain to her how it had happened. She wasn't going to be happy about his shredded jacket either. The bigger problem though was the one ravenstone for the three of them. He had to tell Ross.

The smell of hay and manure hit Robbie as he stepped through the barn door. Balfour trotted over, his tail wagging. The Border Collie pushed his nose under Robbie's tender hand over and over again, begging for attention. Robbie knelt down and gave Balfour a good scratching under his chin. "How you doin', boy? Are you helping?" Robbie sauntered toward Grandpa MacGregor, who slung a huge plastic bag into the wheelbarrow.

"What's that?" Robbie asked.

"Fresh bedding," Grandpa said without looking over. He sounded tired like he'd been working for hours.

Ross was in the far stall shaking a big scoop of white powder on the floor. Grandpa pushed the wheelbarrow into the stall and sliced the bedding bag open with a pocketknife. He lifted the bulky sack high and started dumping it on the floor. Grandpa's knees buckled and his face winced with pain. Suddenly, everything went in slow motion. The bag crashed to the ground, erupting in a cloud of dust. Grandpa MacGregor collapsed, landing on his side with his hands clutched at his chest. He rolled on his back and stuff gurgled in his throat.

Robbie gasped.

Ross whipped around and ran to Grandpa MacGregor. "Angus!"

Grandpa's arms and legs twitched and his back arched. His eyes were fixed and glazed.

"Angus, can you hear me? Angus!"

Robbie knelt next to Grandpa; his own breath rapid and shallow. The old man ground his teeth as his jaws clenched tight. "What's wrong with him?" Robbie whimpered.

"It's a seizure. Tell your mother to call Doctor MacTavish. Now!"

Robbie stood and backed up a few steps, unable to stop staring at Grandpa.

"Hurry!" Ross yelled.

Robbie turned and ran as fast as he could, bursting out the door and racing against the howling wind to the house. He threw open the back door. "Mom!"

"What is it?" She rushed over from the kitchen sink, wiping her hands on a towel. Her eyes grew as big as golf balls, and her jaw dropped clear to her chest. "What happened to you?"

"It's Grandpa. There's something wrong with him," he said out of breath. Ross wants you to call Doc McSomebody."

The same frightened look he'd seen in her eyes for days after Dad's plane got shot down was back.

"Doctor MacTavish?"

"Yeah. Hurry!"

She fumbled for the phone on the sideboard and drew her shaking finger down the list of numbers lying next to it. The return on the rotary dial seemed to take forever as she spun each digit. "Tell me exactly what happened!"

"He picked up a bag of bedding to spread in the stall. Then he fell over and started twitching. His eyes were open, but you could tell he wasn't seeing anything."

Mom brought her fingers to her lips and chewed her nails while they waited a long time. "This is Maisie Finlay. My Dad, Angus MacGregor—He collapsed. I think he's had a seizure....Yes, we can get him to Raigmore Hospital. We'll leave right away."

Mom slammed the receiver back in its cradle. "Let's go, Robbie." She grabbed her purse as they rushed out the backdoor.

The wind pushed them across the yard and howled through the barn's rafters. Grandpa lay unconscious on the stone floor. Robbie and Mom knelt down beside him.

"How long has he been like this?" She looked and sounded as scared as a lost little kid.

"The seizure stopped a minute ago," Ross said.

"Doctor MacTavish wants us to get him to Inverness now."

Ross lifted Grandpa under his arms, and Mom carried his legs. They struggled to the car under the old man's dead weight.

Tears trickled down Mom's cheeks. "Oh, Dad, not now. It's too soon." Her voice cracked.

Robbie opened the backdoor to the Volvo. Mom crawled inside and helped Ross lay Grandpa on the seat.

"Where's Ina?" Ross asked.

"I took her to the Public Hall," Mom answered. "She's at a planning meeting for the Quilters Annual Auction. I'll get her and meet you at the hospital."

"You've got to take him, Maisie. You're family. I'm not. I'll get your mum."

"All right." Mom got out of the car, her hair flying wildly in the wind. "Robbie, maybe it's best if you stay. Will you and Caitie be okay here?" She touched his cheek, studying a scratch.

"Don't worry about us." Robbie was worried enough for both of them.

"I love you. Tell your sister the same for me. And be good!" She tossed Ross the keys to the SUV, got into the driver's seat of the Volvo, and started the car. Gravel spit out from the tires as she sped away.

Ross hurried to the SUV and got into the front seat. "I don't know when I'll get back, but you and Leannan must wait for me."

"Leannan's pretty bad, Ross. She's running out of time."

Ross looked him square in the eyes. "It's too dangerous!" He started the car. "I've got to get your gran to the hospital. Leannan's not in serious trouble 'til she's floating."

"But she—"

"Don't do anything foolish!" Ross slammed the door shut, threw the gear shift into reverse, spun the SUV around, and took off.

But Leannan was floating. How could he get her back to the mountain by himself? He wasn't some superhero—just a kid. Robbie trudged into the house and upstairs to his room. Leannan sat at his desk with her arms folded and her head resting on them. She was asleep and so pale. It terrified him to see Caitie's body like this. "Leannan?"

She didn't respond. He gently patted her arm.

"Aye." Her voice was tiny as though she called from far away.

"My Grandpa's sick. Mom took him to the hospital, and Ross is bringing Grandma there. We have to wait 'til Ross gets back to take you home. Can you last?"

"The blue bells are calling me. I shall be gone by morning."

Robbie shuddered. He couldn't stay and do nothing. They had to go while Leannan could still tell him how to get to the mountain. If she couldn't 'cause he waited too long, or worse yet, she died on the way, there was no hope for Caitie.

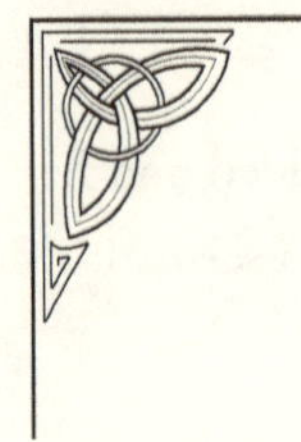

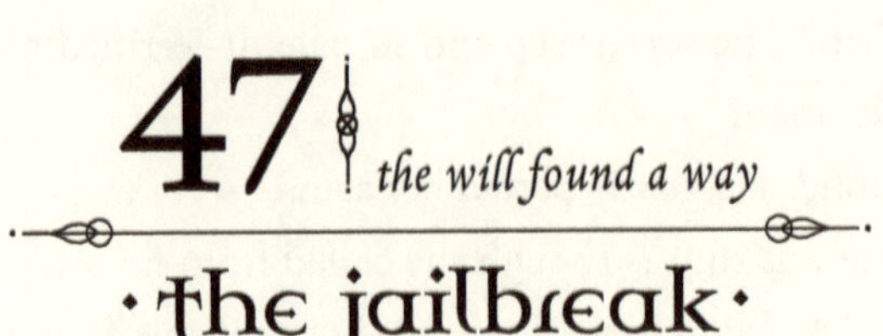

· the jailbreak ·

CAITIE FOUGHT TO KEEP THE TREMOR OUT OF HER VOICE as she answered the angry cobbler standing in the open doorway across the shoppe from her. "The heel on my boot came loose. I didn't want to trouble anyone, so I thought I'd just hammer it back on myself."

"Why did you not let us in?" Corc asked.

"I didn't stop you. The door must have been stuck." The cobblers crossed the floor, scowling like she was a serial shoe thief. She handed one of the bearded old guys her boot, hoping he couldn't tell she'd pried the heel loose.

"This one must have been made after the mid-day meal, when you were sleepy, Orin." The other old guy scoffed as the one with her boot took the hammer from Caitie's hand and nailed the heel back in place."

"I appreciate it." Caitie reached for her boot, slipped it on, and strode toward the door, her pulse pounding in her ears. She casually reached for the gloves' box resting on the display rack and left the shoppe.

CAITIE AND THE GLOVES WERE TUCKING THE FRESH SHEET AROUND Nuala's cloud-light mattress when Lileas came through the door.

"Are we ready to take the carts back to the laundry?" the maidservant asked.

"Not quite. You go ahead. I'll return mine when I'm finished."

Lileas turned to leave. "Then I shall meet ye in the alcove to prepare for dinner when the torchlights turn to their rosy red."

With the bed made, Caitie left Nuala's room. She ducked into Leannan's where she left the cart full of dirty sheets and the gloves nestled in their box. With everything set, she went to the alcove and found Lileas as the torchlights turned.

"It's been a few days now. Has anyone given Mungan something to eat?" Caitie asked.

"No," Lileas shook her bowed head.

"It's time somebody did."

"But King Oseron has condemned Mungan for the queen's murder."

"I've talked to him. Mungan doesn't seem like the kind of guy who'd do anything like that."

"Caitie, though it grieved my heart terribly, I found the evidence in Mungan's chamber."

"Well, our responsibility is to serve everyone in the kingdom, and he's still a Daoine Shi. I don't want his starving to death on my conscience. And I can't believe you do either."

Lileas cupped her face in her hands. "Fill a plate then although I doubt Cormag will allow ye to deliver it."

Caitie put together a tray for Mungan while Lileas poured him a tankard of heather ale. With her back to her friend, Caitie pulled the hammer out of her waistband and slipped it underneath the tray of food. "Okay, wish me luck."

Lileas set the tankard on the tray. "May Cormag be gracious for once."

Caitie entered the Great Hall, but Cormag wasn't there. Alvy stood on Ulvy's shoulders, pulling the last candle stubs from the chandelier. Elvy passed new tapers up to his brother. "Have you seen Cormag?"

"There, guarding the king." Elvy pointed toward the archway to the treasure room.

"That was really nice of you to tell me," Caitie said gently.

Elvy bowed. Ulvy did too. Alvy lost his balance and seized the chandelier, his gargantuan feet dangling wildly in the air.

"Ulvy!" Alvy shouted.

The giant's cheeks reddened. Ulvy grabbed his brother's swinging feet and placed them back on his shoulders.

Caitie smiled, and Elvy looked at her with eyes as large and adoring as a St. Bernard puppy's. Ulvy stooped and Alvy jumped to the floor. Caitie was sure the ground shook beneath them. The trio left the Hall as she wove through the banquet tables to find Cormag standing guard in the archway. As usual, he looked crabby like he had a major branch up his butt.

"I'm ready now," Caitie announced.

Cormag narrowed his eyes. "For what?"

"To take Mungan's tray down."

"Och." Cormag crossed his arms. "The prisoner gets no sustenance."

"Look, I'm just doin' what I'm told. Didn't King Oseron talk to you about this? I thought you and he were real tight. Guess I was wrong." Being nasty to this guy was easy. The bluff she was trying to pull off was anything but.

"Tell me what?" Cormag spit the words out.

"Mungan committed a horrible crime. The king wants him to rot in the dungeon for years. That won't happen if he starves in a few days."

"King Oseron has spoken none of this to me."

Caitie fought the swell of panic threatening to drown her. "Then go ask His Highness. But I'll make it real clear that you're the one questioning him and not me. When I did this morning, King Oseron got real ticked. I was sure I was on my way back to the cell next to Mungan's." She shook her head. "But don't let what happened to me stop you."

Cormag focused his beady, black eyes on her. He reached for the handle on the treasure room door.

"Go ahead. It's your neck. Not mine," she said with a laugh.

He let go of the door handle. "Follow me."

Thank you!

They left the archway and walked through the main corridor around the banquet hall to the passageway leading to the dungeon. Cormag stopped near the entrance at a cabinet hung on the wall and pulled two leather gloves out of it. He put them on as they walked down the long cold tunnel.

"Why do you need the gloves?" Caitie asked.

"The iron cell doors are harmful to us. It discourages the prisoners from hanging on the bars, trying to break them loose."

"I see."

Her stomach churned. Caitie could feel her heart pounding harder with every step. Her right hand holding the food tray ached and her left clenched the hammer handle so hard it cramped. As they approached the cells, Cormag pulled the ancient keys from his pocket. The henchman strode to the door and inserted the key into the lock. Caitie crept up behind him as he fiddled with the stubborn mechanism. Mungan stood up.

"Stay where ye are," Cormag ordered.

Caitie pulled the hammer out from beneath the tray and bashed the back of the guard's head. He crumpled instantly and dropped to the floor. "Ooowh!" Every part of her was shaking. *Please, don't let him be dead!*

"Well done!" Mungan beamed in the dim light.

"Do you think I've killed him?" She set the tray down on the floor.

"I do not think we could be so lucky."

"I only wanted to knock him out." Her trembling hands made it hard to unlock the door.

Mungan quickly stepped out of the cell and dragged Cormag inside. "Unfortunately, he still breathes. We must go quickly."

"Wait. Shouldn't we tie him up and gag him, in case he starts yelling for help."

"With what?"

"These." She pulled the shoelaces out from under her shirt and yanked the scarf from her hair.

"That will work nicely." Mungan bound Cormag's hands behind his back with the laces.

Caitie, still shaking like one of those foot massagers at the Del Mar Fair, rolled the scarf, placed it over his mouth, and tied it tight.

"I am impressed. Have ye ever done this before?" He tied Cormag's feet together with remaining laces.

"No. And I never want to do it again either. I'm way too stressed and I just want out of here!"

Mungan stooped and grabbed the cheese and slice of bread from the tray while Caitie locked the cell. They rushed half-way up the passageway before Caitie turned to him, "Wait here. I'll be back in less than five minutes." She sped the rest of the way up the tunnel, hesitating at the entrance to the main corridor. Hearing no one coming, she stole through it and down the hallway to Leannan's room. She dashed inside, retrieved the laundry cart, and as nonchalantly as possible, she pushed it back to where Mungan waited in the shadows.

"Jump in and bury yourself in the sheets. I'm gonna wheel you back to Leannan's room."

Mungan didn't look too excited.

"What's wrong?" Caitie asked. "I know it's been done a thousand times before in the movies, but it's all I could think of."

"The last time I crawled into the laundry, things did not turn out as I expected." Mungan slung one leg into the cart and then the other and hid himself in the sheets.

"I can't guarantee things will work out now either." She pushed him back to her room with no one noticing.

Mungan unearthed himself and hopped out. "I will forever be grateful for the risks ye have taken on my behalf, Caitie."

"Hold your appreciation. We haven't gotten you out of the mountain yet." She dug through the sheets and pulled out the pink dress. "But look what I got for you." She held it up in front of her.

Mungan looked horrified.

"You can't wreck it either 'cause I want to give it to Lileas when you're done with it."

"I cannot pass as a female."

"Sure you can. Where I come from, men do it all the time."

"But my hair." He reached up and tugged on his dark brown curls.

"I got an idea for that too." Caitie stripped the rose-colored silk sheet from Leannan's bed and tore a two foot wide strip off of it. She covered her head with the mega-scarf, leaving the extra fabric on one side hanging down her front and flinging the other side over her shoulder. It covered her face sort of like a middle-eastern burqa. She raised her hands in triumph. "What do you think?" If you sneak out in the next few hours, you'll blend in with the walls 'cause of the rosy torches."

Mungan shut his eyes for a second, looking pained. "All right, but I shall have on my own clothes beneath, for I refuse to enter your realm resembling a field of blooming heather."

Caitie unwound her burqa and handed it to him. "Be careful!" She stuck her head outside, making sure the coast was clear, and then casually pushed the laundry cart back through the hallway and into the main corridor, dodging

Lileas as she paced between the kitchen and the alcove. Caitie rushed to the laundry room, dropped off the cart, and ran back to the alcove.

"Ye were nearly late." Lileas nodded at King Oseron entering the Great Hall.

He scanned the room before going to sit at his table.

"I'm on it." Caitie picked up a pitcher and headed his direction. She hoped it wasn't Cormag he was searching for. "Good Evening," Caitie said.

"Pleasant evening," Oseron replied. "Have ye seen Cormag?"

"Not lately." She set the plate before him, trying to get the image of the guard bound with shoe laces and her head band out of her mind.

"He should be here by now."

"Maybe he got tied up." It was a bad pun but the first thing that slipped out. She poured the mead into his chalice. "I'll be back in a bit."

Caitie continued serving the others while keeping a watchful eye on the king. Minutes dragged as her mind raced with worry, and the Daoine Shi mellowed with their heather ale. The musicians took to the stage along with the first of the evenings' dancers. Everyone in the banquet hall was chill except for the king. She spied Oseron waving for Durell to come to his table. The guard bent down and cupped his ear to hear the king over the loud musicians. A minute later, Durell marched from the hall toward Cormag's room. Caitie started to panic.

Within minutes, Durell was back at the king's table. She knew he was reporting that Cormag wasn't in his room. The pit in her stomach grew as the she watched the guard enter the passageway to the dungeon.

She had to warn Mungan if he hadn't already left her room.

"Caitie." The call was loud and long and coming from Elvy. "Oh, Caitie," echoed Alvy and Ulvy.

Three burly hands raised on the opposite side of the hall waved her over in unison.

"Not now," she said under her breath.

Elvy stood up and winked at her with half of his face. Alvy and Ulvy did the same.

She didn't have time to help them.

Seeing her standing there, all three waved their arms like the people at the airport signaling planes into their gates.

Oseron gave her a look of disapproval. She scurried across the room.

"We are out of ale," Elvy said.

"Aye, out of ale," the brothers echoed. All three raised their tankards with both hands.

She filled their cups. "There you go."

"'Twas gracious of ye, Caitie," Elvy said.

"Very gracious indeed," Alvy and Ulvy added.

"Aye, as the mortals would say, she is full of the milk of human kindness."

It was the last voice Caitie wanted to hear. She turned to see Cormag flanked by two hostile guards in a half-circle behind her. She whipped her head in the direction of the king's table. Oseron stood feet spread and arms crossed with fire burning in his eyes.

48 *row, row, row that boat*

· the journey ·

2:45 PM
JUNE 29TH

ROBBIE MUSTERED HIS COURAGE AND GENTLY SQUEEZED Leannan's arm. "Let's get you home."

She gazed up at him, and he couldn't tell if it was fear or sadness in her eyes. "Did the nests hold a ravenstone?"

"Yeah. It really works. I couldn't believe it."

A faint smile crossed her lips. "Can ye show me?"

"Sure. Only one problem though—there's one stone and two of us." He reached inside the front pocket of his jeans and pulled out the black pebble. As soon as his hand came in contact with the stone, he started turning invisible.

"Very good, Robbie."

"But how can we both use it?"

"Hold my hand. We shall share its power."

He laced her icy fingers with his and dropped the pebble between their palms. She faded from sight. It was spookier than watching himself disappear. Only the touch of her cold hand reminded him she was still there.

"Aye, Robbie, the stone shall serve us well."

He let go of her fingers and slid them up to curl around the ravenstone. By the time he stuffed the pebble into his jeans pocket, Leannan was visible again and seconds later so was he. "I'll get the camera." Robbie crossed to his nightstand, opened the drawer, and spied Dad's pocketknife with the tiny mustard seed. The woman who gave his great-grandpa the knife hoped it would help his family someday. If they ever needed help, it was today. He plucked it out of the drawer and started to shove the small knife into the back pocket of his jeans but stopped and slipped it into his sock instead like Grandpa MacGregor and his *sgian dubh*. He grabbed Caitie's Lumix and zipped the camera inside his jacket. There was no way he was going to lose that.

"I'm gonna get Caitie's sweatshirt. The wind's blowing hard, and I don't want you to freeze." He ran to her room and returned with the hoodie. He scooted the chair back from the desk that pinned Leannan in place and helped her put it on.

Robbie gently lifted Leannan and carried her out to the shed, holding her tight so the strong gusts couldn't rip her from his arms. Once inside, he laid her down over Ross's bed. She hovered several inches above the mattress. He went to the table where a glass held the primroses. "So, how many flowers do we need?"

"A posy of exactly nine."

Robbie took out the three most withered flowers, threw them in the wastebasket, and placed the remaining nine, glass and all, into a grocery sack to protect them on the journey. He stared out the window. The wind thrashed the trees' branches. "I'm worried about you blowing away out there." He studied the workbench looking for something he could use. He needed something heavy to weigh her down, but then he'd get more tired carrying her. Flinging drawers and cabinet doors open, he searched for a rope. Instead he found Ross's stash of bungee cords. "These'll work." He untangled two brown and yellow ones that were arm's length.

Leannan cocked an eyebrow at the long elastic cords with huge hooks on the ends.

"It'll be okay, I promise," he said, not taking the time to explain. "I'm gonna get the life jackets." He scooped the plastic bag of flowers off the table and left for the dock. The wind howled and whipped his long bangs so they stabbed at his eyes. He jumped into the bobbing dinghy and stowed the primroses in the small space under the bow. To hold the flowers in place, he grabbed the two life jackets beneath the front bench and packed them around the bag. He pulled two other life jackets from the stern and ran back to the shed.

Leannan opened her eyes as Robbie set the two orange vests on the end of the bed. "A flashlight. I almost forgot." He pulled an old, silver flashlight from the back of the workbench and shoved it into the empty pocket of his jacket. He picked up a life vest. "Let's get you in this." Robbie slipped it over her head, clasped the black plastic buckles in the front, and hooked a bungee cord on each side of the strap around her waist before tightening it. He put on the other life jacket.

"Okay. I'm ready. Are you?"

"Aye," she answered faintly.

Robbie picked her up and pushed the shed door open with his backside, fighting the strong southwest wind. He clung to Leannan, afraid a gust would snatch her and send her flying across the loch like a runaway kite.

Once on the dock, he crouched down and stepped into the stern of the rocking dinghy. With one arm wrapped around her, he grabbed the free end of the bungee cord and hooked it to a cleat on the side of the dinghy, switched arms, and hooked the other cord on the opposite side of the boat. Tethered like a hot air balloon, he slowly let go of her to see if the cords would hold. Leannan floated and bounced off the bench near the stern at the mercy of the wind, but at least she was secure.

"'Tis quite clever of ye." The wind carried Leannan's words away.

"Let's hope it holds."

Robbie untied the dock lines and shoved the oars through the rings on the sides of the dinghy. He sat down facing Leannan, put the oars in the water, and rowed.

"Those are mighty, white horses today," she said.

"What are you talking about?"

"The waves, Robbie."

"Yeah," he said, hoping the big waves didn't spill over the sides of the dinghy and sink them. Once heading northeast, with the wind in his face, working the oars got a little easier. "You ought to rest Leannan. I'll wake you up when we get there."

She nodded, and her eyelids drooped closed. Leannan looked so frail. He rowed faster despite being scared of what lay ahead. Pull, lift. Pull, lift. He focused hard on keeping a rhythm going. A boat horn blared, blasting him off his seat. Leannan's eyes popped open, and her mouth gaped in horror. Robbie craned his neck to see behind them and felt the blood drain from his face. The big blue and white Jacobite Cruise boat with its recorded narrator spouting Loch facts barreled toward them with a hundred tourists, eyes and cameras trained on the water, searching for Nessie.

Robbie rowed faster. If he didn't get out of their path, the cruiser would slice them in two. The horn wailed again. Adrenaline surged through his body. He pulled the oars through the waves so fast his arms screamed with pain. The dinghy's stern slid past the veering Jacobite Queen's bow, the wake of the bigger boat, thrusting his smaller one toward the opposite shore. The captain shook his finger at them from the wheelhouse. A group of Japanese tourists pointed at Leannan bobbing up and down, her arms and head flopping at the will of the wind. They shouted in Japanese and snapped thousands of pictures. He pulled the oars from the water and dropped his head, exhausted.

"Robbie?" Leannan asked.

"Yeah, I'm okay." Robbie put the oars back in and rowed once more. The farm became a small speck in the distance. A few minutes later, the rowboat beached on the rocky shore, and Robbie hopped out. He pulled the dinghy as far aground as he could, his boots splashing in the Loch's frigid water. Leannan stirred at the sound of the wood scraping over the rocks.

"We made it to the other side?" she asked, her eyes barely open.

"Yeah." Robbie crawled back in the boat, tossed his life vest on the floor, and pulled the bag of primroses from beneath the bow, slipping the handle over his wrist. He unhooked Leannan's bungee cords from the cleats and took off her life jacket. Cradling her tight in his arms, he got them out of the boat. The dinghy creaked as it seesawed with the waves. He hoped and prayed he'd gotten it far enough ashore so it wouldn't float away. "Where do I go from here?"

Leannan lifted a finger to point. "Over the mountain."

He marched through the tall grass up to the single track road and crossed the empty lane. He lumbered up the hill through tall pines that whispered in the wind to the rocky ridge above the tree line. Powerful gusts battered them, and he feared they'd be blown away. "We're at the top, Leannan. Which way do I go?"

"Down to the path through the valley. Then north to the loveliest of the mountains," she said just loud enough that he could make out the words.

Robbie picked his way down the stony hillside to the valley where the wind didn't bully them. Once on the trail in the valley floor, he studied the hills all around them, trying to figure out which was the home of the Daoine Shi. He should've been able to tell since he'd been there before, but coming from this direction, everything looked different. Then straight ahead, maybe it was his imagination, he couldn't be sure, but there was a hill that seemed familiar. It had a funny rock formation about two thirds of the way up next to a dark spot that could be the cave. "Leannan, does your mountain have a rock that looks like a giant mushroom?"

"Aye." Her answer was slow and so faint.

"I see it then. It's not far."

She didn't respond.

He picked up his pace. He was so hungry that, by the time he found the path up the mountain, his stomach felt like it was grinding itself to bits. It had to be past dinnertime. And even though Leannan weighed as little as a bag of cotton balls, his arms ached from rowing and his legs from hiking for so long. He wasn't in great shape, and if Grandpa MacGregor could see him, he'd be rubbing it in Robbie's face. The heavy cloud cover made it darker when they reached the Daoine Shi landmark and found the entrance to the cave. He set Leannan down inside, propping her against a boulder, but she hovered now a foot off the ground.

Robbie pulled out the flashlight and turned it on. A shiver went up his spine. All the terror he felt the last time he was here came back, but now the stakes were way higher. Caitie was in there, and he didn't know what exactly he'd have to do, or who he'd have to face to get her out. He checked his other jacket pocket for the camera. It was still there. He took the primroses out of the bag and kneeled next to Leannan. "We've made it."

There was no response. He squeezed her shoulder. "Leannan."

She slowly opened her eyes.

"How do I open the secret door?"

"Tap on the portal nine times with…"

"The primroses?"

She barely nodded.

With the flowers in one hand and the flashlight in the other, Robbie scooped Leannan up and headed deeper into the cave. He spied the large boulder where this whole mess began. He struggled up the smaller rocks to get to the big one without smooshing her. Facing the secret door, he switched off the flashlight and stooped to leave it on the ledge. "Leannan, how do I get to Mungan's room once the door opens?"

"Down the passage…" she whispered, her voice barely audible. He could feel her struggling to breathe. "Through the hall..." He sensed her swallow. "To the bedchambers...look for his name."

"Hang on, Leannan." Robbie reached into his jeans pocket and pulled out the ravenstone. The cave was too dark to watch their bodies disappear. He put his hand on top of hers, sandwiching the stone between them, tapped the portal with the primroses nine times, and waited.

The secret door eased open. Robbie stood and carried Leannan into the passageway lit by rosy flames. Just inside the tunnel, his heart skipped a beat. Less than 30 feet away, a huge woman in a pink gown, wearing one of those Afghan head scarves, sprinted toward him and then stopped short. Robbie didn't breathe, afraid even that sound would give them away.

"Who is there?" the woman whispered in a really low voice. She unwrapped the scarf and slipped off the dress tossing both to the ground. It was the guy who pulled Robbie out of his RC truck the night they kidnapped Caitie. "I know someone is there. I saw the portal open."

"Mungan?" Robbie asked.

"Aye, 'tis me. But whose voice do I answer?"

Robbie gently laid Leannan down on the passageway floor. It didn't feel like a good idea to make himself visible. He curled his fingers around the ravenstone, and Leannan materialized.

Mungan rushed to her side. "Leannan?"

The Daoine Shi tenderly lifted her hand and kissed it.

"Where's my sister?" Robbie demanded.

Footsteps pounded toward them from the other end of the passageway. Robbie backed up against rough stone wall. The crabby guy from his real nightmare ran toward Mungan with another Daoine Shi at his heels.

Mungan scooped Leannan into his arms and turned to face them. "Cormag, how unfortunate 'tis to see ye."

"The unfortunate one is ye. Durell, bring what is left of Leannan to King Oseron." A big brute ripped her away from Mungan. Cormag grabbed Mungan's arm and thrust it up high behind his back.

Mungan writhed.

"How did she get here?" Cormag demanded.

Robbie was sure his heart was going to explode. He wanted to save Leannan and Mungan somehow, but he couldn't do anything against all these guys.

"I found her on the floor," Mungan said.

"She could not have made the journey alone. Not in this condition."

"Do ye see anyone, ye fool?"

Mungan hadn't given him away. Robbie stood a little taller.

Maybe he could do something. *Yeah, this wasn't that much different than invisibility in a video game. You used it for your advantage and took any opportunity it gave you.*

Cormag dragged Mungan back down the passageway.

Robbie trailed at a safe distance, clutching the precious ravenstone as he entered their world.

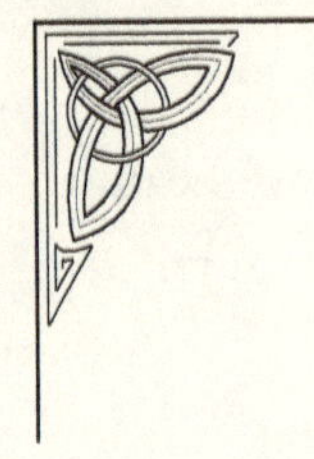

49 *the truth revealed*

·peril·

8:50 PM
JUNE 29TH

CAITIE STUMBLED AS THE GUARD HEYFEDD PUSHED HER toward King Oseron's throne, her arms cramping behind her back under his fierce grip. She could only hope Mungan had already snuck out and was on his way for help.

Lileas bustled to her side. "Your Majesty, may I humbly ask as to why Caitie is under arrest?"

"This mortal has spit in the face of my kindness by freeing a prisoner and harming my loyal servant, Cormag."

Lileas covered her gaping mouth with her hand. She looked deep into Caitie's eyes. "How could ye?"

"I had to try..."

Lileas turned her back on Caitie and stormed away through the gathering crowd as the flames of the torchlights changed to royal blue.

She hadn't meant to hurt Lileas in her shot at getting free. She hadn't had a choice, so why did this feel so bad? Caitie squinched her eyes shut, not wanting to look at anybody.

The crowd murmured and Caitie's eyelids automatically popped open.

The Daoine Shi parted as Cormag led Mungan before the throne. Caitie's heart sank. It was over. She'd never see Mom or Robbie again. She caught Mungan's gaze, and the fear in his eyes reflected back her own.

The crowd moved aside again. The breath caught in Caitie's throat at the sight of her own lifeless body cradled in Durell's arms. She knew in her head it was Leannan. But it felt like one of those out-of-body experiences she'd heard about on TV where a person's soul hovers over their body stretched out on an operating table.

Durell laid Leannan down on the open floor in front of them, only she floated like she was on an invisible cloud.

Cormag puffed his chest with pride. "Your Majesty, we captured not only Mungan but the errant changeling as well."

"She could not have put up much of a fight in this condition." The king drummed his fingers on the arms of the throne. "How did Leannan get here?"

Cormag turned a little sheepish. "We found her in Mungan's arms."

Caitie was as confused as Oseron looked, with his head cocked to one side and brow pinched. She knew there hadn't been time for Mungan to get to the farm and back. And the king probably did too. Caitie combed the crowd with her eyes, was Robbie out there somewhere? She didn't see him.

What was she thinking? He'd never be able to pull off a rescue. Maybe Ross brought her? But he didn't know where this place was. For that matter, Robbie didn't really either, and Leannan couldn't have helped much.

Cormag hunched his shoulders and offered up his hands. "She must have returned on her own and collapsed from the journey."

"From the looks of it, she shan't last. Pity." Oseron crossed his arms and scowled at Caitie. "I am weary of the havoc ye have created." The king glowered at Mungan. "I was lenient with ye, sparing your life when ye took my queen's. No more! Ye will reap the punishment ye deserve!"

Caitie had no idea what the king planned but knew it wouldn't be good.

"Alvy, Elvy, Ulvy, come here at once!" Oseron demanded.

The three giants stepped forward.

"Hold the captives while the guards prepare the flaming arrows," the king ordered.

Caitie shook like a Chihuahua. This stuff didn't happen in real life. Heyfedd, Cormag, and Durell marched off at Oseron's command.

"Bring ropes to bind these blaggards!" the king barked.

White-hot anger flashed in Mungan's eyes. "Ye are an imposter and have no right to mete out punishment to anyone."

"What are ye saying, Mungan?" Earnan asked, making his way through the flustered crowd.

"Silence!" Oseron shouted. He took a deep breath and stared with bitterness at Mungan. "I have watched ye change in the last weeks. Ye are no longer the responsible Searsanach I once knew. Your secrets have corrupted ye, driven ye mad. I am king and shall make ye pay for your crimes."

The seamstresses Pàislig and Ùna wrung their hands. Corc's eyes were wide with bewilderment.

"Garbahn and the rest of the masons, clear out the tables. Elvy and Ulvy, take the prisoners to the wall. Alvy, bind their feet and hands."

Little Friseal brought the ropes he'd been handed by one of the weavers to Alvy.

"'Tis not I who has changed. 'Tis ye—a shapeshifter!" Mungan hurled the words. "And 'twas ye who killed the true King Oseron!"

The crowd gasped. Lileas clapped a hand over her gaping mouth.

"I am truly sorry, Caitie," Elvy whispered from behind her as he guided her toward a column at the far side of the Hall. Ulvy, his giant head hanging low, escorted Mungan to the arch's other column.

Alvy dropped to his knees and tied ropes tight around Caitie's ankles. She fought off tears as her hands were bound, refusing to give the king the satisfaction of seeing her cry.

"Ye were the spider who bit Ballard," Mungan shouted. "Ye tricked him into trying to help steal our gold but feared the truth would come out, so ye killed him."

Lileas pushed her way forward through the buzzing crowd.

"Tianna knew ye were not her beloved. And ye suspected she would give your secret away. She was about to as well, for she left me the note. And ye turned into a mouse in the treasure room after the chess match and scurried down the corridor to murder her. Only Leannan stepped on ye on your way to silence Tianna."

"Nonsense!" King Oseron bellowed.

Cormag strode in with an archer's bow. Durell followed close behind carrying a quiver of arrows, and Heyfedd held a torch high. Cormag stretched out his hand. Durell retrieved an arrow from the quiver and handed it to him.

"No one believes the ravings of a lunatic," the king shouted. "Light an arrow. Mungan pays first."

Cormag, his lips curled in a grinchy smile, put the arrow tip to the flame, igniting it. He brought the arrow to the bow.

"Mungan's not crazy!" Caitie shrieked. "He's telling the truth!" She looked at him as his eyes steeled against the bowman, facing all of this with fierce courage. She wasn't ready for either of them to die.

"Elvy, muzzle the feckless wench!" Oseron ordered.

"I know where the real king's body is hidden," Caitie managed to say before Elvy's giant hand covered the bottom half of her face.

"Where, Caitie?" Corc cried out.

"Fire it!"

Caitie screamed a muffled, "No!"

Cormag pulled the arrow back to aim. He jerked forward like he'd been pushed from behind, releasing the flaming arrow. The fireball streaked through the archway and hit the wall in the corridor beyond before clattering to the floor. Cormag whirled around. "Who did that?"

"Not I." Durell raised both hands in innocence.

Heyfedd shook his head. "Nor I."

Caitie let out her breath, thankful for whatever it was that just happened.

"Let Caitie explain herself, Elvy," Earnan called out, his robe shifting between burgundy and black.

"Fire again," King Oseron demanded, glaring at the wizard. Durell gave Cormag another arrow. The guard, his eyes glinting in the candlelight, ignited the tip with Heyfedd's torch and aimed. Something invisible slapped the arrow away from the bow and out of Cormag's hand.

Elvy's hand slipped from her mouth. "The real King Oseron's body is stuffed in a trunk on a wheelbarrow in a secret passage," she yelled.

"The lass lies. 'Tis merely a delay tactic. Fire the arrow!" Oseron ordered.

"Wait!" Earnan glowered at the king and pointed his wand at Cormag. "Caitie, I am the eldest Daoine Shi, and for nearly a thousand years, I have lived in this mountain and know of no such passage. Ye have been here only three days. How could ye have discovered such a thing?"

"I found it trying to sneak out of here. You get to the secret passage through King Oseron's room. The crown on the statue of the king screws off. You put the key from the queen's statue into a slot in the king's head, and a hidden door opens. I can show you!" Caitie shouted.

"She speaks the truth about a secret passage," Elvy said.

"Aye, she speaks the truth, she does," Alvy and Ulvy echoed.

"How do ye know?" Earnan asked.

"Because we dug it," Elvy answered.

"Aye, we dug it, we did," echoed the other two.

"And ye are going to trust the words of the mountain idiots?" King Oseron roared.

"They cannot lie." Earnan's amethyst eyes flashed with anger and his robe turned raging red.

A Daoine Shi stepped forward from the crowd. "I fashioned the statue in the king's chambers. In the wee hours of the night, at King Oseron's request, I added the secret feature." The sculptor eyed the imposter suspiciously. "Took me nigh a fortnight with my meager magic to make the key in the statue drive the passage door open. 'Twas a hundred and fifty-six years ago. I swore to my king I would never reveal the statue's true purpose. If he is gone, I am bound by the oath no more."

The Daoine Shi crowd turned to one another, whispering their astonishment.

The king screamed, "Silence!"

But the Daoine Shi ignored him.

Robbie materialized next to Caitie, holding his pocketknife ready to lash at whoever tried to take him.

Caitie shrieked. Was she seeing things?

"Now let my sister go!" Robbie shouted.

The crowd gasped.

"How'd you do that?" Caitie asked.

"It's a little trick Leannan let me in on." Robbie tried to slit the ropes around her wrists, but they were too strong for his knife. He slipped it in his pocket and worked at the knots at her ankles with his fingers.

Caitie's chin trembled. "I can't believe you're here."

"Me neither," Robbie said, finally freeing her feet.

"And what happened to your face?" she asked.

"A raven got me."

"What?" Caitie asked.

"Later." Robbie stood up.

"So who are ye truly?" Mungan yelled at the king.

"Aye, tell us," Earnan commanded, now pointing his wand at the throne.

Oseron's head and neck turned purple with rage. "I am Ciaran of the Unseelies!"

"I know our enemies, and ye are no member of Salucevil's Court," Earnan said.

Ciaran's skin paled to gray green. His eyes glowed red with fury. "I deserve to be." The king's pointy ears dissolved into two pinched figure-eights. His chest sunk in and he seemed to shrivel in his robe.

"I have done their bidding for years and deserve acceptance in the alliance. But would they bring me into the fold?" He pounded now bony and gnarled hands on the throne's armrests. "No! I was never good enough." His nose flattened and grew wide. His hair dissolved and his skull elongated like a Bull Terrier's.

Caitie drew back against the column. This was all getting too weird, worse than a bad horror movie.

Ciaran stood, shorter than Robbie. The creature flung off the robe and ripped off his shirt. His emaciated body hopped straight out of his boots into the air and his ostrich feet landed on the throne's cushion. "But a score to settle with your Oseron gave me an idea to prove them all wrong."

The creature scrunched down on his toothpick legs and thrust himself toward Earnan, stripping the wizard of his wand. He bounced off the marble floor, stealing the knife from Durell's belt, and leapt at Caitie. She screamed as he seized her by the neck and flew with her to the platform.

"No!" Robbie yelled.

Ciaran stunk like the dead frog Caitie'd dissected in science. Her body slammed onto the side of the throne as Ciaran's scaly feet landed and gripped the chair's velvet arms. Out of the corner of her eye, she could see the bony fingers of his other hand raising Earnan's wand toward the ceiling. With his arm wrapped tight around her neck, Ciaran clutched the knife so its sharp blade lay cold against her skin.

"Toss the ravenstone up here, mortal, or Caitie dies! Now!"

Robbie pulled the stone from his pocket and pitched it toward the throne.

"Excellent." Ciaran curled his lips in triumph. "The Daoine Shi will at last make amends," he flailed the wand at the ceiling, "or I shall bring this mountain down!"

"Ye know not how," Earnan laughed with contempt.

"Do not underestimate me. I have attended to the masters of evil in this realm. 'Twould be unwise to assume I cannot or will not destroy anything and everything to get what I desire. What I deserve!"

He aimed the wand near Earnan's feet and shouted, *"A' milleadh Stèidhich."* The marble floor by the wizard's boots exploded, creating a three foot crater; shards of marble and granite rattled on the floor in a ring nearly reaching Leannan's limp body. The youngest Daoine Shi whimpered.

Robbie stood frozen; his eyes filled with terror.

"What do ye want?" Mungan asked.

"For years, I've watched Oseron deliver trunkfuls of gold to the Unseelie Court, treasure that rightly belonged to me, yet I received none of it. So I came for the rest of it. But now, 'tis the Daoine Shi's most valuable possession I seek."

Caitie tried to ease her neck back away from the blade, only Ciaran tightened his hold on her.

"Ye speak madness." Mungan strained at the ropes. "King Oseron would never give anything to the Unseelie Court, much less the Daoine Shi gold."

"Aye, he did. Every thirteen years on the 31st of March for more than a century and a half, Oseron has paid for knifing and leaving me to die."

"Your tale is absurd," Earnan said with a dismissive shake of his head.

"'Tis all true. Your good king well-nigh stole my life to save the Queen of Skye. The Unseelie Court does not tolerate such insults and demanded restitution. The night of his last payment, I followed Oseron to the mountain and crept into his portal as a spider. He saw me, raised his hand to smash me, but the fool did not. I watched him for a few days and realized how easy 'twould be to take his place. And so I did. 'Twas not my intention to kill the others, but I had no choice. And I will do the same to all of ye, if necessary. Durell, unbind Mungan so he may obtain what I desire."

Caitie winced as Ciaran dug the knife blade deeper into her flesh.

50 *the prophesy fulfilled*

· the secret ·

9:15 PM
JUNE 29TH

ROBBIE'S EYES ALMOST POPPED OUT OF HIS HEAD WHEN Cormag dragged him through the double doors into the round treasure room. Earnan and Mungan stood at his right, and Caitie shook on his left, her back arched 'cause of the knife the short shapeshifter pressed against her neck.

No torches hung on the walls, but shimmering coins in piles almost as tall as Robbie gave the whole room a golden glow. From behind a mound in the center, a foot tall statue of a buck made out of diamond with bright sapphire blue eyes and a rack of antlers that had to be twelve points ambled toward them. Faceted all over, the deer sparkled so bright, it almost hurt to look at him. It moved with the grace of a real animal and was even more beautiful than Leannan, the day they first met her in the cave.

"I came for the gold, and I shall have it all eventually, but the stag I desire foremost."

"I cannot give ye what ye want. 'Tis not within my power." Mungan sounded like there wasn't any point in even trying.

"Earnan?" the shapeshifter asked.

The wizard shook his head. "Nor can I."

Ciaran's bulging eyes focused on the wizard. "The stag flees when I draw near. And if I pick up so much as a coin, he attacks me. I have tried both day and night to woo him but to no avail. There is a secret to taming the stag, and Oseron knew of it for he smuggled out trunks of gold. Ye must know it as well."

"The stag does what he will. He judges the heart. Apparently, he sees no good in yours," Earnan said.

"Silence!" The shapeshifter glared at the wizard, and a creepy smile curled his lip. "Perhaps with your wand…" He pointed the wand at the stag. *"Thig thugam!"*

Black sparks shot from the wand aiming toward the deer's front hooves.

The white-diamond stag darkened to black, its facets still glistening. In an instant, the buck grew ten times its size and its eyes turned to flaming red rubies. Three inch fangs protruded from its lower jaw. "Eeeeuuuuuuw!" came a guttural sound that shook the room. The stag lowered his head. Red steam spewed from its nostrils and it lunged toward Ciaran, its hooves sending the gold coins clattering. Like a bull in a ring, it nicked Ciaran in the arm with the outermost point on his rack, turned before slamming into the wall, and nailed the shapeshifter with a kick to the stomach from its back hoof.

Ciaran's knife sliced Caitie's skin. She winced and a whimper escaped from her lips.

The gash on the shapeshifter oozed brown blood. Pressing his bony arm to his side, Ciaran's face twisted with pain.

The tall stag circled around a mountain of gold and faced them all, pawing the ground.

"Get me the stag, Mungan," Ciaran ordered.

Mungan stood paralyzed.

Robbie strained within Cormag's grip. "What are you waiting for?"

"'Tis not so simple a choice," Mungan said. "The fate of our entire kingdom may well lie in the balance."

"Leannan's almost dead and this thing has a knife to my sister's throat. You gotta do this!"

Mungan raked back the hair on his head.

Robbie flashed back to the train and Miss Moncrieff's words to him when he was too scared to move. "Indecision becomes a decision." He swallowed hard. "And lost lives never return."

Mungan glanced at Robbie, let out a deep sigh, and stepped toward the stag. He bowed his head and blew the same rainbow vapor toward the ground that Leannan had done in the cave, raising his head as he walked around the stag. Like those fountains that shoot up columns of water in a circle, silver bars an inch apart came up from the floor, encircling the buck in a glowing cage.

The stag faded from black to white-diamond and its eyes turned back to sapphire. It moved only its neck and head, watching Mungan until it was hemmed in.

Mungan stood in front of the cage and stared back, rubbing his chin, as if he was trying to figure out what to do next.

The stag raised his head and reared up on its hind feet. The diamonds from the tips of its antlers trickled down to the ground. Then the ones beneath fell too. His form disintegrated like a salt sculpture from the top down, the diamonds cascading and forming a shadow of the buck on the ground.

They all watched in silence as the diamond picture on the treasure room floor formed a stream that flowed out through the cage's narrow bars. Like the crumbling he'd just seen in reverse, the stag re-formed from the floor up—hooves, legs, body, neck, head, and antlers. The buck slowly cocked its head to one side, gave Mungan a final look, and trotted around the piles of gold to the opposite side of the room.

"I must have him," Ciaran said. "Earnan, ye are the mighty wizard. Capture the stag now!"

"My magic is limited without my wand."

The shapeshifter sneered at the wizard. "And in my hand, it shall remain, trained on ye."

Earnan stuck his hand in the pocket of his robe, pulled out a handful of crystals, and tossed them in the air. *"Glacadh!"* The crystals formed a net above the deer and slowly descended like a sparkling parachute. The stag stretched its neck upward. "Oohweoooh."

Lacy frost like Robbie'd seen on winter calendar scenes covered the net as it floated downward. The icy net touched the points on the stag's antlers and shattered like glass, clinking as it hit the floor. Robbie couldn't believe this creature. Of all the amazing, weird things he had seen before—Leannan decorating the cave, getting shrunk in his own bedroom, finding a rock that turned him invisible—none of it came close to what he saw now.

"I am losing my patience," Ciaran roared. "Get me the stag or the lass dies!"

Earnan spread his arms, palms up. "I have nothing more to try."

"Do as I say!" The shapeshifter dug the blade deeper into Caitie's flesh, drawing blood.

She cried with pain. Tears spilled from her eyes. "Please!"

"Stop! Let me try," Robbie screamed.

"And what do ye know of taming enchantment?" Ciaran sneered.

He knew nothing about it. But he loved animals and knew you had to be gentle with them. "I'm good with animals."

The hideous shapeshifter stared at him for a minute. "Release him, Cormag," Ciaran ordered.

Free of the guard's hard grip, he inched toward the big creature. The sparkling head turned in his direction, and its glowing blue eyes locked on him. Robbie could feel his pulse pounding in his ears. With his mouth dry as cotton balls and legs as wobbly as a pair of sticks, Robbie reached out a trembling hand to touch the buck on its back. The enchanted animal arched his neck. Its needle sharp antlers sliced the air with a whoosh as his eyes followed Robbie's hand.

When his fingertips were within a nail's width of its shoulder, the buck jumped to the top of the adjacent pile of coins, shrinking down to its small size in mid-air. Robbie again moved slowly toward the shy creature and stretched out his hand. The enchanted stag galloped down the backside of the golden mountain, millions of light prisms from its facets reflecting off the ceiling and wall. Robbie dropped his head and closed his eyes. Who was he compared to this creature? It could play this game all day, and there was nothing he could do about it. And if the stag got sick of it, Robbie had no doubt it could kill him if it wanted to.

"Dawdle no longer!" Ciaran demanded, pivoting the blade to slice Caitie's neck.

"Please stop," Caitie begged. Her eyes were closed and her chest heaved.

"Give me a minute!" Robbie pleaded.

"No! Get it for me now or I will slit her throat."

"I'm trying as hard as I can." He had to do something different. Robbie wove between the coin mountains, carefully moving toward the buck. But this time as he got closer, he crouched and spoke gently, "Hey, fella. I'm not going to hurt you. It's okay. Really."

The glowing eyes studied Robbie's movements.

"I just wanna rub your back." The buck didn't run away. Reaching out, Robbie's shaky hand touched the hard, glittering body. It felt cool against his fingertips. Robbie gave the diamond statue a feather-light stroke. The buck slowly turned his head away from him. "That's a good boy," Robbie whispered. He stroked the stag again. "My sister, Caitie, is in trouble. You gotta help me." He craned his neck to look the buck in the eyes. "Can I hold you? I won't hurt you, I promise."

Robbie waited a second and then laid a hand on the buck. Its body vibrated with a pulsing energy. He cautiously inched his fingers over and around the creature's girth to support its belly. The energy radiating from the enchanted statue tingled his hand like it was asleep. "I'm going to pick you up now, nice and slow," Robbie whispered. He raised the statue from the pile of gold coins. The buck remained still and its glowing, blue eyes seemed to read Robbie's soul. "I have to give you to Ciaran. He'll kill my big sister if I don't. I love her. It's the only way I know to get her free." Robbie rose and pivoted, stepping cautiously toward Ciaran and Caitie while holding the buck out in front of him. He stopped a few feet from them.

The statue gleamed in the shapeshifter's wild eyes. "Give me the stag."

Robbie stood taller. "You let my sister go first."

"Do not negotiate with me!" the shapeshifter snapped.

Robbie steeled his eyes against Ciaran's. "You can't hold the statue with the wand in one hand and Caitie in the other. No one's going anywhere. Let her go," Robbie said in a voice braver than he'd ever heard pass through his lips.

Ciaran relieved the pressure on the blade against Caitie's neck. She took a deep breath and slid from his grasp.

"Do not make a move or ye will pay dearly," Ciaran warned her. The shapeshifter then stuck the knife handle between his bony knees, the blade pointing toward Robbie. He reached out a wart-covered hand palm-side up and clutched the wand in his other.

Robbie stepped closer. The buck's leg pawed at the air and its diamond body warmed up. The stag whipped its head in Ciaran's direction and then its glowing eyes met Robbie's. He heard no voice, out loud or in his head, but Robbie knew what the buck wanted him to say. "Give the wand to Caitie."

Ciaran's eye's narrowed. "I am no fool."

"Caitie doesn't know how to use it. She won't give it to the wizard." He looked to her. "Right?"

"I promise." Caitie's chin quivered.

"She is not to be trusted. Now hand me the stag," Ciaran demanded.

The buck balked in Robbie's hand. "No, he'll bolt. Look at him. You gotta get rid of the wand."

"All right," Ciaran looked to the guard. "Cormag…"

The guard stepped forward and reached for the wand. Ciaran eyed him suspiciously and snatched it back from Cormag's closing grasp.

"Perhaps not," the shapeshifter rasped. "Earnan, Mungan, get your backs to the wall. Ye as well, Cormag." With the Daoine Shi on one side of him and Caitie on the other, Ciaran put the wand into her bound hands. "Now give me the stag."

Robbie bent his face close to the buck. "Ciaran's gonna hold you for a little while. It'll be okay." He passed the enchanted statue to Ciaran. The buck slowly turned its head to look into the shapeshifter's face. Its glowing eyes intensified to a brilliant blue brighter than Robbie thought possible.

Robbie backed away.

Ciaran drew the statue close to his chest with one hand and stroked him over and over with his other. "Ye are beautiful, and ye are mine. The Unseelie Court shall now bow to me!"

With a wheeeeesh, the stag burst into blinding blue flame. Ciaran screamed, writhing in agony, but couldn't let go of the magical buck. "Your woes are not over. The Unseelies will destroy every one of ye in only…" The flames engulfed the shapeshifter from head to toe until he was a shrieking mass of blazing blue light.

Caitie screamed.

Robbie couldn't pull his eyes away.

The disgusting smell of burning flesh filled the room. The piercing wails faded. The flames died down, leaving the enchanted statue shimmering even brighter than before and standing on a pile of ashes.

The buck turned, and its glowing blue eyes met Robbie's. Its head barely nodded. With the flick of its tail, the buck trotted toward the pile of gold in the center of the room. In a single bound, it flew to the top.

"Earnan," Caitie called. "Catch!" She tossed him his wand.

Robbie ran to her and untied the ropes binding her hands.

She hugged him tighter than he could ever remember. "Thank you," she whispered.

"You're welcome." Robbie was shaking all over, but he wasn't afraid. He pulled back and studied her neck where blood had clotted over the slice Ciaran had made with his knife. "You okay?"

She reached up and touched the wound. "Yeah. I'll be fine."

"Earnan, we must get back to Leannan," Mungan said, his face full of worry.

Cormag blocked the entrance.

"Move!" Mungan ordered. "And clear the way in the Great Hall for Earnan. Tell Heyfedd and Durell to do so as well."

"I answer to the king," Cormag said, jutting out his chin in defiance.

"Our king is long dead." Mungan grabbed Cormag by the collar with both hands, flung him out of the way and charged out of the treasure room.

Robbie clutched Caitie's hand and rushed out after Mungan, hoping it wasn't too late.

51 *who pray tell, was fairest of them all?*

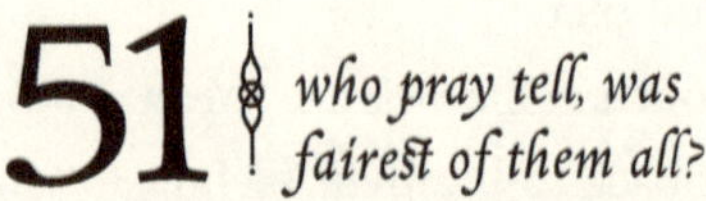

· the transformation ·

CAITIE DUG HER FINGERNAILS INTO HER BICEPS AS Mungan knelt on the floor of the Great Hall and scooped the limp body of her twin into his arms.

"Leannan?" He spoke her name like a desperate prayer. There was no response. Mungan touched her temple. "She still has a pulse." Hope flickered in his copper-colored eyes.

"Then step away and I will change her form back to her own," Earnan said.

Mungan tenderly laid Leannan back down on the cold marble floor.

"It feels so weird to see Leannan like this. It's creepy, like seeing me die," Caitie whispered.

"Don't talk about her like that. She's gonna be okay." Robbie's voice trembled.

Earnan pointed his wand at Leannan's feet and commanded, *"Bi 'nad shithich a rithist!"* Golden sparks shot out of the wand's tip, splitting and forming into two ropes. Earnan drew the wand upward and toward himself. Leannan's body rose, and she hung limp in the air, suspended vertically. The golden ropes encircled her feet and wound up her body like a glistening cocoon. Brown sparkles shot out the top, the cocoon split, and Caitie's clothes tumbled out before the weird rope-thing vanished. The brown sparkles fluttered down into a glittering pile.

A shiny green stem sprouted from the iridescent dirt and turned into a vine, which intertwined into a short log. The vine then split into five branches, which twisted and grew into two legs at one end of the log and two arms and a head at the other. The vine's green leaves turned to the gold, orange, and the rusty red of autumn before withering and revealing Leannan, the hag beneath.

Leannan opened her sickly green eyes and drew her flaky, gray green arms up to her head to cover her gruesome face. She rolled on her side and drew her backward feet into a fetal position.

"Oooogh," murmured the Daoine Shi surrounding Leannan.

Like everyone else, Caitie couldn't help but scrunch up her face in disgust. One face in the crowd didn't react like the rest. Mungan rushed to Leannan's side and held her as she buried her ugly face in his chest.

Whoa. He had to really love her.

"Caitie, I gotta give them your camera," Robbie whispered.

Part of her wanted to say no. She didn't want to lose it. But this was her chance to fix what she'd done to Leannan, even if it was an accident. "Do it now."

Robbie pulled her Lumix out of his jacket and ran to Earnan. "Here."

The wizard's robe shifted to red-violet. "At last, the silver box. 'Tis hard to fathom such calamity came from a mortal's trinket."

It wasn't a trinket, but Caitie bit her lip. Now wasn't the time to argue.

The crowd hushed, and Leannan looked at Earnan, her head with its few straggly strands of gray hair still pressed against Mungan's chest.

"Your magic may be inextricably bound with the mortal's contraption," Earnan said. "I am afraid that when I retrieve it, the silver box may impart its own elements to ye."

"That matters not, Earnan. Please try to restore me."

"Ye have been weakened as a changeling. 'Tis important that ye understand the risks. Ye may never be as ye once were. For all I know, ye may become part fey, part contraption. Or worse, ye may die."

"I would rather perish than live like this," Leannan said.

"Think of what ye are saying," Mungan pleaded.

"I have and 'tis true, Mungan. Please Earnan, may we proceed?"

"Then as ye wish." Earnan flipped the camera over in his hands before pulling out his wand.

He doesn't have a clue what to do. "Wait a second." Caitie walked over to the wizard. "Let me turn it on for you." He handed her the camera, and she pressed the power button. The lens extended from the Lumix. "Aim it so the lens is facing her."

Mungan stepped away from Leannan.

"Tell us again what exactly ye were doing when the camera stole your magic," Earnan said.

"I was adding glamour to the cavern wall." She dropped her eyes in shame.

"So ye were exhaling?" the wizard asked.

Leannan nodded.

"Then open your mouth."

"And I took her picture while she did it," Caitie said, "which means I must have opened the camera shutter at just the right instant so when that sparkly stuff hit the camera lens, it captured her magic."

"How can I open the shutter here and now?" Earnan asked.

"To take a picture, you look through this small square so the person or thing you want to photograph is lined up inside. See?" She held the camera up so Earnan could look through it. "Then you press all the way down on this silver button." Caitie backed away.

"All right. Mungan, can ye help her up?"

"Aye." Mungan gently raised Leannan to her feet and stepped aside.

Earnan positioned the camera in front of his face with one hand and aimed it at Leannan. Pushing the shutter button down and tapping the camera lens with the wand, the wizard commanded, *"Thig a mach agus till innte a rithist!"*

A sparkling rainbow sprang from the camera lens, encircling Leannan's feet. They flipped forward, covered in pretty satin slippers. The swirling, iridescent vapor rose slowly transforming Leannan's rags into the shimmering, white dress she wore that day in the cave. The hunch on her back disappeared. Her shoulders no longer stooped. She stood tall and graceful. The vapor circled her gray green neck and head, turning her complexion Photoshop perfect. The vapor went back into her mouth. The ugly jowls disappeared, and her high cheekbones returned. Her zucchini nose shrank becoming delicate and slightly upturned. The sickly, pale green of her eyes brightened to white and her black-coal irises transformed to their iridescent peacock blue.

The last of the rainbow vapor left the camera lens followed by a loud crack. Caitie's heart sank at the sound. Dad's last gift to her was wrecked. The coarse, gray strands of hair on Leannan's head fell out, and her thick, auburn hair returned as the last orb swirled around her and disappeared into her mouth. Leannan's smile dazzled. The decayed stumps were gone, perfect teeth now in their place.

The gathered Daoine Shi shouted in celebration to see their friend restored.

Mungan glowed brighter than a streetlight. He beamed at Leannan, and she ran to him.

Caitie rushed to Earnan's side as he studied the broken camera. Robbie joined them. "I heard the crack and figured it was the lens," she said.

"I can try to restore it, if ye wish."

Like that was gonna happen. Five minutes ago, Earnan didn't even know how to work the thing. "That would be great." Caitie did her best to sound encouraging, despite the odds being like a zillion to one he could really do it.

"Let us go to my chambers, for I believe we may need a crystal to aid in the repair."

The three of them left the celebration in the Great Hall and walked through the passageway to Earnan's room.

"I don't understand something," Robbie said. "Why did the buck wait until tonight to fry Ciaran? It sounds like he'd had lots of other chances before."

"If the stag had done so sooner, the truth that he had murdered our king may never have been revealed. We can be grateful that Caitie discovered Ciaran's wicked plot and brought it all to light. Ciaran was mistaken though in thinking he could possess the stag." The wizard shook his head. "No one can. He is the protector of the Daoine Shi treasure. And the treasure is not for individual gain, but for the good of us all."

"Why wouldn't the stag let Mungan give him to Ciaran?" Robbie asked.

The wizard stopped, wrapping his palm on the handle to his door. "Mungan's motivation was tainted as was mine. He desired revenge for the murders of Tianna and Oseron. And I admit, I wanted to see Ciaran destroyed. Ye, however, purely sought to save your sister and Leannan, a noble desire for the good of others and at risk to oneself." Earnan ushered them inside and raised his wand. The heavy curtains painted with a moonlit shore scene opened to a small room. Scrolls and books lay scattered on the floor. The rack of potion bottles had been raided. Earnan gasped and his robe turned to a flaming magenta. "Now my *Complete Handbook of Spells* is missing."

"Who would do this?" Caitie asked.

Earnan pursed his lips. "I have a notion, but it can wait on the morrow. Ye have seen enough darkness for one evening. Let us turn to the business at hand and dwell on such mischief no longer." Earnan pulled a sparkling crystal from an alabaster box lying on his writing desk. He placed the crystal on her camera lens and touched it with the tip of his wand. *"Caìrich thu fhèin!"* Red sparks shot out the lens. Earnan retracted his wand and inspected the camera. He smiled proudly before presenting the Lumix to Caitie. "I believe the silver box is now restored."

"I can't tell you how happy that makes me!" She gave Earnan a huge hug. His robe shifted merrily from blue to purple like dancing Christmas lights. "I was sick at thinking I'd never be able to use it again. It was the last present my Dad ever gave me."

"Considering what ye have done for the Daoine Shi, it is a great reward to have been of some small service to ye." Earnan guided them from his chambers, but stopped just outside his door. "Caitie,—"

"Yes."

The wizard looked super serious. "I must apologise."

Caitie shrugged her shoulders. "Why?"

"Your camera is not a trinket after all."

She squeezed his arm. "I'm glad you believe that too."

Lileas hurried toward them bubbling with excitement, the hurt from betrayal now forgiven and forgotten. "Oh, I am so proud of ye." The fairy wrapped her generous arms around Caitie in a suffocating bear hug.

"Robbie, I want you to meet my friend, Lileas."

"Hi." Robbie extended his hand to shake hers.

She grasped it and curtsied. "Caitie, ye were so brave, exposing Ciaran for who he truly was and helping to get Leannan's magic back."

"Robbie's the real hero. Ciaran's just an ash pile now because of him and the deer thing."

"Indeed." Lileas bowed to him. "I cannot stay as I must serve the food and drink for the celebration."

"Great, I'm starved," Robbie said.

Caitie shook her head. "Don't you dare eat or drink anything here!"

"Why not?"

"Eating the food here is how I got trapped in this mountain. Don't do it. No matter how good it looks or how thirsty you are, don't touch anything!"

"Okay, okay. I get it."

Lileas twirled to head back to the kitchen.

"Hey, do you need any help?" Caitie asked.

Lileas laughed. "Of course not. The guest of honour must not serve."

Corc walked over, all serious. "Caitie, I have an apology to make to ye."

"No, you don't. You were right. I did bring a lot of trouble to Leannan and Mungan."

"But ye did a fine job making things right. For a mortal, ye are most decent."

"I'm glad you think so."

"And ye are a very brave lad."

Her little brother smiled brighter and broader than she could ever remember.

LEANNAN'S HEART SKIPPED A BEAT AS CORC DREW NEAR carrying Mungan's dress cloak.

"I appreciate ye fetching this for me." Mungan offered it to her. Leannan nodded and he draped it round her shoulders. The butterflies in her stomach took flight with the first gift, the promise of his protection. She felt him work the latch on the cloak clasp releasing the small band of emeralds in the center of the design. A joy greater than what she found in the outside world sent her spirit soaring. She was floating, only this time her glorious forward-facing feet were on the ground.

"I have a confession." Mungan looked deeply into her eyes. "I was wrong the night of the chess tournament."

"About what?"

"There was a wee mouse as white as a star with a heart as black as coal. I should never have doubted ye."

"And how do ye now know?"

"'Tis a long story, and I shall tell ye every word of it." He stroked her cheek. Leannan quivered all over. "But that night, ye captured a piece of my heart with your wit."

Leannan's cheeks warmed.

He laid his hand on his chest, "The next morning without knowing, ye stole even more through your passion to pursue that which ye love even at great risk. In performing my duty over the last century and a half, I came to believe 'twas best to stay safe. But Leannan, I have never felt more alive than in these last few days where risk and reward have been most great."

An unfamiliar tremor overtook Leannan's chin.

"And then, the day I first saw ye in this gown in the passageway, ye took not only my breath away, but what was left of my heart, for I have never beheld one more beautiful than ye, both inside and out." He knelt on one knee and lifted the emerald ring to her as an offering. "My beloved, Leannan, will ye share my life?"

"But the king…my role…"

"'Twill not be a problem." He slipped the second gift, his token of love onto her delicate finger. He stood and cupped her face in his hands as though he held the most delicate rosebud. Mungan leaned his face into hers and touched her lips with his.

12:15 AM

CAITIE WATCHED MUNGAN KISS LEANNAN. "WHOA!" She and Robbie burst out clapping. Earnan, Corc, and Lileas joined in and then the seamstresses and the triplets too. The rest of the crowd whispered to one another like something was wrong with the kiss.

Mungan extended his hand. She accepted it. He bowed deeply, and they started to dance. The musicians, seeing them, hurried to their instruments to provide a tune. Clearly, it didn't matter to them if the musicians ever even played. The two of them were in their own world, the way Mom and Dad were on their last anniversary. Caitie squelched the lump rising in her throat. Their dance finally ended. Leannan did a 360 pan of the room, blushing brighter pink with every pair of eyes gawking at her.

Caitie didn't get this crowd. The boy got the girl. They should be more excited.

Mungan wrapped his arm around Leannan's waist, and they walked over to Robbie and her.

"There are no words to properly express my appreciation, Robbie, for bringing me home." Leannan bent down and hugged him.

"I'm just glad we made it in time," Robbie said.

Mungan grinned at Caitie. "Ye have quite a quick mind in that head of yours."

"A guy I met in jail told me to use it wisely."

He wrapped an arm around Caitie's shoulder squeezing her close to his side. "And ye did."

Caitie looked up into Mungan's face, and for the first time, she noticed how handsome he really was. But he was already taken and way too old for her anyway, by like hundreds of years.

Across the room, Corc was talking to Earnan. His face was dead serious. The cobbler held a silver cup in one hand and gestured with his other to make his point. The wizard's robe was a happy blue, and he rocked back and forth, curling the end of his beard between his fingers. He gave Corc a nod of approval. The cobbler picked up a spoon from the nearest table and hopped onto the raised platform close to the throne. He banged the spoon on the silver cup, hushing the crowd.

"This night has been most significant for our people," Corc said. "I do not recall in my four hundred forty-nine years ever being so grateful for mortals. We, Daoine Shi, owe a great deal to two courageous human beings. So let us raise our glasses high, to Caitie and to Robbie!"

"Aye, to Caitie and to Robbie!" the crowd joined in unison.

Earnan climbed up the steps to the stage. "Corc has spoken rightly of the importance of this night. For we are now a people without a king. As King Oseron and Queen Tianna perished without an heir, we must choose one to ascend the Daoine Shi throne. I would suggest that we consider one who is honourable and brave, who thinks of the welfare of others before his own, and who will be a kind and faithful ruler. I see only one amongst us who has proven himself to those qualifications. 'Tis Queen Tianna's brother, Mungan."

"Aye. Hail, King Mungan." Corc raised his cup high.

Caitie knew there was one guy who wouldn't approve. But she couldn't find Cormag in the crowd chanting Mungan's name so loud the mountain rumbled beneath them.

Mungan climbed the steps to the platform. "I am honoured. I will do my best to serve the Daoine Shi. However, with one condition will I accept the role. And that is for Leannan to be my queen." Mungan extended his hand to her. There was an awkward silence.

Nuala stepped forward. "I must object."

Earnan turned to Lileas and whispered in her ear. The chambermaid scurried from the Great Hall faster than Caitie had ever seen Lileas move. What was she up to?

Nuala glowered at Leannan. "She cannot be queen. Her lowly station prohibits it."

"But the king can make exceptions for unions as he sees fit," Mungan said.

"For all but royal stations." Nuala crossed her arms and shot him an *I got you there* look.

"Then I shall not be king, if I cannot have the one I love as my queen."

Caitie shook her head. She was ready to deck that dancing witch! While each of the Daoine Shi just stood there frozen in place.

"Be reasonable, Mungan. Ye have not far to gaze to find one worthy of ye." Nuala cocked her hip to one side and rested one hand on it while she rippled the lower half of her silky green dress with her other.

"'Tis a humble and kind heart I find most appealing. Leannan's role as maidservant matters not to me."

Lileas entered the hall with a canvas and carried it to the royal platform. Corc followed with an easel and placed a painting of Mungan on it.

Earnan cleared his throat. "Ahh, Lileas has brought forth a handsome portrait of our prospective king. When did ye paint it, Taog?"

The head artist pulled a pair of spectacles from the pocket of his flowered topcoat and stepped forward to study it. "I have not seen this painting before. 'Tis not my work but a fine example of the craft, nonetheless."

"Well, Mungan, who painted this portrait of ye?" Earnan asked.

"I know not. I never posed for it."

"Then who among us has painted this masterpiece? Was it ye, Leannan?"

She blushed and stepped toward Earnan. "Aye, 'twas me."

Earnan stared icily at Nuala. "Then Leannan must have been miscast as a maidservant. By her work, she is truly one of the finer Daoine Shi artists."

Leannan smiled at Nuala, cocked her head, and shrugged her shoulders.

The crowd roared in approval. Mungan bowed to his new queen, and Nuala stomped out in a big huff.

Mungan, arm in arm with Leannan, came up to Caitie and Robbie. "Is there some way we can repay ye for your goodness to us?"

"Do you think Caitie and I could have our stuff back? You know her phone and my iTouch?"

"Most certainly, Robbie," Mungan said with a laugh.

"And Caitie, what request we can fulfill for ye?"

Nervous about what lay ahead for her, she turned to Earnan. "Can you break the spell that's binding me here so I can go home?"

"I cannot change the laws of our realm. It must be as decreed. However, once ye are free, I can make life easier in your world with a spell for fine fortune."

"You mean like, you could make us rich so we could move back to California?" Caitie asked.

Earnan nodded. "If that is what ye wish."

She'd be back with Sara and the rest of her old friends, hanging at the beach. No more weird food, her own bathroom, ten minutes from the movies and In-N-Out Burger. Caitie looked at Robbie. It was pretty hard to tell, but he shook his head no. Mom was happier here. She'd seen it with her and Grandma MacGregor at the train station, as they worked together in the kitchen, and then the night of the ceilidh when she danced with Ross. "That's a tempting offer, but it would probably end up hurting my family."

"But there must be something we can do to repay ye, Caitie," Mungan insisted.

A grin spread across her face. "There is one thing."

"Name it and 'tis yours."

"It's a big party night, right?"

"Aye." Mungan squeezed Leannan tight.

"Then I'd like to see Lileas dancing up on the stage."

Robbie looked at her like she was stupid for wasting her once-in-a-lifetime offer on Lileas.

"If that is your desire, then it shall be."

Mungan spoke to the musicians and then to the dancers.

Standing on the platform, Mungan called in a loud voice, "Lileas, will ye honour us with your dancing on this grand night?"

Lileas just stared at him, forgetting she was in the middle of filling a goblet. The heather ale spilled over the brim and onto the table before Elvy grabbed the pitcher from her hand. "Ye desire *me* on the stage?"

Mungan nodded. "Aye."

As she came forward, Earnan swirled his wand and commanded, *"Muth aodach."* A rainbow vapor from the tip of his wand swirled around Lileas.

She glided out of the mist in a flowing gossamer dress, her curly hair pulled back from her face and woven with ribbons and flowers. Silk slippers covered her feet. She stepped on to the dancers' stage and took her position.

Caitie clapped her hands together and drew them to her mouth, hoping no one would laugh at her friend.

The musicians began to play. Lileas twirled and swayed, dipped, and leapt, her face majorly glowing.

When the song finished, Caitie and Corc clapped first and loudest. Leannan and Mungan joined in along with most everybody else in the banquet hall.

"She did okay," Robbie whispered.

"It was really good!" Caitie shot him a glance that said, "Watch it, buddy!"

Lileas waltzed over to Caitie, but before she could say anything, Mungan reached out to her and said, "Lileas, ye must honour us more regularly on the stage. Your dancing was lovely."

"'Twould please me much." She hugged Caitie and whispered, "No one laughed at me."

"How could they," Caitie replied. "You were great!"

A little while later, Mungan brought over a small muslin sack with her clothes, all perfectly folded like she'd just bought them at Nordstrom. "Here are your garments and the items I borrowed from ye." He pulled out the iTouch and handed it to Robbie and the phone and iPod back to Caitie.

"Tha—"

Caitie put her hand over Robbie's mouth before he could finish his thank-you. "He really appreciates it."

Robbie gave her a dirty look.

"I'll explain later. So King Mungan, where did you hide our stuff this whole time?"

"Tucked in a drawer for safe keeping. I wanted none of it stolen."

"Now that's funny coming from you," Caitie said.

Mungan cleared his throat and looked at Robbie. "Well now, are ye ready to help Caitie escape her bond to our mountain?"

"What have I got to do with this?" Robbie asked. "You're the ones with the magic."

"'Tis a wee bit more complicated than that," Mungan said.

Her little brother's eyebrows pinched together in confusion.

"I didn't want to make you nervous," Caitie added. "Have you ever thrown a knife?"

"What?"

Caitie only hoped he was better with a blade than a baseball.

52 *the leopards' spots changed*

· going home ·

ROBBIE'S JAW DROPPED. HE COULDN'T HAVE HEARD Caitie right between the music and the fae party animals. He grabbed her arm and pulled her out of the Great Hall into the quieter tunnel leading to the portal. "What did you just say?"

"You gotta throw a knife over my head at dawn to break the spell that's got me trapped in this place."

"That's the stupidest thing I ever heard!"

"It's true. The night after I got kidnapped I was so hungry that I ate their food. I had no idea it would lock me up here in Daoine Shi Land. Now there's an invisible force field or something I can't break through to leave."

Could he even do this? Robbie held up his arms, palms up. "Look, why can't they just walk you out?"

"I don't know. It's some kind of fairy physics. I figured the wizard could break the spell. But he can't. It's up to you."

"What if I miss?"

"You better not. I don't want to be stuck here forever with a knife in my forehead. Now c'mon, there's one more thing I have to take care of before we go."

"What's that?"

"I picked out a pretty pink dress for Lileas. I've got to find it and give it to her."

"What is it with your fairy friends and pink dresses?"

"What are you talking about?"

"When Leannan and I came through the portal, Mungan ran toward us wearing one."

"That's the one. Where is it?"

"Further up the tunnel." He led her to it.

Caitie picked up the gown laying in a heap on the floor. She tried folding it, but the billowing skirt wouldn't be tamed. "Now that it's almost time to go, I'm kind of sad. It's stupid 'cause they kidnapped me and all, but I really like Lileas."

"I know," Robbie said. "Leannan made a pretty good sister too."

"Probably better than me." Caitie sounded serious.

"Just different. C'mon."

They found Lileas humming in the alcove while she laid out bite-size cakes in the shape of crowns on a dozen plates.

"I'm gonna be leaving soon," Caitie said. "At least, I hope I am, and I wanted to say good-bye."

Lileas stopped and wiped her hands on her apron. "Aye, the hour must soon be approaching."

"I wanted to give this to you." Caitie handed her good friend the gown.

Lileas held it against her own dress and smoothed down the long skirt. "Oh, Caitie, 'tis so lovely." The corners of her mouth turned up, but her brown eyes were lost puppy sad. "I will miss ye so."

"I'll miss you too, Lileas. I'll think of you when I'm tidying up." She gave Lileas a hug.

"And I shall think of ye when I dance." Lileas's eyes puddled.

Caitie's chin trembled. "Then you better do that a lot."

"I shall, I promise." She turned to Robbie. "Farewell, brave lad."

EVERY THROW ROBBIE EVER MISSED IN TWO LITTLE LEAGUE SEASONS PLAYED in his head like a string of pathetic bloopers while Earnan, Mungan, and Leannan walked him and Caitie up the passageway to the portal. The wizard spoke some weird spell and the magic door opened. Caitie walked to the doorway with her hands out in front of her and pressed against something invisible like a glass wall. "It's still there." She turned back and paced in the tunnel.

"Aim carefully, just above her head," Mungan said. "Ye have but one chance, lad." He turned, strode through the portal with no trouble and into the dark cave. He would stand outside on the path and call to Leannan as soon as the sun peeked over the mountain.

Leannan bent down a little and gripped Robbie's shoulders. "I have faith in ye, Robbie. Ye saved me. I know ye shall free your sister as well."

He looked into Leannan's sparkling peacock eyes and wished he could believe in himself the way she did. All he wanted was to have this stupid stunt over with. What if he wound up slicing Caitie's face? Worse yet, what if he screwed up—completely missed with the knife, sending it wide to the left or right—and had to leave her here? How would he ever explain that to Mom?

Leannan squeezed his shoulders gently and then passed through the portal to take her place at the cave entrance. Once she got the word from Mungan, she'd pass it along to Earnan, who would be just outside the portal. At Earnan's command, Robbie would throw the knife. All Caitie had to do was stand still in front of her invisible wall and hope he didn't accidentally stab her.

One chance. Maybe he should take some practice throws but that never worked for him at baseball. The more he threw, the more nervous and worse he got.

Earnan unsheathed a dagger with a gleaming blade and fancy handle carved out of ivory. He offered it to Robbie. "This is a finely crafted knife, very balanced. It should serve ye well."

The dagger had to be a foot long and felt super heavy. Robbie carefully handed the dagger back to Earnan and pulled his Dad's pocketknife out of his jeans. "I'd rather use mine. It was a present to my great-grandpa. My Dad gave it to me last year."

Earnan sheathed his knife, slipped it into his robe, and reached out for Robbie's. "Is that a mustard seed in the handle?"

"Yeah. Dad said it stood for faith. That with just a little faith, a person can do great things."

"Your father spoke wisely. 'Tis a fine legacy, Robbie." Earnan handed him back the pocketknife.

"'Tis time for me to take my position and for ye both as well. Do not forget, Caitie, ye must be two paces behind the portal. And Robbie, ye must be another eleven paces from her."

Caitie came back to the invisible barrier and took two long strides from it. Robbie hugged her tight and then counted as he took eleven giant steps heading into the mountain. She stood in front of the portal with her hands in her pockets, flapping her hoodie open and closed, her eyes looking upward.

Robbie fingered the recessed glass over the tiny seed. He thought of the woman that gave the knife to his great-grandpa. *Was this the time she had spoken about?* This was his chance to be there for Caitie, for Mom, and to make Dad proud. Robbie opened the small pocket knife and gripped the well-worn handle.

He thought he heard Leannan but wasn't sure.

"'Tis time, lad," Earnan called.

Robbie took a deep breath and gripped the knife blade in his right hand between his thumb and forefinger. He cocked his arm a couple of times and aimed at an invisible target above Caitie. *One... two...three.* Robbie flung the knife as hard as he could. It flew over the center of Caitie's head toward his invisible bull's-eye.

QUOWONKABONK! The sound of the knife hitting the barrier reverberated in the mountain tunnel like a hammer hitting steel. A spider web of glowing green light grew from the point where the tip of the knife pierced whatever it had hit. The spread and split of each light thread sounded like drum rolls on cymbals. Caitie jerked around and watched the light web expand across the open doorway. When the web reached to the floor, the top, and sides of the portal, it faded away with a hiss. She put her hands out to check.

"Robbie, it worked. I'm free!" Her voice broke.

He let out a huge sigh and jogged over to her.

She lifted him off the ground and spun him around.

"We can celebrate later. Let's get out of here." Robbie combed the stone floor bathed in silvery blue torchlight for the pocketknife. "Here it is." He stooped down to get it. The glass over the mustard seed sparkled in the dancing light. He carefully folded the blade back into the handle and put it into his pocket. He reached for Ross's flashlight that he'd left by the portal door the night before. Caitie jumped off the rock and hugged Earnan.

"Ye are fortunate, Caitie, to have someone who risked so much on your behalf."

"I know that now." She pulled back from the wizard and looked him in the eyes. "Are Robbie and I always going to be able to see the fae?"

Earnan shook his head. "Not unless they reveal themselves or ye take other measures. The glamour that got in your eyes will fade, if it has not already."

"Oh." Caitie looked a little sad.

Robbie scampered down the boulders to the cave floor.

"Farewell, young man. It has been a true honour to know ye if only for a wee while." The wizard's robe glowed a bright blue.

"Bye."

Leannan walked them to the cave entrance. She took Caitie in her arms. "Perhaps 'twould be wise for ye to learn to play chess."

"Okay...." Caitie's face clouded with confusion.

Leannan then hugged Robbie. She smelled wonderful like strawberries and cream. "I hope your grandpa will be well again soon," she whispered in his ear. "I shan't forget ye, Robbie. Ye shall be my hero forevermore."

He hated goodbyes. "I won't forget you either." How could he?

"And be careful on the journey home." Leannan kissed her forefinger and lightly touched his nose.

It was like a warm ray of sunshine radiated through him all the way to his toes. The lump in his throat made it hard to swallow.

"Do ye know the way?" Mungan asked.

Robbie nodded. "Yep."

"Then farewell and fine fortune to ye, lad."

Near the cave entrance, Robbie picked up the bag holding the glass for the primroses while Caitie hugged Mungan.

4:30 AM

"GOOD-BYE," CAITIE SAID.

Mungan kissed her forehead and a tear spilled down her cheek. She wiped it away quick.

"Be wise, Caitie, and stay away from dungeons. Ye never know who ye will meet there or what troubles they might bring ye."

"I'll try to remember that," she said.

She and Robbie hiked down the path in the early morning light with him leading the way. The air was fresh and cool. They reached the bottom of the mountain and started across the valley side by side as the moon faded in the cloudless sky. Caitie pulled the camera out of her hoodie and snapped several pictures as the sun's rays kissed the valley floor. Panning the view, she stopped to take a picture of the Daoine Shi Mountain. "You know, it's really pretty here."

Robbie pointed back at the mountain. "Do you see the rocks that look like a giant mushroom?"

Caitie looked till she thought she found them. "Yeah."

"That's their landmark."

"That makes sense. I served a lot of toadstools for dinner there. I guess the fae are pretty into them." She zoomed her lens in and clicked a close-up of it. "So what's been going on at home the last few days?"

"Plenty." He shot her a worried look like he wanted to tell her something but was thinking twice about it. "Mom got a new car, so don't look surprised."

"That's no big deal. What kind?"

"A silver Skoda Yeti."

Caitie half-laughed. "You're kidding me, right?"

He shook his head. "Huh-uh."

"You let her buy a car named after Bigfoot?"

"I didn't go with her. You wanted to go hiking in the woods that day instead."

"And you believed that?" Caitie shook her head. "You should have figured something was up, right then."

Robbie shrugged. "It sounded like fun."

Caitie punched his arm. "I'm so hungry, I think I could even eat haggis. A turkey and cheese sandwich sounds better though. The minute we get home, I'm heading for the kitchen. Sound good to you?"

"You offering to make me a sandwich?" Robbie grabbed her arm and stopped dead, whirling her around on the muddy trail.

"Sure, 'cause you're the best and bravest little brother a girl ever had."

Robbie rolled his eyes.

"No, I really mean it. Miss Moncrieff was right about you turning into some hero and all, which honestly, a week ago, I would've never believed. But listen to me, you were awesome up there."

"She said stuff about you too."

"I know. And she was right. Things I never believed in—like our friends up there," Caitie shot a glance toward the hill, "taught me some of the things I was so sure about were wrong."

"Like what?"

"Well, Scotland's not boring for one thing." Caitie grinned. "And just cause someone's powerful or pretty or popular doesn't mean they can treat people how ever they want. But you know what I learned that matters most?"

"What?"

"My friends in San Diego aren't the only ones who care about me or that I care about." Her chin quivered for just a second. She zoomed in on his face and snapped a picture. Caitie put the camera into review mode. "You look like Dad." She clicked back to check out the other photos. There in the display was the Daoine Shi landmark. Sitting on top of the rock were Leannan and Mungan in a major lip lock. "Look at this." She handed him the camera.

"Did you see them up there when you took the picture?"

"Nope."

"Then how can we now? I thought Earnan fixed your camera."

"He did. I guess way more than I figured," Caitie said. "You know, Robbie, Miss Moncrieff was right about one other thing. Scotland really is magical."

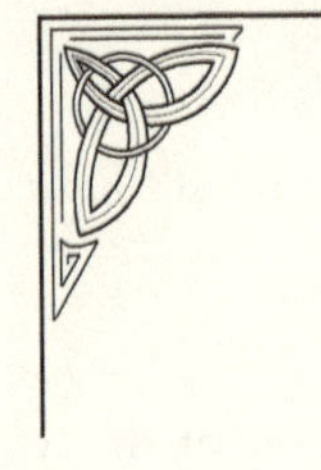

farewell

· epilogue ·

2:30 PM
JULY 3RD

"YOU BEAT ME, GRANDPA. I GIVE UP." ROBBIE LAID THE fishing rod and reel Xbox controller on the coffee table. Maybe he could finally get away.

Grandpa sat on a folding chair in front of the TV, scrolling through the game's lake locations. "Ross, want to take me on in a casting challenge?"

Grandma pulled an old, black plastic box wider than the size of a computer case out of the closet under the stairwell. "Angus, you've played that game enough today. It's only been three days since your attack. I think you should rest."

"We've been over this, Ina. I didn't have a heart attack. It was an arrhythmia. I have my medicine and I'm fine. Come on, Ross. Let's play."

"If you're sure you're up for it." Ross picked up the rod and reel controller.

"Of course I am!"

Mom looked up from her book, *How to Write Your First Novel.* "Please take it easy, Dad."

Robbie walked into the kitchen for a glass of milk when the phone rang. Caitie got up to answer it, leaving Rose sitting at the table.

"Hi," Caitie said. "Yeah, it's me. Oh, hi!" She sounded way more excited the second time.

After years of eavesdropping, Robbie thought he heard Caitie's crush tone. It was a skill he'd developed that usually got him a bargaining chip for later use with Mom. But since they'd moved, he'd gotten out of practice. He was pretty sure she was talking to someone she liked though. It had to be some guy from San Diego.

"Yeah, Rose is here. Do you want to talk to her?"

Maybe he was wrong. He sauntered over to the cupboard, stood on a drawer pull, and retrieved a glass from the upper cabinet.

"Okay. I promise, I'll tell her to stop by the hotel on her way home....Who will have her...what did you call it—payslip?...All right. Oh, and Willie, that guy in San Diego, he really isn't my boyfriend."

That was worth stalling for. Robbie finished pouring the milk and put the jug back in the fridge.

"Sure. We were gonna go for a walk, but we'll wait."

Robbie went back into the dining room to see what Grandma unearthed from the closet. "What are you doing?"

"I have to type the minutes from the Highland Quilters' meeting we had Thursday."

"Why don't you use the computer?"

She set the case on the dining room table. "I'll have you know this old typewriter has served me well for many years."

"Grandma, why don't you just e-mail them to everybody? I can teach you how."

"Robbie, I'm too old to learn the computer."

"Do you have a list of people to send it to?" She gave him the Highland Quilters contact list. "Look, Grandma, here are all their e-mail addresses. If you send it by e-mail, you'll save time and the money for copying 'em, and stamps."

"When you put it that way, perhaps I should enter the computer age."

"C'mon. Let's go upstairs. I'll get you started."

While Grandma sat down at his desk, he made her an e-mail account and showed her where to put the addresses in her message.

"Do I put 'Meeting Minutes' in the subject box?" she asked.

"Sure. And then the rest of what you want to say goes in the big space below."

"This is marvelous." Grandma started typing.

He looked out the window at the Loch. Something weird was flying toward the house. He squinted to see what it was. It wasn't flapping its wings. In fact, it didn't have wings. It soared up and out of sight. He went over and put his nose to the pane, trying to find the mysterious object.

Seconds later, he did a double take. Leannan, only in miniature, floated in front of him on a flower stalk. She pointed toward the shed and took off.

"I'll be back, Grandma."

She was hunched over the keyboard, studying the monitor. "Fine, dear."

He scurried to the wardrobe and dug out his bright white tennis shoes.

He smiled as he slipped them on and laced them tight. Like Miss Moncrieff said, "A brave man always stands out."

He raced outside to the shed and opened the door expecting to see Leannan, but she wasn't there. Had he just imagined her? He walked outside and headed toward the dock.

"Robbie."

He turned and saw Leannan by the side of the shed. She was tall and beautiful again. "I wanted to see that ye made it home safely."

"We did. Is everything good back in the mountain?"

"Much better."

"I missed you. It was kind of exciting while you were here."

"And I have missed ye as well, my friend." She looked down at his feet. "The last time I spied those shoes, they were stuffed in the back of your wardrobe. I thought ye did not fancy them."

"I changed my mind. They feel pretty good now."

"They suit ye."

He felt his cheeks get warm. *Did she know Miss Moncrieff too?* "Tha… I'm glad you think so."

"Now that I know ye are safe, I suppose I should not dally."

He didn't want her to go, but he couldn't really invite her in the house to hang for a while either.

He didn't know quite what to say. "I hope you live happily ever after, Leannan."

"I would like to wish ye the same, but I know that is not the way in your world."

"Yeah, but it'd sure be nice if I had a little bit of your magic. Life would be a lot easier if I could just twirl and my homework or chores would be done."

"Robbie, the magic in my realm ye envy is just a façade."

"You mean what we saw there isn't real."

"The good and evil in my world is as real as in yours, but what makes things lovely and easy is not. There is little depth to our beauty. 'Tis fashioned in a moment but cannot last. 'Tis pleasing to the eye but not satisfying to the soul." She reached for his hand. "We envy ye mortals as your hard work brings a sense of accomplishment we can never understand. Ye can see beauty inside, where we busily search on the surface. No, do not envy us, Robbie. Be glad for what ye have."

She squeezed his hand and let go.

"Will I ever see you again?" His eyes blurred. He looked down and blinked, embarrassed for her to see him like that. Robbie looked up, and she was gone.

· acknowledgements ·

THE BOOK IN YOUR HANDS WOULD NEVER HAVE BEEN PUBLISHED if not for the help and guidance of so many supportive friends along the way.

First, I'd like to acknowledge Ross Boardman of the outdoor adventure company Boots-N-Paddles. Ross led my family on a magical morning of weaselling near Inverness, providing the seed for the story.

Carolyn Wilson, our first friend in Drum, graciously opened the Glen Urquhart Hall and her home to us and made the introduction to Morag MacCallum who gave *Captured* its Gaelic spells.

Naomi White, dear friend, kindred spirit, and Highland tour guide/interpreter, has also been the best Scottish editor an American could have in keeping the dialogue true.

A heartfelt thanks to Elizabeth White for proofreading *Captured* and reminding me, once again, that even though we Americans and Scots may speak the same language, our understanding of the meaning of words can often be miles apart.

Award-winning author and editor Carolyn Wheat saw potential in the first draft and led me to a critique group including talented writers Matt Coyle, Judy Hamilton, and Cathy Worthington, who all provided inspiration, encouragement, and the challenge to write more in less pages.

Laura O'Brien, another fine writer who introduced me to the Society of Children's Book Writers and Illustrators (SCBWI), has provided guidance and advice all along the way for which I am very grateful. She also formed a second critique group with writers Amberlie Phillips and Jill Coste that ensured *Captured* was the best it could be.

Edie Ham, fellow SCBWI member, assured that it could be done.

Linda lee Franson encouraged me to pursue the manuscript's publication and worked long hours on the final editing. Her patience, keen eye, and dedication were truly appreciated.

Lisa Victoria, whose artwork inspired one of the main characters before the first draft was even written, has captured the pivotal scene in an incredible painting for the book's cover. Graphic artist Joni Stringfield saw the vision, and her talent has made the book beautiful.

I would like to acknowledge my parents, Joann and George Birk, for my mother instilled the love of stories and my father passed on the gift of telling them. She encouraged me to dream, and he taught me to persist in pursuing them.

My children, Kristen and Matthew, gave Caitie and Robbie voices, and I am grateful that they are captured in time within the pages of this book for me to always remember.

Finally, I want to thank my husband Jerry, my first and last editor, who read this fantasy over and over, making it better, defending its value, and being honest always. Without his support—encouraging me and spending hours alone while I worked to revise and revise again, I could not have done it.

www.ingramcontent.com/pod-product-compliance
Lightning Source LLC
Chambersburg PA
CBHW030828310726
48980CB00006B/687/J

* 9 7 8 0 6 9 2 6 6 8 8 0 1 *